HALE

HALE

The Prophet's Journal
Book II
A NOVEL

JK NOBLE

NEW YORK

LONDON • NASHVILLE • MELBOURNE • VANCOUVER

HALE
The Prophet's Journal Book II
A NOVEL

Published in New York, New York, by Morgan James Publishing. Morgan James is a trademark of Morgan James, LLC. www.MorganJamesPublishing.com

Proudly distributed by Publishers Group West®

Morgan James BOGO™

A **FREE** ebook edition is available for you or a friend with the purchase of this print book.

_____

CLEARLY SIGN YOUR NAME ABOVE

Instructions to claim your free ebook edition:
1. Visit MorganJamesBOGO.com
2. Sign your name CLEARLY in the space above
3. Complete the form and submit a photo of this entire page
4. You or your friend can download the ebook to your preferred device

ISBN 9781636981529 paperback
ISBN 9781636981536 ebook
Library of Congress Control Number:
2023934203

Cover Design by:
JK Noble and
Chris Treccani
www.3dogcreative.net

Interior Map Illustration by:
JK Noble

Morgan James PUBLISHING **Builds** with... **Habitat for Humanity®** Peninsula and Greater Williamsburg

Morgan James is a proud partner of Habitat for Humanity Peninsula and Greater Williamsburg. Partners in building since 2006.

Get involved today! Visit: www.morgan-james-publishing.com/giving-back

For my readers who have helped me change the world one
book at a time. Your purchase supports the Encourage
Literacy Foundation which provides books to children
across the globe. Thank You.

DARK SHIELDING PROPHECY

THE GRIFFIN CLAN

ELDER'S DOME

THE STAGE

TREEDALE

BANSHEE FOR

PRIESTESS SANCTUARY

ARKETCHA TRIBE

N
W E
S

THE EXTRAORDINARY DIVISION OF MALPHORA

LIGHT

ARDOR

ENDURANCE

MARIGOLD COTTAGE

KINGDOM OF BIMMORUS

OBSERVATORY

ACADEMY

ROYAL PALACE

EMSEQUET

BREATHING BAY

ISLES OF NEPENTH

GORGES OF NAVMALA

TEMPLE AND CEMETERY

PROLOGUE

September 5, 2009

I am restless. The dreams are always the same. Though lately, the strength of these premonitions has consumed my body and soul, and I cannot wake from them as easily as before. It has become too much to endure. Only today I've woken in Naomi's terrified arms, after hours of screaming, only to be told she could not stir me. I've been asleep for three days. Since I ignored all the warnings, I am responsible for my current suffering. I realize now that the higher forces refuse to take my carelessness as an answer.

The vision begins with clouds descending from the dark skies, attempting to mask death and gore. Pieces of bodies are scattered along the muddy terrain and floating in the rivers, staining the waters red. Pools of flesh are melting out from blood-rusted armor and into the soil. The dead are reduced to an endless feast for the impatient vermin. The putrid smell of their rot is somehow singed into my nostrils, and each half-decayed face haunts me even after the dream.

I run through the field in horror, toward a dim light. Eventually, the glow intensifies, and the fog disperses. I come before The Eyes, standing between Rioma and Deor. They admirably gaze up at Bayo, who reveals a devilish ear-to-ear grin. At this moment, I know the violent deaths were his doing. Bayo finally won his long-awaited war. The Griffins are now the ruling nation over the worlds.

But The Eyes between us are not as I know them. From their trio, the orb of Orcura turns to black, drops from its infinite rotation, and lands by Bayo's feet. Thus, the entire world of Orcura has died.

Young Griffin warriors emerge from the shadows, kneeling before their eternal king. Bayo's arms expand to absorb their devotion when the setting blurs.

I find myself at the beginning of the same premonition. Every corpse I'd previously passed, I must pass again. I rush through them, avoiding the bloody, dismembered figures. Following the only light in this blackened world, I expect to meet the same faces. But once I burst through the haze, it is not Rioma and Deor bowing before Bayo. It is Hale. He is an adolescent, and the brutality in his expression surpasses that of his older brother. The young Griffins kneel before them both.

I cannot help but stare into Hale's hypnotic eyes while he looks at the two hovering orbs with hunger. He is not the warm toddler I once knew. Bayo and the orbs fall out of view as the boy's presence overwhelms me entirely.

The sun peeks from behind the mountains and rotates backward in the sky from west to east, then stops midday. The vision wishes to show me yet another outcome. The battlefield comes alive, yet Hale and I have not moved. Horrific howling hails from every direction. Wild warriors whirl past. I recognize their faces. They wield their weapons so valiantly, and my heart sinks as they collapse to their deaths, in the very positions their corpses lay at the start of my premonition.

Throughout all this, Hale's Griffin uniform morphs into one of black and blue. He looks up. With one blink, his brown eyes are replaced with white beacons piercing through the clouds above. His arms extend as if floating on air, and he rises off the earth in his human form.

From the hillside in the distance, Bayo's personal battle pauses as he catches sight of his brother. He is horrified and transforms expeditiously.

His monstrous claws pull up the earth as he dashes toward Hale. He spreads his wings and soon is airborne. Only moments away does his flying cease abruptly. As if paralyzed, Bayo's wings and muscles stiffen, and he tips over in the sky, plummeting at a dangerous speed. Not a soul comes to his rescue.

He slams against the terrain.

Here of all places, in this barren, death-trodden land, does my closest friend, the great Griffin King, lie misshapen, his blood pouring out from him.

I wish I had woken then. I wish I was able to look away. But I could not. I sink to my knees and reach out to him, but there is no time to mourn.

Death and annihilation do not end with him.

A clear wave of energy emits from young Hale's body and spreads through the battlefield. Those that occupy the sky drop just as Bayo had, and those below holler in torment before their final collapse. All the while, Hale continues to hover above them like an apocalyptic angel with blinding beacons for eyes. His stance does not waver. Not until his plague befalls every living creature and thing.

Green grass becomes brittle and frail in seconds. Grand trees flake away to ash. The air is stagnant, and any promise of wind dies with the world. Even the eternal fire of the radiant sun overhead smolders, and the realm turns black. Before long, nothing exists, and the only source of light that remains is Hale's eyes.

Until they shut.

What I've seen is unexplainable. Bayo might destroy the world, but not to the extent his brother could. Until this point, I would have argued that such magic was impossible. There has yet to be a Griffin in existence that soared the skies in their human form while their eyes produce a blinding light, uncorrelated to any of the powers bestowed on us by the Welcoming Moon. Even Bayo could not massacre an entire battlefield. Yet Bayo's brother has consumed the world whole in mere moments.

It is no coincidence that Hale is gifted with a power that could surpass Bayo's ultimate power of Endurance.

I've told Bayo about my dreams numerous times, but he won't see reason. I've held on to him for so long, hoping he could change. But I see now that I cannot stand beside him any longer. Bayo will not stop. The many centuries passed have long since molded him. Sadly, he is not the man I once fought for.

I am fearful of the possible futures yet to come, especially now that the variety of outcomes are increasing. I know I won't live long enough to see which manifests into being. I can only describe my certainty as intuition, which is now validated since the premonitions. Not I, Greon, nor Ianna are present in any of them. Perhaps the dreams are warning me that my plans to stop Bayo are futile, that one of these four outcomes is destined to be.

However, I cannot stand idly by as Bayo plots. I now know the extent he is willing to go. And if not me, then who will take my place in stopping him?

My heart is broken as I face the decision to break the trust and bond between my dear oldest friend and myself. Despite the fact that he is past saving, I have decided to do whatever it takes to save him, his brother, and the three worlds, even at my life's expense.

While it is a decision I have made on my own, regardless of my endless rebuttals, my wife and daughter have taken the same oath.

I am afraid I'm damning my family along with me.

I pray for a favorable outcome.

Felix

CHAPTER 1

July 10, 2021

Bayo's Griffin form is but an insignificant speck in a rumbling grey sky. He strains his wings, attempting to cut through mighty winds. The howling overpowers his eardrums. For each mile he overcomes, he hurls backward three times the length. Suddenly plummeting, Bayo manages to stay aloft and skim the violent sea below. The mild surface of monstrous waves drenches his midsection. He scrapes through the skies desperately but cannot ascend. Then the ocean recedes, only to grow before him at a massive height and speed. The epic whoosh of its expansion is an unbearable, piercing sound. Bayo is unsurprised, however.

Not even when the monumental structure towers over his head and quakes his core does he feel the least bit of panic. Blackness gains on him. *If this is meant to be my death, it is well deserved.* It topples over him, breaking against his bones and limbs.

Why should I live if he is dead?

The pain overtakes his consciousness. While Bayo swirls in the depths of the chaotic sea, he hears Hale's screams from only earlier that day.

"I trusted you!"

"But remember, Hale. Your past is not real. I'm real." Even in a dream, he is spinning Hale his lies. Even in a dream. Guilt takes over. *No, wake up. Do not allow yourself to falter. There is still a chance . . .*

Bayo's eyes burst open.

He redirects his gaze to the roaring surface and feels the push of the current sweeping him away. Subtle moves set his arms and legs on fire. He contemplates his end. A few minutes more and he would be out of air. Nevertheless, he admits it is beautifully silent here, beneath the world. Here he can permit the sea to carry off his endless mistakes as if they never mattered.

Then bits and pieces of a memory almost forgotten flash before his eyes. *I trusted you!* Hale shouted.

I will bring my brother back, Bayo thinks.

Bayo's irises come alight in red, the color of his supreme power of Endurance. Gathering his strength, he rockets upward. His majestic paws kick and push through the forceful tide. The blustery wind no longer seems to be a challenge. While bolts of lightning strike the ocean, and heavy rains descend, Bayo pushes on unfazed. Every bone, limb, muscle, and tendon work profusely despite the ache. *I will bring him back.*

Peering through the downpour and fog, Bayo makes out a shadow of land. He allows himself a glint of hope.

A rocky cliffside stands before him, and Bayo grabs on. His wings are too worn to fly to the top. He'll have to climb. The muscles of his Griffin form swell while he hoists himself up the slippery slopes. Recklessly, he slams his paw against the rock until his claws latch on. He shrieks as the rock cuts through his skin, but there is no other way. Reaching the end of this jagged climb would feel like the accomplishment of a lifetime to most, but for Bayo, it is but another step closer to an ambiguous conclusion.

Bayo transforms and collapses. The forest around him is but a blur, and the blood of his tattered body seeps to the ground. Fresh bruises mark his open skin. Each wound stings with sea salt, and yet he forces himself to his feet.

"Hale!" he hoarsely bellows into the vacant woods.

Bayo stumbles through the muddy terrain. The downpour is further blinding his sight, and he has no choice but to use his power of Endurance to scope the land. Empty.

But how could that be? He fell right here . . . when the siren sang.

Overcome with terror, Bayo sprints forward while calling Hale's name. *Could the boys that followed Hale have taken his body? Or perhaps Hale was strong enough to conquer the siren's voice?* Bayo's mind races with disastrous thoughts he dares not wish to manifest. Hours pass. Hopelessly, Bayo's knees falter. Here lies the muddied Griffin King. Weeping.

Eleven long years. Finally in my arms, and now gone again.

Bayo remains paralyzed in grief until the storm settles and the sludge beneath him clays, to which then he gathers his wits and flies off.

Rioma stands in the doorway of the Elders' Dome with a shawl around her shoulders. The rain pours around her as she scopes the sky for Bayo. Finally, she catches sight of him descending through the clouds. He descends at an unsafe speed, then transforms to his human form midair and lands on wobbling feet. He gazes at her with hazy eyes before stumbling through his first steps. Rioma rushes, though not before Bayo falters on the damp grass. With her shawl in hand, she throws it over his body and lifts him.

Defeated, Bayo exclaims, "I couldn't find him!" Tears pouring freely.

"You will use The Eyes," she says.

Through a hoarse voice, he shouts, "You don't understand! He dismantled them. Many of the spells I've put on The Eyes over the centuries have come undone. I won't be able to use them to find him."

Rioma pats Bayo's back unaffectionately. Bayo jerks away from her touch.

"The siren must have k-killed him," he says, swallowing the lump in his throat.

"You would have found his body——"

"He had his friends with him," Bayo explains. "They could have taken the body." His voice is breaking. "T-tossed it into the ocean for all I know."

They walk through the front door.

Bayo grabs hold of the railing and heaves himself up with his remaining energy while Rioma stares. She notes that the only other time he's been this distraught was when Felix stole Hale away twelve years ago. She finds it curious that the most powerful man and beast in all the worlds is so easily broken by a single boy.

Muddied footprints and droplets of water lead the way to Bayo's study, where he locks himself in. His soaked hair falls over his eyes, and his clothes cling onto his shivering body. Hastily, Bayo rummages through his countless shelves and trunks, pulling out one dust-covered journal after the next. All the notes he's taken over the centuries of his existence are a reminder that his torment is unending. Scribbles concerning his hunger to learn about mythical treasures and his drive to take back the world did not depict an immortal life well spent.

Bayo flips through the pages like a madman. Droplets from his hair fall over his old handwriting. Too lost in a spur of memories, he finds himself unable to concentrate. He gazes at the center of the room. The events of earlier that day, once again, replay in horror. The last moment Hale ever spoke to him rings in his ears.

I trusted you!

Bayo cannot hold the swell in his throat any longer. Tears pour from his bloodshot eyes. A moan of grief escapes his lips when he recalls the look on Hale's face when he pulled his sword between them. It was the realization of pure betrayal. Every slash of Hale's sword, each erratic push and thrust, was meant to strike Bayo's body. But how could Hale ever understand? He won't. Bayo is sure of it. Not so long as the greatest years of his life were in Felix's care.

"Curse you, Felix," he murmurs. *I kept him alive and well for a thousand years! A thousand years! Only a few more, and my plans would have been completed! He and I would have lived happily. I would have raised him in a world where we could live as ourselves without fear. Free and prosperous . . . You stole him from me and raised him as your own. You took the most precious years of his life away and claimed them with no right. A childhood I was saving for him. How could you, Felix? How could you?* He throws all his books onto the floor in his anger.

After slamming his back against the wall, Bayo slides down onto the floor. He heaves and clasps his hand over his mouth. *He thought I used him!*

"What have I done!"

An open book beside him on the floor flips a page. It coincidentally falls open to a locating spell. He catches sight of it. *Maybe this would . . .* He pulls himself to his feet and shuffles to the orbs with the book in hand. With weary arms, he works over them with grand hand gestures. The orbs glow bright yellow. *It is working.* Bayo brings his pendant and map underneath the orbs, then chants the ancient spell. Though he completes the ritual precisely, the pendant does not move. Again, he repeats the spell, and again there is no effect.

Growing tense with frustration, he tries one final time. "Come on," he mutters. "Come on."

He stares at the orbs intensely.

"Show him to me," he directs.

He waits a moment, then another. There is no change. He grips his book. His pale hands shake while he rereads his notes. *But I did everything right. What could it be?* In Hale's absence proceeding Felix's betrayal, he was protected by what Bayo and Greon could only assume was blood protection magic. This theory proved true when Bayo found and brought Hale back to the Griffin Clan after Carly's death. However, this time is different. Hale is unprotected, as Felix and his family are now dead. The book falls from his hands and onto the floor with a thud. Bayo nearly topples over and catches himself on the rim of the table.

Choking on his sobs, he thinks, *There can be only one reason I cannot find him.*

His grip almost crushes the wood beneath his fingertips.

Hale must be dead.

The next morning, Rioma knocks on the heavy door to Bayo's study as gently as her nature allows. There is no answer. She can feel her every vein pulsating with intense heat. To remedy her aggravation, she thinks she should knock louder in case Bayo hadn't heard the first time.

As she lifts her hand to the door, Deor enters her mind and warns, *It is not wise. He is grieving.*

She scoffs. *Grieving! Grieving what? That low-grade ingrate whom he'd spent a year manipulating to be his heir? Mary is gone, and all he's concerned about is that boy!*

In her entitled fury, she picks the lock and enters the room. To her amusement, papers and books are scattered in every direction. The orbs hover in the center of the study, directly above Bayo's unconscious body—which lies wet and cold on the wood-paneled floor. She stomps through, trampling on his belongings without care, and kicks him awake.

Bayo's bloodshot eyes open, and she could tell he'd been crying a great deal. She grimaces in disgust.

"Leave me before I break you," he grumbles.

"Will you stop sulking? We still have all of Malphora to rule! Were all these years of your epic plans wasted? And while you mourn your brother, have you ever thought just for a moment about Mary? How could she leave me like this? After all I've done for her? I've raised her! I cared for her! And Ianna," she sneers, "that ungrateful—"

The moment Rioma spoke her last word, an aching surge strikes her. She stumbles back. The veins from her reddening temples ripple as she fights to stay on her feet. Bayo presses his power harder onto her, his fingertips curling into his palm, as if he were crushing her very soul.

Rioma clutches her chest. The free air refuses to enter her lungs. Losing herself in anguish, she topples over. She locks eyes with Bayo. His blank and careless stare fuels her anger, and she, too, begins to use her power to radiate heat from her body.

At once, Deor's cold chuckle rings in her mind. *You asked for it.*

Bayo rises steadily, and despite herself, Rioma yearns for his gentle touch. Would he take her into his arms and make amends? That would be all to satisfy the beast within. But in one swift move, Bayo yanks her arms. She can feel the disconnect of her joint. *Of course this would be his reaction. I shouldn't be surprised,* she tells herself. All the more reason to allow her fire to ignite. After all, he isn't the only one who's lost somebody. He isn't the only one in pain.

Flames dance on Bayo's sleeve, and smoke gradually fills the room. Bayo tolerates it but lets her have what she came for. He unleashes his power until Rioma is no longer able to hold in her screams.

Bayo seethes, "My brother, whom I have sheltered a thousand years, *is dead*. Because of a foolish decision my *closest* friend made in hopes of defying my plans for the world I envisioned. A world in which *our people* would be safe. My brother is *dead*," he repeats, enraged.

He continues, "After everything I had done to protect him, to make him strong. None of Felix's visions were accurate! He never told me Hale would die! Felix took fate into his own hands instead of trusting me. If not for Hale, then what is left for me? For whom do I build an empire if not for him? Not for the children you and I shared—no, they died in the civil war because you didn't protect them! And you come to me now with your pathetic halfhearted sobs about Mary. I have said this to you before, Rioma, and I will say it again.

"You have done nothing for Mary. She was born at a time when I refused any of us to procreate. But it was I who allowed the child to be born. Since infancy, it was I who gave her all her heart's desires. Clothes she wanted? *I provided them.* Treasures from the Human Division—*I provided them!* Toys to no end—scattered around the dome! Who procured these items—*I had!* The latest inventions of the Human Division—done! She wanted to travel to the Human Division—*I made it so.* She wanted to go on quests for me—*I made it so.* She was alone—*I gave her attention and care.* After six hundred years I sheltered her, nurtured her, taught her to be strong, and acted with her as a blood relative, did I not? *I* am the one betrayed—not you, my dear," he hisses.

He goes on, "And yet, somehow it seems that it was I who cooped her up here and put her against her will. And apparently, it was I who forced Felix's hand against me! When in actuality, it was I who gave them everything! It was I who pushed Mary out the door and into the Human Division—where she had always dreamt to be. It was I who provided Felix with knowledge and pleasures. He wanted a wife. Done! He wanted a child for the barren wife. Done! He wanted to be well learned in strange magic—to my demise, it was done! Then he wanted Hale! And by his will, IT WAS DONE!"

He lightens the pain he has over her, and at once Rioma's muffled screams cease.

Bayo continues, "You come here in all your rage with a plan to blame and aggravate me over losing Mary. As if she meant something to you at all. If you had it your way, she wouldn't know how to speak, let alone have the courage to leave the Griffin Clan! It was I who raised her to be independent. And she came back every time, pleading to stay. She would call the Clan her home, bring me gifts, and try to show her worth to me. And each time I told her these doors would always be open for her. Did I not?" he shouts.

"You did, Bayo!" Rioma says. If ever she was going to wave a white flag, it would be now.

Bayo thrusts her backward and walks to the window. "And now she has fled as a victim from a villain. Just as Felix fled from me with *my baby brother* in his arms as if he was his savior!" Bayo swallows and wipes his eyes. "Hale comes to me eleven years later, with an earful about his *wonderful father*, Felix. Felix made himself a *father to my brother*, and I am somehow meant to stand idly, with the capability to understand and make amends with the past . . .

"I spoke with Mary before I brought the young Griffins back into the Clan. I told her she had a choice in participating. She could have refused. I expected as much. But she agreed. I gave her a choice, just as I gave Felix a choice all those years ago. But here I stand corrected!"

After pausing briefly, he laughs. "You also bring up Ianna . . . Now, Ianna I understand. It wasn't easy being housed with the likes of us. First Deor—which caused the mess of Mary in the first place! And unwillingly! *Then you,*" he growls. "You repulsive, envious, vain arsonist! Ianna could have nothing and no one with you on her tail. Thank the heavens you hated Greon; otherwise you would have him just so she wouldn't. But you successfully stole her newborn and bewitched her to hate her mother. Not to mention you constantly set Ianna's skin afire as if it would make her any less beautiful than you!"

Bayo looks down at Rioma's crimson cheeks. She glowers at him.

He turns his back to her. "I, too, took part with my endless demands and orders . . . and my lack of respect for her. Her only solace was Greon, and even that she could not have, as I took him away and to his death. Honestly, I couldn't care less whether she's gone. I'm quite happy for her; she finally took control of her life. It only took a thousand years.

"But Mary and Felix . . ." He shakes his head. "Their betrayals, I would never get over. Not for as long as I should live. You will do well not to bring their names up again. And you shall never, *ever* have the name of my brother upon your venomous lips! That boy was worth a billion of you! Your pain will never be as great as mine, Rioma. You haven't experienced the level of betrayal and loss I've endured."

Rioma storms out of the room and slams the door shut. Bayo pays no mind. He hovers in front of Felix's portrait hanging on his wall.

They must not have understood how much I loved them.

CHAPTER 2

June 2, 2021
ONE MONTH EARLIER

A warm breeze floats through the trees, and the setting sun paints a melody of vivid colors throughout the cloudless sky. Strolling hand in hand is River and Grace, basking in the summer warmth.

While the pair spends nearly every day with one another during their training, they seldom have time alone. Now that training has converted to mixed sparring with each class of Griffin, there is more opportunity for leisure.

It seems the Elders are plotting a mysterious war at the expense of the adolescent Griffins. At this realization, Grace, River, and Evan decided they would leave the Griffin Clan as soon as they could. This notion is but a fantasy, considering an invisible barrier physically traps them. In the meantime, River and Grace are spending this day wisely, making for the cliffside to fly about the waterfalls.

River is blushing, though he can't help it being next to her. He admires the sun-kissed glow of Grace's skin and the highlights in her auburn hair. She notices him staring and meets his gaze. Instantly, River melts at the contact of her brown eyes and sighs uncomfortably.

Grace stops in her tracks. "What's wrong?"

He shakes his head and mutters, "Nothing, just . . ." he trails off.

"Just what?"

River blurts, "What would you do if you really want to do something, but you're not sure if it's a good idea?"

Grace smiles. "I would ask you what to do."

He flashes a shy grin. "No, Grace, come on."

She shrugs. "I don't know. Your question doesn't make much sense."

"What if you weren't sure if the action . . . would be received . . . well?"

"Are you doing something bad?"

Kicking a pebble in his path, River says, "Depends on what the other person thinks."

Grace huffs, "Well, you won't know until—"

River grabs Grace's hand, and at once her heart thumps at the touch. He is shaking. It is then he does the most unpredictable thing imaginable. He kneels, mumbling, "Here goes nothing."

Grace stiffens.

"Grace," he begins. His hushed voice speaks her name so sweetly. "I've been in love with you from the moment we met fourteen months and ten days ago when I first arrived here. The same night your brother, Evan, took me by the collar and threw me on the stage to fight him, and you stepped in and gave him that nice bump on the head with your shoe."

Grace laughs.

River squeezes her soft palms. "I love you more when I see how you are with the people around you. You are the odd one out when everyone else is having a blood-fest. You befriended the worst people and changed their ways. With them, you formed your own society and showed them a different way to survive." He lifts her hand to his lips and kisses it. "You were everyone's hero before you were mine, and for all the times you saved me, thank you."

She is quiet, and for a second, River regrets his words.

But then Grace strokes the side of his face and whispers, "You saved me quite a few times, too, you know."

Tears well in her eyes, striking River with emotion. "Why are you crying? You're making me all teary, too! I'm emotional enough as it is! This is totally not manly!"

They laugh.

"I have something for you," he whispers.

He nervously pulls out a mysterious object from his jeans pocket and dares to utter the following words: "I felt this way about you for a long time. I know we're only eighteen years old."

His fingers unclasp to expose a beautiful pear-cut emerald ring with a golden band. Grace gapes.

River, still shaking, is finding it hard to manage his nerves. "Will you mind being with me like forever . . . and ever and ever?"

Without warning, Grace pounces. River lands on his back. Her gentle hands slide around the base of his neck. Their lips are only millimeters apart. Grace slowly gazes down at his lips and watches them move while he speaks.

"So that's a yes?" River asks, grinning.

As if in slow motion, her eyes flutter closed, and she leans in. River's heart nearly flies from his chest. His breath is knocked right out of him, and he swears he's never felt so happy.

Her face hovers over his, and her lashes graze his cheeks before whispering, "Yes."

River, beaming, slides the ring onto her finger. "You probably shouldn't wear this around everyone else," he warns.

Grace nods. "Where did you get this? It's so beautiful!"

"There are boxes of jewels in a secret trove beneath the Elders' Dome. I saw them while I was there helping Ianna with her tasks. Mounds of those gold coins we used to collect, too. She noticed me eying this ring and asked me if I wanted it. I told her I would earn it. I helped her with all her tasks for months—and she sure needs the help."

"You're amazing," Grace says in awe. Many loving moments later, she asks, "I wish we could tell Evan and Hale."

River hangs his head. "That might not be such a good idea. You know how Evan might react, and Hale's spending all his time with Bayo and Leon now."

Grace stands, extending her hand to River to hoist him up. To keep from straining her, he takes her hand yet pulls himself to his feet.

"Yes, I know . . . I don't understand it. Hale could never be like them," she offers.

River mumbles, "He's like a good apple mixed in the wrong pile. Maybe he has no other choice . . . Speaking of apples . . ." Digging into his pocket, River reveals a shiny red apple. "You hungry?"

Intertwining his fingers in hers, she shakes her head with a smile. "What else are you hiding in those pockets of yours?"

"Oh, I got a turkey leg for later, a shiny new guitar, a high school diploma, a college degree, a license to drive. I also got the house we're going to live in together one day. Oh, and also last week's check, 'cause we got to pay the mortgage and the bills."

Grace's airy laughter comes to a saddened halt when she remembers they will never have that normal life River just mentioned.

He notices her sudden sorrow and squeezes her tenderly. "Everything will be okay."

Grace melts into his arms, and suddenly it feels as though she could conquer any hardship with him by her side.

Just then, they catch a shimmer among the trees in the distance and immediately recognize the tree dome River lived in months ago.

"There it is! My old baby!" he exclaims, rushing to it. "Oh, right." He recalls the horror Leon made Grace experience within, just months ago. "And back to the cliffsides we go!"

Grace shakes her head. "No, I want to see it."

"Grace, it's okay. We're wasting daylight," River says.

She pulls him forward. "Let's stay. We used to have so much fun here. I can't let a single memory ruin it."

River watches Grace march forward and feels deep admiration for her strength. Not but a minute later, his excitement gets the best of him, and he gives Grace an earful of all the cool things he learned about the tree dome, like the built-in bathroom in the trunk, the secret hiding places, and the filtered water.

Listening intently, Grace looks at the tree dome with fresh eyes. Eventually, he ends the conversation with, "Whoever built this thing was a genius."

Grace's friends are nearby. They've spotted her and call to her. River immediately backs away. The tree trunk conceals his presence. Nobody can know about his relationship with Grace. It is too dangerous. Grace removes her ring inconspicuously and places it in her jeans pocket.

River whispers, "Go, I'll meet you later."

Although Grace does not wish to leave his side, especially right at this moment—the most magical moment of her life—she must, at least for a little while. Grace departs, and River circles the trunk in search of its ladder using his fingertips to stroke the bark. It seems empty. All the better for River to reenter the one space in the Griffin Clan that's given him security and shelter, just for old times' sake.

Suddenly, River's arm slips inside the trunk. Pausing in astonishment, he pulls himself out from its unfeeling depths only to resubmerge his arm to explore this strange magic he's stumbled upon.

There's something in here. It feels like a . . . book. He pulls out a black leather-bound journal with intricate designs carved on the cover. Once unlocking the latch on its side, a yellowed and loose page floats to the ground beside his feet. He lifts the paper and reads its contents . . .

September 7, 2009

Dear River,

I am Felix, the Elder Prophet. If you are reading this, I am dead and have thus failed in foiling Bayo's plan. Bayo seeks to make an army of the young Griffins of the current generation to help him reign over Malphora. I know that magic keeps you from leaving the Griffin Clan, but that boundary will open in exactly one month.

I have prepared my journal and hid it in my home—which I know you are quite fond of—to assist you in the journeys you must face ahead. In it, you will find maps of the Extraordinary Division and all my knowledge of the creatures, nations, fauna, herbs, potions, and remedies that you will need. Study it as much as possible before the month passes. Within the book are four cloaking pendants—one for you, Hale, Evan, and Grace. It is imperative that you wear them only when you've left the Clan, and important for Grace's safety while she remains.

Bayo needs Hale's assistance in completing his task, solely because Hale possesses a power which supersedes his own. He is straining Hale's humanity to accomplish his goals, while you, River, must counter it at all costs. I wish there was another way, and I deeply apologize for the struggles you will face. But you are my last hope. Your love for my son might not only save him, but also the worlds in the process.

Felix

CHAPTER 3

July 1, 2021
ONE MONTH LATER

Hale has just fled from the Elders' Dome, and Evan is on his tail during an epic chase until Bayo uses his grand power of Endurance to send electrocuting pain throughout his body. The next thing Evan knows is that he's in the middle of the open sea.

Not long after, Evan emerges and immediately hurls all he's swallowed. Unable to see clearly past his salt-burning eyes, he squints to make out the shape of birds fleeing the treetops of the uncharted land in the distance. Those birds have paved the way for a black Griffin carrying a screaming boy to ascend the heavens. Evan instantly recognizes River and Hale. He wastes no time paddling forward.

With great strain, Evan transforms, pounces out from the water, and flaps his wings. Finally, he is airborne. He gains on River but cannot fly any closer, as there is an invisible barrier blocking him. It is River's power of Shielding. Evan squawks, but River does not hear over Hale's cries. Evan is bewildered. *What happened after I fell into the ocean? Is he hurt?*

River glances sideways, and when Evan assumes his protective shield would dissipate, he finds it is, in fact, expanding. River doesn't recognize him. The bubble grows at an immense speed, not allowing Evan a moment to adjust. Knocked from the skies, Evan plummets to his doom once more and squawks in panic. Luckily, Hale's wailing ebbs, and River notices Evan with enough time to swiftly swoop and hook his hind claws into the skin of Evan's back until Evan regains his momentum. Poor River releases his tired grip and Hale awakens, letting Evan experience the torment firsthand.

Hale is contorting, and River is struggling to keep him from slipping from his paws. His arms and legs twist rampantly, and though his eyes are open, it is clear he is not truly awake. River attempts to break Hale from his trance with a slight shake, but the howling intensifies. Hale's face is wet from flowing tears, and his Griffin brothers are at a loss for answers.

Suddenly, the bloodcurdling screams cease. His companions behold Hale's limp, unconscious body worriedly and note his steady breath. For a while, the Griffins roam the heavens in peace. The sunlight warms their fur, and an endless blanket of cloud is beneath them. At last, they are free of the Griffin Clan and all its troubles. This is supposed to be their salvation. *Maybe the worst has passed,* Evan thinks. Little does he know the extent of Hale's condition . . .

Hale wakes in a frenzy, raging and convoluting in River's helpless arms. Desperately, River descends to the nearest clearing and rests Hale on the green grass. Once in his human form, he tries to snap Hale out of his daze. Though no matter how much River shakes him or calls his name, it is as if Hale is blind and deaf. The earth trembles as Hale's agony amplifies. There is a nervous sweat at River's temple as he pulls three pendants from his pocket and puts one over Hale's head, then his own, and gives one to Evan.

"What is this for?" Evan asks.

"Just put it over your head," says River abruptly while flipping through the pages of Felix's journal. His skin has paled to a sickly shade of white.

"What happened to him?" Evan asks while putting the pendant around his neck.

"I don't know. I didn't see what happened," River blurts.

"What happened to Bayo and Leon?"

"I saw Bayo take Leon and fly away," River says.

"Did they hurt him?" Evan asks.

River snaps, "I don't know! I'm trying to figure it out!" He skims through the book and exclaims, "I read this book three times over, and there was nothing about screaming in pain like this!"

River is fuming. How could Felix leave him this guide to protect Hale and yet not explain how to heal Hale from whatever ails him now?

"His body is turning black," says Evan. "His skin is bruising."

River lifts Hale's shirt and gasps. The skin on his torso is forming black bubbles. As they appear and darken in color, Hale winces and cries. Moments later, when the blackness on his skin fades, he loses consciousness.

River returns to the book that is shaking in his palms. "There has to be something here that can help."

CHAPTER 4

Before the sun peeks from the summits of the Arketcha Tribe, a lively spirit with a fearsome cerulean glow speeds through the grasslands. It is invisible to the mortal eye and no larger than the average palm. The earth judders some miles back, and the soul carries on at a faster pace, calling to the one person who can see and hear it.

"Palla! Palla!"

The humble bungalow of the Spirit Guide comes into view. The alarmed orb storms through its wooden walls, not bothering to use the door, for it has no need for doors, of course.

"Palla!" it shouts, shaken.

Palla springs from her bed. She knows that voice all too well. It is a trusted spirit messenger she'd left stationed at the boundary between the physical and spiritual world. The ground trembles once more. Palla holds herself steady and opens the door to witness the commotion.

"An additional rift has appeared," explains the messenger.

"Gather our spirit friends; we need them!" Palla commands, and with that, the messenger disappears. Palla throws on her robe and calls, "Dagiel? Are you here?"

Immediately, a levitating yellow orb appears on her right side. "Always," he says.

"Good." Palla returns to the doorway and extends her hands out in front of her. Her naturally brown irises flash neon green as she speaks the angels' language. It didn't seem so long ago that the angels bestowed Palla and Kala with their infamous powers over those existing beyond the physical planes.

In the woods, some distance away, is where Palla senses the intruder. She shoots waves of pulsating white energy at it. Just as Palla's power strikes, a giant monster is revealed to all creatures of the physical world. It towers threefold over the jungle; trees tremble at its every step. It resembles a translucent arthropod with luminous vermillion eyes. When it spots Palla, it releases a deep-throated howl that sends the forest animals scurrying to safety.

Unintimidated, Palla straightens her posture and, with an extended finger, tells the ghoul, "*You* will not have this tribe, Socha!"

At once, Palla sprints toward the nefarious creature while calling for the support of her friends in the angels' language. The scape is abruptly ablaze with the light of hundreds of multicolored orbs surrounding their valiant Spirit Guide.

Socha mocks her. "You will not get the best of me this time, little Spirit Guide! I am not alone!" Socha elevates itself onto its hind legs and welcomingly spreads its remaining pedipalps wide.

Suddenly, the screams of the Arketchian people travel through the jungle. Nearly knocked off balance at another tremor, Palla realizes the horror of the situation. *Oh no!* She is forced to speak the tongue of the angels once more, exhausting herself before the true battle has begun. Pulsating energy explodes from her soul, expanding to the brink of the tribe on all sides, farther than she's ever allowed it to travel before. Like a lit lamp in a dark room, Palla's power reveals malevolent, unworldly spirits flooding the Arketchian skies and valleys.

Breathlessly, Palla prepares herself for the massive battle she must now fight.

"Is this the army you bring to defend yourself, little one? *Human souls?*" Socha cackles, "Seems your sister has abandoned you!"

The legendary demon spirit, Socha, has the ability to learn the secrets of the mind, similar to that of Griffins of the Dark. When it was just a small, insignificant creature free in the physical world, it enjoyed creeping into the minds of citizens, instigating their lives, and causing discord. That was before Palla and Kala defeated and reacquainted it with the spirit realm.

Here it is, hundreds of years later, much larger, and ready to reclaim its right over chaos in the Arketcha Tribe.

"Dagiel! Send half the spirits to the border. They must hold off whatever else is coming through! I will be there shortly," Palla orders.

"Yes, Palla!"

Palla and Socha have come face-to-face, and her army is too few to defeat it. It would surely absorb their energies to magnify his own. So, with her chanting, she casts them into invisibility.

Socha laughs. Black smoke radiates off its essence. "You dare face me alone?" it taunts.

But Palla has no choice. She must put an end to Socha once and for all without sacrificing any other entities.

Socha raises its leg to smash her while Palla lifts her arms and focuses on her energy. Dissipating into a large puff of smoke, Socha engulfs Palla, spiraling around her like a tornado. Lost in its dark aura, Palla finds her head spinning, and her chanting turns into incoherent slurs. Eventually, she falls to her knees. Outside the cyclone, her spirit friends smash themselves against Socha. Yet their efforts are futile. Some dash overhead to come to Palla's rescue, but Socha has closed her in.

The loud chuckle of the demonic spirit escalates in the cocoon. Seeping into her memories with a distorted whisper, it says, "You are nothing. On the verge of destruction without your spirits to support you . . . Without your sister."

Palla grabs her aching head. "It's not true," she mutters.

"Oh, but it is. Look how inadequately you fulfill your duties. Down on your knees in moments of battle."

"I will defeat you," Palla declares. It is more of a hopeful affirmation rather than a statement.

Socha's voice drops a tone as if signifying pity. "Poor, lonely Palla. Everyone has left you, haven't they? After all the sacrifices you made, where is the reward for your efforts? Wouldn't you rather be like your sister and run off to freedom?"

Ragefully, Palla rises. Her eyes alight with a cosmic green color. The rage has given her the boost of power she needed. Warningly extending her arms on either side, she commands Socha, "Go back to the spirit world or I shall eradicate you!"

"Your world is mine to command!" shouts Socha.

Palla strikes the beast, giving it her all. She hollers while her diminishing power pours out from her.

It senses her lack of strength. "You are weak!" it taunts. Palla struggles to hold on and keep her tired eyes open while the cyclone draws nearer. It is useless; she has no power left to come to her defense. Throwing her hands out one final time and speaking the angels' tongue sends a trickle of blood down her nose.

Socha closes in. She's prepared to be eaten whole and collapses on the ground to make it easier for the wicked spirit. *What should I care? I've lived long enough.*

Palla's spirit friends shriek in dismay. If they should lose their Spirit Guide, there will be no power left to keep them in the physical world. If they are not quick enough to enter the spirit realm before Palla's demise, their very souls will cease to exist since they have stayed in the physical world so long after their deaths. It will be *ultimate* death. A death feared by all who know of it. Yet none of Palla's spirit friends leave her side in this crucial hour.

Palla is fading in and out of consciousness, and she finds herself agreeing with the wicked Socha. Perhaps death is her escape from the harsh world. Perhaps she will obtain her long-awaited freedom in the next form of existence. Perhaps the centuries of battling will come to an end. She should welcome death. She should.

Her eyes flutter open. The black shadow is yanking her very soul away from her body when the blurry image of her colorful spirit friends comes into view. Palla inhales drastically. She cannot die, not so long as their very existence is bound by her power!

When Socha's cold energy meets Palla's skin, shivers travel up her spine. But Palla seems unaffected by the uncomfortable cold as she spurts, "I am stronger than you know."

A nuclear pulse explodes out from her, fragmenting the nightmarish ghoul. "NOW!" Palla commands her spirit friends. They charge forward. Before she knows it, Palla lands harshly on the ground.

When she opens her eyes, Socha is long gone. She pulls herself up with great strain and haste. Dagiel places himself under her arm for support.

"How long have I—" she asks.

"Not long," he answers.

There is a great commotion coming from the Arketchian square. Palla's battles are not over yet, and she hasn't a clue about what's happened to Socha. She must finish this before it gets out of hand.

Palla gets to her feet. "Let's hurry, Dagiel. Our people are in danger!"

After a mighty and successful battle, Palla trudges through the buzzing forest late that same evening. Socha had escaped back into the spirit realm. Its prolonged life might be the reason for another battle yet to come. But for the time being, Palla has once again saved the Arketcha Tribe from mass destruction, and she is on her way home.

Palla would have otherwise enjoyed the breathtaking view. The graceful melody of warbled chirpers envelops the land. Thousands are hovering inches above the foliage to create a stunning light show. Warblers flash their glowing wings, making them any color they so please. This nightly trollop in midsummer signifies the warbler mating season. While the males of the insect species strut their stuff, Arketchian citizens are lulled to sleep by their calming melodies. Warbled chirpers bump in and out of Palla's way, yet she is indifferent.

I've seen them for countless nights of my immortal life, she reminds herself. *What if for one night, I just keep my eyes shut?* She closes her eyes and passes through. Palla knows the way well enough, but still, she sighs. *Even the insects, in all their beauty, can find their genuine match. They shed their light for the world to see, all for the sake of love. But I . . . I shed my light . . . for no one to see . . .*

Socha's menacing figure and horrible words cloud her mind. *You are weak . . . You are nothing . . . Look how inadequately you fulfill your duties . . . Poor, lonely Palla. Everyone has left you, haven't they? After all the sacrifices you made, where is the reward for your efforts? Wouldn't you rather be like your sister and run off to freedom?*

Dagiel leans in and asks, "Would it have been so hard for our people to give you a bit of bread and water?"

"How could bread and water satisfy an eternal being?" she says sarcastically.

"Oh, please. They know the extent of your immortality," he counters.

"No. They don't. They'd rather not know how mortal I am."

The flames of Dagiel's orb grow in his rage. "Each passing generation becomes worse than the previous."

Palla nods. "I believe that is why the rifts are appearing and the strength of the wicked spirits are increasing. At least I have you all to stand by my side in times of battle . . ."

The space around Palla is abruptly overwhelmed with the light of her spirit friends. She sighs with relief. At least they see me, she thinks. A faint smile graces her face when their orb-like forms dance through the fields. She hums along to their tune. It is an Arketchian folk song about a warrior swept away to battle and losing the love of his life. His love is named Nirahoo, a popular name for an Arketchian girl when the song was written about five hundred years ago. The current generation couldn't possibly know this song. But between Palla and the spirits, nostalgia is everlasting. Together they sing.

Nirahoo, Nirahoo
The winds will push through trees to you.
Nirahoo, Nirahoo
Blue, the ocean where I first met you.
Nirahoo, Nirahoo
Float me to battles too grand for two.
Nirahoo, Nirahoo
We will meet again, it's true.
Nirahoo, Nirahoo
The name of the gentle flower, you.

Palla makes out the shadows of her small bungalow and worries she cannot walk much longer. Yet at every trip and stumble, she is at once supported by the forces otherwise invisible to mortal eyes. A gloomy thought crosses her mind: *I am no different than they are . . . a ghost on an eternal mission.*

Coming upon the front stoop to her home, Palla removes her hood, unveiling her long, sleek brown hair swaying over her waist. After unlocking the door with a brass key she keeps around her neck, half the spirits rush inside. Palla laughs along with their playfulness. The other half, her older, faithful half, remain outdoors to give her privacy.

While habitually lighting several candles and torches, Palla mocks herself. She didn't need that much light with the spirits running around. They flutter around her belongings, her small bed, a chest for her treasures, one dresser for her clothes, a firepit off in the corner, and a table with a chair beside it.

"Palla, why not a mirror? I saw a merchant selling some beautiful ones at the square!" says a spirit.

Palla's long grey robe drops to the floor revealing a pink A-line slip clinging to the curves of her body.

"I don't want any mirrors, Fae. Thank you," she says.

The light of Fae's sphere dims with disappointment, though she is not the only one who has noticed Palla's disdain for her reflection. The living speak about it as well.

Sitting at the edge of her bed, working a brush through her hair, Palla feels the need to elaborate. "It bothers me that I do not age."

All the spirits gather behind her and suddenly nudge her up and out the door. Palla immediately objects. "I just got home! Where are you taking me? Please, allow me to retire," she pleads. "It's been a long day."

But they continue to push her without so much as an explanation. It is then that Dagiel cozies up beside Palla's right ear and says, "They have planned a surprise for you."

"Well, I hope it is worth my while. I'm about to fall asleep right where I stand."

"I think so," says the yellow spirit.

Dagiel is Palla's childhood friend, the closest thing she ever had to romance. In Palla's sixteenth year, Dagiel wooed and courted her with respect to the Arketchian custom. Palla often dreamt of her life with Dagiel, until the angels entrusted her and her sister to act as guides for the tribe. Guides that were gifted with immense spiritual power and immortality yet were never allowed to wed, as their powers rely on their purity.

Palla had bid farewell to Dagiel without so much as a complaint. Though this crushed her soul, she told herself every day since then that it was an honor to make such a sacrifice.

She watched Dagiel marry another, have children, and grow old from afar. All the while, Palla refused to think about what could have been. If she'd done that, she would have surely been as careless as her sister.

In Dagiel's old age, he called to Palla for spiritual services on his deathbed. She performed them without question. It was then he took her hand and with his dying breath, he said he wished their lives were different, and though they couldn't be together, he would spend the rest of eternity keeping her company in his spirit form. Palla knew more than anybody that staying in this realm was dangerous for a spirit. The longer a spirit kept themselves from moving on, the stronger the chance they should become a malevolent spirit in the physical world. However, when Dagiel died, he kept true to his word, no matter how many times Palla asked him to move on.

Palla never minded the company of her oldest friend; in fact, she rather enjoyed having him around to keep her grounded. But she would never admit it—for his sake if he should ever decide to leave her.

The spirits escort her down the steps and around the bend of her tree. Up they went, climbing a small hill. They pass the radiating greenery of the extraordinary jungle, all the while singing and humming a joyous melody. Palla covers her mouth while she yawns.

"We're almost there," says Dagiel. "Don't fall asleep just yet."

Palla feels the spirits surrounding her body, allowing her to lean on them. "We will carry you, Palla," they whisper.

"Thank you, my friends. Tell me, Dagiel, do you miss sleeping?"

Dagiel thinks about this question. "I do not recall it entirely. I remember my body needed it as yours does. I remember some nights were pleasant, and others were hard, filled with nightmares."

Palla yawns once more. "Yes. I've been trying to keep the night-terror demons from the tribe for years! They are slippery little things."

"Indeed," Dagiel agrees. Then a moment later, he says, "We have arrived."

The spirits flow through the leaves and shrubs, but Palla must move them aside with her hands. Once the greenery is well out of the way, a steamy hot spring living beneath a starry sky comes into view.

"The spirits found this the other night," Dagiel explains.

"Oh, it's lovely!" Palla beams, rushing toward it. "Thank you, all," Palla says.

The yellow light of Dagiel's aura brightens with glee. "I will make sure you have your privacy," he assures.

He is about to float away when Palla asks, "Would you . . . not go too far away, please?"

Dagiel's spirit bounces in the air. "I will keep a distance and keep you safe." With that, he vanishes, and one by one, the light of the spirits that kept Palla's company also disappear.

Palla drawls a deep breath. "I can't remember the last time I was so pampered." About to remove her dress, she cautiously looks over her shoulder to the dark forest, afraid to expose herself. She bites her lip and removes her dress in haste, stepping into the steaming water slowly.

"I can't remember either," a strange voice says from behind. Palla jumps and covers her body with her hands.

There is no one there.

Palla sinks quickly into the hot spring to preserve her self-image.

"Dagiel?" she calls. "Dagiel!"

The detached voice chuckles. "Oh, pet, I've sent him away. I've sent them all away. Seems that little of my power still resides after my death."

Palla holds her breath. The voice is familiar. "Show yourself," she commands, her irises blazing a neon green.

The spirit's sinister cackle circles around Palla's head to make her dizzy. "Oh, you were always such a bore! Come on, take a guess!"

Angry by the interruption and quite afraid of the threat of power, Palla quickly uses her power on the spirit. After a few chants, the spirit hiding in the shadows of invisibility bursts into a visible dark-blue light, taking the form of a curvaceous woman with long, straight hair.

Palla recalls the features at once. She nearly jumps from the water. "Kala?"

"Yes, little sister," Kala says with a bow. "I am dead."

Palla isn't the least bit surprised at her sister's untimely end due to her despicable life choices, but still, she cannot help but feel pain for her loss.

"Oh, please." Kala reproaches. "I do hope you are not pitying me! After all, death is still life. You and I know that more than anybody."

Palla huffs, "Yes, that is true. And considering death was always your idea of freedom, I don't suppose you could enjoy that freedom somewhere in the other worlds?"

Kala strokes her sister's hair. "That sounds lovely, but you see, I have missed you so much over the centuries. I think I should like to reconnect . . . build a bond, stay at your side—like that precious old flame of yours. Dagiel, was it?"

Palla crosses her arms. "I might be kind, Kala, but I am not a fool. You can't move on, can you?"

Kala swivels in the air, continuing to make Palla dizzy. "No, I am fully capable of that. It's just where I am meant to be going, that is the dreadful part," she explains. "And I have debts to pay, you see."

"How long?" Palla asks.

"Seven hundred years. One for every soul I stole and all that rubbish." She rolls her eyes. "I am doomed to make amends on this earth by aiding you. I'll just be one of the other several miserable spirits floating around you while you sleep. Perhaps even sinking into your dreams for fun . . ."

Palla laughs. "You do know the more awful things you do, the more time you will have to pay? Have you forgotten the Arketchian law? You are in prison, sister."

Kala sighs. "All right, all right! Perhaps some good deeds and reports won't hurt." She winces at the thought.

Palla frowns. "I'm sorry," she manages.

Kala for once sounds serious in her reply. "Sorry, yes. It seems that no matter which path I would have chosen in my life, I would have still ended up here, with you, doing this work. There is no escaping fate."

Palla nods in understanding. "If only you stayed."

"Were you rewarded for your good deeds yet? Have the angels come to remove the burden of eternal life?" she asks earnestly.

Palla shakes her head. "No."

Kala shrugs. "Then what is seven hundred years compared to the eternity you must face? It is I who should apologize to you, little sister. I never did understand why you were so committed to the job. Helping people for nothing in return. Yes, I thought it was fulfilling—to a degree. But I was angry, as the gift chose me when I had not chosen it . . ."

She continues, "I believe if I would have had a choice, I might have chosen your path. It was as if the lives we lived and planned were not important, sacrificed without care. Our family grew old and died while we stayed young and alone. The love of my life fled to some other woman . . . I honestly don't know if I would have chosen the gift. I just wish I was asked."

Palla looks up to the dazzling sky, thinking about all the things her sister just said. Likewise, she thought the same but never spoke about it. That was the difference between her and Kala, she concludes. Palla bore the weight of it, the pain and loneliness, knowing she helped so many people, even if she is no different from a ghost.

Then Palla thinks back to her sister's selfishness in life. *Oh, how I blamed you for leaving me to do the work of two for eternity. How angry I was with you for betraying me. Yet I am not happy to see you this way . . . I feel your pain. Still, if I was presented with a choice between the gift and mortality, I would have chosen the gift.*

But Palla will not say how she truly feels when it is so clear her sister needs her understanding.

"I know."

CHAPTER 5

October 10, 2009

In my wildest dreams, I never thought I could envision something so pure or so beautiful. I finally found solace in my decisions.

Hale, the little boy fast asleep for a millennium, is my son. I can feel it in my soul, as if the truth had been dormant within me for centuries and has now awoken. It's all clear to me—the reason I was previously incapable of allowing him to sit in an eternal sleep as a potential pawn in Bayo's plan, and how that alone unsettles my core a thousandfold more than Bayo's thirst for power.

As lucid as the light of day, in my vision, Hale is awake. The sunlight shines behind him as he walks through a front door. He wears an unusual bag strapped to his shoulders. When he meets my eyes, the misery fades from his innocent face and he dashes straight toward me!

And when his short arms wrap around my neck, I knew he was mine.

We separate and I watch him mature into a young man. I recognize his adolescent form from my previous visions of the massacre, but before me is a different version of the same boy. His presence emits kindness and warmth, and he gazes at me with admiration. It became probable that he had been asleep all this while until I was ready to be the father he needs. I understand I won't be doing the right thing, but hopefully, I will be doing right by him.

Once I told Naomi the news my premonition shared, she wept with immense joy and responded, "If he is your son, then he must also be mine." My heart soared. Countless images of memories yet to come filled my mind . . . memories of us as a family.

Though I undeniably feel justified in my future actions, I am still and will forever be plagued with woe as I imagine Bayo's grief. First by my betrayal, then at the loss of Hale, and later at the several years of loneliness he will endure after our departure. There is no doubt that he truly cares for the boy. There is not a day that has passed that he does not stay with Hale's comatose body. He would use Ianna's power to move him, clean him, change his clothes and his sheets, and take him for walks and picnics on the beach. All the while, Bayo would hold Hale's hand so he wouldn't forget the feeling of physical touch once he was woken. And before all retire to bed, Bayo reads to him from books of grand adventure and heroism.

There will be consequences for this, and I will bear the rightful weight until my wrongdoings catch up to me. While I believe I can defy fate by waking Hale and stealing him away from Bayo's influence—thus saving all of Malphora—there is that question that hangs over me: Will my action be the catalyst that drives Bayo's anger so much so that he will find a means to manipulate and use Hale for evil in spite of me? Or will this forsaken decision I make be the saving grace Hale would have never otherwise had?

Is fate inevitable?

Felix

July 30, 2021

The Banshee Forest is a place a skilled explorer of the Extraordinary Division would smartly avoid. River, on the other hand, is not a skilled explorer and makes the grave mistake of descending from the clouds to tend to Hale in the smallest clearing within these woods. He doesn't realize what this place is, considering the sun is up and it is silent. However, upon leaving, neither River nor Evan can manifest their Griffin forms. This is when an unsettling pit forms in River's stomach.

"What's going on?" Evan asks, attempting his transformation several more times.

River hastily opens Felix's journal, and Evan looks on earnestly. River finally finds the page he was looking for. It is as suspected.

"What is it?" Evan repeats, dreading the fateful answer.

"We're stuck."

The Banshee Forest is not for the faint of heart, nor is it a place for a Griffin. Dark magic afflicts this horrid place. For those traveling in a group, be cautious, as you will suddenly feel an urge to turn against one another. The magic also prevents the transformation of all kinds of shape-shifters. Here, even a werewolf would remain in its human form during its moon-controlled cycle. Legends of nearby nations speak of shape-shifters daring the tedious travel to the forest to collect its soil, hoping to cease their transformation. Though wearing the soil on one's person was an instantaneous cure for their multiple-formed affliction, the cursed soil lured them into the forest to meet their doom.

Likewise, if any being of human consciousness should die in this forest— and all have—their souls tether to the land, hence morphing them over time into banshees. Banshees are frightening creatures. Since they are stuck in the physical plane, they take the form of their rotted vessels, though they are no more than spirits. Nights are filled with their wailful moans, cries, and screams. They appear and disappear at random, hoping to touch a living creature and pull it through the veil of life and death. One could smartly avoid a banshee by hiding in the shadows, not moving or speaking until sunrise, or using light to cast them away. The latter is efficient considering the creatures of the night who are attracted to the cries of the banshee . . .

—Excerpt from Felix's journal.

River curses under his breath for allowing such a mistake to happen. He should have known better. After all, he'd studied the book for a month and, in it, the map of the Extraordinary Division.

"How long until sunset?" he asks.

Evan checks the position of the sun. "Three hours, I would say."

River looks down at Hale, who cannot be touched or moved. *What would happen if Hale wakes up during the night? His screams would attract them.*

Finally, River says, "We have no choice but to stay here until sunrise, then leave by foot."

That is if Hale will be in any condition to leave the following morning. How would they carry him without striking up his physical turmoil? Like River said, they have no choice.

"I need you to make a ring of fire around us," he tells Evan.

Evan does as River commands while staring at the strange book River is carrying with him. River notices Evan's gaze and shuts the book. *Evan's too much of a coward to read the book himself.* He pauses in his tracks, shaking his head. *Why am I thinking this way . . .*

Their stomachs grumble, and a flock of femus scurries past. This species of bird can be compared to a large hummingbird and are equally as colorful. Its tail fans out into individual feathers ranging in shades of green and blue. Its breast is white and furry, and it has a tiny snout like a dog, and with small, pointed ears and soft eyes. River instinctually traps them within a shielding bubble and hands them over to Evan, who kills them swiftly, guts, then cooks them on several sticks over his fire.

"Don't come out of the circle of fire," River warns once the setting dims.

But what should they do when Hale's screaming begins, and the creatures come for them? There is only one solution: River must create a shield around the trio, though that means he will have to stay awake the entire night, for the third night in a row. River's face is already drooping, and his eyes are shutting. He hardly has the strength to lift his arms. But this is the only way they can survive. He takes a meditative stance and creates an invisible barrier surrounding them.

"Don't let me fall asleep," he tells Evan.

Evan takes in River's sunken eyes and pasty skin yet does not for a minute feel that River wouldn't come through. He throws a hateful glance while River's eyes are shut. *He's just so perfect.*

—*Excerpt continued*

The most dangerous of all predators of the Banshee Forest is the vyrtrusk. They are calculating creatures that thrive off suffering. Vyrtrusks share the face of a buffalo, yet they have a third eye. Their long and swooping horns grow from their forehead, just above the additional eye. A shaggy and black coat of fur mounts on their large hump. They lean on hoofed hind legs, while their long and clawed arms are used for galloping over the ground and dismantling their prey.

They feast on tormented flesh, enjoying any mortally wounded creature, however a creature not yet dead. Their coats are often caked in old blood, the scent they most enjoy. Habitually, vyrtrusks will seek out an animal in perfect health to inflict pain on it. They then consume it slowly, ripping out one limb at a time.

The third eye of a vyrtrusk has an intelligent quality—almost human compared to the other two on either side. It is rumored that one gaze into their hypnotic third eye will cause their prey to relive the most painful moments in their lives.

Vyrtrusks prefer living in places of anguish and chaos, which explains their presence in the Banshee Forest . . .

The world around Evan's ring of fire is pitch black. Apparitions fade in and out through an eerie fog. Their faces are grotesque, deformed, and rotted. Their clothes, tattered. The words they speak are inaudible, though it is certain through their howling that they are hurting. They tug at themselves, pull at the base of their hair, and sink their long fingernails into their skin. What's worse is they've spotted three living creatures beyond the fire. Luckily, they have no interest in approaching . . . that is, not until Hale awakes.

The moaning of hundreds of banshees could not top Hale's current suffering. With pain so alluring, the ghosts lunge toward the trio at whim, itching to pull Hale through the veil of death. But they cannot pass River's protective shield, no matter how much they bang and smash against it. Evan is on the verge of losing his sanity from the constant shouting. He attempts to increase the height of his fire to keep the ghosts at bay, but it is no use. They want Hale.

If River continues to concentrate on his breathing and remain centered, the trio might survive the night. After some time, River tunes out the horrific noises beyond his wall.

All the while, Evan stares him down with envy. He wonders how River isn't frightened by the sounds of these monsters. Evan slumps down against the trunk of a tree and finally, once Hale's cries die down, he calls to River.

River dares not interrupt his meditative stance, and grunts.

Evan is fuming. "What are we doing? We need to go back for Grace."

River is perplexed by Evan's random statement, but he understands the forest has been tricking his pack brother. Steadily River answers, "We can't go back right now. She will be okay. The forest's dark magic is making you angry—"

But Evan refuses to let River go on. "What do you mean we can't go back right now? How can you just sit here and help *him* after he ditched us?" he says, gesturing to Hale. "If Bayo wants him so badly, why don't you just bring him back to the Griffin Clan? Maybe Bayo can help him. That way we could get Grace out."

River's eyes finally open. Evan struck a nerve. "You think I don't want to go back for Grace?" he says.

Evan snips, "If you wanted to, you would have done it by now! Who knows what Bayo and the other Elders are doing to them now that Hale is gone!"

Trying to regain composure, River says, "Evan, you need to calm down. You know Grace is perfectly capable of taking care of herself. She'll find a way to leave from the inside, and she will find us."

"It's been a week!" Evan roars. "Why are we here, protecting Hale, after everything he did!"

River grimaces. "He's our friend."

"He almost killed you!" Evan counters.

"You already know that he wasn't himself."

Dark-red flames burst and lick Evan's forearms. "Oh, is that right? But he was himself when he left us for Bayo. Ditched our pack to join him."

River shakes his head. "He was manipulated, just like you were by your old friends."

"Don't compare me to him."

River is having difficulty keeping calm. His shield is losing strength as a result. Banshees lunge at them on either side, and their howling begins to attract a rustling in the nearby shrubs. River attempts to keep his shield steady by raising his arms.

River says, "You're right. I shouldn't compare, because you're worse. You didn't leave your old friends. They left you after you ran back to them like a needy puppy. Then they nearly murdered you. If it wasn't for Grace reprimanding you, you would have still been the same person you always were."

Evan's skin reddens. "How do you know that? How do you know what Grace said to me?" The fire coursing through him turns orange, and its flames heighten.

River doesn't answer. It is obvious Grace had told him.

"Why is she talking about me with you?" Evan presses.

River scoffs. "We were talking, and she just told me. Why does that bother—"

Evan stands with balled fists. "What else has she told you?"

"Evan—" he begins.

River rises to his feet. The creatures beyond the force field sense the weakening barrier. Shadows more than double the size of a banshee are circling the perimeter. Was it a vyrtrusk River saw? He isn't sure. Sweat drips down his forehead. Hurriedly, River presses his power harder and concludes this conversation isn't nearly as important as surviving.

"I really don't need to explain myself to you," he tells Evan.

But Evan cannot care less about whatever is closing in on them. His anger takes over, and in no time the fire blazing on his bare arms turns yellow, signifying the increase in heat.

Evan laughs in disbelief. "I can't believe this. How didn't I see it? You're always hanging around her, looking at her the way you do."

He spins around, and fire shoots from his arms, aimed at River's head. But the fire reaches as far as River's brick-like barrier. Just when River assumes the fight is over, Evan attempts another attack to break through the shield.

River holds out his arms in front of his face. He isn't strong enough to keep up with two force fields at a time, especially with the lack of rest. The shadows are closing in. *Where have all the banshees gone?* The forest is silent.

Thinking back to Felix's journal, River starts to panic. "Stop it, Evan. Nobody asked you to come here and help Hale. If you don't want to be here, you can leave. Hale is our friend. He saved your life. He saved Grace's life twice. All this happened within a few days of knowing us. He was in trouble, and we didn't see it until it was too late. He deserves our help. But nobody is forcing you to stay. You need to stop, or those creatures will get in."

Evan continues to fume, but he steps back. The flames on his arms are smoldering red. His back is to River when he asks, "Tell me, does Grace feel the same way for you?"

River shakes his head in disbelief. *After everything I just said, this is what he's concerned about?*

Fireballs speed at River's face. He impulsively blocks them with his power. They sparkle like firecrackers against the shield. Evan circles around him searching for an opening. But River covers himself on all sides. However, his second force field is shrinking despite the massive strain on his power. The monsters are closing in.

River's heart is pounding in his chest. If those things on the other side of his shield are vyrtrusks they will be dead in minutes. He needs to end this, fast.

"You do know the barrier is back around the Griffin Clan, right? We can't go back, and we can't get her out," River explains.

Suddenly Evan stops. "How do you know?"

"I flew back and checked on the first night, while you were sleeping like a princess. This whole week you haven't mentioned her name once apart from now. What happened, Evan? I thought you cared about her?"

Evan is silent.

River shakes his head in disapproval. "Do you honestly think I would ever hurt her?"

No response.

River adds, "You aren't stuck with us, if that's what you think. You can take the journal. It will help you survive out here. Maybe you could even find your way home since you made it clear you don't want to stay and help."

Evan's nostrils flare. "If I wanted to go, I would have gone."

Finally, River snaps, "You know what? I wish you would go. What did you contribute this week while I was keeping us alive? All you've done is show off your passive-aggressive attitude about the journal, then refuse to look at it when I've been handing it over to you. Now you're throwing fireballs at my head when you know I'm the one keeping us from those creatures, all because you're jealous Grace has affections for someone other than you. And you complained about looking after Hale. Hale took you in and made us a pack when I didn't want anything to do with you. And I listened to him, even after all those times you beat me 'til I knocked out. You threw both of us on the stage our first nights in the Griffin Clan, have you forgotten? We saved you from Leon—how many times? And to top it all off, now that Hale needs your help, you don't want to help. You're pathetic, and you always were. If you don't want to help, don't get us killed. If you so much as stand near me, you will regret it."

River observes the forest outside the shield, searching for a sign of the monsters. Yet all is still and silent. *Maybe they were scared off by the light?* He tosses the journal to Evan and allows his force field to dissipate for the moment. "Leave."

Evan stands stagnant while his eyes pierce through River's soul. After a moment of waiting patiently, River creates a surge through the air and Evan flies backward, landing on his bum.

"Don't test me," River warns.

Glaring at River, Evan snatches Felix's journal and fades into the darkness.

The calm forest floor is short-lived, for as soon as Evan steps out from the ring of fire, the banshees reappear, leaving him no choice but to dash farther into the woods. His thundering pulse rings in his ears, and for the life of him, he cannot decide if he is furious or afraid. How can River throw him out like that, especially here? Banshees are catching sight of him. They roll through the ground with reaching arms. All Evan can see are their corroded faces and gaping mouths. Suddenly, a large animal breaking branches sounds nearby.

I have to get out of here, Evan thinks. With his hands outstretched, he spews his fire at the ghosts, and they reel back in horror. But their cries and screams only increase in volume, and Evan can't help but watch the shadows lurking behind the trees instead. He spins, and a cyclone of fire bursts from him, sparing him enough time to flee the scene and climb the nearest tree. From above, he spots the surreal glow of the spirits resuming their nightly prowl as if they never crossed paths.

He's safe for the time being. Behind his shut eyes is River's perfect face and charming eyes. There is nothing River cannot do. This week of trying to survive proved that, while Evan sat idly by twiddling his thumbs. Smoke fumes from Evan's nostrils. Kindness, looks, good humor, smarts. River has it all . . . and now it is clear Evan isn't the only one who noticed. How didn't he see it? He guesses he was too busy training, hanging out with other friends, and surviving the nightly battles Bayo ordered.

Now he knows the reason behind Grace's smile through the horrors they lived through and the reason behind the blush on her cheek. Shouldn't he be happy for her? She is his sister, after all. And he is perfect. Everything Evan is not.

"She loves him," he mumbles. Evan stuffs his hands under his arms to keep the fire from igniting. "It just had to be him of all people. My polar opposite . . ."

That's the reason, isn't it, he thinks. River's qualities always bothered Evan. It's why Evan can't help but hate him and why Evan used to single him out from the crowd and go out of his way to hurt him. Evan tenses up. But when did it all change? He remembers Hale's kind smile. *Hale was so accepting, even after everything I did . . .*

Just then, the forest shudders with the sound of a human scream in the direction Evan came from. He jumps. The voice doesn't belong to Hale . . .

It belongs to River.

I didn't see a vyrtrusk, I didn't see a vyrtrusk, River repeats. *It is all in my head . . .
Okay, I don't feel too good.* River grabs his crown and fumbles back in the grass.
This can't be happening, I can't give in. His vision is blurring. *It's going to be okay.
I just need to keep the force field up until morning . . . then somehow carry Hale out
of here . . . without transforming . . . with no help.* He closes his eyes. *Nothing new.*
He lets out a long, drawling breath and forces himself to return to his meditative
stance. *I can do it . . . I can . . .* Slowly River falls over and loses consciousness,
and the force field disappears.

Thump, thump. The ground shakes. Groggily, River's eyes flutter open. There
is a hoof in front of his face. River looks up and screams. But the blistering
cry does not faze the vyrtrusk from grabbing Hale's shoulders. While River's
innocent touch is enough to send Hale reeling, such fits couldn't compare to the
touch of a violent beast.

Hale's mouth gapes open to its widest capacity, and he expels an excruciating
cry. River's heart nearly stops. *NO!* Instinct takes hold and at once, he creates
a barrier between the creature and Hale, but the vyrtrusk fights River's weary
efforts with ease, pulling Hale closer to itself by the second.

The creature's jaw unhinges to open wider, revealing long, pointed teeth
and tongue. While its viscous drool drips out, River rushes to crawl until he is
directly beneath it. Hale's feet are dangling inches above River's face. His pain-
filled screams unnerve River. There is not much time. River strikes the vyrtrusk
with a powerful shield. Finally, the vyrtrusk releases Hale, and River catches him,
though it is no soft fall by any means. All the while, the beast smashes against the
invisible barrier furiously. It pulverizes River's energetic shield, making him feel
as if he's taking the blows against his actual body.

With a clenched jaw, River struggles to keep afloat, while Hale contorts in
his arms. His head feels light, and he knows it is just a matter of time before
his body gives in. Through his hazy vision, past Hale's head he sees the beast's
menacing third eye beckoning his gaze. *Don't do it,* River commands himself, but
his head is turning to meet it. *Shut your eyes.*

The inviting violet glow of the hypnotic third eye shines through the dark,
and River finds that he cannot keep his eyes closed for long. Whatever happens,

it is out of his hands. The force field is giving in. Shadows of the remaining vyrtrusk pack gallop into view.

"Hale, I'm so sorry. I tried," River wails.

Suddenly, Hale's body goes limp.

River catches on as soon as the screams cease. "NO!" He shakes him violently. "Snap out of it, you hear me! Hale!"

Just when River assumes the worst, an eerie, raspy howl creeps out from Hale's throat and escalates in volume. The beasts howl in tune with the otherworldly cry, arching their humped backs to the sky. They continue to claw at the soil, preparing to attack. Desperately, River presses his power full-on. The beasts smash into the barrier savagely, breaking it in with their tremendous muscles and antlers. Slobber continues to drip from their mouths.

River can take no more of the brutal beating, but he needn't struggle for long. A vyrtrusk is hit from behind with a sparkling fireball. *Evan.* River is instantly relieved. One after another, Evan tosses cannon-like balls of fire at the beasts. Strangely enough, the vyrtrusks make no sound of distress after impact.

Through all the commotion, Hale's moaning cuts off.

"Carly!" Hale yells.

It is the first time Hale has spoken since the accident. *Will he wake up?* River, in shock, places a hand on Hale's cheek, urging him awake. But as soon as Carly's name leaves his lips, Hale's head falls to the side. There is suddenly a lifelessness in his body. Frantic, River takes Hale's wrist and applies pressure. *I can't feel a pulse.* It is just as River feared—the pain from the fall was too much for Hale to bear.

"Hale!"

The smell of singed fur fills the air. The well-distracted beasts jarringly turn their attention to their assailant. But the others, the ones who were yet to be harmed from Evan's fire, remove their attention from Hale and instead lock eyes on the wounded of their own. In the blink of an eye, they spring into action, tackling the impaired. They topple over one another and seize fighting limbs. There are no howls of agony, just a series of snaps, chewing, and moaning in immense gratification.

Evan rushes toward the boys with Felix's journal in hand. The light of his free, flaming hand reflects onto the monsters, illuminating blood-drenched mouths gnawing at the flesh of their own.

River brings Evan into his shield. "He's not breathing. Make a fire around us," he tells him.

As asked of him, Evan presses his palm on the cool ground, and a large fire grows around the trio while River pumps Hale's chest repeatedly. There is no change.

River screams, "Hale!"

CHAPTER 6

When the veil of life and death crumbled, Hale saw his sister Carly's spirit hovering over him. Carly reaches out to the smoky figure emerging from Hale's body, but she cannot grasp it in time, though if she had, she wonders if she'd be able to put it back inside his body. Nonetheless, it disperses into the sky.

Something that can only be perceived as an all-consuming luminance replaces her surroundings. It is a warm, inviting presence, and she feels an unexplainable connection to it, like reuniting with an old friend. Enveloped in the loving and powerful energy, the presence lessens her fear and turmoil. Her darkest memories have deconstructed and now feel like a dream, as if the constructs of reality are altogether different. Dark emotions and earthly desires are now eradicated from her being, leaving only what she has learned in life. She twirls, finally free of all burdens that bound her to the physical world.

But the light withdraws.

Carly follows it, and as if it were a thinking entity, she calls out, "Wait, please! My brother—"

An unsettling feeling courses through her soul. She is met with vacancy at every turn and is very afraid. But the scene develops.

It is difficult to put into words what the mortal eyes cannot or should not behold. The place Carly finds herself now is free from all material constructions. The elements as we know them—air, water, earth, and fire—are absent. Carly wonders if the loving presence she met is truly gone, or if it is still here somehow, built into everything in existence, watching lovingly, and offering a guiding hand . . .

Sixteen beings materialize into the airy space and advance. Their essences are gigantic and look to be made of pure flame, the color of burnt copper. The flames are intense and alluring compared to an ordinary spirit—such as Palla's spirit friends or Carly herself. The bottoms of their essences seem to have only a single leg with a round and bare foot. No toes. Stretching out from their backs are four eagle-like wings. The sound of their flapping matches the rush of grand waterfalls.

The beings approach in rows of four. The beings in the first row have the most beautiful faces Carly's ever seen. They are perfectly symmetrical, devoid of any blemish or mark, passing for man or woman, both at once, or neither at all.

The three additional rows of ethereal beings hover just above the previous and are equally stunning, though not at all what one might imagine. In the second line, the beings have the heads of lions with long and flowing silken manes. The third row has the heads of oxen with dazzling gemlike horns. And in the last row are beings with citrine eyes and the heads of eagles. They form a concentric circle around Carly, remaining in each of their rows.

One with a human face, brilliant blue eyes, dark skin, and long blond curly hair, beckons Carly forward. "Come closer." Its voice is a strange mixture of gentleness and diplomacy, yet neither female nor male.

As if compelled by the wholeness of this being, Carly follows its command.

The same being gestures to its right. "Look." Where it directs its hands appears one large orb twirling with two colors: green and yellow. Carly stares at it. It is familiar, and she tries to remember where she knows this spirit. The orb bounces with what she registers as glee, giving off a sparkling glow at Carly's approach.

The blond being tells the orb, "She does not recognize you."

The orb understands, and at once the colors pull apart until it becomes two distinct orbs, one completely green and the other yellow. In a flash, the orbs stretch and morph into two human shapes.

Carly gasps. They are her loving parents, Felix and Naomi.

She embraces them. "Mom! Dad!"

They hold on to her tightly. The pristine spirits of her parents are free from the marks of their deaths and are younger than when they died. Logically, Carly is aware that she hasn't seen her parents in years, but here, where time is heightened, she cannot help but feel it wasn't that long ago. Still, she missed them. Terribly.

The being addresses the three spirits. "I am Assella, the angel of judgment. Felix, Elder Prophet of the Griffin Clan. Naomi, wife of Felix and master of the Light. Carly, daughter to Felix and Naomi, master of the Dark. We've brought you here as true witnesses to Hale Onadore's life, to assist us in deciding his fate."

Felix is outraged. "What do you mean, decide his fate?"

Assella answers, "For the moment Hale is dead, and unless this court proves his worthiness to survive, his spirit will not be returning to its current body."

With a wave of Assella's hand, a striking book, illuminated in purple, appears in the center of the space. The book opens, and most of it, including the pages, is black. The writing within is blood red. Just a few pages within are white. The dark energy that emits from the book matches its appearance, and Carly notes that all energy here matches their appearances exactly, unlike in the physical world . . .

Felix proclaims, "That book does not belong to my son!"

Naomi places her gentle hand on Felix's shoulder to settle him.

"Yes, it does," Assella counters. "Let the trial begin!"

CHAPTER 7

Hale stands on a shimmering snow-colored cobblestone bridge suspended somewhere deep in the cosmos. Wispy clouds spiral along the pathway. The heavens are so vivid. The Prussian blue above fades to a cosmic aquamarine, and the galaxies in the distance are lively shades of purples and pinks.

Hale beholds this mystical place in awe.

Glowing, gaseous stars hover statically. The nearest star levitates a foot beyond the bridge to Hale's right. Curiosity beckons him, and he reaches out to touch it. Heat radiates from it, and Hale stops himself. *This must be real . . .* he thinks.

Gusts of warm wind push from behind. When Hale fumbles forward, he notices the abrupt end of the bridge. At its end is a golden moon. The wind continues to urge him forward with a light whistling sound. Just as he is about to follow the wind's current, he hears muffled voices.

Hale turns to see an apparition of himself lying unconscious on the cobblestone and gasps. Apparitions of River and Evan materialize beside his double. River is resuscitating Hale's opaque body with angst while Evan checks for a pulse.

Evan anxiously looks over. "River, those things are coming closer."

River mutters through his clenched jaw. He breathes into Hale's mouth repeatedly. In horror, he exclaims, "It's not working!"

Hale attempts to contact River by placing a hand on his shoulder. But at Hale's touch, River's apparition dematerializes into smoke, then rematerializes a moment later.

"Concentrate on the force field. I'll do that," Evan says, trying to pull River away.

River's brow is slick with sweat, and he is reluctant to leave until Evan presses his hands over Hale's heart steadily. River extends his arms on either side to strengthen his protective bubble.

Hale follows River's gaze to spot the creatures they are referring to, but he cannot see a thing apart from the bridge.

"Is there a pulse?" River asks.

Evan is silent.

This further proves to Hale that this isn't a dream. The apparitions are depicting the waking world. Hale is *dying*. While he comes to terms with the hard truth, he suddenly senses a presence standing behind him.

He turns to meet Carly's eyes.

She is radiant. Her face is plump, and her cheeks are red. There is not a single mark or bruise on her flesh. A white sundress flows behind her. Hale remembers it—it was her favorite dress in life. She smiles at him.

Hale rushes into her open arms.

"You're here!" he says, squeezing her tightly.

"I'm here," she says with a voice as soft as velvet.

There is an urge to cry or shout for joy, though Hale does not know which. Yet he knows for certain that no words can describe how much he missed his sister. Now that he is reacquainted with her authentic beauty, he feels immense hatred toward himself for forgetting the small bits and pieces. Like how her eyes twinkle in the light, and how her freckles spot her cheeks and nose. Or how it feels to wrap his arms around her. To hold her. It feels like home. How strange it was to be apart for so long. Here now, it is as if she never left. They just picked up where they left off. Maybe the reality he's known is really a dream, because this moment feels more real than any moment he experienced since she died . . .

She strokes his hair.

Hale musters the courage to ask, "Did I die?"

The wind picks up speed.

"Come," she says, entwining her fingers with his. She walks along the path.

The wind turns into a light breeze. Carly and Hale continue in silence, though Hale cannot help but stare at her. Did her hair always flow behind her that way? Still, there is more to Carly on this surreal bridge than there was while she was alive. She is herself, and at the same time, she is so much more . . . Hale cannot put it into words. Regardless, that is the least of his concerns. *I wish this moment can last forever.*

"I think it's for the best," he says.

"What is?"

"That I died. I get to be with you. Nothing will ever hurt us again, and—"

She ceases her stride. "Hale. You can't die. I won't let you."

Flushed with emotion, he objects, "B-but it's better this way." He recalls all the people he ever hurt with his power. "If I die, I wouldn't h-hurt anybody anymore. If I live, I—"

"You what?" Carly interrupts. "What would you do if you live?"

Hale's voice cracks, and his sobs are about to burst from him. "Carly, I'm a monster."

She holds him lovingly. "No." She shakes her head. "You just forgot that you're not a monster."

Once they part, Hale notices that they have mysteriously appeared at the end of the bridge, though just a moment ago they still had some distance left to travel. Before him is the stunning golden moon. It is as tall and wide as a whale. Now that they are close, Hale can see it isn't a moon at all but a magnificent floating disk. Its surface is sleek, and the edge ripples as if it were a flat vertical pond. Hale peers into the disk and makes out their reflections.

In his wonder, he asks his sister, "What is this?" He raises a finger to poke it. At his touch, it ripples, yet his finger mysteriously remains dry.

"Look into it," Carly advises.

Hale does as she says, and their reflections are unexpectedly replaced by Bayo's face. Hale leaps back in fright, but Carly takes his hand. Taking a deep breath, Hale stares deeper through the golden window and submerges into a black cloud.

The cloud fades away, exposing the parlor room in the Elders' Dome. Behind the paneled windows stretching across the wall is a raging storm. The fireplace crackles subtly. Hot white drinks in china cups and dessert rest on the table, Bayo's favorite. Hale takes a whiff. Its aroma is so real, it's like he is truly there. But he knows better—this all happened before. *This is a memory.* Yes . . . he remembers this night. This is one of the first nights he did not return home to River and Evan.

Voices sound from behind, and Hale faces the direction they come from. Entering the parlor room is Bayo striding proudly beside a slightly younger version of Hale. Taking his younger version into account, Hale thinks, *Why did I look so different?* This only happened less than a year ago . . . Hale cannot place what changed about him. It isn't his build, weight, or height. Not the length of his hair, or his clothes. The younger Hale is a different person altogether. He treads humbly and gazes up at Bayo with deep admiration. Meanwhile, Bayo speaks with grand gestures and a wide grin, evidently absorbing Hale's esteem.

How didn't I notice this before? I was so clueless . . . so in awe . . . I used to be so . . . innocent and open-hearted . . . So this is my older brother. I see it now . . . we do look alike. Hale's heart sinks.

Placed on the table beside the teacups is a stack of books. *Ethics books from the Human Division,* Hale vaguely recalls . . .

The Bayo and Hale of the past sink into their cushioned seats and sip their tea.

"Do you think ethics are important?" Bayo asks while young Hale flips through the endless pages of text.

Young Hale nods.

Bayo goes on. "There are countless ways to perceive a situation. But what is truly important are your actions during a difficult situation. For example, when do you think murder is justified?"

"Never. But if you have to, in self-defense," Hale answers.

Bayo shrugs, as the answer isn't quite to his standards. "Yes, that is true. But I believe there are more instances than that. How about during a duel where both parties agree to the terms fairly? This can be a single match or during battle. In both cases, whoever shall die will die with honor. Another justified case is if you must stop someone who is planning or doing harm."

Young Hale interjects, "You don't need to kill a person to stop their actions. You can talk to them and try to make them understand what they are doing is wrong. And if that doesn't work, you can prevent their actions without killing them."

Observing from the corner, the true Hale's eyes widen at the realization that he would never say such a thing at this point in time, and he is horrified that he would now agree with Bayo. *I changed . . . so much.*

Bayo counters, "And if that does not work, what would you do? If they persist and become violent?"

Young Hale shrugs off the question. "I would ask for help."

Bayo challenges him. "And if there is no one to help?"

Stammering for an answer, young Hale says, "If I couldn't"—he trails—"then I would outsmart them and wait for the best moment to escape."

Bayo smiles. "And if they pursue?"

"Run to survive, trap them if I have to," younger Hale offers.

"And if you cannot keep this person in prison?" Bayo counters.

Young Hale struggles to manage his hostility. "My sister and I were abducted, locked away, and tortured for months. We let him do what he wanted. At one point, I was so desperate that I begged him to end our lives. And even after everything he ever did to us, we didn't hurt him, and we didn't kill him. We did the right thing, and we waited for an opportunity, and we escaped."

Tears well in current Hale's eyes. Hearing himself speak about his pain felt no different from a blade piercing his chest. Strangely enough, that experience seems to have happened in some distant dream. Why did Hale distance himself from the trauma when his younger version was so in tune with his emotions? But of course, this memory is the pivotal moment of his detachment! *Why didn't I think it was odd for Bayo to single me out from the rest? He made me feel that special . . .*

Bayo listens intently to Hale's sad story, and his cold, expressionless face morphs into one of pity. He places a hand on Hale's shoulder, holds his gaze with Hale's welling brown eyes, and says, "I'm sorry you had to go through that.

You didn't deserve that pain. But I see that your experience has made you into a strong young man."

Hale shakes his head, forcing the lump in his throat down. "I am not strong."

Bayo counters, "Yes, you are. You grieve those you lost. That does not make you weak. You wish you could have changed your fate. Perhaps you wish you tried harder to protect her. Tell me, what would you have done differently if you could relive that dark period of your life? Would you have stopped your assailant by whatever means necessary?"

"I tried," Hale whimpers.

"Yes, you did, and you did wonderfully for someone who did not have the resources you have now. You learned and have become so much since then. Despite this, I'm sure you wish you could go back in time and do it all differently."

Hale nods.

"But what would you have changed, specifically?" Bayo asks. "You've done everything you mentioned that should have been sufficient. Your abductor was able to take advantage of you and your . . . sister because you were submissive. You waited for an opportunity, you escaped. But you did not win. So how would you have changed the course of your fate if you continue to choose not to take that awful man's life?"

Young Hale doesn't respond.

Bayo concludes, "It is justified. Don't you agree? Your sister would have lived, and there would have been one less villain in the world."

Young Hale nods unsurely.

"Don't hold this over your head, Hale. You did what was best. But times have changed, and you are more than capable to take on such challenges. Take this as a lesson learned. Strike down your opponent before they act on their maliciousness, like that awful man had done to you."

A black cloud seeps out from the walls and smothers everything until Hale blinks from the dream in front of the golden disk. His face is wet with tears. Appalled, Carly squeezes his hand. Clearly, she, too, watched the memory unfold.

Hale sets his sobbing free. "Bayo did this to us. *He* killed our parents, *he* had us tortured. He pretended and lied this whole time. He made me trust him."

Carly agrees. "I know. But you have to keep looking."

Hale wipes his face and returns to the disk with all the bravery in him. It ripples as it consumes his consciousness.

He shoos the clouds away impatiently and spots his fourteen-year-old self just about to enter the front door of his old home. He notes the red and bleeding knuckles his younger self attempts to hide in the pockets of his coat. *Oh*, Hale thinks. *I remember this day.* Fourteen-year-old Hale tries to act as innocently as possible when he walks in. Little does he know the principal already called his parents, and he is about to get a rude awakening.

However, current Hale is enthralled at the sight behind the door. There stands Naomi, cross-armed and frowning. She and young Hale already began an exchange, while current Hale glides toward his mother. *Wow. Look at my mom! I forgot how beautiful she was.* He reaches out for her but cannot feel a thing. *Right*, he thinks. *This isn't real, they are just figments.* His fingertips hover millimeters above her cheek, and he imagines her looking him in the eyes.

Felix emerges from the other room, and suddenly young Hale silences. His father shouldn't have been home so early. And judging from his tight jaw, he's in a terrible mood. "Sit," Felix commands, pulling out the chair in the dining room.

Dad! Current Hale laughs in astonishment. *Look how angry he was with me. If I knew better, I would have never let him get so upset . . . if only I knew I didn't have long with them . . .* In fact, his parents died a few months after this very memory took place.

"We want to hear the story from you first, before making any rash decisions," Felix says with a tight grip on the back of a chair. "What happened today?"

Flushed with embarrassment, young Hale mumbles, "A boy in school started a fight with me . . . and I finished it." He shrugs his shoulders without care.

Carly walks into the dining room and young Hale stiffens. Present Hale can see the wheels turning behind his double's eyes and smiles. He hated for Carly to know he'd done something bad.

"You dare shrug your shoulders as if this incident is of no importance?" Felix bellows. His veins pulsate from his neck. "Tell me how he started this fight."

Young Hale doesn't dare avoid eye contact with his father. His lips are pursed tight when he explains, "He's a bully. He shoved me and called me a loser. He wouldn't stop, so I made him leave me alone."

Current Hale is taken aback. *Why don't I remember being so angry? I look scary . . .*

Felix roars, "You've misused your training! You swore you would never use it unless it was necessary." He forcefully pulls out young Hale's hand from his pockets. "And you come home with sore fists, hiding them in your pockets like some street mongrel!"

Naomi interjects, "Maybe Hale was only trying to defend himself. Don't be so hard on him."

Felix snaps, "Is that what you see in his face? Do you mean to tell me you are oblivious to pure hatred and evil in his expression? Do you honestly think he was trying to protect himself? He can knock down a six-foot man with his bare fists, and he almost punched a hole through a boy's chest because he called him a loser. No." He returns his attention to Hale. "Tell your mother. Were you defending yourself? Did the boy get physical with you?"

Young Hale's cheeks turn bright red.

"Face your mother and tell her the truth," Felix demands.

Shamefaced, Hale shakes his head. Finally, the confession.

"Why did you do it?" Felix asks.

Silence.

Felix continues, "I just got off the phone with the mother of that child. After dismissal, the boy fainted at home. His parents had to take him to the hospital."

Young Hale's mouth nearly drops. It is no fun reliving this moment. Current Hale hangs his head in shame. *One of the greatest regrets of my life.*

"Yes! You put that child in a hospital! He had a heart condition! You punched him repeatedly in the chest! Imagine how his parents are managing. That is their child, their loved one, their hard work, and their pride and joy. A living being who feels pain like anyone else!" Felix slams his fist down on the table and shouts, "I taught you to defend yourself in the off chance you come across a violent stranger! In case someone would ever hurt you! I didn't teach you to fight so you could feel powerful!"

Felix intensely stares into his son's eyes and then growls, "Was it worth it? He's fighting for his life right now because he called you a silly name. Are you proud of yourself? Do you think you taught him a valuable lesson?" With that last word, Felix storms out and into the master bedroom.

Naomi hovers silently. The disappointment in her eyes forces young Hale to avoid eye contact. Eventually, in a low voice, she says, "Your father is right. I don't recognize my son . . . Life is precious, Hale. It is not yours to hurt, and it is not yours to take away." Naomi turns her head to the sound of Felix calling her. She goes to him and shuts the door.

The current Hale watching this memory feels an indescribable urge to follow his mother into the room. He walks through their bedroom door, entering mid-conversation.

Felix collects his wallet and jacket as if he is preparing to leave. "We must now go to the hospital and try to make amends . . . Everything we've done has been in vain," he says, holding in his tears.

Naomi strokes his arms, and Felix melts into her at once. "You've already foreseen the boy living through this. This is only one incident. Hale understands he is wrong," she assures.

"We taught him the difference between right and wrong. Armed him with knowledge and strength. He almost killed someone with this rage I didn't know existed in him. I was wrong. We cannot change fate."

Naomi whispers, "He is our son. We will continue to protect him, nurture him, teach and guide him as best we can. He will make you proud. Trust him."

Felix's voice breaks. "He suddenly looks so much like him. Don't you think?"

Hale regains consciousness in front of the disk. It takes a bit of time to process what he's just seen.

"I-I reminded him of Bayo. Why am I here? Why these memories?" he asks Carly.

She answers him, "Because they are the turning points of your life. This last memory pulled you back to your humanity, while the first pulled you from it. You are confused and hurt by your love for Dad and Bayo."

"They both lied to me," Hale whispers. "I don't know what is right anymore, Carly."

Carly says, "Then you have to find the answers in yourself. You can accept Bayo's or Dad's truth, or you can have the courage to create your own."

The golden disk vibrates lightly. Hale raises his hand to its surface once more and finds he can now submerge his hand through it. "Where does this lead?" Hale asks, curiously.

Carly smiles, urging him away. "It is a mystery."

"Do I deserve to live, Carly, after what I've done?" Hale asks.

"You are who you make yourself to be, before or after the mistakes you've made. I only hope you will choose a path that will not cause you suffering. And yes, you deserve to live. I will be with you even if you cannot see or hear me, rooting for you every step of the way." Her warm smile fills his heart. "Endurance doesn't have to be a way to inflict pain. Use your power of Endurance to overcome pain, and flourish despite it. Remember who you are."

Hale wipes his tears. His voice cracks when he says, "Please don't tell me you're trying to say goodbye."

Carly kisses Hale's forehead before pulling away. "I have to go."

The strange wind picks up again. Carly looks to the golden disk yearningly.

"I-I don't want you to go," he pleads. He can hardly make out her features and desperately wipes his tears away to see her clearly.

"I will never leave you. And you made me a promise, remember?"

A flashing memory replays in the back of his mind. *Promise me you will live a good life*, Carly had said just before she died in his arms.

"Please don't leave me again," he begs her.

She shakes her head. "You will see me soon enough." Her voice is becoming more ethereal by the moment. Even her essence is turning opaque.

Hale takes in the cues. Carly is leaving. He can't live without her, not again. "No," Hale mouths.

All the same, Hale forces himself to stop reaching out to her. Defeated, his arms fall to his sides. The shedding tears have come to a halt as he contemplates his fears and puts them aside. Carly needs to go on.

"You d-deserve so much goodness," he blurts before it's too late. "I love you. I will never stop missing you."

Carly beams. "I love you." Her words are barely audible. She walks into the disk, and her soul fades in a silvery flash. The mystical wind, which forcefully led Hale to the golden disk, is sated with Carly's departure, and the air on the bridge stills.

Carly rematerializes before the angels and her parents during Hale's trial.

Assella is reading aloud from Hale's book of life. "It is marked that the spirit with the given physical name of Hale Onadore is born a Griffin in the year of 1009. To mother Geeah of Shielding, father Drenon of Light, and brother Bayo of Endurance. In the year 1014, during the Griffin Clan's civil war, Hale's mother and father died, leaving Bayo as his rightful guardian.

"Bayo brings Hale to the Welcoming Moon in his fifth year, long before Griffins traditionally receive their powers, in hopes that the invaders who sought the deaths of Bayo and his company—later to be known as the Elders—will not harm the child, Hale. Felix prophesizes the night of the Welcoming Moon and does not see a threat in attending. He is mistaken, for after Hale receives the power of Endurance, the group is ambushed, and Hale is dropped from the skies.

"To spare his life until a cure was found for his condition, Bayo places Hale in an enchanted sleep. Bayo finds the cure and refuses to wake Hale until his plans for total domination are completed. He does this as a result of Felix's premonitions in which Hale might turn against his brother in time of war. In Hale's thousandth and fifth year, Felix, Naomi, and Carly steal Hale away from Bayo, due to the several prophecies Felix has received convincing him that Hale should be in his care.

"It is thus prophesized that the boy contains the power to abolish all existence in the physical worlds. Whether he will do this is unclear. As it is unclear of his joining with Bayo, thus unleashing Bayo's tyrannical rule over the worlds thus named Malphora and Orcura.

"Felix and his family have since failed in their plan of rescuing Hale and molding him for goodness, for they perished in what is called the Human Division of Malphora, offering him back to his rightful guardian, Bayo, who successfully molds him for evil only one year later."

The light in Naomi's soul dims while Felix mutters, "That cannot be."

Assella turns the grand page. "Behold! All the evil Hale thought in that time." A long list is visible in a very small script. The list goes on, and the book flips pages on its own accord. "And here, all the unintentional evil he wrought onto the world, and here are his intentional evil actions."

Carly, Felix, and Naomi are in disbelief, though silenced by the proof while the angels deliberate.

"It is well known that Hale's immeasurable power exists to destroy the worlds, for good reason. The evil that has befallen those physical worlds is too grand and must be eradicated by him," says a lion-headed angel.

An eagle-headed angel chimes in, "Even if the worlds are somehow redeemed, Hale was born to the physical worlds, which gives him free choice to act as he will. He has chosen the dark nature he was born with, glorifying Bayo and his teachings."

All the angels agree.

"Yes!"

"It is true."

"Evidently, Felix's, Naomi's, and Carly's training did not make a difference to Hale's life path but only brought him closer to Bayo in due time for his plans to dominate Malphora," says an ox-faced angel.

At this note, Felix's essence alights with fury. "May I speak?" he asks.

Assella nods.

"Not I, my wife, or my daughter took part in *training* Hale. Hale is our son. We didn't know he was our son until I received a premonition. In that premonition, I saw Hale's goodness matched with the way he was as a mortal Griffin, just shy of his fifth year. The amount of heroics that child has done in the time of the invasion would baffle you—and where are they listed in this confounded book? Show them to me!"

The book remains still, while the angels look on to see the truth of Felix's words. Then Assella waves a hand over the book, forcing its pages to flip. There, a new white page near the beginning materializes, and written on it is every good thing Hale has done before his accident at the age of five.

"I *love* my son," Felix says. "My wife loves her son, and Carly loves her brother. We taught him the difference between right and wrong. We did not *train* him like a domesticated animal. After we woke him, he did not remember his life during the war a thousand years ago. Perhaps it was because he was asleep for so long. It was not hard for him to adjust to the Human Division. It was especially not hard for him to be a good person while we raised him in the Human Division. Where in this book does it mention that?"

Assella again waves a hand over the book, and suddenly, several black pages burn and are replaced by glistening white pages depicting Hale's childhood with Felix, Naomi, and Carly.

"Include his good thoughts, good intentions, and good actions during this time, please," Naomi says.

Assella does. The book is whitening by the moment.

Felix goes on, "Now reveal his needless suffering, or does that count for nothing? Endless pain follows him. Between the deaths of his birth parents, the war, the accident, and being in a coma for a thousand years, then at the loss of Naomi and myself—"

"And I can attest to the time proceeding," Carly interrupts. Assella nods for her to go ahead. "Hale and I were kidnapped by Greon, who acted out of fear for what Bayo might do to his own family if he had not succeeded in retrieving Hale. We were physically abused and neglected for months on end. On the day of our escape, Greon drowned Hale to get answers from me. When Hale fell unconscious, Greon revived him. We fled, with his burning fever, and were attacked in the woods where Hale used his powers unknowingly on Greon when I was stabbed. I then died in his arms."

Felix and Naomi hold steadfast to their brave daughter's hands.

Naomi then adds, "You cannot believe that Hale's presence in the Griffin Clan was any less horrible. How many times did he escape death while he was there?"

The black book fills with more white pages once Assella forces it to reveal Hale's suffering.

Carly then adds, "In the time my spirit was lost in the Human Division, Hale has done many great things in the Griffin Clan. I've seen them when I entered his dreams a year later. He's helped several people from death and mistreatment. Norton, River, Evan, and Grace, among others. He is not what you say he is. He is not evil. He will not choose evil."

A lion-headed angel questions her. "How would you know what Hale should choose? Even your father thus titled on Malphora as the Elder Prophet of the Griffin Clan remained unsure of Hale's path during life."

Carly says, "My family and I did not sacrifice our lives without reason. I know what Hale will choose. The moment he saw the truth about Bayo, Hale realized what he allowed Bayo to do, and he fled. Hale severed his alliance with his brother, broke the barrier Bayo placed around the Griffin Clan, and made amends with those he truly loves only minutes later."

Suddenly, one golden page is added to the end of the book.

Carly continues, "Do not forget he paid for the mistakes he's made under Bayo's influence as soon as his path crossed with the siren. The siren didn't have the opportunity to take his life, as she did not finish her song. He is in excruciating pain, only surviving this long because he is an Endurance Griffin—"

Assella holds out a hand to stop Carly from going on. Carly and her family cannot tell whether there are more white pages than black, and they hold on to each other desperately.

Assella says, "The possibility of Hale returning to his brother has become obsolete, as he has fled from him, and Bayo presumes he is dead. Therefore, three possible futures are still in consideration. If Hale's soul returns to his body, will he destroy the worlds with his power, thus cleansing them of their wicked ways, will he fight alongside goodness, or shall this be his time of death—leaving the destiny of the worlds to their superpowers?"

Another human-headed angel says, "In the hope the worlds will heal by fighting for goodness, and in the belief that Hale can conquer his gift of destruction, I will vote for Hale to continue life."

A third human-headed angel says, "I do not believe Hale is able to fight against his gift, as the affliction of Endurance gives him great pleasure. And I do believe the world must be cleansed. His power was given to him for good reason. I vote for Hale's life."

The fourth human-headed angel then makes its decision. "Let the superpowers defend the worlds; Hale's life offers no guarantee. Better not to risk the consequences. I vote for Hale's death."

Assella is quiet while staring at Hale's book of life and deliberating the final vote. "Hale's immense power was given for a reason," it finally says, "but that reason cannot be deduced by the likes of us. Furthermore, Hale has proven on more than one occasion his boundless capacity for good. While it remains utterly important that he keeps on this path or is removed from it entirely, the outcome of his death might also result in a world catastrophe. I believe the gift to be a test of his character, and a test he will consciously pass. I believe him to be greater than we take him for . . . I vote for his life!"

Felix, Naomi, and Carly's leap of joy is interrupted when Assella warns, "Do not exalt, spirits. We do not have the final decision."

Hale's book of life shuts closed, and suddenly the group of sixteen angels morph into four distinct beings. Each being has four faces on one head. The human face in the front, the lion's face to the right, the ox's face to the left, and the eagle's face in the back. To behold them in this form is absolutely terrifying, which could have been why they have chosen to separate parts of themselves while near Felix, Naomi, and Carly. They get into position—two in the front and two in the back—and raise their hands up simultaneously.

In the space above their heads forms what looks to be a sapphire crystal. It grows upward at an infinite length and becomes a throne. The space they exist in booms, and Carly looks down, nearly jumping.

She is hovering over the three worlds. Thurana, Orcura, and Malphora, where she lived in life. Clouds float beautifully in the skies of Malphora. Mighty storms seem so tiny from where Carly now looks on. The separation of the Human Division and Extraordinary Division is so prominent from where she stands, like a massive cut around the perimeter of the world.

The ocean sky of Orcura is just as she imagined. Peering closer magnifies her vision. She makes out mighty sea creatures within that ocean sky; then her vision focuses on the center of the world, where the different floating islands rotate around the light source, the Loom. To her surprise, she can also spot the Orcuran people traveling between islands on airborne animals!

Thurana, the desolate world, is filled with serpent people performing horrific acts of violence. Carly does not linger on them for too long, for the stars come into view all around them, including the moons orbiting the worlds, distant planets, and galaxies from the three distinct universes combined!

She gasps in wonder. *How is this possible?*

A mighty quake unlike any tremor Carly experienced before comes from above. Neither the angels, Carly, nor her parents waver from their hovering spot, however. She senses its power, like the rupture of volcanoes! Accompanying the tremor is the familiar presence that enveloped Carly when Hale died. Though she knows it is the same energy, it's in an entirely different form—its true form, sitting upon the sapphire throne.

The being seems to be made of blazing fire, and she cannot look directly at it. It is a million times stronger than if one were to look at the sun in the physical world. A large rainbow aura encompasses the being, which includes colors Carly did not even know existed because her vision was limited. It is as if each color represented a different aspect about the all-encompassing being. It is hard to explain the essence that felt so powerful, intimidating, and yet so loving.

Golden and glowing orb-like spirits hover near the throne, an equal amount to its left and right. The orbs transform, just as Carly's parents had, into the shapes of their once physical forms. These spiritual beings were not at all like the genderless angels, for the ones on the left resemble women, and those on the right resemble men. All of which wear shining diamond-like crowns. They look like stars. Instinctually, Carly understands these are grand peoples from all points in time that once lived in the physical worlds, now spirits joined together as kings and queens beside the Most High.

Hale's book of life soars upward until it disappears. Not but a second longer—if seconds existed in a place that is not bound by time—a thundering voice emanates from the being on the throne, as powerful as a typhoon, though not comprehensible to Carly, Felix, and Naomi's spirits, who share a look of astonishment.

"Hale Onadore will continue life," Assella translates.

Hale's family rejoices, their meager essences illuminate.

Unfortunately, Assella adds, "But he must prove his stance in life. The trial keeps on!"

CHAPTER 8

H ale inhales sharply and his eyes come wide. He faces a starry sky, not
very different from the sky on the cobblestone bridge. Is he still there?
No, he couldn't be . . . the stars are farther away, and the golden moon
is gone. Still, he isn't sure. *It's quiet,* he notes. Unaware that he cannot yet grasp
sound, Hale groggily attempts to move, but it proves difficult to twitch even a
finger. His tender body is throbbing everywhere.

Hazily, Evan and River come into view above him. They are staring. *Why do
they look so shocked?* Hale's brows furrow as their lips move. *Are they speaking to
me? I don't hear what they are saying.*

But wait . . . Carly was just with him. She held him and kissed his cheek. Cringing,
Hale decides it's worth a check. Using the sum of his strength, he looks around.

"Carly?" he calls. "I can't lose her again."

River is too stunned for words.

Hale continues, "She was just here. Where did she go?" His voice is hoarse.

River takes Hale's cold hands, and Hale tries to read his lips. "Hale.
Everything will be okay."

But it is far from okay. The white noise in the back of his mind fades, and the sounds of the forest are amplifying. *What is that howling . . . and banging?* He sits up, and the boys give him a hand.

"Everything hurts," he mumbles, holding his throbbing crown. Determined to find where his sister went, Hale forces his head up and points. "She was standing right over there." But instead of his radiant sister, Hale is met with grotesque monsters. Left, right, no matter where he turns, their grimacing, bloody faces bang at an invisible wall. And before River warns him not to look, Hale meets the hypnotic gaze of their third eyes. River jumps in the way of Hale's view, but it is too late. Hale's eyes roll back.

The glance into the violet cyclone of the vyrtrusk's third eye returns all of Hale's worst memories.

Suddenly, Hale is in front of his mother's dead body. Every inch of her skin is burned and black. "I don't want you to see Mom," he recalls Carly saying. But who would stop him? For the life of him, Hale didn't believe his parents were dead. The doctors and nurses must have been wrong. But here Naomi is, in a freezing drawer at the morgue, covered by a zipped-up plastic bag. Even this temperature can't subdue the strong smell of her charred flesh, like burnt red meat. The contents of his stomach rise.

There is a jolt.

Hale is now standing before two dug pits. This is his parents' gravesite, on the day of their funeral. He wears a stiff black suit and clutches on to his grieving sister. They are gone . . . Carly's voice rings in his ears, "It's just you and me now." Their parents slowly descend into the freshly dug ground. Carly topples over and sobs. Hale grabs hold of her and swears he will never let her go.

The scene changes, and Hale is walking home from school, eager to run into Carly's arms after a long and hard day, when he is grabbed from behind on an empty street. His screams are unending. "Please. HELP!" No one comes to his rescue. A heavy hand clasps his mouth, and Hale peers over to see the assailant's face. But Hale does not know him. He can't believe this is happening. After an unsuccessful fight for freedom, Hale's mouth is bound with a rag, and his hands are strapped behind his back. Through muffled, heart-wrenching cries, he is stuffed into the trunk of a car.

The vibration of the revving engine cascades over to the dark trunk while Hale attempts to smash the taillights. His efforts are short-lived when the car travels over several harsh bumps. Hale struggles to hold on. Something rolls over onto him. It is a comatose person with long hair. The flowery perfume the person wears is familiar . . . she smells like . . . Carly . . . Hale screams through his tied mouth.

"Carly," he manages through the rag. "Carly, wake up!" He squirms to shake her, but she does not wake. Hale assumes the worst, and who could blame him after the mysterious deaths of his parents?

Carly's weight on Hale prevents him from moving, though he can feel her breathing lightly. The car comes to a complete stop, and the trunk opens. The light of day blinds Hale's eyes, the swelling red lump visible on Carly's forehead. Hale, exhausted, continues to scream for help. The three are somewhere in the woods.

Another jolt.

Every single night in that cellar replays. The iron cuffs ripping into his wrists, the helplessness, the endless hours of torment. Sick, cold, and hungry on a concrete floor with bare necessities.

Another jolt.

Greon's dagger enters Carly's back.

Her last moments.

She was the last thing he had.

Her last touch, with her blood-smeared hands.

The countless hours he spent digging the pit he would place her in as she lay near him.

The mounds of soil he heaped over her dead body.

Hale screams in the waking world. In a flash, his overflowing eyes burn a dazzling white. Evan and River fall backward at the impact. But the visions are not done with him yet.

Bayo's glowing image appears like a saving grace, bringing meaning and purpose to Hale's life once again. Finally, Hale had someone else to love, and who loved him in return, as his family had. Someone who mentored him, understood his hidden aspects, and was patient with him. Just when Hale felt powerful and unstoppable, he learned that the man he idolized was an imposter. All it took was opening a single door.

The man he worshiped, obeyed, and loved was a murderer. Bayo murdered my family. *All the pain Hale went through in his life resulted from Bayo's selfishness and schemes.* He never loved me. What a fool I was to believe someone could love me that way again. How could I let him change me? I'm no better than him. I am a monster!

After a dangerous fall, Hale spots a gorgeous girl standing at the edge of a cliff. He swears her voice is the most blissful thing he's ever heard. For that moment, all his problems and thoughts melted away. Then came the pain. The bruises formed on his body, and it felt like something was clawing and beating him from the inside. His blood boils and bubbles. He so desperately wants to wake up, but there is no escape, not even behind shut eyes. Passing out did not relieve him. Every single touch, even resting on the ground or the plush back of his Griffin friends while they flew, was pure anguish.

And suddenly the siren's spell returns all at once.

Hale's torment is unbearable. His eyes blaze into the pitch-black sky. His veins protrude from his body while he howls at the stars. The woods are silent, part of his voice, and everything is engulfed in his light.

River hastily places a force field around himself and Evan.

A wave materializes from Hale's body like a radial wind. The pack of vyrtrusks stumbles backward. River and Evan scatter to hide behind evergreen trees that have shriveled to brittle planks poking out from the ground. They endure the blistering wind and Hale's tormented howl until it dies down.

It is over.

River peeks out from what was once a trunk. The radiating light pouring from Hale's eyes is no more, for Hale's eyes have shut.

Every tree, blade of grass, and flower has withered and greyed. The once ghastly vyrtrusks turned to black stone before crumbling to ash and floating away. The spooky fog of the woods has cleared, along with the banshees. All that remains safe and sound in the Banshee Forest are its three Griffin visitors.

River and Evan perk up in amazement. Instantly, they sense the darkness of the forest is abolished. How strange that everything has died, yet the forest is suddenly so alive. Even their hearts that were turned against each other feel brighter and lighter.

The boys step cautiously toward their pack brother when glowing white particles arise from the land and glitter the scape.

Hale is sprawled on the soil. His chest rises and falls steadily. Miraculously, he made it out of the vyrtrusks' epic punishment alive, and he is at last free of the siren's plague.

"I was wrong. I'm sorry," says Evan to River.

River pats him on the back. "Me too."

Evan holds out Felix's journal. "Take it, it's yours."

River slides the book in his satchel. "You can look at it anytime. What's mine is yours, brother-in-law," he says.

Evan pauses. "Brother-in-law?"

River is trying not to laugh.

"What do you m—"

Just then, the forest begins to hum. Beings are creeping out from behind the withered trees.

"They are coming towards us," says Evan. "Are they banshees?"

"I think they used to be," says River.

The soft hum of the spirits intensifies as they approach. They are aglow in white light rather than the opaque and muted grey and blue they were. Individual happy faces smile down at Hale, gathering around his sleeping body.

Evan is about to protest, but River stops him.

"I think it's okay," River says.

The whispers of the brilliant spirits echo through the clearing, creating warmth in the crisp air.

"Savior," they whisper.

Hundreds of arms create a web of hands resting on one another, then finally resting on Hale. Hale's skin shimmers and warms. The bruises on his flesh left from the siren's plague dissolve, and even the dark veins left from the lightning bolt alleviate. Hale releases a long and peaceful breath. His lips curve into a faint smile whilst he dreams.

At last.

One by one, the spirits turn into large particles of light that rise into the eternal atmosphere and depart from the physical world.

CHAPTER 9

Bimmorian beetle-crickets sing the night away while Marcus sprints toward the palace in a dashing ensemble. He is dressed in a gold robe and slacks embroidered with royal-blue and purple embellishments. Though this is the most expensive he's ever looked, he doesn't think the colors suit his pale skin and ash-blond hair. Rather, the suit would have highlighted the perfect blue complexion of a natural Bimmorian. Alas, he cannot turn down a gift, especially since Camden handpicked the suit.

The enchanted lanterns on either side of the bridge pick up Marcus's approach and come alive with a yellow flame as he crosses. His pointed shoes click against the stone. Marcus is late, not that he cares, considering he feels like a gold-painted fool. He looks down at his outfit, shakes his head wearily, and lets out a long sigh.

"I can't believe I'm doing this," he says as if he had any choice in the matter. After all, what privileged student of the Royal Academy would turn down an invitation to the annual Summer's Solstice Ball? Especially if the general of the kingdom insisted.

Marcus enters the palace. Inviting cool air whooshes past him, and the bright white interior echoes with muffled music. He recognizes the instrument immediately, the sincerous. Marcus once spoke of a young girl who played such an instrument when he'd first arrived in the capital a year ago. Camden later casually mentioned that he found the same musician and invited her to play at this ball. Though Camden boasted of her talent, Marcus knew Camden only invited her to please him. This action should have been sufficient to break his internal angst, but Marcus cannot help but worry.

He makes his way through the several elaborate corridors and to the ballroom. The music grows louder, and Marcus quickly checks his breast pocket and sighs in relief. *Good, I didn't forget it.*

The fifteen-foot-tall double doors to the ballroom are guarded by a few palace guards. The vibrations of the music matches the thumping of his heart.

He recalls Camden's words from yesterday. *"For Malphora's sake, you look like a ghost! You are going to a ball, not a battlefield!"*

Marcus then nervously rambled, "I've never been to any sort of party in all my life. I heard from the students that at such events, you must dance. One could not possibly dance in front of frequent dancers at such an event if one had never danced before. If one does not dance, what would others think of that person!" Especially in this golden getup.

Camden simply laughed and offered to teach him a few Bimmorian moves. But at the sight of his extended hand, Marcus turned red. "No, thank you!" He didn't want to embarrass himself.

Now approaching the ballroom, Marcus couldn't possibly hate himself more for making such a decision, for the guests are all dancing. When he comes to the end of the hall, the guards unexpectedly whip their sabers in front of the door to prevent him from entering.

"Invitation?" the guard on his left asks flatly.

Marcus pulls a small card from his breast pocket and swallows. None of his exchanges with Bimmorian guards were pleasant. The moment they see his pale skin, they turn sour. He'd never experienced prejudice until he came to the capital. Marcus grew up in his secluded town at the edge of Bimmorus, where the Griffin refugees lived. There were so many rules to follow and permits their family had to have to be able to walk freely in the rest of the kingdom since King Owen's passing. Marcus wishes he could use inventor Lady Thelmure's ring, which projects the illusion of blue skin, but Camden took it from him, saying something along the lines of, *"Marcus, you are like a fine pearl in the blue sea. A rarity, a treasure. If I ever see you hide your true self again—so help me!"*

The guard gives his papers a once-over and grunts. "You must wait until the performance commences before entering."

That suited Marcus just fine. He could watch the talented Bimmorian girl flick her sincerous from the doorway.

"Then you will be announced in," continues the guard.

Announced? Marcus turns paler than he already is. No one invited to such an event would dare turn up late for the sole consequence of ridicule by the most influential people in government. Not to mention, it was disrespectful to the king. But being so young and new to this world, Marcus had not realized his entrance would be publicized. He takes several steps back, contemplating escape. *Camden wouldn't be that mad,* he thinks.

Someone calls his name from behind. It is Evangeline, the princess of Bimmorus, waving hello gleefully from the end of the hall. She is escorted by two guards on either side.

Her glittering, light-blue, and silver freckled skin is brought out by her stunning—and, ironically, gold—gown. Its train and sleeves flow behind her. Golden sequins cascade down the dress. And as she moves, the tint of the dress shimmers in electric lavender. A delicate golden band is at the base of her head, bejeweled with precious stones. Her long and curled blonde hair sways side to side.

Marcus takes a breath. There is no doubt in his mind that Camden had purposely bought him this suit to match the princess's gown.

Evangeline flashes a charismatic smile and points to his clothes. "Marcus! We match!" she giggles. "Did someone tell you what I would wear this evening?"

Feeling foolish for not bowing sooner, Marcus attempts to remedy his mistake. He awkwardly bends his torso forward and stutters, "N-no, Your Majesty. I had no idea."

"What a coincidence!" she exclaims. "Imagine how positively stunning it would be to walk into the ball together. Arm in arm. Not to mention better for your sake, considering you're late."

Marcus blushes. In this brief moment, he wonders how this disastrous moment has turned into the most significant thing that ever happened to him. Before he can answer, the performance ends, and the guests of the ball stomp their feet to show their appreciation for the talented girl with the sincerous. Just then, rhythmic drums bang to signify an entrance into the ballroom.

"Let me take your arm, Marcus," Evangeline whispers.

He repositions himself and she grabs hold. The pressure of her delicate fingers, even through his suit, makes his heart race. His forehead is damp with sweat.

The guard to his left stomps his grand staff on the floor and hollers, "Welcoming, Evangeline Belflore, princess of Bimmorus, and companion, Marcus Theoden of the Royal Academy."

They walk forward with offbeat timing as Marcus clearly misses his cue. The crowd kneels before their princess.

In the blink of his eyes, Marcus is transported. The moon whirls forward, though it is opaque, covered slightly by cloud. *What did that mean?* Marcus is somewhere dimly lit and damp, perhaps underground. It is noticeably colder. A puff of smoky air expels from his mouth. Strangely enough, Marcus is not wearing his golden suit for the current occasion but instead tattered clothes, stained with blood and earth. The Bimmorians are still in front of him, exactly as they stood in the ballroom. He looks to Evangeline and gasps.

Once perfect long hair is cut unevenly from shoulder to ear. She is battered and frail. Her open skin is marked with bruises and wounds. Her clothes are that of the destitute. Oddly enough, she smiles at him. There are tears in her eyes.

"We made it," she whispers, squeezing his hand tight.

The necklace Marcus currently has in the breast pocket of his golden suit is resting on Evangeline's neck. His heart skips a beat. He realizes the Bimmorians were not just bowing to the princess but to him as well. *How strange.*

The crowd in the ballroom is staring at the strange pale man their princess is clutching on to, not for any of the obvious reasons but rather because he seems to have fallen asleep with his eyes open. Evangeline recognizes Marcus is consumed by another vision and moves to improvise until he wakes.

With a simple extended hand, the Bimmorian subjects rise from their bent positions and gaze upon the young princess—and the unblinking golden fool beside her.

"Happy Solstice!" Evangeline begins.

The king is staring daggers her way. Evangeline swallows nervously. It was a mistake to have come so late, and with a Griffin boy, no less. To top it off, it appears she is basking in the light of her inappropriateness by calling attention to herself. She's going to hear about this later.

And yet, the crowd responds in unison, "Happy Solstice!"

She clears her throat wondering what else she might add. "Please pardon me for the interruption. I only yearned to say . . . that on behalf of myself and my family, we wish only good tidings and a fortunate year ahead for you, your loved ones, and all of Bimmorus." She glimpses briefly at Marcus and bites her lip. He hasn't woken from his trance. Subtly, she tugs on his arm to try to stir him. "May your crops be plentiful, healthy, and grow tenfold the usual amount! May your health thrive! May all your endeavors succeed! May you be happy beyond comprehension! Long live this great nation!"

The Bimmorians are stunned. The princess never spoke aloud to her subjects.

Finally, the silence breaks when a goblet rises from Camden's hand. His drink sloshes to and fro, dripping on the hem of some guest's gown. His voice booms throughout the ballroom, and he flashes his charming smile. "Long live Bimmorus!"

The others join in with exuberance.

Camden's voice is unmistakable and reaches through to Marcus's strange vision. Marcus searches the parallel world for Camden, but Camden's face is absent among the underground crowd. It is haunting, especially since Marcus is usually deaf to the real world while experiencing a premonition. He had not even heard Evangeline's speech, though they are standing together. There is no doubt about it. The fact that whatever Camden just said is audible, though he is not in the vision, is a clue for Marcus. He is sucked from the dream the way a wave pulls back into the ocean. Before he knows it, he is back at the party.

Evangeline gives a long sigh of relief and leans in. "There you are!" she whispers. "Make haste. My father is about to explode."

Marcus glimpses in the king's direction. The princess isn't exaggerating. William's furrowed brow could house a flock of femus, and his fiery face might have enough heat to warm the room twice over. Evangeline whisks Marcus down the steps and into the crowd where they meet many curious adults who question quite too many things.

"My! You look beautiful, Princess! Is this your betrothed?"

"Princess, what a wonderful speech! Is this young man a Griffin? I had no idea Griffins lived in Bimmorus—"

"Your Majesty, you are the spitting image of your mother! May she rest peacefully. How do you find growing without maternal care?"

Marcus is horrified.

All the same, Evangeline smiles graciously. "No, he is not my betrothed," she answers. "And yes, he is a Griffin, as a matter of fact. He is a prophet. He could tell you your fortune with the touch of a hand. I would allow you one small insight, as you are an elite. But do know, his gifts are *strictly* used by the *royals*. I give no one else in all of Bimmorus such a privilege. Consider yourself very lucky. You may hold out your hand."

Marcus blushes and wonders why Evangeline just lied. He cannot tell people's fortunes! His gift is entirely random—and a nuisance, he would add.

A man eagerly holds out his hand for Marcus to take. All that is left for Marcus to do is pretend. Once taking the man's clammy hand into his, Marcus gives a slight jump, as if frightened by what he's seen, and stares blankly in the distance.

"Well? What is it? What do you see, boy?" the man asks.

Marcus drops his hand and looks at the man solemnly. "Outlook not so good."

The man is stammering for words. "Wait, I—"

Evangeline smirks and turns to the woman who spoke of her mother. "Thank you for your lovely compliment. I am very proud to resemble her in any way I can. Of course, I would like to have her with me, but no, I am not in a position of lack. I am the princess of Bimmorus, and as such, I am provided for in every way imaginable, including personal happiness, fulfillment, and familial love."

With not a moment more to spare, Camden steps into the conversing circle with another drink sloshing in his hand. He silently gazes at the hovering elites and guzzles down his beverage. Though Evangeline has them put in their places, the mere sight of Camden sends them running altogether.

Camden lifts a brow. "Well, that was entertaining." He nudges Evangeline. "Who knew you had such wits about you?" She smiles, quite pleased with herself, until he says, "No doubt from me, as we know that couldn't have come from William."

Evangeline playfully shoves him. "I did not require saving, cousin."

"No doubt," he agrees. "I only wished to experience the mischief firsthand." He tells Marcus, "You can sense the fortune of others by touch, aye? That was by far some excellent acting. My drink almost shot through my nose at the sight of Pollard's face!"

The three laugh.

Then Marcus remembers. "Camden. Can I speak with you?"

Camden nods. "Yes, I need to speak with you as well."

Evangeline is unbothered. "Oh, there are the girls from the academy! I'll be with them." She departs.

Camden inquires, "Your vision at the top of the stairs?"

Marcus moves close to Camden's ear and tells him everything he's seen.

Camden scratches his stubble. "What could this mean?"

Marcus shakes. "You know what this could mean."

Camden sighs. "Not this again! Marcus, those are just warning signs. They could be a parallel future, for all we know."

Marcus is enraged. He draws close to Camden and extends his first finger. "There is nothing ulterior about what I've seen, and you know it! I've already had five visions. First, the royal towers falling and Griffins roaming our skies." Marcus nearly points to the king. "Then of your—"

Hastily, Camden places a hand against Marcus's mouth to stop him from speaking further. "Yes, Marcus. But you've also had these visions before we completed the barrier around the kingdom. There will be no such happenings befalling Bimmorus. I took care of that."

Marcus's hands ball into fists. "You were not in my last vision. You know I'm right. There must be something we can do."

"What more is there to do, hmm? Do you have any suggestions?"

"I'll tell William," Marcus offers.

Camden laughs. "Telling William is possibly the *worst* thing you could do. Not that he would believe you anyway." He grabs hold of Marcus's shoulders. "Listen to me carefully. If anything devastating should happen, it is meant to be that way. Whether the dark situation befalls the kingdom or any of your dear friends. And do not think I do not heed your words. I will take extra measures to protect the kingdom upon your warnings. Now with that said, this is a party for *Malphora's* sake! Speaking of which, you were very late."

Marcus tugs at his costume and huffs, "Yeah, I'm sorry."

Camden shrugs. "It did work out to your benefit. Walking in with the princess. Matching her dress exactly. You both looked like a pair of twinkling stars."

Marcus gives him a snide look. "Did you have anything to do with that?"

"The dress, yes. Evangeline is often drawn to vanity and well-put-together men, such as myself." He smiles jokingly. "But the rest I cannot take credit for. That fate's doing." He slaps Marcus's back.

A servant brings another round of drinks and offers it to the two gentlemen. Camden replaces his glass and thanks him. "Marcus, I have a surprise to share with the guests." He pulls out his pocket watch. "It should arrive in precisely one hour. So I suggest you enjoy the party and make haste with your romantic plans."

Marcus blushes. *Does he have to be so loud?*

Camden leans in. "She likes you, you know. She wouldn't walk in with just anybody and declare a grand speech on their behalf." He shoves Marcus toward the academy girls, shouting, "Go get her!"

Marcus has half a mind to hit him playfully, but all he can do is give him a stink face. All the while, Camden continues to urge him along with an ear-to-ear grin.

CHAPTER 10

The dark and chilly cave glitters with mounds of precious stones, gems, and tokens. Embedded in its rock are shimmering crystals the length of half the average person. With a wooden torch in hand, Bayo shuffles down winding stairs of stone. The fire beside him illuminates his half-dead face. He continues with a slumped posture.

As a man who once took value in his appearance, Bayo seems like a different person. Whoever knew him and knew him well would know Bayo never wore black. Yet here he was, in all back, passing his glittering treasures among the protruding limestone stalagmites, carelessly.

Each treasure in this cave represents another memory of Bayo's eternal existence. Over the years, he'd convinced himself he needed these treasures to prepare for the war he is bringing to Malphora. But now, he wonders if he would put any use to them at all.

Lost troves from many countries are among this collection. Their heaping mounds soar above Bayo's head and continue to the end of the cave, leaving a narrow path for walking. Coins and jewels clatter at his feet. He enters the rocky depths and ganders at the several open chests containing expensive jewelry. Worthless items to him. He left them for Rioma and Ianna's pleasure; however,

Rioma never allowed Ianna to wear them. The chests are open and dug through. Jewels that did not appeal to Rioma are tossed aside indifferently, much like what a furry pest does searching for its next meal in one's heap of rubbish.

It's been approximately twelve years since Bayo last visited his massive treasure trove. There were so many things here that he had not thought about in centuries, like the platinum tokens stacked high to his left. Immediately, they bring back the memory of how he, Felix, and Greon stole this cursed money from the Isles of Nepenth. To a mere mortal, the touch of the silver would decay their flesh within minutes. Needless to say, the Elders were unaffected—not that he told his companions about the possibility of their deaths upon touching the items . . .

The jewels lessen as Bayo sinks deeper into the cave. Submerged in moist darkness, a faint moaning amplifies. His torch illuminates several crates where he keeps a swarm of undying creatures that are formally known to be extinct in the Extraordinary Division. Zylans. At first glance, you would not assume they are creatures at all but piles of grey sand. Endless moaning marked by starvation betrays their innocent appearance. For a single drop of blood would stir their infinite sleep and devour any life in proximity to satiate their bloodlust.

Bayo approaches a dead end yet incredibly steps through the stone wall. Long ago, Felix used magic to mimic what they'd seen in the Kingdom of Bimmorus when they found the Three Eyes. Beyond the wall is the true hidden wonder of Bayo's treasury.

Bayo tightens the grip on his torch at the recollection of the bond he once shared with Felix. Felix was the only man he ever trusted. As Bayo's most trusted friend, Felix was the only one who knew about Bayo's secret places. To the rest of the world, Bayo's treasured place exists beyond the waterfall where the bioluminescent bay twinkles in the night. *Of all the ways he could have betrayed me. Of all the ways to make a mockery of my plans. Did he have to stoop so low? Did he have to destroy me?*

Past the stone is a breathtaking sky, spotted with moving stars. Grand planets soar in the distance. Bayo removes his shoes and sinks his toes into the plush grass, the softest grass in all of Malphora. He sighs as the smooth blades caress his rough soles. It is a bittersweet moment to recall building this scape with his once greatest friend. Bayo is brought back to the countless memories he spent here with him. Day after day, they would contemplate their plans, hide away from the other Elders, and enjoy their collection. This mystic place, stagnant from time, is still as dazzling as ever.

Bayo strolls to the still ocean that makes no sound. Upon creating this world, he wished the sea would be without a single wave or current. Now, as Bayo walks along the white beach, he admits that this silent world is eerie without Felix. He has half a mind to destroy it this very moment. His rage intensifies, and he throws his torch into the water before slumping down into the sand. It is a strange spot to pick to sit, considering this is where Bayo and Felix last spoke to one another.

"What are we doing?" Felix asks while sitting on the shore after a wondrous flight to a distant planet.

"We are resting," Bayo chuckles.

"Are you not bored?" asks Felix with a frustrated tone.

Bayo is puzzled. "Bored? We have everything anyone could ever want. Riches, pleasure, leisure, freedom. Everything is in our control, and soon the outside world will follow." He places his hands behind his head and enjoys the perfect weather.

Felix gestures to the still ocean. "The ocean is not supposed to be controlled. What is the point if it doesn't move?"

Bayo scoffs. "I could will this ocean to move whenever I please. That is the beauty of it."

Felix grimaces. "It shouldn't be so."

Bayo groans as he sits up. "What are you going on about?"

"What am I going on about? This life—our lives are without purpose."

Bayo shrugs. "The sun does not set for us; we are Elders. What is the rush! We will conquer everything in due time."

Felix says, "We waste away here."

Bayo says, "Every step must be thought through for our plan to—"

Clearly agitated, Felix shouts, "Yes, yes. The plans. The grand finale! To which you fantasize Griffin domination, and you will surely achieve it with your loads of treasures. Then finally, you will wake your brother from his endless slumber. When will these plans take place? What more tools must you acquire before you decide to give it a rest?"

If anyone else had spoken to Bayo in such a manner, he'd have them withering in torment. But not Felix. Never Felix.

Calmly, Bayo explains, "I require nothing else besides the allegiance of Thurana before anything commences."

Finally, the truth.

"Thurana!" Felix rises to his feet. "After I've warned you against it. After I've shared my visions that showed the horrors they would do to our world! Why bring the serpent people to Malphora? Is there no end to your madness?"

Bayo growls, "You are testing my patience, Felix."

Felix turns red. "My words are that worthless to you? I've never had a false premonition!"

Bayo glowers. "Yes you have."

Felix pauses. Now it was clear why Bayo would never listen to him. "I have only been wrong once. Nine hundred some-odd years ago!"

Finally, Bayo snaps. "I don't care if it was a billion years ago! I'll never forget the trouble you've caused."

"You're on a mission to destroy the world in spite of me!" Felix shouts.

"We need Thurana's help. We are just one nation taking on the world," argues Bayo.

"Exactly! Who needs the world? Look at the world you already have!" Felix gestures to the great scape in front of them. "It's infinite. We can create anything we want here. We are free to play and explore and live in this fantasy we've created. Not to mention you also have The Eyes, for Malphora's sake! We can travel and enjoy any place in the three worlds!"

Bayo groans, "No, Felix. I will not stop until everything is in order. Everything must be in order. I've thought it all through. They have the numbers, but we have the power of the Welcoming Moon. The serpents won't be able to take over the Griffin nation. We will win. Then Griffins will finally be free and prosper."

"I'm leaving," Felix says flatly. "I'm taking my family and we are leaving the Griffin Clan."

Stunned, Bayo pauses. "Where will you go?"

"Anywhere! All the years I've dedicated to you. All these years and we've watched your madness grow. You are dead inside, and I wish I could help you, but nothing is as important as getting what you want."

"And what is that exactly?" Bayo shouts.

"Power! Bayo, the superior Griffin of Endurance! Bayo, the almighty Griffin warrior! Bayo, the mighty Elder of Endurance! Bayo, the king of the Griffins! Bayo, the emperor of Malphora! Do you approve of all your titles and the one yet to come? You will have your throne, all the treasures in the worlds, and countless nations at your feet, begging you for mercy! But you have lost your soul! And you sure as hell lost me! You won't even remember I'm gone, I can assure you! Do you even remember Hale?"

That last one hit a nerve. "You do not speak of my brother!" A surge courses through Bayo's body and strikes Felix so tremendously that he falls to his knees. "You who put him at so much risk. You are the sole reason for his condition. You should be grateful I've forgiven you after the mess you've created."

This is the first time Felix has felt Bayo's power.

Felix moans through the pain. With a clenched jaw, he says, "Make all the excuses you wish. You're just lying to yourself. You wear his cure as a necklace for safekeeping! You have the power to wake him! All the warnings in the worlds couldn't stop you! You are incapable of doing the right thing! You are a coward. Bayo, king of the cowards! You've got Greon beat!"

Bayo releases the agony he inflicts on Felix at once. "Why don't you understand?"

But he thinks, I do not dare wake him with your confounded premonition hanging over my head. The premonition of he and Hale as enemies if he should awaken in time for this war. But Bayo thinks it pointless to continue his defense.

In a cold whisper, he says, "I won't stop you. Take your family. You may use The Eyes if you wish. Find value in your life that you're lacking by my side."

Felix growls, "You're a lost cause."

"Get out! Leave!" Bayo roars, as he is moments away from striking Felix down with his power.

Felix departs from their treasured world in silence.

It is a memory Bayo wishes he could forget, but here he is, in the very spot beside the still ocean, reenacting it in his mind. His chest aches as he thinks back on it, and he rises to his feet.

True, Hale is dead. But even though Felix stole him, Hale did not die by Felix's hand. He died by the accursed voice of the siren. Half the siren stuck within a mortal vessel, to be exact. And the other half Bayo has hidden here, in this fabricated dimension. It rests in a crystal box forged by the fire of the last Dragon of Malphora at the very bottom of this vacant sea.

He motions his hands, as if he were pulling them apart with great tension, and the ocean parts in two to reveal the crystal box glittering in the light of the suns. Bayo treads steadily through the parted sea and takes the box into his hands. The bouncing entity is visible through the sheer crystal cage.

He glowers, "I will avenge my brother's death."

CHAPTER 11

arcus musters up the courage to approach the gaggle of Bimmorian girls. Evangeline is only a few steps away, her back facing him. Just when Marcus extends his hand, the music picks up, and a swarm of guests pushes between them, advancing to the dance floor. Marcus loses sight of the princess in the commotion. He squirms through while contemplating what he might say.

Should I ask her to dance? No, I can't dance! I would look like a fool—and I already look like a fool! Maybe I should take her away from the crowd and do it there? Ah, but that's not romantic! There she is!

Once again, young Marcus is interrupted when a dashing and young Bimmorian man in purple kneels before the princess and offers her a dance. Marcus's heart stops at the sight of Evangeline's smile. Without a second to spare, she runs off with the attractive blue-toned stranger.

Evangeline leaves behind her friends, who are busy hiding their scowls behind their smiles. On the other hand, Marcus couldn't care less about what the girls thought. Not when it should have been his hand Evangeline is holding. He sinks away behind the several people looking at the dancers and watches the pretentious Bimmorian elite have her attention. He huffs at the sight of them twirling like femus in spring. Her partner lifts her off the floor and spins gracefully. Marcus's mind goes wild. *He hasn't even broken a sweat. Who is this guy? He doesn't go to the Royal Academy. Why is she so taken with him? She won't even spare a moment's glance away from his eyes!*

Marcus has no choice but to avert his attention since his jealousy is too much to tolerate. He looks for Camden, but he has long since left to attend to his personal matters. And though Camden is not beside Marcus, somehow Marcus can hear his voice saying, *Stop that sulking! It's a party, for Malphora's sake! Ask one of the other girls to dance!*

After drawing out a long exhale, Marcus stomps his way over to the group of Bimmorian girls with nothing to lose. He hasn't even given himself a moment to consider their disgust when approached by a Griffin boy. Every girl turns away as he approaches, but he doesn't mind. He makes eye contact with Guenana, who he always thought to be the kindest of all the girls in school. Guenana just so happened to be a harpy who came abroad from her nation in the Outlands to study. At the sight of Marcus, she bats her abnormally long eyelashes, and to his surprise, she smiles and accepts his offer.

His heart skips a beat. *Now what?*

He can hear Camden laugh. *Now, take her to the center of the ballroom and show her off like the prize she is!*

Marcus curses the little Camden inside his head. Nonetheless, he gently pulls Guenana to the dance floor. All heads point in their direction, but he is suddenly too determined to pay mind. With a swiftness he didn't think he possessed, he faces his partner and places a hand at her waist. Marcus continues to mimic the dancing of others and does not dare to part eyes with Guenana, though he so desperately itches to look at Evangeline.

When Marcus spins his partner, he spots the belts restraining her perfect pearly wings.

He leans in and asks Guenana, "Why did you restrain your wings? They are beautiful." Lady Meir always encouraged her students' abilities, so Marcus had often seen Guenana fly about in the academy.

Guenana beams, "Thank you!" Then she sighs. "I was told I was not allowed to attend the ball if I did not wear this. It would offend the elites."

Marcus's jaw clenches. How could the Bimmorians invite those of different nations to study in their kingdom but restrict them of their nature? It is no different from not allowing a Griffin refugee to transform in the kingdom! King William is a dastardly man, and Marcus is sure that things would be much different if King Owen were alive.

All at once the guests scream and push backward, causing Guenana and Marcus to stumble. Marcus peeks past the countless people. There is a massive rift cutting through the air in the center of the ballroom!

Within the black-hole-like slit comes forth a womanly figure. As she steps through, she materializes in this plane and becomes entirely visible. She is a tall, striking woman with long limbs and dark Prussian-blue skin. Her intimidating glare cuts through the startled guests as if she is searching for something—or someone.

Her head is wrapped in a colorful multi-toned scarf. In every which way she turns, the scarf appears to be changing color, and peeking out from it are short, curly locks of platinum-blonde hair. A silver bodice clings to her slender body, which is more like laced armor swerving in intricate designs. Silken fabrics drop from her waist, accentuating her curves with long slits. When the light of the dim ballroom hits her, her luminescent skin shimmers with an aquamarine highlight. But most striking is the bejeweled silver collar around her neck. Embedded in the settings are large cut gems, for his statement piece showcases her royal stature in her world.

The rift grows wide enough to allow armed soldiers to come through. One row after the next encompasses the woman while the Bimmorian guests continue to gasp and retreat.

It is his majesty, King William, whose reaction is most satisfactory to behold, just what Camden was hoping for. It was the same facial expression William had when Camden's magical dupe, Annabelle, the former ambassador and Camden's ex-fiancée, tried to stab him in the chest in the middle of the night. The same expression he made when Camden returned to the palace after exile. And when Camden's plans to secure the kingdom passed without his knowledge. Or the time he found out his daughter was actually his brother's daughter. Or when he first discovered his diseased wife's spirit in her old parlor.

True, despite his numerous faults, the current king of Bimmorus had many setbacks. But his gaping mouth, twitching tongue, inflated nostrils, shuffling feet, wild hair, and lopsided crown is a particular treat for Camden, who stands off to the side.

It is times like these where you see the difference between a set of twins, Camden thinks while he cuts through to greet his otherworldly guest.

"Bow before Talzra, the grand empress of Orcura, mother-nation of Bimmorus!" Camden declares.

Thumps echo the space when everyone takes a knee, including King William.

With a thick accent, Talzra orders, "Rise."

All follow her command. Talzra notes the shock among the Bimmorian people and says, "Camden Belflore, general and former prince of Bimmorus, your people are negligent of my timely presence."

"Please forgive them, Empress. They were uninformed. May I escort you to your seat?" Camden gestures to William's golden throne.

The empress frowns. "This puny throne does not compare to the grandness of my own." And yet, she allows him to escort her toward it.

"Of course it wouldn't, Your Majesty. What is the entire world of Orcura compared to our small kingdom?"

William moves out of the way and continues in a bowed position. "Your Majesty, it is a pleasure to have you attend our grand celebration."

"Grand?" The empress waves her hand dismissively. "Well, I suppose this is grand, considering."

Camden calls forth all the servants of the ballroom to attend to the empress with all the food and drinks they can offer. A careless wave of the empress's hand has the plates fly from the servants' grip like a gust of wind pushed through the corridors. This was Empress Talzra's gift—like many people of Orcura, she can control the elements.

She crosses her very long and dark legs, which peek through the slit of her gown, and says, "Be swift and present me my gift, Camden Belflore."

William's face gives a great twist. He turns to his nephew. "What gift, Camden?"

CHAPTER 12

Greon slashes through the thick shrubs of the jungle with a blade. He is damp with sweat, and his shoulder-length blond hair clings to the back of his neck for increased irritation.

"Would you stop that noise!" he barks.

Garet, the quirky Irishman he's picked up in the Human Division, struggles to keep up. Panting, Garet wipes the sweat off his face with an equally sweaty hand. "I can't 'elp it, mate! It's blazin' an' sticky! Dere's no water!"

Greon scoffs. "I told you to drink from the Decon."

"I'm naht abooeht to drenk frahm de belly o' a lettle fochrry creature!" Garet counters. "Dat's an awfoehl din to do!"

Greon remarks, "But helping a witch steal away souls in exchange for a potion in your pocket wasn't as awful, I take it?"

Garet huffs. "I've decided ta change me ways. Now dat de wetch is gahne, I'm retoehrnin' to me mahrality—and you shooehldn't be talkin'! I'm sure you've dahne wahrse."

Greon nods. "I have. But I'm not pretending I'm someone else, am I."

Garet throws his heavy trench coat over his shoulder.

"Why are you *still* carrying that? It's slowing us down."

"What if I'll need it? Doesn't it rain 'ere in dis wahrld?"

Greon looks back at the ignorant human, quite annoyed by his deep-seated denseness. "*Yes,* it does. Your idiotic questions torment me. It is time, I think, that I explain things. It will pass the time along . . . I will start at the beginning. Malphora is this entire universe, not just the ground beneath our feet. Long ago, the humans and extraordinary lived on the same plane of what they have taught you to call Earth. However, humans waged wars against magical beings and beasts. Your human ancestors were diligent in ending entire species like dragons, certain sea monsters, and so forth. In truth, the humans weren't just looking to conquer land. They were after the world's ultimate treasure, which the extraordinary peoples protected yet did not use. *The Three Eyes.* At this time, the ancient peoples of the extraordinary took it upon themselves to use their talents, the Three Eyes, and the oldest tree to cut Malphora in two, creating what we call the Great Divide or Great Severance. This was approximately seven thousand years ago, before the epic flood of the Human Division which killed off the giants, another enemy of the extraordinary."

Greon can sense Garet's confusion, but before Garet can verbalize his thoughts, Greon explains further. "Yes. Malphora has two different planes of existence, both with the same constructs of reality. All physical properties remain the same, including the elements and nature. According to ancient maps, the landmass that is now the Extraordinary Division on Earth was in the Atlantic Ocean. The Great Divide has shrunk your Earth and universe, so to speak, to bring half here to this separate plane. Yet the two planes remain connected somehow. When the ancients divided Malphora, they took the Three Eyes for safekeeping, leaving the oldest tree in the Human Division. A being, for example, can pass between the two planes if they have the Three Eyes in their possession or the assistance of the oldest tree. Both act as the gateway."

"So, you traveled to de 'uman Division usin' de Three Eyes?" Garet asks, finally catching on.

"Yes."

"Why dedn't you retoehrn usin' de ahldest tree?"

Greon sighs. "If I had continued my journey to the oldest tree, I would have died before I arrived. You see, my life is prolonged by the annual Welcoming

Moon that only occurs in my country, the Griffin Clan, due to what we believe to be caused by the moon's energy matched with the radioactivity of the land. I was fortunate enough to learn the rumors about the witch gifted with magic while in the Human Division and fortunate enough to find that it was Kala, an old acquaintance. My circumstances were beneficent to you as well, I believe."

"Aye . . . abooeht de Three Eyes. Do yooehr people in de Greffin Clan keep dem now? What ahther powers do dey pahssess cahnsiderin' de 'umans were so adamant to 'ave it?"

Greon nods. "Yes. My former master, Bayo, has them. The nature of the Three Eyes is very complex. They are called the Three Eyes, frankly, because there are three of them. Three levitating glassy orbs representing one per universe or world. We use the terms loosely. The first represents our universe, Malphora, the second for the universe of Orcura, and the third for the universe of Thurana. The other universes are very different from the constructs of this universe. From what I can describe, Orcura is an inverted world. Their sky is made of ocean where sea monsters roam, and land exists within the bubble, orbiting their light source, a crystal, not a sun. They call it the Loom. Thurana has evolved into a desert wasteland due to the harsh conditions, thus their people have evolved into violent serpents. Each of these worlds has its own set of the Three Eyes."

"How interestin'," Garet says, taking in all the information. "Tell me abooeht dis place, de Extraordinary Divide. What is it like 'ere? De territahries, de peoples, and species."

Greon nods. "I am a Griffin of the Griffin Clan. As a Griffin, I have two forms, one as man and the other as beast—"

Garet interrupts, "I've never seen yooehr secahnd fahrm. We cooehld 'ave flown to ooehr destination."

Greon answers, "My wings are injured. Cut them against the rocks in the ocean just before I came to that rancid pub and found you."

Convenient, but Garet doesn't linger. "'ow does one becomb a greffin?" he asks.

"It is hereditary, while our powers come from the annual moon I have mentioned before. It is custom to attend the Welcoming Moon as a young Griffin coming of age. They will be blessed with one of six powers. The first, Endurance, is the power to inflict physical anguish onto any being with only your mind. It is most feared among the clan. Ardor is the power to produce fire from one's body and control the element. Light is the power of which I was blessed, the ability to create illusions."

At once, a bright-yellow butterfly appears in front of Garet. He inspects the illusion on all sides, trying to find a flaw. "Incredible!"

"Then there is Shielding." Greon pauses as his thoughts flood with Ianna and her elegance as she performed her magical barriers. "The love of my life is a Griffin of Shielding, the best of her talent. She can create invisible barriers of all shapes, even as sharp as razor blades, to protect and attack. Though she would never do such things unless . . ." he trails off. "Afterward comes the power of Dark. A power which I most despise. A skilled Griffin of the Dark will enter your mind unwillingly, leaving no thought or memory untouched, and one of greater caliber will mold your mind and actions."

"And de last power?" Garet says, clearly counting.

"Prophecy. They are the strangest of the bunch, for the Welcoming Moon chooses to bless a single Griffin per generation with this power. They are plagued with random and violent visions . . . doomed to fear the future for the rest of their lives. To attend the Welcoming Moon more than once is taboo, as a Griffin will be cursed to attend forever more or face death. To attend constantly will give you immortality. The Welcoming Moon only blesses Griffins, however."

"Tell me abooeht de ahther nations," Garet says. And so, time went on pleasantly through the lush jungle while their minds were preoccupied with territories and their unique magics. Greon spoke of the Arketchians next and elaborated on their lack of technology.

"Boeht 'ow is it pahsseble dat we 'umans and you extraordinary share de same universe yet are naht as evahlved in terms o' technahlogy?"

"It is a very simple answer," Greon explains. "The Arketchians do not have need for technology, as their magic is so grand. They have spells for every possible need. They also prefer their strict culture and traditions, which have aided their stagnancies.

"A community in the universe of Orcura colonized here in Malphora. They built a kingdom called Bimmorus. Of all the nations in the Extraordinary

Division, Bimmorus is the most advanced, and *that* is only because they have bred with humans, thus dwindling their magic of controlling the elements, so they must rely on technology. Bimmorus has had its fair share of tragic events, like plagues and famine, which hindered its growth. Now that Bimmorus has regained its strength as a kingdom, magical technology is more prominent. Yet not everyone is as fortunate to use such technologies. Poorer citizens do not have the luxury and live similarly to peasants of your Dark Ages. Their modes of transportation are evidently similar with a horse and carriage as opposed to the flying crafts the elites of the kingdom use."

"And 'ow do you know so moehch abooeht de 'uman Division?"

Greon answers, "I've visited many times with my master over the centuries. I am more than a thousand years old. We are well versed in human life, its countries, rules, traditions, histories, and so forth. Bayo often enjoys human luxuries and has vacationed there on numerous occasions with the help of the Three Eyes."

Garet has no more questions, as he is too exhausted to continue the conversation. And after some silence, he mumbles, "'ow lahng oehntil we've reached ooehr destination?"

Greon looks back at his new companion and recalls the little nymph who once helped him escape death. *Even that chatty creature was more useful than this odd human.* He huffs.

Suddenly, the trees above their heads quiver. The native birds fly from the tops in a swarm. Greon overlooks it and instead observes the dimming sky. It would be dark in a few hours.

"Best to find a place to camp. The sun will set soon," he says.

Greon is a ways away when Garet comes across a beautiful flower. Its stem is thrice the size of a person, with enormous petals acting as a canopy. The smell alone is alluring. It is so sweet . . . just like his favorite dessert.

He takes a whiff. "Mmm," he moans. *Joehst like Granny's bread and boehtter poehddin' . . . I 'aven't smelled sahmethin' so good sence she died.* Garet beholds the strange flower. It was unlike any flower he'd ever seen. Each of its petals shows off several vibrant colors. Liquid drips down its stigma, one drop at a time. This is Garet's lucky day. *Water!* He catches the droplets into his mouth, and stays to collect them, when miraculously, the water increases to a steady stream. Garet cannot seem to part with it, not while the refreshing liquid tastes just like his granny's pudding.

Garet feels a tear across his hands. He stops drinking. He's bleeding and his vision doubles. The forest sways left and right while tears continue to appear on his body at random. Hazily, he watches his blood soak into the ground, and he swears that the stem of this flower grew twofold right after.

Lethargy takes over, and Garet lacks the will to move. "Greon," he calls faintly.

"What is it now?" Greon asks, annoyed. He instantly notices the blood and the flower drooping over Garet. "What have you done? I told you not to touch anything!"

Garet's knees are buckling, and Greon catches him in the nick of time. The ground vibrates, jolting the pebbles at their feet. Half drugged by the poisonous flower, Garet attempts to turn his head toward the vibration. His head rolls off to the side, and he gasps. The jungle is covered every which way he looks. This is Garet's ability. He sees approaching death.

He clumsily gets to his feet, shouting, "Shadows! Roehn!"

Pouncing from the depths of the forest on all sides is a massive black wave of stampeding Shigbis! Garet and Greon have nowhere to turn or hide.

"Where ded dey comb frahm?" Garet asks.

"They sense blood, you imbecile!" Greon answers.

The pack is gaining on them, and Garet feels foolish to have been duped by a flower. He dashes through the jungle with Greon leading the way, but his strength is short-lived, and his spinning head has him zigzagging. He inevitably falls face-first in the dirt. Garet looks back briefly and finds that all light and color of the day have been snuffed and replaced with *black shadows*. In a flash, his own shadow materializes behind him. He gasps. Never before this moment has he seen his own shadow. Greon's hands are pulling at his arms, and soon enough Garet is on his feet.

The Shigbis are seconds away.

All the while, Garet exclaims, "I'm goin' to die!" while Greon drags him across the jungle floor.

But this is serious! From what Garet's gift has taught him, death is fated, and one cannot avoid it unless it's transferred to another living being by magic. *Dis is de end fahr me,* he thinks. *What an idiot I am fahr combing 'ere!* Garet has half a mind to give up this instant. His lungs are burning and the whole world is spinning anyway. *It wooehldn't 'oehrt dat badly. Maybe after de trampling . . .* He glances backward.

Shigbis climb the trees. Shigbis left, Shigbis right! They're sinking their teeth into any living thing in their path! Leaping off tree trunks and swooping at them from above!

The sea of black Garet now sees are not just Shigbis—they are shadows!

Greon pulls him forward and uses his mighty power of Light to make himself and Garet invisible. False images of them dash in the other direction to divert the Shigbis. A boulder rests directly in front of them. They jump over it and hide in its crevice. Hastily, Greon rips a piece of his shirt to wrap around Garet's hands while hundreds of Shigbis leap over their boulder. The rest of his wounds are hidden beneath his clothes. Meanwhile, Garet is having a breakdown, marked by a series of yelping and Human Division cursing.

"If naht de beasts, dat poisahnooehs flower'll get me. I'm dahne fahr!" Garet says.

"Hush up," Greon commands in a whisper. "I cannot mask sounds. They cannot smell us because so many are rushing past. But they will eventually. Keep that wrapped."

Garet applies pressure on his wounds, but his head aches too immensely. His adrenaline rush is ebbing, and he can't keep his eyes open much longer.

Greon shakes him eagerly. "Don't sleep."

Hazily, Garet mutters, "I see me shadow, mate."

The stampede of Shigbis has finally passed. Greon is busy slapping Garet's face to wake him when the sound of sniffing reaches his ears. Greon must remain silent and composed at all costs. This shouldn't turn into a travesty since Garet is passed out.

He spots a lone Shigbi coming around the bend of the boulder. Its large nostrils twitch with each inhale as it stalks toward them. Greon keeps up his illusion of invisibility, but the Shigbi is unconvinced. It puts its nose against the ground like a dog and sniffs its way to the blood.

Using the proximity to his advantage, Greon presses his hand over Garet's mouth and uses his other hand to conceal the man's wound. As long as they stay silent and Garet's blood is not exposed, they should be able to survive this.

The Shigbi draws nearer and approaches Garet's face, where he'd smeared his blood. *Sniff. Sniff.* Perfect timing, for this is the precise moment Garet decides to open his eyes. Despite Greon's hand clasped over his mouth, he lets out a muffled scream.

The Shigbi bares its teeth.

"You are by far the most senseless man—" Greon begins as he is about to meet his doom.

A shining green venom emerges from its sharp teeth. But instead of sinking its teeth into human and Griffin flesh, the Shigbi stumbles back, yelping. Before the two know it, the Shigbi collapses and takes its last breath. They take a closer look to see what's killed one of the strongest predators in the jungle. A single dart sticks out from its back. Immediately, Garet's shadow vanishes.

With one eye half open, Garet cries, "Greon! I'm naht goin' to die!"

Greon gives him a snide look. With half a mind to end the human's life, Greon thinks, *He shouldn't be too sure about that.*

But this is astonishing news to Garet! Death is not fated! More importantly, it can be avoided if such a miracle should occur! One does not necessarily need to turn to black magic and transfer the death to another person. Finally, Garet feels a strong sense of purpose with this gift—or maybe this heightened state of emotion and enlightenment is a result of drinking from that poisonous flower. But whatever the reason, Garet finally understands his gift is not a curse. Yes, daunting, but important. Its extent of good isn't simply warning someone to prepare for their untimely death! He can find ways to save them from their fate altogether!

"You may come out now," says a woman's steady voice from behind the boulder. "You are safe."

Garet blinks awake, and he stumbles to his feet. He and Greon meet their saviors. Five Arketchian men stand waiting and armed around what Garet believes is . . . a goddess! Who is this enchanting woman? She is illuminated in all directions; orbs of light float around her. He's never seen anything like it. *Is she a saint? An angel? She's gahrgeooehs!*

Greon recognizes her straightaway. The Spirit Guide of the Arketcha Tribe, "Palla," he says in greeting.

She bows her head slightly. "Elder of Light. We have crossed paths yet again."

While swaying drunkenly, Garet thinks, *'ow does 'e know dis gahddess?*

"The spirits sent me to come for you and your companion," Palla explains. "You may follow me."

Groggily, Garet attempts a step forward and declares, "Beautifoehl lady!" With that last note, he blacks out.

A wet cloth is placed on Garet's forehead, stirring his sleep. His pounding head, weariness, and wounds are clear signs the liquid from the strange flower continues to take its toll. Yet to his amusement, he wakes to what he would consider a magnificent view! Before him is Palla, his savior, wiping his forehead with a damp cloth.

"'ello, beautifoehl," he says.

"What is your name?" she asks in what Garet perceives is a thick accent.

"G-Garet," he stammers.

"Curious. In my language, your name means riverbank," she says.

"My lahvely!" Garet exclaims, clearly still drunk.

She tells Greon, "He's quite the charmer, your friend. Even drunk with poison, he attempts to flatter."

Greon is sitting on a wooden chair in the corner of the room, guzzling water from a clay cup. "Mmm, where he comes from, drunk with poison is the best time to flatter . . . I must ask you for a great favor, Palla. We seek shelter."

Palla nods. "I am happy to give it."

Garet has dozed off.

Greon says, "Thank you. Do you mind my asking . . . why did the spirits send you to help us?"

Palla answers, "They sense imperative energies emanating from both your beings and connecting to me like long vines. This means our paths must cross, you see, though I am unsure why." Palla is sidetracked by Kala's voice buzzing in her ears, and she laughs. "I can say for certain that my sister is very put off by this reunion."

Greon turns white. "Kala is here?"

Palla nods with amusement. "Show yourself, sister."

"I will do no such thing!" Kala declares.

Greon exclaims, "Even death is not death!"

Palla's brows furrow. "Were you there when she died?"

He sighs. "A long story. She wanted to feast upon my soul. It didn't work out to her benefit, as this human lying in your bed saved my life."

"We had a bargain, Greon," Kala exclaims. "I did my part. And you certainly made a mess of things. By all means, do tell us about how you managed to set the destruction of the world in motion after Felix and I sought to save it! Now you seek refuge in the Arketcha Tribe, of all places!"

Palla is confused. "What does she mean, Greon? What have you done?"

Greon hangs his head in shame. "I've done horrible things in service of Bayo. Things I am not proud of, things I'd like to forget, but I see them every time I shut my eyes." He means to go on but finds the words hard to emerge.

Palla attempts to ease his pain. "You are safe to speak here."

And so Greon openly tells Palla and her spirit friends all that has happened in the Human Division. "My master, Bayo, had commanded me to use the magic which I learned from Kala all those years ago, to travel into the Human Division, find his young brother in a short span of time, and bring him back to the Griffin Clan. Hale was living alone with Carly, Felix's daughter at that time, for Bayo and Rioma took the lives of Felix and Naomi but found Hale not. However, when I found Hale and Carly, I could not transfer him back to the Griffin Clan. He was magically protected from moving between the divide. I worked long and hard to find the solution through magic, but nothing had worked. Bayo then threatened Ianna and Mary's life, and I became desperate. I resorted to hurting Carly and Hale . . . they escaped eventually, and though I meant to retrieve them, young Carly fell into my blade, and she was too weak to fight the blood loss. Upon her last moments, I learned that a gemstone pendant cloaked them from magic, and I re-created them to finally become free from my master. I then traveled the Human Divide to search for the oldest tree which could have granted me passageway back into the Extraordinary Division, and ironically, I found your sister instead. Kala had escape Bayo with Felix's family and has since then lived alone, posing as a miracle witch whose terms of service included an exchange of human souls to preserve her life."

Palla is fuming. Kala appears as an orb of blue light, eagerly trying to explain herself further, but Palla won't hear it.

Greon goes on. "That evening, Kala showed me that Hale had somehow returned to the Extraordinary Division where Bayo had already begun to manipulate him for evil."

Palla nods her head. "So the High Elder continues with his plans, then?"

Greon nods. "Yes."

"It must be fate," Palla concludes. "Why is Hale important for Bayo's plans? Why has Bayo gone to such lengths for him?"

"From what I know, Hale's power is prophesized to surpass Bayo's," Greon answers. "Bayo would use him as a weapon."

Palla takes in the information for a moment, then calls her sister into visibility. "Kala. Is what he says true? Is this young man of great importance?"

Kala's orb bounces in the air. "Yes, Palla. He is of utmost importance."

"It seems to me that there is a great shift in energy," Palla concludes. "I do not know if these occurrences are connected. We have too few answers. Yet between the expulsion of the siren from the tribe, the incessant rifts between the spirit and physical worlds, and the happenings in the Griffin Clan, I believe we should be preparing for the worst."

CHAPTER 13

Multitudes of pink and purple hues splatter across the thick sky. Heavy clouds roll in. Between the steep mountainsides, in a canyon stands enormous, bent, and twisted rock formations and large pools of rainwater across the muddied ground. A pair of panting Griffins soar overhead. They make for the small plateau to rest.

Crash-landing on the narrow boulder is Mary and her mother, Ianna. They shape-shift into their human forms. Both women are soaked, and red splotches mark their skin. Ianna's chest heaves. She hadn't flown this much in hundreds of years. In her defense, she wasn't allowed. To calm her breathing, she clutches the wet stone on all fours. Though Mary is exhausted, too, she does not hesitate to give Ianna a sideways glance while slumping down on the wet rock.

"Perhaps we could stay here for the night?" Ianna suggests. "I'm afraid I can't go on."

"We should not have come through the Gorges of Navmala," blurts Mary. She blows on her stinging palms. "The rainwater is too acidic to drink, we have no food left, nor warm clothes to last the night. The harpies are threatening us to leave. You should have listened to me," she snaps.

Ianna swallows to ease her dried throat. "Better a few nights of turmoil to arrive at our destination quickly." She coughs in the sleeve of her dress.

Mary counters, "And how will you manage without water?"

Ianna says hoarsely, "I'll make do. I've managed through worse."

This has been the longest she's ever spoken to Ianna in all the centuries of her life. Mary stares. *She is strong... I will never have to see Rioma again. I never have to fear looking at Ianna or speaking to her. Ianna is beautiful, too. Do I have her eyes?*

Ianna catches her gaze and at once, both turn away. Why did it feel so weird to acknowledge one another now that they were finally free? But physical freedom differs from freedom of the mind. Rioma's spiteful face haunts Mary's thoughts, and Mary can still hear her sinful words on repeat, as if Deor himself had engrained them in her mind.

She never wanted you. You are Deor's daughter, after all. She would have ended your life in her womb if it weren't for me. I saved your life and gave you the love and attention a youngling desires from their mother. She was never a mother to you. You should not speak with her. She does not deserve you, Rioma would say.

Mary picks at her nails. *Why did I listen? Why was I too blind? I believed her and never asked Ianna why she didn't want me, no matter how much I wished I did. Every time I tried to get close, Rioma would burn her. I stayed bitter and brokenhearted for seven hundred years. Ianna was all I ever wanted, and she's next to me right now as if time hasn't passed. As if the pain never existed.*

Ianna recognizes the concern in Mary's expression. "Give me a few minutes to catch my breath, and we will resume our flight. I remember there was a nice grassland not too far—"

Now Mary feels ashamed. "I didn't mean to make you feel bad."

Ianna smiles and takes Mary's hand. Mary nearly gasps. They've never touched before this moment.

Ianna says, "I know. It would be better for us. We could find food and drink there and get good rest. Do not worry."

Mary nods. She allows Ianna's hand to rest in hers, though she cannot lie—it feels awkward. Ianna senses her unease and gently lets go. They sit in silence for a long while, staring at the maze of rock structures they would soon have to swerve past. The wet stone mildly stings their bare skin as both contemplate the journey to their destination.

Out of nowhere, Mary blurts, "Why didn't you want me as your daughter?"

Ianna is taken aback. "I always wanted you, Mary."

"Then why didn't you take me from her?" she asks.

Ianna lets out a long breath. "I couldn't. I would have if Bayo had taken my side, but he hadn't cared for the battles between Rioma and me. She took what was most precious to me in all the worlds knowing that I could not prevent it with my power and knowing Bayo would leave me defenseless."

"We could have left," says Mary.

"No, we couldn't leave. We didn't have the tools to hide from Deor's mind or The Eyes back then. Greon knew this and was always hesitant to leave. He wanted to wait for the right time." She sighs. "I listened to his warnings. He rather we had our lives in the hands of those who wronged us than to chance death."

Mary is silent.

Ianna continues, "When you were just an infant, Rioma acted as my wet nurse. It had been the first time she was ever kind to me, and I was fooled into believing she could ever sympathize with my pain. It was when she would not let me hold you that I knew she was planning something. I risked taking you from her room one evening. She caught me, of course. She and Deor are closer than you think. At the time, she hadn't said a word. I thought myself a victor that night. After she pretended to be happy for me, I fell asleep with you in my arms while she rushed to convince Bayo to take you to the Arketcha Tribe. Greon stood firmly against it, though Bayo took Rioma's side in the end. There she hired the Dark Shaman to place a curse on you."

Mary's nostrils flare. "Why would she do that? What kind of curse?"

Ianna becomes tense. "Free yourself of your anger, Mary. Her offenses against you were only done to hurt me. The curse was to keep you from loving me. This is what was told to me, though I do not know if it is true."

Mary's blood boils by the moment. "Why would Bayo allow such a thing?"

Ianna places a hand on her shoulder. "With Greon as a witness, Rioma declared your life for Bayo's cause. You were to be his loyal servant. Your love for me would have sided you against him since I was not treated with any sort of kindness." Ianna spots water welling in Mary's eyes. She wipes her daughter's face and smiles. "I hope once we get to the Arketcha Tribe, we will be able to find out if you were truly cursed in such a way, and if so, possibly remove it."

Mary takes time to process. Then she says, "I never loved her, you know. I don't think I loved anybody, except—"

"Except Greon," Ianna finishes. "I know. I was so happy that he was able to be there for you since I could not be." She strokes Mary's long hair and instantly, Mary feels a massive weight lift off her. "There are so many things I wanted to tell you throughout the years. So many things I wanted to teach you and keep you from," Ianna says.

A swell rises in Mary's throat, and she tries to hide her emotions by turning away. Mary asks her, "The night you smuggled me those potions, you were badly hurt, weren't you."

Ianna shrugs. "Nothing I couldn't handle."

Even though Mary felt so indebted to her, she still has so many questions. She bursts into tears. "But why would you make me see those visions! I saw a future where I died at the hands of a boy I cared for deeply! It was so painful!"

Ianna looks horrified and throws both arms around her daughter.

So, this is maternal love.

"I know what you're feeling," Ianna says. "I should have told you what the potion did, but I was afraid I would be found out. The potion does not show the future; it shows your greatest fears."

Mary's eyes widen. "This whole time, I thought I had seen my future!"

"You feared the one you cared for would kill you? Why?" Ianna asks.

"I met the same soul hundreds of years ago when I lived in the Human Division. We shared grand adventures! I've never been so happy!" Then Mary frowns. "He died. He was so young . . . I returned home, and Bayo sent me to visit the Arketcha Tribe, where I met a woman named Palla. She called herself the Spirit Guide and told me I will meet him again. I found him in the Griffin Clan and recognized him right away. There was no mistaking his kindness, humor, and gentleness."

Ianna nods. "Noble qualities—I can see why you loved him."

Mary shudders. "I was ordered by Bayo to kill his friends. One of which was the girl who owned his heart."

Ianna hugs her daughter tightly.

"I managed to trick Bayo into believing I finished the job. But I saved the two and left him to be with her."

Ianna says, "So you were afraid of him taking revenge if you had heeded Bayo's command?"

Mary nods.

"You did well, Mary. You have done the right thing despite Bayo's consequences. Bayo no longer holds the keys to your future. Perhaps the stars have aligned for you and this soul in the past, but maybe his return was meant to teach you this lesson rather than to have him as your life companion. The pain you've experienced with him this turn has helped you break free. Cry no more, Mary. You are free."

Mary blinks, and slowly her lips widen into a smile. "I am."

CHAPTER 14

"What gift, Camden?" beseeches the king.

Camden smirks but does not answer him. He looks to the empress. "Your Majesty, my gift is too magnanimous to fit in our small palace walls."

The empress raises a brow. "Oh?"

Camden calls forward finely dressed soldiers from the doorway, who hold up a golden and empty litter on their shoulders. "May I escort you to my gift?" He holds out his hand elegantly and leads her to her seat. Whether Talzra appreciates the details put in this night's affair is a mystery, for her face remains stonelike, though she abides by Camden's gestures. Once she mounts the litter, the Bimmorian servants rise, and Talzra overlooks the crowd with perfect stature.

Camden signals his announcer and the announcer then proclaims, "Our ball will resume in the palace garden."

Empress Talzra's Orcuran fleet encompass the Bimmorian servants who hold her litter. What seems like an army passes through the halls of the palace. The crowd of inquisitive guests eagerly follows both parties into the courtyard.

Camden strides in front of them all, one even step at a time. Though he walks with a great sense of confidence, his mind is betraying him. *There is no room for errors,* he tells himself. *If I cannot perform this miracle, it will be the end for Malphora as we know it. The Orcurans will immigrate here and take over our entire world if their Loom is not saved. We lack the numbers and ability to take on a full alien invasion.* He runs his fingers through his hair. *Think well, Camden. The scientists wouldn't have given me a finished product if they had not deemed it worthy.*

The palace garden buzzes with futters, best described as the jellyfishes of land. Camden takes his place in the middle of the flowered clearing. His body is stiff, and there is a nervous sweat at his temple. *The fate of Malphora rests in my hands,* he exhales. *This entire universe.*

Talzra interrupts Camden's terrifying thoughts. "Do tell us, General Camden Belflore, where on Malphora resides your gift?" She looks up to the sky instinctively, though she finds no resemblance of a Loom in sight.

With a shaking hand, Camden reaches for his breast pocket and reveals a beautiful sparkling crystal. It is no bigger than his palm.

Talzra's face drops. At the sight of the luminous rock, she exclaims, "I do hope you are not mocking me, General. Do you expect *this*—"

Camden does not bother to come to his own defense. He merely throws the crystal up into the air, and it fires several hundred feet into the sky, like a sparkler, though he had not lit a thing. Suddenly there is a crackle from above, like several shots of thunder. The Bimmorian guests duck for cover. Even the Bimmorian servants have a troublesome time not dropping the empress's litter. Needless to say, Empress Talzra is not amused, though she and her fleet keenly look on muttering prayers for success.

Fabricated storm clouds emerge from the crystal and blanket the skies before spiraling like a tornado.

"Come on," Camden mouths. "Come on."

Then the clouds dissipate, and the lighting ceases to showcase the transformation from night to day. With hands over their eyes, all behold the magic the general has performed. The small crystal has grown monstrously and hovers far in the atmosphere. Its warmth is as inviting as the Malphoran sun. The invention is indeed a dupe to the Orcuran Loom. It rotates slowly, half illuminating the world while half remains in darkness.

Camden smiles. He focuses his attention on the empress, eager for any sort of approval, and to his delight, her eyes are wide with disbelief.

He steps forward. "Have I pleased you, Empress?"

Her expression quickly returns stonelike. "How often does the rotation complete a single cycle?"

"An equivalent to twenty-six hours Malphoran time, the length of an Orcuran day," Camden answers knowledgeably. It is clear how much thought he'd placed into this crystal. "We wanted to make an exact replica, and we've done just that."

The empress is unsatisfied. "When will this crystal die?"

Camden shakes his head. "It has the expected lifetime of six billion years. Just like your Loom."

"How have you managed to create a light source that should last as long as the natural Loom?" Talzra snaps. "Nothing man-made in this world has ever had such an extended lifetime!"

"Indeed." Camden leans in. The Bimmorian servants lower the litter so that he may whisper the necessary information in Talzra's ear. "We've sourced our sun's energy, harnessed it, and duplicated its nature. By nature, it will continue to live. A confidential secret between my government and myself."

Talzra then asks, "How do you suppose we bring this to Orcura if it is now set in your sky?"

Camden smiles. "I will show you."

He leaves Talzra and reveals a vial in his pocket filled with a luminous magenta substance. He throws the vial into the air, the same way he had the crystal. But the vial is not magic and has not shot into the sky the way the crystal had.

As it descends, an ash-blond Griffin dashes above the crowd, nearly scraping the hairs on Camden's head. It catches the vial and skyrockets toward the blinding light of the new Loom. The Griffin is none other than Marcus! Camden jumps enthusiastically as Marcus soars. What a risk Marcus is taking to transform in front of the king who would condemn his entire family without so much as a thought! Undeniably, King William is fuming. But there is nothing Marcus should fear, not with Camden's title returned to him. If the king wishes to punish Marcus, he must wage war against Camden.

Once Marcus nears the warm Loom, he tosses the vial at it. Lightning and thunder quake the sky once more, and day returns to night. The crystal shrinks to its natural size, and Camden catches it in his careful hands. A servant offers an intricate box and key. Camden places it inside and locks the box before handing it over to the empress.

He tells her, "Considering the measurements of altitude in the very center of your world where your Loom lives, this crystal should grow to the approximate size. Here is another vial with the same shrinking substance that should shrink the natural Loom, as this crystal and yours are essentially twins. And these scrolls"—Camden pulls out a scroll from inside his vest—"contain the rest of our data."

The empress reaches out for her gifts and studies them. "In all my years, even our technology has not found the cure to our suffering." She hides both in the folds of her dress. "Will our enemies find and use this technology to their advantage—taking the new Loom with the concoction in your vial?"

Camden says, "We've already thought about this possibility. There is only one vial remaining, for single use to replace your Loom. The substance is compounded of very rare materials, and only Lady Meir of the Royal Academy and I know the formula."

"Ah, yes. Lady Meir. She is trustworthy."

Camden is perplexed. *Is there nothing and no one this woman does not know?*

Talzra warns, "If you are giving me a faulty contraption, I will end you and this entire kingdom."

Camden nods. "That is precisely why I would never hand over a faulty contraption."

Talzra notices the gentle wind made by Marcus's wings as he descends. Everyone backs away from him in horror and disgust. A beautiful light engulfs his beastly body while he transforms.

"You have a Griffin ally," Empress Talzra states flatly.

"He is a great friend," Camden says.

William approaches the empress with terror in his eyes. "Your Majesty," he says, bowing, "I sincerely apologize for this terrible display! I will see to it at once that this . . . Griffin is taken care of!"

Before Camden retorts, Bimmorian guards close in around Marcus.

Just then, the empress raises her hand, and her fleet comes in between Marcus and the Bimmorian soldiers. Her lips curve into a smile. "That is unnecessary. You will be wise to keep as many powerful allies as you can, William Belflore, especially in such times."

William is motionless, and his blue face reddens as he understands that his deal with the empress is void, since Orcura is healed. Camden has made a mockery of his rule and destroyed their only chance in war with a single rock. He stares daggers at his nephew, who suddenly resembles his reckless father more than he does.

The empress nods to the empty space before her as if signaling invisible onlookers. It seems her people were keeping a close eye on her from Orcura. A large rift cuts through the air. Her fleet replaces the Bimmorian servants holding up the litter.

Just before departing through the portal, the empress locks eyes with Camden and says, "If this should work, General, I thank you."

William calls his guard to escort him away from this madness and wishes Camden at least had stayed in exile. It seems his nephew is buying back his power in the kingdom, forcing William to ponder his next moves . . .

CHAPTER 15

The pressure of the locket against Marcus's chest is a constant reminder of a plan left unfinished. The glossy hair of the princess swaying while she danced in the arms of a young Bimmorian man is all he can picture while he walks alone through the vacant palace courtyard. This place is so well kept and filled with colorful flowers and wildlife. It reminds Marcus of his old cottage back in the town designated to Griffin refugees.

He sighs. *Maybe it's best. She should be with someone who everyone would accept*, he thinks. The tall flowers of various colors have shut for the evening, and the beetle-crickets were somewhere in the thick of them, hopping and buzzing.

While the Human Division would receive the most daylight during the summer solstice, the opposite was true for the Extraordinary Division, which receives the most moonlight. Marcus lies down on a stone barricade made for the garden and looks up to the vivid night sky.

Oh, how Marcus hates the moon! It whirls him through hundreds of visions, pulling him up through the sky and dropping him to some memory of the future or past that does not belong to him. The violent storm of the moon cycling backward or frontward as it attempts to tell him the time that passes by is just too much to handle. He cannot seem to keep count, as it travels too quickly!

And the future visions are only glimpses of possibilities, leaving Marcus deeply worried all the time.

Like when he foretold Lord Genrik's madness. Then there were those strange moments of intuition he gets, where he'd know something he shouldn't. Like that night when he and Camden found the Book of Peace and the spirit of Camden's late aunt. Now he has constant visions about the towers of Bimmorus falling. And tonight, that strange vision in which he remained half-awake, standing beside a battered Evangeline in some underground setting before surviving Bimmorians. He wipes a tear, hoping to never have to see her in such a condition. *I hope the technology for the kingdom's barricade is ready,* Marcus thinks. *Then maybe these visions will stop, and everything will be solved.*

"Marcus?"

He knows that voice. *Can it be?* It is. Princess Evangeline.

She smiles. "My cousin said you were here."

Marcus's heart is beating. "Is that all he said?" he mutters. What joy did it give Camden to orchestrate Marcus's romantic evening? Marcus would never know.

"Should there have been more he said?" Evangeline asks.

"Evangeline, wouldn't your father be upset for you being out so late . . . especially with me?"

Evangeline crosses her arms and scrunches her button nose in the most adorable way. "Listen carefully, Marcus Theoden. My father is up in the parlor room in a fury for the display you and my cousin have caused. He is wondering why Camden has decided to make him look foolish in front of his people and the empress of Orcura. While he deliberates his counterattack—which I'm sure my cousin is well prepared for—he is ignorant of the fact that Camden has created an even greater ally in Orcura, for they are now indebted to us for the continuation of their world.

"Not only this, but with you and the rest of the Griffin rebels at Camden's side, we have a stronger chance of facing whatever it is you see in those visions of yours. Camden also has impenetrable technology, the help of a few of the best inventors and scientists this kingdom has to offer. Therefore, you have absolutely nothing to worry about."

"William is still your father," Marcus says, taking Evangeline's hand. "And you should listen to him. You'll have a big role to play someday in the future. I'm sure you won't be a princess forever."

Evangeline steps back nervously. "Have you seen that—in one of your premonitions?"

"N-no," Marcus stammers.

"Then why bring it up, Marcus? I am not fit for such things. I can hardly pass my grades, let alone run a kingdom on the verge of war," Evangeline says.

"Yes, Camden once said the same, and he is more capable than the man who wanted the crown," Marcus offers.

Evangeline takes her finger to her lips. "Watch what you say. You don't know who might hear," she whispers. "Anyhow, I just came to see if you were all right and to congratulate you for tonight's success."

As she pulls away, Marcus grabs hold of her forearm. "Wait," he says. "Don't go yet. I wanted to give you something . . ."

He pulls out the locket from his breast pocket and places it in Evangeline's hand, too timid to place it around her neck in case she does not like it.

It then occurs to Evangeline that Marcus *does* feel the same way for her. But the complications of their situation will take hold, and Marcus wouldn't stand in the way of authority. Evangeline knows he is right, and she should not cause trouble.

She looks at the round, golden locket and is at a loss for words. Engraved on the outside is a detailed image of her favorite flower, the pentiblom, that only blooms at night, and especially so during this particular solstice. She places her long fingers over the object and opens it. At once, the courtyard is engulfed with a mesmerizing and realistic projection. Evangeline steps back to witness the image in full. A beautiful melody plays from the locket, and in the mist, Evangeline's opaque likeness made of golden particles appears to her left, working her way to the center of the courtyard. Someone emerges from the right. She is a beautiful woman, sharing similar features.

"Is that my mother?" she asks Marcus in disbelief.

Marcus nods. "Yes."

The projection of Adene takes her daughter's hand, and they twirl around the courtyard in a beautiful Bimmorian dance specifically meant for a mother and her daughter. This is a dance Evangeline could never participate in unless Camden was present to take her hand and fill that painful void. This is her dream come true, to be able to dance with her mother. It was a wish she'd only mentioned to Marcus briefly, a fleeting detail that would have been overlooked by all others.

The melody clips, and the illusions of Evangeline and her mother embrace before they dissolve. Evangeline begins to cry, clutching the closed locket.

Assuming this means she has not liked the gift, Marcus quickly explains, "I'm so sorry, Evangeline. I thought you would like it. I was hoping . . . this way your mother could always be with you . . ." He meets Evangeline's overflowing sterling eyes. "Please don't cry," he says.

Evangeline throws her arms around Marcus's shoulders. "I will cherish this always. Thank you."

CHAPTER 16

The northern forests are so different from those near the Arketcha Tribe. It is not lush, and the greenery lacks vibrancy. Even the native animals seem less ferocious with their plush coats and grass eating. Likewise, the unexplored territory is accompanied by unknown rules. Brisk nights were among the worst, for in the Arketcha Tribe, winter is just a mild version of summer, and more preferred for the cool ocean breeze.

Nonetheless, Ellionna, her cousin Robin, and Robin's father, Atomi, tread the land toward the promise of the Kingdom of Bimmorus. Was it a kingdom or a myth? The trio is unsure, for no Arketchian has ever been known to venture off to Bimmorus, though plenty of nomadic beings like the harpies and centaurs have been invited to study. Of what worth is study in the Arketcha Tribe? The Arketchian people preferred magic to basic knowledge. Magic creates solutions to all needs. Perhaps the Arketchian people would have been more advanced in the absence of magic, or in the company of other striving countries. Alas, these were not their blessings.

"We must tread east, for the Griffin Clan lies in the west," says Atomi.

It has been six months on the road, six months since Ellionna was exiled from her home for murdering two young men—not that she wanted to. It was the siren's soul who shares her body that sought their deaths. Half the siren's soul, to be exact, as the other half is locked away in a crystal box, forged by the last Dragon of Malphora, as legend has it. It is a bittersweet exile. Ellionna gets to be with her usually grumpy cousin. They were not able to spend time together in the Arketcha Tribe because Robin was learning her warrior craft at the Temple of Chiba. And her uncle, Atomi, made a miraculous reappearance after the previous chief murdered the rest of their immediate family a decade ago.

Having Atomi near is a blessing to Ellionna, who misses her late father, Amoz, dearly. Like her father, Atomi is wise and loving. He often tells stories about Ellionna's parents in the evenings beside the fire, and she adopts his memories as if they were her own.

It is a blissful exile considering she no longer has to marry Prince Sokos, her betrothed. Oh, how she loathes Sokos! Of all the people the siren should have killed in the Arketcha Tribe, Sokos would have been a perfect choice. Ellionna remembers he was once a timid young boy who was hesitant to approach her. Though when he did, the two realized the siren never emerged in Sokos's presence, almost as if it liked him. As the two grew, the cruel prince would often torment Ellionna, knowing she was of no threat.

Even if Ellionna had not been exiled and was married off, it would have still been worth it if it meant she could continue to be with her grandmother, Livia—who is all alone now, without family or help. Ellionna often wonders if her grandmother is safe and healthy and if the neighbors remember to check on her every once in a while. Every rising sun is a constant reminder that Livia is getting older, approaching her final sun whenever that should be.

But Ellionna would rather not think about that if she can help it. She'd rather think about the Arketchian foods she is missing as she gnaws on the last of the dried ruminant meat. Dumplings, steamed rice soaked in fresh herbs, and a roasted oxtail soup! *Mmmm . . .*

Unfortunately, every step is a step away from home, and a step away from a home-cooked meal.

"When I get to Bimmorus, I'm going straight to the market then will make us dumplings!" Ellionna exclaims.

"We don't have Bimmorian money," Robin reminds her.

Atomi says, "We will find a way. There is always honest work in any country. Ellionna shall make us the finest dumplings we ever tasted . . . I really miss oxtail soup."

Ellionna gasps. "Me too, Uncle! You have read my mind!"

Robin rolls her eyes.

"Mind reading is a gift bestowed upon some Griffins, I believe," Atomi mentions.

"Why can't we go to the Griffins, Uncle?" asks Ellionna. "Maybe they will be kind to us."

"Not after you killed one of their own," Robin says.

Ellionna shouts, "He did not die!" The thought of killing yet another innocent being is too much for her to bear. She must believe the boy was strong enough to have survived her voice. Even though it is impossible. Even if no other male has ever lived through the voice before.

Robin says, "He's probably dead by now."

Ellionna clenches her fists in fury.

Atomi says, "We must avoid contact with the Griffins at all costs. No more discussions."

All at once, Ellionna's body becomes transparent. Likewise, her surroundings are fading to black. She calls out for her family, and they reach for her. Though try as they may, Ellionna is on the verge of transporting to some place unknown.

A one-sided oval window with a rim made of smoke hovers above the Three Eyes. An onlooker can spot the lands of the Extraordinary Division within. Bayo firmly stands over his treasure, working them with grand motions of his arms and a steady incantation. He looks to be pulling apart the air. The movement of his body adjusts the view within the window. He is scouring the deep wood in search of something . . . or someone.

A trio of travelers comes into view. Their deep olive skin signifies Arketchian origins. Bayo motions his hands as if pulling a rope with immense tension, and the window's view whirls clockwise, stopping in front of the young woman with long, dark curls. Gripping the edge of his oak table, Bayo soaks in the sight of the siren's vessel, the person who took Hale's life.

Bayo's gentle words in a dead tongue turn the scape within the window black.

"Robin?" shouts Ellionna. Her accent thick. "Atomi?"

Her quavering voice brings forth a sickening smirk on Bayo's lips. *Now there is no one to protect you,* he thinks.

Materializing in an unilluminated and dank setting, shivers immediately rush up Ellionna's spine. It is cold here. She wraps her arms around her torso.

"H-hello?" she calls.

Daring her foot forward, Ellionna feels for an exit. Her hand discovers the surface of a stone wall, and she continues along its path, unsure of where it will lead.

A blinding glare sparks from behind abruptly. The space is illuminated for the moment, allowing Ellionna a slight understanding of her surroundings. She is enclosed by rock structures, which leads her to believe she is in a cave. But she cannot spot a path to freedom. The mysterious brilliance morphs into a tear in the air. The gash elongates and pulls apart. Out from it emerges a man. Just as he steps through, the supernatural doorway shrinks in a second's time. Darkness resumes.

Cowering, Ellionna sinks down, and as far away as the boundary of the caves provides. It occurs to her that this man has the ability to transport people, and it must have been him who has brought her here. But why? With every approaching footstep of this stranger, the more uncomfortable her throat feels. The irritating and burning sensation is the siren itching for an escape. But Ellionna must not let it. She cannot by any means allow the immortal creature to take another life.

Mustering her courage, she confronts the stranger. "Who are you? Why have you brought me here?"

The lump in Ellionna's throat swells further. She swallows while grabbing at it with her hands. The siren is using Ellionna's fear against her. At once, the aquamarine amulet at the base of Ellionna's chest—given to her by the priestess of the old magic—lets off an inner glow. Her irises have flashed the same color. It is the pattern of the gem working. In that moment's flash, a vague silhouette of the man becomes visible inches away. Ellionna backs away, ignorant of the stone directly behind her, and hits her head.

Shaking, she pleads, "Please release me. I cannot control the siren." How long would the power of the gem help her keep the voice down?

There is no response.

"Who are you?" she asks again, just above a whisper.

There's a loud bang beside her left ear. Ellionna jolts, assuming the stranger has smashed his hand against the rock. She can feel his hot breath on her as he seethes, "You killed my brother."

Ellionna gasps. *The boy at the cliffs, the one with vein-like markings on his body.* An aching guilt looms over her while she recalls an incident in the distant past with a different set of brothers she ended in the same manner.

The man grabs her upper arms forcefully. Wincing, she warns him a second time. "Please, I'm trying to contain myself."

His hand seizes her neck—where the siren's inner manifestation hid—and squeezes. But Bayo remains unafraid, for the siren had sung to him the same day it did to Hale, and he was able to overcome death. On the other hand, he desperately wishes his death would have come.

Ellionna is gasping for air. But suffocation is not enough to satisfy Bayo, for he must press his power of Endurance into her. A painful surge courses through Ellionna's body, and her knees falter while the torment accelerates. Her lips part to release her whimpering, and she is not allowed even that as her assailant's rough hands grip her airway, muffling her cries. The siren is writhing as well. All the better for Bayo, for it cannot set its awful power free to do to him what it had done to Hale.

During the torment, the siren senses something . . . familiar. A part of itself that was missing for centuries. It is somewhere . . . hidden in the rocks of the cave. It calls to its distant half with a serene hum that only the two can detect. With newfound strength, the siren emerges as soon as Ellionna's consciousness flees. Only for a moment, though, but long enough to speak with a gurgling and unhuman voice.

Water drips from the corners of Ellionna's mouth. "You hide what belongs to me."

Astonished, Bayo releases the girl, and she collapses on the cool ground. Both she and the siren are surely asleep.

CHAPTER 17

Ariah Theoden takes a long look at her surroundings. The new home of the Theodens is placed directly in the capital and was an insisted gift from the general and family friend, Camden Belflore. Camden urged the move because he believed the Theodens needed to stay close to Marcus just in case he should need his parents. But the Theodens knew this was truly Camden's way of thanking them for their help in undoing his exile, as it was also a form of his protest. The mere existence of Griffin refugees in the capital strikes at the core of Bimmorian propriety, which traditionally allows no such thing.

The home is decorated entirely with Eliath's fine carpeting skills and Ariah's upholstery. The infamous Hall Tree that forced Marcus and Eliath on a whirlwind adventure stands to the left of the arched front door, in the sitting room. How furious Ariah was to learn those gripping details! *If I'd been there, I would have set everything aflame,* she thinks, giggling at her absurdity. Two love seats are placed in front of the fireplace and bookshelves over the mantel, matching their first home. *Everything seems to be in order,* Ariah thinks.

The official doctrine of the previous king, King Owen, that gave permission for all Griffin refugees to live in Bimmorus hangs proudly in their new home. It is so large that it takes up half the wall. The document came with the home when they moved in. Camden called it his housewarming gift. Hundreds of signatures crowd the bottom, two of which belong to Eliath and Ariah. Ariah gazes upon the certificate, stroking her penmanship in memory of the epic day. It was a miracle they'd survived the Griffin genocide and a miracle that she and her company survived the journey to Bimmorus, with her unborn child nonetheless!

An inviting aroma floats in from the steaming dining room table, seated for a party of ten at the least. Today, the anniversary of Griffin acceptance in the kingdom, is a day of celebration!

With a flip of a grand switch, only built into the loveliest structures in Bimmorus, balls of floating energy grow and hover just below the ceilings in each room on the first floor. Their inventor, Lady Thelmure, is one of the brightest inventors in all of Bimmorus, and also a family friend. She named these lively spheres Star Lights, and for good reason. As many landbound creatures wish to be one with the heavens, these contraptions may illuminate a space the way a gaseous star should. Yet Ariah looks dissatisfied. She turns the dial next to the handle, controlling the hue and saturation of the light. Hundreds of colors pass, and not one of them pleases her.

"That looks nothing like the stars," says Ariah, sighing. As a Griffin, she would know.

She shuts the switch and flicks her wrist toward the candelabra. Out from her fingertips shoot small flames landing onto their corresponding wicks. In no time, the home is aglow in yellow.

Ariah claps her warm hands together. "Now that's perfect."

The hardwood floors vibrate, and there's a light clatter at the dishes on the table. An even whooshing sounds overhead, and Ariah rushes to open the door. Above her flourishing farm is a flock of flying Griffins! Eliath's blond and greying fur glimmers in sunlight as he leads the way. Francis, a fellow Griffin refugee and neighbor in their secluded Griffin town, is at his left, his wife and child behind him. Tailing their guests is Ariah's son, Marcus. His ash-blond fur is unmistakable. Marcus loops in the sky joyously. There is a screaming Bimmorian clutching on to him for dear life. Ariah's squints her aging eyes. *Is that General Camden?*

"Marcus! Cut that out!" she hollers as if he could hear nearly a hundred feet above her. If only she knew Camden had asked for an adventurous ride and is enjoying every moment.

What joy it is to see her people descend, transforming in a dazzling white blaze into their human forms, greeting her one by one while she welcomes them into her home.

Camden towers a good few feet above her. He is dressed in a glossy white robe ending at his knees. Its trim is embellished with silver stitching to match his silver freckles. The robe is tied at the waist with a leather belt. Black knee-high riding boots, perfect for the occasion of riding a Griffin. And of course, the crescent necklace his father, King Owen, had gifted him before his passing. But his hair, shocked by the wind, sticks out in every direction, making Marcus belly-laugh.

But Ariah is quick to work her fingers through it. "Stop that, Marcus."

"Thank you," Camden says, remembering his late mother's gentle touch while Ariah fixes his hair.

"Camden, you look as dashing as ever!" says Ariah. They embrace. She touches his necklace and looks up at him quizzically. In a hushed tone she asks, "Won't this transform in our presence?"

Camden shakes his head. "Hasn't Eliath told you? He's configured its system to transform on my command. I no longer need to fear the presence of magic around it."

Ariah gleams. "What good news! Do keep that protected." She frowns at Marcus before entering the house.

Marcus shrugs and Camden slaps his back playfully.

"Ariah!" exclaims Francis's wife. "How stunning!"

Francis nods. "Yes. It will do well to remember that for every tragedy we face innocently, we will be rewarded beyond our measure."

Eliath smiles. "Aye. Ya sound more like yawr pa every day, Francis."

They laugh.

"Ah, I wish. If only he'd be here to say such things 'imself," Francis says. His wife can sense the grief in his tone and clasps his hand.

Camden butts in. "I know the horrors you've all faced. Let us reinvent this dark moment, dedicating it to the one's we've lost. May we think of them in good health, recompensed for the injustice brought upon them in their new lives, wherever they might be."

In that moment of silence, loved ones grab on to one another's hands. Their eyes meet with the tremendous document on the wall. A document they'd signed years ago and have not seen since. Proof of their strife, and their survival.

"Marcus, what is it like in the Royal Academy?" asks Francis's thirteen-year-old daughter, Lor.

Marcus explains, "It's amazing. There are so many people just like us! Harpies, centaurs, and fauns, all with their own cultures and beliefs. Honestly, simply meeting them is enough to understand we are so much alike. Our forms do not matter."

"Yes, well said, Marcus," begins Thora, a Griffin refugee.

Thora was once an educator in the Griffin Clan. Now she is a tradeswoman for the sake of making a living.

Thora goes on, "These three species so mentioned are not at all to the scale of the Griffins, Arketchians, or Bimmorians. Long-lasting and grand countries compared to these nomadic species. Harpies, centaurs, and fauns migrate yearly to different destinations of the Extraordinary Division. They do not believe in settling in one place long. And that is where Bimmorus's corruption lies—"

Up until this moment, everyone has lent a keen ear to Thora, and it is clear that she meant to go on, until she locks eyes with Camden and blushes.

"Please, I mean no offence," she tells the general.

Camden says, "I have not taken any offense. I would have very much liked you to continue your thoughts, as I might be able to aid the situation in the capital."

Thora is hesitant until Ariah approves. "Camden is most trusted. A man of his word," says Ariah.

Thora says, "I meant to say if Bimmorus was truly a kingdom that sought to create allies in the Extraordinary Division, they should have additionally allied with the superpowers of the realm. Bimmorus has preferred not to reach out to the Griffin Clan and the Arketcha Tribe in all the years the Royal Academy was established. Of all the Griffin refugees, even Bimmorian born, Marcus was the only one picked for the academy. No doubt, because he is the prophet of this generation."

"I see . . . I would like to see this vision of unity complete," Camden says. "Perhaps one day it will be so. Until then, there are many powerful forces preventing this joining, preferring their borders, their rule, and their magic. In regards to Griffin students at the Royal Academy, I, too, believe more should attend. Leave it to me—"

Suddenly, Marcus's eyes roll backward, and he falls over in his seat, shaking tremendously. Eliath and Ariah rush to his side.

"Marcus, dear!" Ariah exclaims.

"I thought he was past this!" says Eliath.

Camden instantly takes Marcus into his arms and onto the cushioned couch in the seating area. Everyone crowds around him, and none can wake him from his trance.

When the vision came to sweep Marcus away, there was no sort of warning. One moment, he was at his mother's table enjoying the conversation, and the next he was falling from the skies. Of all the premonitions he's ever had, this had to be the most violent and terrifying, for as he falls in the dark abyss, there is no telling when he will land, or if he will land. He tries to take hold of it, the way he usually does, like lucid dreaming, the way his instructor, Lady Meir, taught him. But it is no use.

Marcus lands roughly in an undefined setting, and because it isn't really real, he gets up. The scene morphs, and six arched doorways surround him. Above each doorway is a moon; all are cycling backward. Dizzying with the intensity of his vision, Marcus finds counting the cycles futile. When the one to his left ends its cycle first, the strange hallway rumbles. Marcus assumes the doorway beneath this moon showcases the first event he must witness.

Marcus enters the first archway. Inside is a boy nearly his age. He is wearing shackles on his wrist that keep him pinned to the wall while he pleads for mercy. In the center of this room, a man looms over a young woman. His face is hidden by shadow, and she is hanging on for dear life.

Another rumble. Marcus peers over his shoulder. The second moon has completed its cycle. Within the archway is a dark forest. The young man and woman from the previous archway rush to hide behind the trees. Epic and gruesome moments pass. For every time Marcus urges his eyes shut from the madness, tremors jolt up his legs, forcing him to look.

"Your amulet, do you still have it?" says the young woman just before her death.

Marcus is urged to the third archway. Within its doorway, young Griffins in their beast forms are fighting viscously when this same boy enters the scene. A gaping mouth signifies his shock at the sight.

This must be the Griffin Clan . . . and these visions are all following the same person. But why is he so important? Marcus thinks.

Horrible matches end with the death. But the young man's life is saved by another young man with black hair.

"I'm River, by the way," says the savior. "What's your name?"

"Oh. I'm Hale."

Hale.

Another rumble. The fourth moon has finished its cycle. And the others are moving slower by the moment. Epic battles showcase Hale's courageousness and righteous actions when he defends the innocent. The more Marcus watches, the more he is in awe of Hale. For every obstacle Hale overcomes, he remains true to his character.

The fifth tremor nearly knocks Marcus off his feet. He moves along to the next doorway with buckling knees, trying to keep his balance. A lavish golden dome comes into view, and there, Hale meets a man . . . who shares similar features.

"Hello. I'm Bayo."

They look so much alike, especially so in the eyes, Marcus thinks. *Are they related?* But they couldn't be, as this man explains the history of the Griffin Clan, and Hale speaks of his father, Felix. An extravagant bed appears, and Hale sinks deeply into it.

At the sixth quake, Marcus is thrust backward, hitting his back, hard. In the waking world, Marcus has jolted upright and plops back into his cushioned seat, startling his parents and their guests.

"Marcus, dear. Wake up!" says Ariah, giving his shoulders a slight shake.

But Marcus is deaf to the waking world.

Flints of particles sparkle in the light of the final archway. The earthquake-like tremor forces Marcus to crawl to it. Only when he reaches it does it calm.

Hale whirls a sword with precision—not that he needs it, for as soon as his opponent is out of reach, Hale's eyes narrow, forcing his opponent to beg for mercy from the might of his power . . . Later, the ghost of his sister, Carly, leads him up the stairs and through a closed door where mysteries unfold instantly.

"Hale, he wasn't your father. He stole you! From me!" Bayo presses his hand to his chest. "You are my brother. Do you see the resemblance?"

During an epic chase, Hale reunites with his longtime friends. Their success is short-lived, for Hale collapses when he hears the siren's ethereal voice. Marcus, however, cannot hear it, as the scene is mysteriously muted, but he understands that Hale's visible pain resulted from the beautiful olive-skinned girl.

A light appears from behind. Marcus turns to the center of the hallway, where a tall man with blond hair and blue eyes waits. Though Marcus can't explain it, he instantly feels a connection to this person. *What is it about him that is so familiar?* he thinks. Familiar in the sense that their inner beings somehow match.

"Marcus, the prophet of the current generation!" says the man, smiling.

"Who are you?" asks Marcus.

"I am Felix, the Elder Prophet."

"You're the man who stole Hale away from Bayo!" Marcus says, putting the pieces together.

Felix nods. "I needed to."

"I know," says Marcus.

"My son has fled the Griffin Clan. He and his two companions are making their way to Bimmorus. You must allow him into the kingdom at all costs. The survival of the worlds depend on it."

The moons overhead darken into a new moon phase. Likewise, the scenes within the doorways have vanished except one, which exudes a blinding light.

Felix adds, "My last premonition is something I'd very much like you to see." He holds out his hand for Marcus to take. Marcus, however, is hesitant. He already had too many visions at once, and they've significantly worn him down. Yet Felix's kindly gaze is one most trustworthy.

When Marcus takes Felix's hand, both their eyes flash an electric green, identical to the moon that has bestowed them with the power of prophecy during the annual Welcoming Moon celebration. Whatever Felix now shares with Marcus makes him laugh with wonder. The light of their eyes returns to their natural state.

Felix is walking into the lit doorway, his voice becoming fainter with each absconding step. "I am proud to have you for a successor. Tell my son—"

Marcus, too, seems to be fading away. Losing time, and understanding exactly what Felix wishes to say, Marcus assures him, "I will."

"He's coming to," sounds Camden's voice.

Marcus opens his eyes to a dizzying army of worried people hovering over him. He feels too weak to sit upright, so Ariah gently lifts his head to feed him a glass of water.

Grabbing Camden's hand, Marcus whispers urgently, "I know you planned to put the barrier up today. But you mustn't do it."

"Why?" Camden is baffled. Up until now, Marcus has been pressuring him daily to create the magical barrier around the kingdom.

"Because the Griffin Prince must come to Bimmorus," Marcus explains.

Chapter 18

June 1, 2021
ONE MONTH EARLIER

Fifty rows of Griffin soldiers are lined in front of Ianna, separated into two classes—Griffins of the Light at her right, and Griffins of Shielding at her left. Their intimidating armor consists of shining black coiled metal—which is most curious, for when the young Griffins transform, the armor morphs with their beings, molding perfectly and providing protection to both forms.

Tugging at her heavy armor for some relief in the scorching sun is Grace. She is daydreaming about a swim at the waterfalls with River, who is just in view to her right among the Griffins of Shielding. The back of her neck is damp with sweat even though her hair is twisted into braids for maximum comfort.

River's unmoving, ridged stature is most unlike his typical fidgeting. This is usually the moment of their day when he'll sneak a charismatic smile or wink her way. Yet when River does turn, there is no mistaking the worry hidden in his green eyes. Grace catches his Adam's apple quivering and a hasty wipe of his eyes. She's never seen River so distraught, not even during their most dire circumstances.

Something's happened. It suddenly feels as though the sturdy ground beneath her has faltered. Though she desperately wants to take River into her arms, Grace must keep in line at all costs. She reverts her attention back to her instructor.

Ianna's black hair has grown down to the base of her back, and it is styled in a snakelike waterfall braid that travels from side to side on her head. She is neither armed nor wearing armor but instead is wearing a light-blue silken robe covering her from elbow to knee. Her soldiers work at her command with ease. Ianna paces and tenderly adjusts those with poor stature.

"There you go, just like this," she says.

How remarkable it is for the Elder of Shielding to be so well versed in all things of the Light, a talent separate from her own. And how fortunate they were to have Ianna, whose students face no casualties during her training, unlike the other Elders' students.

When Ianna addresses the crowd, her words project loud enough to reach most, though her tone is gentle, like that of a mother.

She says, "In times of battle, you will meet chaos. There will be nowhere to turn when your companions are pushing forward and the enemy is closing in. You will feel afraid upon collision, and a greater fear during combat.

"But you will find support with your comrades. For in my teachings, I've shown you how to combine your powers to never reach a point of individual combat. Our advantage is in our powers. You, Griffins of Shielding, will be tasked to push through, conquer, and protect the other Griffins that lack your protective abilities. Griffins of Light, your task will be to dissuade the opponent with illusions so that we may enter successfully."

She continues, "In times of old, High Elder Bayo and we Elders defended our country against whole invading nations. Six beings against hundreds. We established this Clan, and for hundreds of years proceeding, the Griffins thrived." A look of grief strikes Ianna's face. "The grandness of our history waned, but now, we have the ability to regain what we lost."

Something is odd about her last words, perhaps in the change of tone. To Grace, it seems that Ianna does not believe what she herself just said. With a wave of her hand, Ianna signals the Shielding Griffins to begin their sequences.

To observe Griffins of Shielding perform their sequences is like watching water dance. They have a fluid and elegant way about their movement. Every hand gesture and twirl of their bodies is pure artistry. River, along with his brethren, extend their arms out as if pulling a grand energy from their chests to procure a shield. A beautiful glimmer showcases the shape and thickness of their shields, a new effect Ianna has taught them to display their usually invisible powers.

It is obvious that River is trying not to look Grace's way when he performs. But their eyes inevitably meet for a split moment, and he frowns, breaking Grace's heart. *Have I done something to upset him?* she wonders.

The Griffins of Light start their sequences as soon as the Shielding Griffins come to a halt. As if they are one with the wind, they cut through the air. Their strategic movements matched with their mental powers create a combined illusion of a Griffin a hundred times the average size. Its pearly fur descends from the mountains in the south and roams the skies toward the east. In this moment, the minds of all the Griffins of the Light are intwined. For in their subliminal communication, they are able to aid in this grand illusion.

And for every sense of the word, this epic Griffin is real. The ground judders at its passing, and the ears of the soldiers are filled with its squawking. This is something a lone Griffin of the Light could never conjure. Not even the great Greon can manipulate the perception of sound.

Simultaneously, the soldiers of the Light pounce, kick one foot high, spin, and land on their right knee. In that instant, their illusion vanishes in a puff of smoke right in front of Ianna's stony face.

Grace's chest heaves with lost breath; her clothes beneath her armor cling to her damp skin. That was the most she's ever exerted herself during training, and she can tell that the mental and physical push improved her stamina. But is Ianna proud of their illusion? Grace peeks past the heads of her comrades and watches a proud smile grow on Ianna's face.

"Well done!" Ianna exclaims.

She transforms without warning, illuminated in the light of her essence, and takes to the skies. Finally, training is over for the day, and Grace is free to spend the rest of her time with River. While the young Griffins take to the skies,

Grace waits for River, but she cannot see him anywhere through the eager crowd. Minutes pass, and now she is deeply worried. Did he leave without her?

There's a sudden tug at her waist from behind. She immediately recognizes his touch. River's soft hands on her waist and the closeness of his body feels like home. It was all that Grace needed to settle her nerves. River wasn't upset with her. Something else must have happened.

River leans close to her ear and whispers, "Meet me at the waterfall." His voice is as smooth as velvet.

She places her hands atop his, instinctually, and River's grip on her tightens to a point where she can feel him shaking. Grace yearns to take him into her arms, but before she turns to face him, River pulls away.

Grace desperately wants to bolt to him, gently place her lips on his, and wipe the tears from his beautiful eyes. She wishes as much for the boy with the golden heart, but she knows better.

Not here.

The restriction of being close to those she loves boils her blood. How desperately she craves freedom!

River transforms. When his form molds and the light of his soul is exposed, Grace believes that she has never seen a soul so pure and beautiful. River gallops through the skies. His raven-like fur glimmers with a blue iridescence as he shrinks in the distance, leaving Grace hoping everything is okay.

It feels wonderful to stretch one's wings! Grace closes her eyes and takes in the light breeze flowing through her auburn feathers. She is supported by the wind, which carries her worn body toward her destination. The scape forms before her. Cyan sparkling waters are directly below, and just beyond, grasslands turn to rolling hills over the winding cliffside.

The sound of burbling intensifies, and the grand waterfall finally comes into view. It is surrounded by plentiful rocks and shrubbery, but Grace cannot find a trace of River. Mist gently coats her midsection when she tilts her body and swoops down and to her right in search of him. A luminous rainbow appears within the opaque downpour near the edge of the waterfall, and through it is the silhouette of a young man. Moving closer to the violent current, Grace peers into the cave on the other side of the waterfall. And as suspected, River is inside.

His armor is thrown carelessly onto the cool and wet rock. River's loose shirt clings to his torso, and his hair is wet. He allows himself a faint smile upon seeing her.

This should have allowed Grace a bit of relief, but the concern behind his weary eyes prevents it. She lands within the cave and transforms. The air here is so cool and refreshingly shaded, though the sunlight continues to shine through the gushing wall of water. Immediately, Grace reaches out for River, but he pulls back. Something he's never done before. Suddenly uncomfortable, Grace just stares. River refuses to hold her gaze.

"Something is wrong," she says, finally. "You've been off the past week. I'm worried."

Why wouldn't he look at her? She can't even see his eyes with his hair over his face like that. Grace dares a step closer. River's chest is suddenly heaving, she leans over and spots his overflowing eyes.

"I'm so-sorry," he sobs. He takes in a breath and forces himself to face her. "I kept something from you that I couldn't tell you before."

Unexpectedly, he strokes her head, cascading his hand down the base of her back. In his free hand, he holds a chain that he then places around her neck. Attached to it is an obsidian pendant cut in the shape of a short wand. She inspects the beautiful piece of jewelry and is puzzled. The necklace's twin is hanging from River's neck. He pulls it out of his shirt for her to see.

"This pendant protects us from all magic, including the power of the Dark. With this we can speak freely," River says, taking her hand. His are cold and shaking. "Do you remember the day we promised each other we'd always be together, then we visited the tree dome?"

"Yes," Grace nods.

"You went with your friends while I hid behind the trunk, and I found something." He continues to tell her about Felix's journal, and his mission written within. "Hale is in danger. His father said I had one month to study the information in the book. He gave us four pendants, one for all of us."

Grace takes in the information, then nods with enthusiasm. "That's great. We can finally leave the Griffin Clan, and Hale will finally be away from Bayo. When are we leaving?"

River pauses. It seems he hasn't explained the situation well enough. "Grace." His voice is breaking. "Only Hale, Evan, and I are leaving. Felix has implied that you stay behind."

"Oh," she says. "He didn't mention why?"

River shakes his head solemnly.

"When?" she asks. River squeezes her hand tighter, forcing her emotions to rise from within. "No," she mouths.

River speaks just above a whisper. "The day after tomorrow, after Hale's battle with Leon in the arena."

Grace shakes her head in disbelief. "No!" she cries. River wraps his arms around her tightly. She sobs heavily against his sturdy chest. Her fists clutch onto the back of his shirt. "Why didn't you tell me?" she asks furiously. "All month you could—" She is suddenly gasping, searching in his bloodshot eyes, eyes that she thought would be hers forever. The darkest of thoughts cross her mind. "I won't know if you all will be safe. I wouldn't know—and the Elders are stealing away the rebels in the night—"

River's tears pour freely. "I know. Listen to me." He shakes her shoulders. "At all costs, make them believe you are not a rebel. Rewire your brain. Whatever you do, don't let a single thought of being against Bayo cross your mind. You support Bayo. You are his soldier. And at all costs, don't think about us; especially don't think about Hale. You don't know where we are. You know nothing about the journal. Do not even think about the pendant, and do not wear it often or the Griffins of Dark will suspect something. Do you hear me?" He shakes her once more. He's never been so forceful before. His tone is as cold as ice. "Do you hear me, Grace?" River repeats loudly.

"Yes," she whispers, processing her living nightmare.

"If Felix didn't foresee you doing something of importance here, I think you would have come with us. I think you're staying here to fix what Hale could not."

Her only solace in this crazy reality is leaving and might never return. Is this their last moment together?

Grace is bawling. "How do you know?"

River reveals his signature captivating smile, and suddenly the world feels less burdensome. "I can feel it. It's you, Grace. You are the one who's going to fix everything in the Griffin Clan."

River's intuition is seldom wrong. Grace takes a deep breath and nods. "You too. Take care of them."

"I will. This isn't the end, Grace." River pulls her hands up to rest on his shoulders, and then he rests his hands on her waist. Their temples touch, and he begins stepping side to side. "I'm going to see you again. And when I do"—he pecks her lips—"I'm going to marry you."

Grace forces a smile. She strokes his face and hopes to never forget this moment no matter how much time will pass proceeding it. "You are my every happiness." She shudders, a tear falling down her cheek.

River wipes it away and kisses her forehead. Then he pulls her in close and begins to step side to side while humming a soothing tune. His singing is like sunlight after an eternity of darkness. His heavenly voice is so soothing and delicate.

The skies glitter with stars,
I watch the sun rise, swell, and fall
But no light shines as bright as your heart
I'll run to you when you call
Because of you, I am strong.

Destiny calls me to move on
How can I go and leave my heart?
I can't change the world on my own
I'm no hero, please know,

You are my light, you are my heart
You are the reason, I don't fall apart
You are one that makes me strong
My heart breaks to leave, the timing is so wrong
When I find you, we will sing our song.

I've seen the world crumble and break
How can my small soul make things okay
If only my hands could carry you far away
But fate won't let me stay.
Will everything be okay?
I wish I can hold you tight and say,

You are my light, you are my heart
You are the reason, I don't fall apart
You are one that makes me feel strong
My heart breaks to leave, the timing is so wrong
When I find you, we will sing our song.

I am no hero, you are mine
I've seen the skies glitter with stars
I watch the sun rise, swell, and fall
No light shines as bright as your heart
No light shines as bright as your heart.

River immediately picks up the tempo. Suddenly, he is bubbling with enthusiasm, and his romantic words bounce off the cave walls.

Grace attempts to quiet him down, but he simply spins her out of his arms and chuckles. "Let's not waste the time we have left being sad."

She nods and smiles.

"Dance with me!" he exclaims.

So she did.

July 1, 2021
ONE MONTH LATER

The cool interior of the dome shines with the amber fire of a few torches. Tia and Maya, Grace's pack sisters, are fast asleep in the two top bunks. Grace, meanwhile, is just about to get into bed. She is exhausted from endless sparring and plops on her mattress to rub her aching muscles.

Ianna is no longer their instructor, as she has disappeared without so much as an explanation, leaving Grace often wondering whether she is alive. The remaining three Elders never spoke of her vanishing. Shielding and Light Griffins are now split between Bayo's and Deor's duties. Soon the Clan will leave to wage war on neighboring nations the young Griffins know nothing about.

She bites her lip, holding in a painful moan when she feels an open wound beneath her clothes. Pulling up her shirt, the long gash across the midsection is revealed. How didn't she notice before? Perhaps her mind is too preoccupied. The wound isn't deep, only a bleeding scrape. She dresses it with a solvent the three shared atop the nightstand and wraps it with gauze.

What was the point of sparring to extreme lengths? Daily injuries of Bayo's army were unending. Grace removes her outerwear to inspect other possible wounds and halts her thoughts. I shouldn't think this way. Hastily she pulls River's pendant out from under her mattress, throws it over her neck, and hides it under her shirt. *There. Now I'm free.*

She drops back onto her bed, and though she noticed the scrapes and bruises marking her open skin, she decides she does not have the strength to do anything about them. River's smile, so lifelike, is visible behind her shut eyes. Blood pulsates across her stretched-out body, and she is throbbing all over. Tossing over, she imagines it is River's body she rests her head on rather than the bulky pillow. It's been about thirty days since he'd left with Evan and Hale.

River, I pray you are alive. I pray you, Evan, and Hale are safe. Words cannot describe how much I miss you, or how frightened I am to be here without you. Come back to me soon.

His words replay in her mind: *I'm going to see you again. And when I do, I'm going to marry you.* Will they ever have that opportunity? Grace clutches the engagement ring in her pant pocket and envisions the world she and River would be part of if they returned to the Human Division.

She sighs deeply as she imagines herself with books in her arms and a backpack strapped to her shoulders. The college campus grounds are a vibrant green. Perhaps it is spring, her favorite season. Evan and Hale are tossing around a football in the courtyard, laughing and shouting playfully. River, sitting atop a shaded stoop, is strumming away on his guitar, looking up into the slightly cloudy sky while coming up with new lyrics and melodies. He notices Grace approaching and immediately smiles. The charming strumming of the guitar picks up, gathering the attention of other students. Maybe Maya and Tia would be there, too, Grace wonders, happily including familiar faces into her fantasy. And River would sing the song he wrote her.

Picturing River doing what he loves most and being totally in his element is like witnessing starlight. The deeper pitches of his words matched with his feathery runs were a signature style of his, and she imagines the allure would be too great not to turn heads. But she among the sea of many would be the only person who gets his attention.

Then what comes next? she wonders. Holding hands, taking classes, studying, spending every free moment together, goofing around with Hale and Evan, and inevitably graduation. Though unsure what career path she'd follow, Grace knows that the story must end someplace peaceful. They'd be loving parents to their children, in a happy home, something that she and River never had. Never to be taken away to their deaths again. Never to have to fight for a cause they did not believe in. No need for confusion or needless pain while struggling to survive. No Griffins. No dictators. No Bayo.

The dome quakes. Grace's eyes grow wide. *Oh no!* She's done the unmistakable. She disregarded River's warnings to be mindful of her thoughts. But she's wearing her pendant that protects her from magic, including the power of the Dark. Perhaps they weren't here for her . . . Maya and Tia groan from their bunks above.

"What was that?" mumbles Maya.

Tia tiptoes toward the thin window beside the door, making her curly hair bounce. "You know what that was, Maya," she says with a shaky voice, her almond complexion illuminated by moonlight.

"Grace, did you?" Tia asks.

"I-I don't know," Grace says, hastily removing the pendant and hiding it under the mattress along with her engagement ring. "I would never be against High Elder Bayo. He knows I am his loyal servant."

"Yes, as am I," says Maya, now clutching Grace's arm. She's a small girl, with short black hair and mocha-colored skin.

"Long live the High Elder of the Griffin Clan!" Tia declares.

"What do you see?" Grace asks, stepping forward.

Tia is backing away. "They—oh no!"

The front door of their dome bursts open. Three young and armed Griffins storm through. Maya screams. Grace's eyes are wide. *They must be here for me. But I—long live Bayo!* She thinks desperately.

The soldiers extend otherworldly spears, long shafts pulsating with a blue aura from either pointed tip. This weapon is called the huanim. Only the Goonies were allowed to wield them, and as rumor had it, the weapons were a gift to the Griffins from Thurana, a world of serpent people who are allies to High Elder Bayo in the upcoming war . . .

A single touch of the enchanted spear sends electrocuting shocks to its victims, not unlike the power of Endurance. *Why would Bayo allow the young Griffins to use this against one another?* Grace checks herself once more. *Bayo is a genius of combat, a strategic ruler.*

The young Griffin soldier at the front has his arms extended out in front of him. No doubt he'd used his power of Shielding to push though the locked door.

Maya falls to the floor in horror, deep fear consuming her. "Long live High Elder Bayo! Long live High Elder Bayo!" she bellows.

Grace had never seen one so close before. Goonies. There was something strange in the way they walked. Their limbs so stiff, and movements almost robotic. She peers closer. The light of their shaft illuminates their faces, and she gasps.

"Jacob?" she says.

A boy she once knew very well, he was a part of her rebellion when everyone first arrived in the Griffin Clan. He even helped save River once . . . Jacob's pupils dilate as if recalling the name. *Maybe he remembers?* Grace thinks.

She dares to try again. "Jacob. It's me, Grace. You remember me, don't you?"

"Grace! Stop! Stand back," says Tia protectively.

"Tia, you are coming with us," says the Shielding Goonie. Even the way they speak, enunciating each syllable placidly as if using their own foreign language, is strange.

Grace looks to her trembling pack sister. "No," she objects. "Tia would never go against Bayo. You're mistaken. She loves the High Elder. She says so daily."

Grace takes slow steps toward her pack sister. The three soldiers turn their heads eerily to their new threat. With one swoop of the hand, the Shielding Griffin throws Grace across the room, smashing her spine against the bottom bunk.

"Ugh!" Grace moans.

But this isn't enough to stop the valiant warrior. Grace makes her way to her feet while projecting ten illusions of Tia surrounding the soldiers. The stiff, expressionless soldiers begin slashing their shafts. The solution is short-lived when the real Tia jumps back in fright while the shafts cut through her clones.

The Shielding Griffin hastily blockades Tia on all sides with a bubble-like shield. With strong motions of his arms, he looks to be tugging on the air and pulling it back. At his movements, Tia is dragged out the door. Grace steps forward; the two other soldiers turn to her with their shafts pointed.

"Stand down," says Jacob.

Grace pauses. His eyes were not looking into her eyes the way they should. It is a cold, expressionless, and eerie stare. Tia is nearly out the door, and she looks to her pack sisters for what she knows will be the last time.

"I'll find you," Grace says. "Don't worry."

"Don't, Grace," Tia says. "Please don't fight them. Long live the High Elder." The door slams shut.

Grace yanks the knob that should be unlocked. "Ahhh! Come on," she grunts.

Maya stutters, "G-Grace. S-stop."

The pressure against the door caused by the powerful Shielding Goonie vanishes, the door opens, and Grace stumbles backward into Maya's arms, then dashes into the night. Maya follows her, just in time to watch the Goonies transform in the distance. They hoist Tia up in the air, as she is still entrapped in a now opaque aqua-colored bubble. Grace comes to a screeching halt along the grassy ground. Tia looks utterly horrified.

Neighboring Griffin sisters are peeping their heads out from their doors in dread. Reminding themselves not to repeat Tia's mistake, their whispers spread throughout the scape. "Long live the High Elder."

Grace retreats to her dome, racking her head until she meets Maya's eyes. Automatically, Maya begins to apologize.

Enraged, Grace balls her fists. "You know Tia would never go against Bayo. She knows her place more than anybody. She wouldn't allow herself to think a single thought against him."

Maya bites her lip. "It could have been a fleeting thought. Deor—Elder Deor senses everything, long may he live."

"You are a coward," spits Grace, storming away.

"What are you going to do?" asks Maya.

Absolutely nothing, Grace thinks. She cannot disobey, no matter what she's on the verge of losing. A lump rises in her throat, and she is on the verge of thinking about all that she has lost. Tia's shaken grimace as she tells Grace to give up is enough to set Grace off the edge.

"It's good she's gone," Grace whispers as she wipes her tears. "It's good she's gone," she repeats, now loudly, to Maya. "She was a traitor."

The neighboring Griffin girls look on with astonishment.

"The show is over!" Grace tells them. "Long may the High Elder live!"

"Long may he live," they repeat, shutting their doors. Grace retreats to her dome and jumps in bed.

Maya does not think her actions are curious in the least and does the same after burning the torches out with her power of Ardor.

"Maybe it doesn't hurt. Maybe it feels good. All the Goonies are more powerful than we are," says Maya.

"Yes," Grace says, recalling the Shielding Griffin who singlehandedly stormed through a locked door and entrapped their pack sister with enough force to carry her through the sky. "Our powers are tied to our emotions."

Maya says, "Who knows what potential they have now that they don't stand in their own way . . . Goodnight."

"Goodnight." *Breathe, Grace. Everything is okay. We are just going to get some sleep, and everything will be better in the morning.* After minutes of repeating this inner mantra, Grace slips her hand under her mattress and hastily pulls the protective pendant over her head. *There,* she thinks. *They'll think I'm asleep.*

Grace allows her power of Light to wash over her body. She peers into the long mirror pushed against their wall to inspect her work and cannot see her reflection.

Good.

Maya tosses in her sleep. She was always a heavy sleeper. It is so bizarre how one moment can change your perception of a person. Grace sighs. She can't blame Maya, though. She is only fourteen, the youngest age among the Griffins. It's a wonder she's even lived this long. Everyone just wants to survive.

She leaves the dome in silence.

Thigh-long blades of grass rub against Grace's legs. Splattered specks of light in the sky are her only guide through the prairie. Hunched low, Grace creeps toward the large golden dome that shone with a luminous orange light through its windows. The Elders' Dome. The pendant River gave her dangles from her neck, protecting her from all magic, and her power of Light conceals her from visibility.

It seems the shortcut she's taken offered her a few minutes advantage to the path the lifeless soldiers took. She can hear the flapping of their wings overhead. Grace nears the front entrance when the three transform a few yards away. Like clockwork, Rioma emerges. She is as dazzling as ever. Her statuesque figure is dressed in a lavish purple gown. Too lavish for the casual occasion of opening the door, but this isn't a new behavior for the Elder.

"Thank you," says Rioma, addressing the soldiers who cuff Tia's arms.

Grace sneaks through the small gap between Rioma and the door. Her heart is pumping with adrenaline, and she can hardly hear Rioma speaking past it.

Tia does not struggle. She knows it's futile.

"Welcome, Tia," Rioma says. "Come this way."

With a deep breath, Tia enters the extravagant dome, neither intimidated or in awe of its luxuriousness. Grace, too, reminds herself not to fall for the allure of the dome's interior. She is here for answers that only she can uncover with her power of Light and her enchanted pendant. Tia ascends the winding steps and Rioma follows; Grace is at their tail. Stepping in time with their steps to prevent noise, Grace advises herself, *Breathe, Grace. You can do this.*

Once at the second floor, Tia slows her pace. Grace can tell she is very frightened but admirably brave. Will she be able to save her pack sister?

Rioma, too, has noticed Tia's angst and unremorsefully says, "All will be well."

Grace has half a mind to punch the Elder in her smug face.

The young girl then dares ask Rioma, "Why was I called here? I am Bayo's trusted servant, long may the High—"

Without even the slightest pause, Rioma answers, "You will be meeting with Elder Deor of the Dark. He will be working with you to heal any previous mental wounds. The young Griffins have experienced tremendous turmoil during their previous lives in the Human Division, and we wish to relieve you all that pain. What do you think about that?" She flashes a magnetic smile.

Tia's slumped posture changes. She is erect and confident, speaking with an exuberant tone she didn't have a moment ago. "Yes. That sounds lovely."

Lovely? Tia never spoke that way. Shivers rush up Grace's spine.

Rioma immediately drops her gaze before leading Tia to an unlit room. Grace does not follow her inside. The door slams shut behind her. Voices sound from within. Grace leans closer. It is a man's voice . . . *Deor's voice.*

"Do you know where you are, Tia?" he asks.

"Y-yes."

Rioma rushes down the steps, the bottom of her dress in her hands. It is as if her facade has slipped once Tia entered the room, and it is clear the Elder is disturbed by what will proceed . . . Strange, Grace almost thought the Elder believed her own lies.

Grace lingers with her ear against the door.

"To whom do you place your allegiance?" Deor asks.

"High Elder—" There is a loud thud, like Tia has fallen on the floor, followed by a piercing scream.

Grace jumps back, bringing her shaken hand to her mouth.

"Your mind speaks differently," Deor says.

"Bayo! Bayo is my king!" Tia yells.

Grace's tears are interrupted when something catches her eye to her left. It is Bayo leaving his room and descending the steps. Should she take up this keen opportunity or fight for Tia's life, risk being exposed, and lose her pendant? The clock is ticking, and Grace needs to decide quickly. No, she will live to fight another day. The more answers she'll find, the better equipped she will be in saving the Goonies. And what better way to find answers than following the High Elder himself.

Grace tiptoes behind Bayo and follows him out of the Elders' Dome. Bayo transforms yards away and takes into the sky. His transformation is one with exceptional power, almost illuminating the night, to reveal a Griffin of fine magnitude. The length of three ordinary lions, muscular limbs, long talons, and powerful tail. The sleekness of his coat along with his subtle movements accentuate his mysteriousness. If Grace hadn't thought the High Elder was entirely evil, she'd have thought he was beautiful, especially in his Griffin form.

Bayo's enormous and haunting wings unfold. A single flap sends a warm breeze through the grassland. Grace is left to contemplate her next move. *I can go back to my dome right now and avoid any harm . . . or I can see what he's hiding. Is it worth the risk?*

River's voice is so clear in her mind, it is like he is standing right next to her. *I can feel it. It's you, Grace. You are the one who's going to fix everything in the Griffin Clan.* Grace doesn't believe she is that powerful to stop the evil happenings in the Clan, but River's faith in her gives her hope. For River, Evan, Hale, and everyone else who's suffered here, she must try her best.

Grace transforms.

Bayo cuts through the misty clouds with ease, and Grace strains to keep up. Finally, he descends near a mountainside surrounded by many waterfalls and caves, transforms on a plateau near an opening, and lights a torch. Grace has never been here before. She creeps behind him in awe of the crystal stalagmites that glitter the space.

Bayo leads her to a narrow descending staircase. Shivering, Grace wraps her arms around her torso. Was it cold in here, or is it her nerves? She cannot tell. *Everything will be okay,* she tells herself. *You have to see what he's hiding.*

There are so many corridors in the labyrinth cave. The long walkways are flooded with mounds of gems and jewels. With one careless step or shuffle of the foot, it would be game over for Grace. She makes sure to be wary of her every move. The Elder's polished shoes come to a slow halt.

She looks into the black abyss, trying to recall the series of steps she took to get here. *Was it left, left, right?* She can't remember exactly, and her thinking is interrupted when the cave judders, compelling her to grip on to stone for balance. *What was that?*

Bayo has pulled a lever that opened a secret passageway. There is no light source within. He steps through. Grace rushes inside before the entrance returns to its natural state, before the light of Bayo's torch fades with him, leaving her here wondering how to get out or, worse, waiting for Bayo to bump into her on his way out of the narrow path.

The cave quakes with intensity. Half panicked, Grace wonders if the cave will collapse in on itself. If so, she must spend her last moments trapped with the High Elder. She regrets coming, though she forces herself to breathe at an even pace. *You have to stay calm. It's the only way you can keep up the illusion of invisibility.*

Down another set of winding stairs, Grace finally understands what Bayo has traveled all this way for. Or better—for whom. She assumed she'd find Elder Ianna here, yet at the cold bottom is a shackled girl no older than Grace herself. The girl's arms are chained above her head; her legs are dangling inches above the ground. It must be so exhausting to be held in that position. The thought of the girl's painful limbs and popped sockets sends shivers up Grace's spine.

Her head hangs with exhaustion. By the light of Bayo's approaching torch, Grace beholds her beauty, long brown spiraling curls, and a deep olive complexion. A large azure crystal rests on her chest, embroidered into her leathery lavender-colored top and cape. Whoever this young woman was, she did not dress like a Griffin. *What could he possibly want from her?*

The girl senses the light of Bayo's torch, and with a lack of strength, she lifts her head a few inches, revealing hazy eyes and a metal brace around her mouth.

Bayo grins. "How have you been enjoying your stay?" he asks, drawing nearer.

Neither fear nor anger are present in the girl's empty expression until her head springs back and muffled cries sound through the iron brace, startling Grace half to death. *Bayo is using his power of Endurance.*

"You think yourself brave, don't you?" he whispers in her ear. "You think yourself strong."

Ellionna keeps her eyes closed and winces through the pain. Grace looks on in trepidation, a bone-chilling sweat at her temples.

Bayo says, "You are holding yourself quite well. But I am not impressed. Your strength will be short-lived, as so many before you. Nobody in the world, not even the vessel of the siren, is a match for me."

Siren? Grace has heard of such mythological creatures in the Human Division. Something like a mermaid who seduces sailors to their deaths. How wrong the myths were, for this girl is no mermaid; she is just a girl . . .

Bayo continues, "All the years you've stolen from my brother, I will steal from you, one painful day at a time for all the pain you've inflicted on him while taking his life."

Grace is clutching her chest in shock. *Hale is dead. Evan? River? Could they be—* She's shaking. *But that can't be true!* River told her they would run from Bayo, that Felix foretold their leaving will be successful. Tears fall to her cheeks. *No, it can't be true.*

Bayo continues to torment this defenseless girl, leaving Grace no choice but to stand idly by. After long, excruciating moments, the brutality ceases and the screams silence. Ellionna's head drops in defeat. She's out cold. There's a gleam in Bayo's eyes, one of pure satisfaction. But it seems he is not finished with her yet.

Ellionna awakens and her woeful screams resume. The sound echoes through the cave and in Grace's ears, shaking her to her core. The corners of Bayo's lips curl into a sick grin.

The struggle to keep up the illusion of invisibility is proving difficult in the presence of pure evil. Grace thinks, *I shouldn't have let River go. I should have made him stay . . . No, they can't be dead. I don't believe it!*

This time, when Ellionna's head falls forward, she does not wake again. Grace peers closer, making sure her chest is rising steadily. The Griffin King leers as well, yet his attention is on the blue crystal at the base of the siren's chest.

Cracks form within the aquamarine gem until it shatters into countless pieces. Its sharp and fragmented shards clink on the cool ground.

Eerily, Ellionna's head jolts upward. Though her eyes are wide open, her brown irises are replaced by misty white scleras. Her paralyzed face is most off-putting, evident in the drooping of her facial muscles, like water pulled by gravity.

"There you are," Bayo says as he undoes the shackles around the siren's mouth.

The siren cackles with a deep gurgling voice that sounds as if it is underwater. It says, "Ohhh, Highhh Elder Bayo of the Griffin Ccclan! A thousand and some years of existenccce, and you still don't know hhhow to play your cccards right!"

Its sinister ear-to-ear smile stretches the beautiful girl's face unnaturally, making Grace's hair stand on end. As it speaks, water pours out from her mouth and drips down her chin. "You hhhave something I want," it growls. "And I cccan give you whhhat no othhher cccan!"

"What might that be?" Bayo asks.

"Oohhh hhhow slimy you are! Slimy as an eel! The othhher hhhalf of my soul is in your possession. I cccan sense it! Give it to me, in exchhhange for my allegianccce."

Bayo laughs. "Your allegiance! You will never show allegiance to any being."

The siren counters, "The Arketchhhians hhhave kept me imprisoned in their hhhuman vessels for cccenturies! Cccenturies of deprivation! Starved! You are in need of a weapon. And I am in need of souls . . ."

"And what will you gain with the other half of your soul?" Bayo questions.

"Only more cccontrol over this vessel."

"Wouldn't you rather be free?"

"The occceans are a vast domain . . . but imagine hhhow much I can ccconsume . . . in battle!"

The being shrieks suddenly. Bayo is working his power of Endurance over it. Water floods out of its mouth. Nonetheless, Bayo grips her neck tightly. His face reddens with rage.

"You took my brother's soul!" he says through a clenched jaw.

Choking against his grasp, the siren mutters, "Wrong! I cccan no longer ccconsume souls. Not until the othhher hhhalf of my own is returned to me. For now, I only kill."

Bayo shakes his head. "The more souls you consume, the more power you will obtain! You will be a threat even to me!" He releases her, prepared to leave, when—

"Let us make the ultimate pact," says the siren.

Bayo pauses, pondering the limitless possibilities. "You would bind yourself to me for eternity?" he asks.

"I would."

There is a long pause while the wheels churn in Bayo's mind. Finally, he says, "You have a deal."

Bayo places the shackle back on the creature's mouth and pauses at the foot of the winding stairs, inches away from Grace's shaking and cloaked body. Can he hear her breathing? Maybe her heartbeat? Does he detect her scent? It can't be that he can see her with his power of Endurance; after all, she is wearing Felix's protective pendant. But why is he hovering? He turns back as if to ask the siren a question, but Grace understands he's noticed her somehow. She creeps backward, going up one step at a time while removing the pendant around her neck and swallowing it. The moment she's been dreading has dawned upon her.

Bayo ascends the steps as though all is well, though slower than he usually would, and yet Grace cannot climb backward up the stairs fast enough. She contemplates turning her heels and running. Somehow she'll hide against the wall and wait patiently for Bayo to reveal how he pulled the lever. She plans to leave sometime after him, even though she is unsure of the way out.

Mid-thought, Bayo's right-handed torch swings round. In a flash, the fire leaps onto her skin and dances across her midsection. The flame consumes fiber after fiber, the heat confuses her senses, and she feels freezing cold before her skin burns. Instantly, Grace attempts to extinguish it with furious movements while doing her best to continue her illusion. But this is a fool's game. Bayo already knows.

Grace wants to scream, but she holds in her yelping. Her power of Light glitches in her anguish, and like the flicking of a light switch that is common in the Human Division, she becomes visible, meeting his blazing eyes.

It's over.

The fire smolders, and smoke fills the space. It smells of her singed flesh, like tanned leather. Grace sinks to her knees, her vision is turning black, and she is unexpectedly lifted by his sturdy arms. His eyes do not meet hers. The cave quakes—Bayo must have pulled the lever. What shall come after, Grace will not know. Her life rests in Bayo's hands . . .

CHAPTER 19

Hale sits at the foot of the bank that faces a row of mountains in the grand distance. The setting sun illuminates a few constellations and what Hale assumes are planets. River and Evan are busy preparing a meal behind him. A mouthwatering aroma of smoked fish fills the air, and though Hale's stomach grumbles, he has no interest in joining his pack brothers.

River approaches. Hale can tell it's him even without looking, perhaps by the gentle way he walks, or maybe he instinctually feels his presence. A steaming leafy plate is held out to him, but Hale shakes his head.

"I don't want to eat, thank you," Hale mumbles.

River sighs. Hale hasn't eaten in a few days. "You need to eat," River says.

Hale ignores him.

River doesn't feel comfortable enough to sit next to Hale. Hale made it pretty clear he wants to be left alone. It is almost as if River offended him in some way. Maybe the Hale that River knew a year ago won't come back. Maybe this is who Hale is now. River puts a pause to his thoughts. *No. He's just confused,* River thinks.

River dares extend an olive branch. "Do you want to talk about it?" he asks.

Hale refuses to look his way. "No."

Days later, Hale hacks away at a piece of wood with Evan's pocketknife. He's kept his distance all this time, continuing the long, lonely days without acknowledging his pack brothers. However, the small tasks he's given himself to keep his mind busy don't settle his unending thoughts . . .

I just lost my sister for the second time. Now for good. A familiar swell rises in his throat, matched with his puffy, bloodshot eyes. *I'm never going to see Carly again. We could have been free if she didn't force me to keep that promise. She didn't believe me. I am a monster. I'm better off dead.*

The bark is gradually forming into a woman's figure by the work of his hands. Carly, he meant it to be, just as he saw her on the cobblestone bridge. A slight flick of his wrist leaves the hem of her dress uneven. *Everything Bayo ever said to me was a lie.* Slash. *He tricked me for a year.* Slash. *Had me tortured.* Slash. *Planned to use me to help him rule over Malphora. Planned to create the ultimate murderer. If he's my brother, doesn't that mean I am just as evil as he is?* Slash.

Dad—I mean, Felix. He isn't my dad. He's the Elder Griffin Prophet who stole me away from Bayo. He never once told me who I really am. Did he have to lie to me? Couldn't he have at least prepared me with the truth so that I could have dealt with this when the time came? How should I think of my family? Are they imposters? Traitors? How could they keep the truth from me like this? Were they good people at all?

The figurine is ruined. The wooden mass is nothing more than an unidentifiable blob, and worse still once Hale has furiously tossed it against the trunk of a tree. He can't sculpt wood like Evan can . . . The knife is still in his hands, and it reflects the sunset. He stares at it.

I hurt people. He repeats their names in his mind. *I'm a monster.* He tosses it into the water, a knife the three have used this long to survive. A most reckless action.

But the frenzy does not end once the blade submerges, for after it, rocks fly out from Hale's tight grip. One upon the other like a meteor shower attacking this pond. *Why is it so easy to be like Bayo?* He recalls using his power of Endurance on the Griffin Clan and the thousands of screams that followed. *Why didn't I feel anything when I hurt them? Why was it so easy?* While his victims begged and clutched the dirt in agony, Hale does not recall feeling remorse. Unable to believe what he's done, Hale wonders, *Who am I?*

Like a madman, Hale continues sending the rocks into their murky doom, grunting heavily with every pitch. Evan emerges through the bushes, steadily calling out to his pack brother, yet ends up wrestling Hale for the stones he clings to. Perhaps they are to be the stones of his burdens.

"Everything is okay," Evan manages.

"Leave!"

Evan succeeds. Hale was never a match for Evan's physical strength, and even more so without the use of his body while tormented by the siren's song. The stones return to the ground, and the pair gaze into the horizon in silence. Hale's face is wet with tears and red with embarrassment. He turns from Evan, hoping he'll leave. Yet Evan lingers. The pain Hale carries is all too familiar to Evan, who has more than his fair share of regrets. And though he knows Hale would like him to go, he finds his feet are well rooted and his comforting hand is meant for Hale's shoulder until his sobbing ebbs.

Hale is resting with his back facing the warm fire. But he's deeply uncomfortable and rolls over. The crackling sounds like a sweet lullaby. Maybe it's the nostalgia of his childhood camping trips with his family. All the same, Hale can't sleep. He hadn't slept since he first woke in the Banshee Forest. A long breath expels from his lips while he sits up to feed the fire.

If I never went to the Elders' Dome that night to meet Bayo, maybe . . . if we didn't go camping that weekend, maybe . . .

River is fast asleep to his right, and his light snoring is oddly musical. Back when Hale first came to the Griffin Clan and met River, he used to always catch River singing or coming up with poetic lyrics whenever he thought he was alone. Hale can only imagine what a wonderful artist he was when paired with the guitar that Mark spitefully smashed long ago. Hale then notices River's book wrapped tightly under his arms and thinks, *I wonder where he got that book, and why he holds it so close at all times.*

River moves slightly in his sleep, and the book slides from his hands. Hale finds himself reaching out for it, but he hesitates. *Maybe it's his diary, or where he keeps his songs.* But then, why would Evan read it sometimes? And why would it be so thick? This would be the first time Hale has gotten a good look at it. The brown leather is worn with age, as are the pages, yellowed. Yet the intricate engravings on the cover are illuminated by the fire, in gold, and Hale can make out a Griffin's head in the delicate swerve of the abstract design. Curiosity gets the best of him. There has to be a good reason why River is guarding it, and it would surely pass the time until morning.

Hale takes the heavy book in his hands and unclasps the metal locks inlaid with gemstone. He's seen such beautifully crafted books in Bayo's possession. Books from the grand ages of Griffin history that depicted wars and battles and sacred texts. The ancient writing was always odd to Hale, for he often found he could read a word or two. Bayo must have known considering he had never allowed Hale to read from books written in the Griffin language, as there would then be a need to explain Hale's literacy . . .

Hale opens the book to the first page. He is shocked. The writing is in English. *This handwriting is so much like . . . my . . .* His arms go limp. *My dad wrote this?* Like a swarm of locusts after rainfall, Hale's mind is engulfed with questions. *Why did my dad leave his journal to River and not to me?* His eyes fly across the pages.

'I am restless. The dreams are always the same. Though lately, the strength of these premonitions has consumed my body and soul, and I cannot wake from them as easily as before.'

Hale finishes the journal entry. His face is tearstained. *My dad knew he would die if he took me from Bayo. I am the reason they are dead.* He recalls Carly's departure on the cobblestone bridge through the golden disk. *It is my fault! She didn't have to take care of me after they died! Why did she?*

Felix's journal proves what Hale suspected all along. But Hale is meant for far worse things than he thinks he is capable of. He is the destroyer of worlds. *Carly was wrong about me! If she knew the truth, why didn't she let me die? They are dead because of me!*

The next thing Hale knows is that he is dashing through the woods, jumping over the bushes. Whimpering, he skids to a halt before a lake.

Because. Of. Me.

The water pools in his shoes and makes him heavy. He drags his feet forward until the water is at his neck, then his nose, then his eyes. The agony left behind by those he loves is too great.

I have nothing left. No one left.

His head is fully submerged, and he forces himself to breathe in. Bubbles emerge to the surface while water burns in his lungs, choking him. This is the only remedy for the aching gloom within, he is certain of it, just as he is certain that he can't do anything good in this world.

All Hale wants is to be with Carly. Carly was his one rock whose love and intentions were never questionable. *This is how I should have died*, Hale thinks, recalling the time he was drowned in the cellar. And once he's dead, he'll return to the cobblestone bridge in the cosmos and follow Carly through the golden disk to eternal peace.

His head feels light, and he tolerates the familiar stinging in his lungs while they fill with water. Just before death claims him, something grabs him by the torso.

Back on the shore, River and Evan hover over Hale. They are soaking wet. River is clearly panicked and panting from the rushed swim.

"I can't believe this is happening again," River says as he desperately pumps Hale's chest.

"He did this because he read the journal," Evan says.

"He did it for a ton of reasons," River says flatly.

Hale begins to cough, and the water expels to his mouth. River and Evan push him on his side. Hale resumes consciousness and lies back to face the heavens. For a split second, he thought he'd done it. It is when he understands the heavens are too far out of reach that he realizes he is still alive . . .

Evan spots River clenching his fists in fury. "River," Evan begins.

But it is too late. River lifts Hale by the collar of his shirt. "What were you doing? Do you want to punish yourself? Is that it?" River shakes him forcefully.

Evan puts a hand on River's stiff shoulders. "Cool it."

Now Hale remembers what happened. He's been saved yet again. Not at all what he's intended. He's back to face the consequences of his actions, and he can't help his tears any longer. "I just wanted to go back to my sister."

"Why?" River asks, shaking him once more.

No answer.

"River," begins Evan.

"No more silent treatment," River shouts. "Talk!"

"I-I don't belong here," Hale explains, choking on sobs.

River's lost it. "I can't believe this. I can't believe this!"

Attempting to remedy the situation, Evan says, "Everything is okay now. It's all over. It'll be fine."

"Fine? He's trying to kill himself. And he's going to keep trying!" River grabs Hale by the collar once more. "You listen to me—"

Hale shakes in his arms. The confrontation he's been dreading is now upon him, and he can feel his power of Endurance jolting from within. He can't calm himself down, and he fears the worst. He tries to push River away, but River's enraged grip is thrice the might of Hale's.

"Get away! I could hurt you," Hale pleads.

But River is steadfast. "Go ahead! It's a choice, Hale. You have a choice."

Evan senses the situation escalating. He pushes River off Hale. "He doesn't get it, River. Leave him alone."

"No, *you* don't get it. I'm dangerous!" Hale says, pulling back and tripping. He scrambles to his feet and is prepared to run, but River lunges forward with fingertips of steel pushing through Hale's skin and bones.

River exclaims, "And what? We are *all* dangerous! We *all* need self-control. Evan and I got you out of the Griffin Clan, using your dad's journal as a guide. You were sick and unconscious for a month. You just came back from the *dead* and now you want to kill yourself! What's the point that we all tried so hard? What's the point you were given a second chance? In the end we have to see your dead body floating in a lake! Your family risked everything for you! What did they die for? What did your sister die for? You think they took you in because you're some sort of prophetic monster sent to destroy all the worlds?"

Hale has never seen River so furious. Before this moment he'd never heard River's voice escalate. River was always the calm and cool one, the one who makes light out of the darkest situations. The gentle support.

"Yes!" Hale exclaims. He *is* a monster sent to destroy the worlds. Not even the devil and his demonic minions can do the damage Hale is prophesized to do. The weight of this knowledge is too much for anyone to withstand. Why did he come back to life if this is meant to be his fate?

River counters him. "You are selfish to take the coward's way out. They saved you because you are really their son. They loved you, and they knew you are capable of doing greater things." River grabs Felix's book he'd left on the shore. After opening it to the exact page, he shoves it in Evan's hands and orders him to pass it along to Hale.

Evan does as he is told while River explains, "You didn't read the whole thing. How are you prepared to drown yourself after reading only one page, you—"

Evan checks him once more. "Cool it, River."

Hale's eyes graze over the old paper while River quotes the letter by heart. "'Hale is my son. I could feel it in my soul, as if the truth had been sleeping within me for centuries and has now finally awoken.' I memorized it. You had amazing parents. I've never had anybody feel that way about me in my life. I picked scraps off the street to have something to eat. I slept under bridges when the shelters were full. Imagine that in the winter! You think I couldn't have thrown myself off Kennedy Bridge? You were surrounded by love all your life! Even Bayo loves you!"

Hale shoves the journal back in Evan's hands angrily. "Bayo used me!" he exclaims.

River counters, "And what? You're *hurt?* Boo-hoo! He chose power over you. He chose to have you asleep a thousand years just so you wouldn't get in the way. Then he chose to manipulate you. Either way, he made these choices—as sick as it sounds—so you wouldn't get hurt . . . You're upset he turned out to be the bad guy, aren't you? I think you saw it all along but didn't want to lose him. *You miss him.*"

Enraged, Hale seethes. "I don't."

River snaps back, "Keep lying to yourself—"

"River," Evan buts in.

"When did you become the peacekeeper, Evan?" River returns his attention back to Hale. "I know you're still blaming yourself for what Leon did. You tried to save that boy. It wasn't your—"

Hale is exposed. How did River know what he was thinking? Is there nothing that can be kept to himself?

"I don't deserve your help!" Hale blurts.

"Yeah, well while you're sitting there thinking you are all alone, you've completely forgot you have family right here."

Evan adds, "That's right, Hale. We are here."

River continues, "You are our best friend, our brother. You are kind, smart, great in a fight, and always do the right thing. But you just got lost on the way because the sense got talked right out of you, that's all. Now we have a mission to complete, we can't let this war happen, and we can't let any more people die. Don't let everyone's sacrifices be for nothing. Wake up."

Hale blinks as though he has blinked awake from an intense dream. Suddenly he is seeing the world in a new light, and in that world, there is hope. He whispers, "You're right."

CHAPTER 20

Soaring several thousands of feet into the sky is Bayo in his Griffin form with Grace knocked out cold in his paws. *I should have killed her a year ago. I knew she was trouble.* But there is something she has about her, something cloaking her from magic. What is it that protects her? Is it similar to what Felix and his family used? He needs to know.

When he arrives at the Elders' Dome, Deor immediately emerges, clearly finished with turning Grace's pack sister Tia into a Goonie. Deor's eyes are fixated, and when he touches Grace's temples to enter her mind, he cannot detect a single thought.

"Positively interesting," Deor says.

Bayo dumps Grace's unconscious body in Deor's arms. "Find what cloaks her."

Grace flutters in and out of sleep. Her vision is foggy, though she can faintly hear a conversation between two men just above her. One has a thick and unique accent. Something presses against her stomach.

"It is an inventive magic. A gem of some sort, hidden inside her," says the one with the accent.

"How much to remove it?" asks a cold, distant voice.

Grace desperately tries to sit upright but lacks the will. The sound of sacred chanting and drumming courses through the space. Enchanted by the music, Grace slips once again into darkness.

It is but an Arketchian shaman working alongside Deor. The shaman uncovers a set of cleaned animal bones of various sizes from a black cloth and pours thick blood from a vial into a wooden bowl before dipping the bones in it. He hovers over Grace and keeps the bones over her midsection. Blood carelessly drips onto her, staining her clothes. Grace's stomach heaves as he chants. Gradually, the crystal she's swallowed pokes out from her belly as if attracted to the bones like a magnet.

Deor stands in the far corner, obscured by shadow, the way he most prefers. Whilst the Dark Shaman works the crystal higher up Grace's torso, Deor finds the content of the shaman's mind most devilish and intriguing. But most importantly, he uncovers that the Dark Shaman knows of magic to conceal minds from Griffins of the Dark. Why, then, did he choose to allow Deor free access into his thoughts? Deor smirks. It seems the Dark Shaman recognizes a common ally in the Griffins . . .

As the Dark Shaman continues working over the auburn-haired girl, he comes to understand the crystal was forged in the fires of Emsequet and embedded with intricate magic only someone as skilled as himself can create.

How intriguing . . . Deor thinks.

Will you discard her? the Dark Shaman asks Deor, mentally.

No, you may not have her, Deor answers, knowing exactly what the Dark Shaman intended to do with her.

Grace stirs in her sleep and suddenly her eyes are wide, reaching for her neck. She turns her head and hurls, once, twice, three times. Something clanks onto the floor. Before she can grab it, the shaman takes the wet crystal into his hands. He is a dark man with many piercings and tribal tattoos on his rotting face. He's appears thrice her age. His hair is wrapped in a scarf, and he is dressed in wrapped purple fabric.

"You have the soul of a warrior," he says, as if he knew from just a simple gaze into her eyes. "You will be fighting on the other side of the war soon." A slimy smile reveals yellowed teeth coated with viscous saliva attached to his upper and lower jaw like spiderwebs. It is most irregular teeth for a person so young. Grace has a vague sense that the rest of his innards are equally decayed. All the same, his words send shivers up her spine, and it is clear he is pleased with her demise.

Grace's worst fears are now upon her. Not only has she been caught tailing High Elder Bayo, but she's lost her one chance of protection and survival, which could potentially ruin River, Evan, and Hale's chances of escaping the Griffin Clan. She might as well have killed them and then herself, as she's destroyed everything in one evening! River was wrong. She wasn't going to fix things in the Griffin Clan. He shouldn't have trusted her with the truth, or with the pendant. If only he would have taken her along.

A rift opens behind the Dark Shaman. Through the six-foot gash in the air is a tropical scene of an azure sky and palm trees. The caws of seagulls sound just beyond. Grace recognizes her one chance to escape and jolts up. The Dark Shaman only laughs at her foolishness. Her arms and legs are cuffed to the cot she's resting on.

The sorcerer takes his leave through the rift and tosses the crystal behind him. Deor emerges from the shadows, swiftly catching it in his hands. Grace shudders. The time for punishment is upon her. Felix's journal, everything she tried keeping secret, is now open knowledge without her pendant. Grace feels naked under Deor's speculative eye.

This is the first time Grace has ever seen Deor up close. Suddenly, the horrifying stature of the Dark Shaman isn't so frightening, for while Deor looks perfectly young and physically flawless, there is no mistaking the cruelty behind his eyes. The hard truth hits. Deor can do whatever he likes with Grace's body pinned to this cot.

Stay strong, she tells herself. As long as she hardens her mind, it will be unbreakable, even if Deor enters it, even if he'll physically hurt her. This isn't Grace's first tough scrape, and she'd almost lost her life to Leon in a similar situation. Leon could do no wrong as Bayo's protégé, even with unspeakable intensions. Luckily, Grace was saved by River, Evan, and Hale. But who will save her now?

Grace can't give up. Deor cannot win. Not when everyone she loves can be found out and killed. She takes a deep breath and closes her eyes. *I will make it through this.* She allows herself to drift off into a sweet daydream.

Before she knows it, River waits for her behind her shut eyes. They are walking hand in hand through a peaceful wood, sharing laughs and making sweet memories. His vivid green eyes calm her nerves. He tells her he loves her, and Grace feels as though she can conquer the world. The light of her soul is impenetrable as long as she remembers love.

Grace tries to open her eyes and face the satanic Elder with newfound courage but finds that she is still in the woods with River. The daydream starts to feel like reality. Time continues, and she wonders if being trapped in the Elders' Dome is the true daydream. *Yes . . . That was just a dream. I'm safe.* She never felt so grateful for safety and laughs at a joke River makes. Then the sun sets rapidly, and Grace wonders how such a thing is possible.

"River—the sky." She points to the horizon.

River looks puzzled, as if he hasn't noticed the change. Once he follows her gaze, it becomes too dark to make out his silhouette. Thankfully, his hand is still warm in hers, though not for long. The air becomes brisk, chilling Grace to her core.

She tugs on his arm. "River, please say something."

His fingers won't uncurl. Likewise, his entire body is as stiff as a board. She pats his chest. He isn't breathing.

"River!"

Then it occurs to her. This is a dream, and the person next to her isn't the real River. It is all an illusion created by the Elder of the Dark!

Don't let him win, she tells herself. *You are a Griffin of the Light, Grace. You can make anything happen. If it is dark, you can make light.*

Grace takes a deep, chilling breath. At least her shaken voice is soothing. "Focus." Another breath. "I am the light."

Out from her core emits a yellow glow. Though terrified and half out of her mind, she tries to squeeze out of River's hand. She looks up and finds that it is not River's face she is gazing at. It is a figure with black, scaly skin, white irises, and a twisted smile . . . its features look like Deor. This figure is meant to be the form Deor has chosen for himself in the constructs of Grace's mind. His inner being is indeed a monster.

Grace holds in her screams. *Don't let him win. You're stronger than he is,* she tells herself. For every time she tugs and pulls from him, she has somehow pulled herself an inch closer, much like falling into quicksand. Deor cackles. He is secreting a freezing black mass that gradually creeps up her forearms, blackening the veins in her arms. The cold is dulling her senses with dark emotions. Wickedness, anger, and hopelessness. Her muscles clench while she combats the seeping evil.

She repeats her mantra, "I am light," and a bubble grows out from her core, warming the air. Yet she cannot help but wonder if fighting is useless. Is a single ray of light enough to illuminate an entire murky sea?

River's glowing smile materializes once more. This time it is a figment of her creation, not the Elders'. Grace sighs with relief. It seems she's regaining control over her body. River holds out his hand for her to take. Without hesitation, she grabs on with her free hand. Beside River, another shape forms in the light she's created. It is her brother, Evan.

Though they are simply illusions, she tells them, "I don't think I can get through this. I'm sorry I failed you."

River says, "You can do it. Keep fighting, Grace."

Grace nearly cries at the sound of River's voice. It is so unbelievably lifelike, and she has missed it so much. The emotional boost just might be the ticket to enhance her power. She allows her energy to spread throughout the scape, and to her surprise, River's figment uses the power of Shielding to create a sturdy force field between Grace and Deor.

"Grace! We got you!" Evan exclaims. A flame bursts from his hands and lands on Deor's scaly skin. Deor falls back, finally releasing her.

Grace feels a surge of hope. *I can beat him!*

Evan continues throwing fireballs Deor's way, but Deor simply slips into shadow.

"Do you see him?" Grace asks the figments.

"No," they say, continuing the search.

Out of nowhere, the bright light encompassing her body and protecting her from harm fades away. Grace gasps. *What's happening?* She hasn't stopped using her power—why is the light dimming?

"Evan? River?" she calls.

The young men have frozen in time. She touches them with her inner light, yet blackness has instantly turned the figments into hard stone. Eerily, their necks turn. The movement of their joints makes loud cracking sounds. Grace wants to run, but there is no escape. Her legs are cemented to the ground.

Just then, Deor emerges and the space echoes with his sickly cackle. Grace understands there was never any light she could manifest to keep him at bay. This was all a game created to *entertain* the Elder. A game of cat and mouse in which the mouse has been caught all along.

Six ice-cold hands grab her in the void. The cold evades her and turns into an agonizing burning sensation.

"Please stop—AHHH!" she screams.

Grace trembles without control until she freezes over. All her memories are fading, and soon enough, she can't recall the warmth of the sun, the touch of a loved one, or a sweet kiss.

There is nothing left.

Empty.

The stone figures crumble to dust. But it matters not. She can't remember who they are. *Where am I?* she wonders. *Who am I?* Her eyes are stuck staring at Deor's atrocious inner being and can't even bring to mind why she need be afraid.

He leans in and whispers, hauntingly, "You're mine."

Deor strides through the long corridors of the Elders' Dome with his new trinket dangling from his hands, which is still moist from the innards of the Griffin girl.

Now what shall the Elder of the Dark do with this information his High Elder has commanded him to find? Shall he hand the crystal over to Bayo? If he does, Bayo would take it as a sign that Hale might have had a similar pendant cloaking him from magic and that he might be alive, which Deor suspects to be true, as he visited Grace's mind and learned all about Felix's *foolish* journal.

This must have been just the magic Felix used to cloak him and the rest of his demented family all those years ago, Deor thinks. *Ahh, Felix! Even long after his death, he continues to be a massive pain!* Deor smirks. This is nothing he cannot handle. Bayo is finally on track with his plans to seize Malphora, and Deor will not allow anything to get in the way of that.

Deor senses Bayo in his study in the floor above, rummaging through endless books, as he usually does at this time of night.

Oh, Bayo, soon you shall not recall the young girl who followed you. Not her name, her face, or the magic you claim cloaks her. For you have indeed gone to your hidden caves to speak to the siren, but you have gone alone. Your brother shall remain dead, and you will complete your plans. You will . . .

Grace awoke, but her body is not where she left it, neither is it lying down peacefully while she slept. Instead she finds it running through the woods in the dark of night . . .

Grace swears she was just tied to a plank in a dark room, and gradually she grasps the situation. It's probable that she's been awake for several hours without realizing, and it is her inner being, her consciousness, that was asleep.

All the same, Grace is dashing through the trees, miraculously sprinting over every rock and obstacle with stamina she wouldn't ordinarily have. Strangely, she hears footsteps stomping exactly at the same time as her own. A simple desire to pivot her neck proves that Grace no longer controls the movements of her body. But the footsteps are approaching on her side, and Grace makes out their shapes from the corners of her eyes. They are armed Griffins in their human form. They aren't blinking, nor do they stop for breath. *They look so lifeless.*

Goonies.

If Grace was running alongside them, that would mean . . . *This can't be happening!* She tries to skid to a halt, but her legs do not obey her. Panic settles. She roars and rages from the inside, desperately urging her true self through, yet her muscles refuse to release a single twitch on her account.

Oh, how badly Grace wants to scream or cry! But her inner being remains suppressed. Her worst fears have come to life.

I'm a Goonie! They must all feel this way, Grace thinks. *Trapped within their own bodies. Are they awake on the inside, too? Or are they still asleep within themselves?* Either way, this is torture. *It is better to be dead.*

A single tear falls from her right eye and flies away behind her as she runs. A tear! A tear is more than nothing. That is something to hope for. She continues to struggle. *Move your hand, Grace. You can do it! Move your hand! This is your body. Your actions are your own!*

She's regaining control by the moment. Her pace has slowed, and she even twitches a finger. Hope floods in. *Progress.* She continues like this for some time, and the painful straining weakens her consciousness as a result. Sleep beckons her. *Don't sleep. Don't sleep. You need to stay awake. You need to take back your . . .*

Suddenly, Deor's wicked laughter invades her mind as though he'd been there all the while.

He growls, *Let your hope die. As I said, you are mine!*

The woods in front of her eyes dim from view. Grace finds her inner being slipping into obscurity. Fighting her drowsiness, she comes to terms with her stupidity. The Elder has fooled her once again, waking her to play his vicious game.

But how can she know what Deor is thinking or the games he enjoys playing? If he's connected his mind to hers, would it be possible that the connection is double-sided? Can she find a way into his mind through the darkness of her own?

Intuitively, she feels that he cannot read her thoughts here, wherever she is now. He thinks she is sleeping and has left for the time being. With her lingering might, Grace rises to confront the void and bangs on the walls that confine her. Hours of pummeling later, a piece of the wall weakens and, finally, shatters like glass.

Peering through the small and foggy opening, Grace reunites with her vision to the outside world. Like a bystander, she creeps on the actions of her physical body. At least deep in her subconscious, it is safe for her to be awake. Maybe here, she can find some answers, build her strength, and take back what is hers. Maybe she might find her connection to Deor and evade *his* mind. But that is a feat to accomplish in due time . . .

The Goonies come to a halt and creep carefully behind large trees. They are targeting a pair resting in the woods near a small fire. A teenage girl, no different from themselves, dressed in armor, is sleeping with her sword in her hands and a large wolf curled up against her torso, twitching its legs in its sleep.

Griffins of Shielding enclose the space with a force field to keep the targets from escaping. The Goonies reveal their glossy huanims and surround the pair on all sides. Likewise, Grace finds the exact spear in her hands. She's never used this weapon before, as only Goonie soldiers are allowed. Bolts of lightning-like energy shoot out from its pointed blade.

"Stop!" screams Grace while she bangs on the walls.

But her body dashes forward, going for the kill!

CHAPTER 21

EARLIER THAT DAY

"We need to get Ellionna back," declares Atomi.

Robin, the usually keep-it-under-control warrior, has been a bit off since Ellionna's disappearance a day ago. To her standards, she's failed as the siren's official guardian. Her soul purpose in this world is to protect Ellionna with her life. She is assuming the worst and hating herself for it. But what else can you expect from a young woman who has lost her mother and siblings at the hands of a sick murderer when she was just a child?

"We don't know who's taken her or if she's still alive. I've never seen magic like that—" Robin begins.

Atomi stops her. "No. We know exactly who has taken her, and we must think fast. That boy she sung to on the outskirts of the Griffin Clan is on the verge of being avenged. It is no secret the Griffins have supernatural abilities that are above us Arketchians."

No matter Atomi's words, Robin continues to insist that her cousin is no more. "Don't you think she's already—"

"Do not finish that sentence," says Atomi. "We shall not lose any more members of our family, if it is the last thing we do."

"What can we do, Father? There is a barrier around the Clan. We cannot enter."

"Perhaps we shall act as a nuisance, reaching closer and closer to the Clan as much as the barrier allows, and we will remain there. Yes . . . they will surely come find us."

"We are only two people, Father!" Robin shouts.

"My wolf phase is beginning tonight, Robin. I will be of more help then."

"Father!" This is ludicrous. Not only have they lost Ellionna, but Atomi is offering a suicide mission!

Atomi objects, "We have no choice, Robin. We are without help, and we must try. They will not kill her. They will rather use her as a mighty weapon. A weapon to end all wars . . ."

That is true . . . She had not thought about that possibility. Robin sinks into the grass and grasps at the roots of her jet-black hair. "We're going to die."

It is the middle of the night when the pulsating ground wakes Atomi. The black fur of his wolf form reflects the light of the orange fire he sits beside. He nudges Robin with his paw. Robin's eyes open wide. She furiously grabs the grip of her sword, whipping it from her scabbard, and scares her father half to death! But he should know better than to be frightened—Robin is an anxious sleeper and always comes to in such a state.

Atomi whines and paws at the ground to make a second attempt at explaining what he feels. Robin understands and presses her palm against the soil to feel the vibration. *They are coming.* She does not bother to put out the fire, as it is the one thing leading the Griffins to them. The two lie back down, pretend to sleep, and allow their enemies to gain on them openly.

Minutes later, the duo is nearly bored out of their mind while waiting for attack. Robin peeks over at her father, and humorously enough, he shrugs his wolf shoulders. Oh, but here they come in the distance! A group of . . . young soldiers?

Soldiers no older than Robin herself. How strange. What did the ruler of the Griffins take this Arketchian pair for? Was this an insult to their skill? Did the Griffins assume a bunch of teenagers were enough to take on an Arketchian warrior of Chiba and her werewolf father? Robin is enraged. If she threatened her own tribe, they would have sent the best and strongest warriors to take on a warrior of Chiba and her wolf! She has half a mind to go against her father's orders and destroy every single one of them just to prove her skill.

Just then, a strange blue bubble forms around their campsite and the Griffins advance. *Their eyes are blank*, she thinks.

"Rise!" they command in unison.

Robin jumps. *What type of magic is this?*

She and Atomi are on their feet, and Robin holds her hands up. "We surrender."

"You are ordered to leave, or suffer the consequences," they say. Their accent is weird to Robin.

Atomi paws the ground once, twice, no three times. He means to initiate his third plan. Robin is shocked. He does not think they can conquer the enemy, and Robin has no choice. They must retrieve Ellionna.

Robin answers the Griffins. "We shall suffer the consequences."

There is no grand battle, death, gore, or struggle. Robin and Atomi both disappear from the woods, just as Ellionna had, and appear someplace cold and dark with stone walls and no visible exits. They call out for Ellionna and find her not. Wherever they are, they are alone and trapped . . .

CHAPTER 22

Waxed pebbles are spread throughout the small square of the Bimmorian factory district. It reeks of rot. Each step made on the path sounds like stepping in sticky slime or chewed gum. The lonely smog-filled track is graced by one visitor, a woman of light-blue complexion, covering her sickly body with rags and hiding her face beneath a black veil to keep from inhaling the poisonous air. She is Annabelle, General Camden's former fiancée, likewise the former ambassador of the Bimmorian kingdom.

The hem of her long dress merges with the tar and she yanks it free, but the goop does not release her. It is as if the slime beckons her to join with it. She imagines it speaking to her. *Come, stay. You belong with muck and filth!* Annabelle grabs hold, heaves, and *boom!* She's successfully collapsed on her side, pummeling her worn rib cage. Groaning, Annabelle attempts to pull herself up with whatever dignity she has left. Thankfully not a soul is here to witness this embarrassing moment. Long black vines cling on to the drapes of her apparel. Losing hope and grip, she drops onto her backside and groggily looks up at the muted sky with misty eyes, desperately wishing for some rain to aid her escape and wash away the smell of sulfur.

Just a town away, where the smog does not exist, anyone can spot the golden sun. But what use is the sun to Annabelle when everyone in town uses their best arm to pummel her with rocks? She can remember their hurtful words so clearly.

"There she goes!" said a woman. "The woman who disgraced all of Bimmorus!"

"Look at her run! The general won't save you now! And neither will the Griffins," a man called out to her.

It is true—Annabelle hasn't any place to go. Not to her decade-long diseased father who suffered from the last outbreak of femu-pox, nor her mother who disappeared with a fisherman up in the north. Not with any distant relative, for they have been disgraced by their relation to her, and not with any friend for the mere fear of being caught and executed alongside her.

Annabelle's picture is encrypted on every projecting device in the kingdom because she is a wanted woman. However, only wanted by the government, to proceed with her expected beheading. It's strange to Annabelle why nobody who she'd come across in this prolonged year has yet to bring her in to collect the reward money. Yet it is more baffling that the reward is only one hundred zaire. One hundred! Even a live animal is worth more than one hundred zaire!

Ever so, often a Bimmorian guard passes by, and Annabelle would run off to sleep in the piles of hay the sranus built in the countryside. It is the only comfort she could find considering no one allows the likes of her inside their homes.

"You? Let you in my home! I'm sorry, miss! I would not let a traitor into my home! I am a proud Bimmorian! Off with you now!" a woman said.

The sranus perspired profusely when not caked with the mud they bathed in. They, too, have their fair share of worms poking through their leathery flesh, but at least they are friendly—well, friendlier than people. Annabelle has never known about the wildlife in Bimmorus before now, but she adapted upon experiencing true hunger. It is more than a once upper-class woman can deal with. Her stomach growls to no end, and her fatigue gets the best of her each day. If she were her usual self, she'd have said she'd rather die than to befriend a wild creature who feeds on small beasts and bathes in the mud.

So why here, in the factory district, does this little outcast sulk? To make a long story short, even the sranus got tired of her using them for food and giving nothing in return. To prove their distain, they've gifted her with several infested bite marks on her forearms, from which, Annabelle learned, one should not snatch a meal from another's mouth, no matter how hungry.

Annabelle often thinks back to Camden, and though part of her curses his name for ever releasing her from prison before execution, her other half wishes that he wouldn't have let her go so easily. Couldn't he have taken her back and continued to love her unconditionally? Sparing her life and setting her out into a cold and cruel world with nothing is far more painful than dying, though she has the option of going back to the capital and give her life up to the king.

Yes, she dreams of Camden every night, especially during frigid evenings. With no blanket to cover her scrawny body, she imagines him lying with her, holding her as he once did with silken sheets on their once grand mattress. Oh, how she regrets the decisions of her life, even as she lies in this stinky goop! But how can life be so cruel when her intentions were for the better of all? She only wanted what was best, especially for Camden! The constant replay of memories they shared is her only solace.

If only he knew that, she thinks. *I once vowed to make him the happiest man in all the worlds. I would have kept my word.* Annabelle sighs and hoists herself to her feet. She yanks at her hem, and her skirt rips to pieces.

Tears she has not shed in months resurface. In the midst of sobbing, she inhales the smog and finds it hard to breathe. Annabelle wheezes and gasps for air. She pulls the cloth tighter to cover her mouth and nose, but it is no use. While sprinting through the factory district, her shoes get stuck in a wild glop. She yanks again, but to her dismay, her shoe is perpetually stuck and begins to bubble, releasing green smoke before melting away.

Annabelle cannot believe her luck, and she very well cannot have her bare foot on the acidic ground, so she holds it up, planning to hop along, when a sizzling sounds from the second shoe. She's sinking by the millimeter and before she can jump away, the heat intensifies against her soles. There are no options left: Annabelle must run. It feels like hot, sticky coals. With every step, she is stripped of another layer of skin.

Through the clearing smog, Annabelle spots a body of water. Were things finally turning up? *Just a little more,* she thinks, urging herself forward.

Annabelle frantically plunges into what she believes is safety, neglecting the fact that this is no ordinary lake or pond. It is a cesspool! The brown-and-green bubbling liquid reeks of toxic fumes. She gags and runs out. Her legs, thighs, and feet are blistered and bleeding.

Incapable of taking much more of this fated punishment, Annabelle topples over onto the grimy gravel and screams in torment. Her breath weakens, and the vision fades from her eyes. *This must be death. Let it come and take me,* she thinks.

She clutches her bleeding calves, and her airway tightens. *I should not have come through here. I thought it would be quiet. I thought . . . nobody would laugh at me here.* Silently, she chokes. These are her last cognizant thoughts before her eyes finally shut.

Just then, the air above her splits open into a horizontal rift, and a mysterious gust of wind pulls her through the other side . . .

CHAPTER 23

May 16, 2010
TWELVE YEARS AGO

Kala, the former second Spirit Guide of the Arketcha Tribe, is busy at work in her bedchamber of the Elders' Dome. She whispers sweet Arketchian words into a bowl filled with mixed and crushed herbs. While shaking the bowl to awaken the magical properties hidden within the herbs, she wonders what her life would look like if she hadn't professed eternal love to the king of the Griffins and ran away with him.

The contents of the bowl smoke, so she adds a slightly viscous and clear liquid to it. The herbs melt into the liquid and the concoction turns bright yellow. After pouring its contents into a vial, she hands it over to Naomi, Felix's wife, who stands anxiously in the corner. This potion is a replica of one she had made on the very day she met Bayo years ago, who sought her help in waking his slumbering bother . . .

"*Is there a time limit to this potion?*" *he asked her.*

"*What?*"

"*Will this expire in time?*" *he clarified.*

Kala shook her head. "No, its potency should last lifetimes . . ."

Once Bayo's charismatic smile and manipulative words lured her away from the Arketcha Tribe, Kala beheld the small boy named Hale and asked the Griffin King, "Why do you not wake him?" After all, she had created the potion to do just that.

But instead of waking his brother, Bayo had placed the vial on a chain and wears it around his neck. He never removes it, and he never answered her question.

This new potion is but one step toward escaping the cruel master Kala once fawned over. It's about time for her to regain a sense of life instead of depleting her energies in a golden palace, endlessly creating magics in Bayo's hungry service. Now that Kala has renounced being the Spirit Guide, she has lost her spiritual gifts and has been reduced to meager sorcery—something any Arketchian housewife is capable of. Given she might be the best sorcerer in Malphora, Kala still regrets her life choices and wonders if she'd repeat her mistakes if Deor hadn't been present when she and Bayo first met.

Could *he* have pushed Kala's mind toward renouncing her gifts? If only she had known at the time about the blocking potion that keeps Deor's telepathic abilities at bay! Kala sighs and concludes, *It couldn't have been that hard to manipulate a person who was on the verge of breaking.* The task of being a Spirit Guide is not for the faint of heart, and she wonders daily how Palla, her sister, is managing on her own.

She submerges her hands in a watery mixture of clay until the concoction's texture is consistent. To this, she adds several loose, highly pigmented powders and, finally, a single strand of her hair. At the sound of her chanting, the clay emulsifies and expands. The elegance of her movements while she works her hands in the air is soothing. With each flick of her wrist, Kala sculpts the clay, magically, until it takes the shape of a woman.

"*Nikoletfiti. Nikoletfiti. Uh te fente, uh te baneh. Hikofesh te. Hikofesh te.*" Or what the Arketchians would understand as, "Rise. Rise. Oh, my likeness, oh my prize. Limbs of mine. Limbs of mine."

Long, sleek black hair grows out from the newly fashioned scalp and the clay hardens, then softens to a dark-colored flesh. Lavender material explodes from the bust and wraps itself across the torso, forming a tight asymmetrical dress, just as Kala is wearing right now. A bystander inexperienced with dark arts might think Kala is a mad woman, but by her own standards, she is an experimental genius!

"It's uncanny," Naomi whispers.

"Indeed," Kala agrees. "Hopefully this will do the trick."

Kala flashes a winning smile at her completed creation that is just about to peel open its eyelids. Not even the great Bayo in all his glory can prevent Kala from reaching her full potential. And so, she names her creature from such of old, created from the earth and raw fire.

"My golem."

Felix stands at the foot of the magical doorway of the parallel world he shared with Bayo that leads back to the treasure trove. He looks back to his oldest friend one last time before he departs. *I wish things could be different*, he thinks. A chain carrying an obsidian pendant rest in his palms. He pulls it over his head.

"Goodbye, Bayo," he says just above a whisper.

Felix vanishes, while Bayo stares furiously at the still waters. The very blood in Bayo's veins boils with fury and he thinks, *How could he want to leave? I've given him everything he's ever wanted!* And yet, the most powerful Griffin in all of Malphora feels too weak to stop his friend. Or perhaps he is calling Felix on his bluff.

Felix makes haste. He needs to get to the Elders' Dome before sundown. His wife and daughter should be hiding in Kala's chambers with their protective pendants. Dashing through the cave, Felix thinks back to Carly's dismay when she'd asked about Ianna.

"Can't we bring Ianna with us?" asked Carly.

"No," Felix responded. "She would never leave without Greon or Mary, and telling her would be risky on account of Deor."

Though he cannot help Ianna now, Felix hopes that one day her story will change for the better. The friendship they shared throughout the millennia would make Felix's departure especially difficult, but he must carry on. There is too much at stake.

Felix arrives at his tree dome. Naomi and Carly have taken all the essentials. Now that his last exchange with Bayo has inevitably proved Bayo will not see reason, Felix must take an extra precaution. He rips a paper loose from his journal and scribbles a brief letter to a teenager he's seen multiple times in his premonitions. A boy with shaggy black hair, green eyes, and a happy smile who is, as of now, a small child growing up in the Human Division. *River.* In the years to come, this young man will be a brick-like platform beneath Hale's faltering feet.

As he writes, Felix feels the hardened weight of his decisions. His choice will affect more lives than just that of his family. He pauses. *Are their lives mine to sacrifice? But what choice do I have? They would certainly die if Bayo succeeds.* Felix places the letter at the front of his journal and hides the journal within the magically cloaked hollow in the trunk. *Hopefully, River will never have to find this, and I can keep Hale safe all his life. This is just a precaution for a future that might or might not be.*

The swelling sun tucks itself behind the mountainside. Its light is fading quicker than Felix expected. He sprints through the woods with a single bag in hand. Bayo is due to return to Hale's sleeping quarters for their evening read. Palpitations thunder within Felix's chest. *I need Kala's sleeping cure to wake Hale. Hopefully she's finished it . . .*

Ianna was not expecting Felix to burst through the front door of the Elders' Dome. "Felix!" she exclaims in shock. "Deor didn't tell me you would be arriving. I would have opened the door for you."

Felix smiles at her. This would be the last time they see one another. "Thank you, Ianna." In these last words, he meant to say, *Thank you for all the times we've shared, for your friendship, and all that you've done. I'm sorry it has to be this way. I will miss you.* Felix dares not linger. He bolts past her and up the stairs before she might question him.

How long before Bayo returns from our pocket world? Felix wonders. *Would he try to find me and keep me from leaving? Or would he give me time to leave without a last goodbye out of bitterness?* While heartbreaking, fingers crossed it is the latter. Felix knocks on Kala's door lightly, then proceeds to Bayo's study with his spare key. Bayo has allowed only Felix to have the spare. Carly, Naomi, and Kala emerge like clockwork. Their belongings in hand.

Felix urges them inside while keeping a lookout. Within the study is a separate room where Bayo keeps the Three Eyes. A precise wave of Felix's hand over the orbs creates a six-foot-tall portal to the Human Division.

"Hurry," he whispers.

Kala and Carly enter. Naomi, however, is hesitant to leave without her husband.

"I will be quick," Felix assures.

She nods and departs into the strange realm.

Felix rushes to Hale's bedroom. But just then, the front door to the Elders' Dome opens and he can hear the brief exchange from below.

"Welcome home, Bayo," Ianna says.

Bayo grunts, "Was Felix here?" He shoves past her and stomps into the parlor room.

"Yes, he went upstairs," she answers.

Felix's heart is pounding, and he immediately regrets not letting Ianna in on the secret.

Bayo pauses, staring up at the second floor. "So, he's really leaving . . ." Thankfully, he continues to the parlor with clenched fists.

Felix doesn't have much time. Bayo can come upstairs at any given moment to confront him. He enters Hale's chambers.

The windows are open, and the flowing shades are drawn, bathing the room with marigold light. A gentle spring breeze passes freely, and at the center of the space is a four-post bed, draped in white and fit for a king. Lying in it is a little boy, seemingly no older than five years old.

Hale's dark-brown hair is brushed perfectly away from his innocent face. His torso expands slightly with each passing breath. At the sight of him, Felix feels a sense of calmness in the midst of this madness. My son. All this trouble is certainly worth it if it should mean he will finally hold his son and give him a good life.

Approaching the bed cautiously, Felix places Hale's pendant over his head, then gently slides his hands underneath the child's body to lift him. Hale is frail and feathery, with little meat on his bones. *Soon you will be free, running through the grass and living your life*, Felix thinks as he shuts the door to Hale's room.

Taking long, quiet strides, Felix makes his way to the study when ascending footsteps sound from their staircase. The veins in his temples are visibly throbbing, and he takes care to lock the study door as silently as possible before rushing to the open portal.

"Felix?" Bayo calls. "Are you here?"

No answer.

Bayo uses his power of Endurance to scour the dome. Even so, he does not sense Felix's presence because of his protective pendant.

At the foot of the stairs, he asks Ianna, "Are you sure he was here?"

Ianna nods. "Yes. He only just arrived before you had."

Bayo thinks, *Perhaps he left already. How did he manage to leave so quickly with his family?* But Bayo puts an abrupt end to his thoughts, as he has more important things to do. He checks his pocket watch, and as suspected, it is time for him to read a book to Hale. *Felix will be back. He'll know what a fool he was leaving all that he has here. All that I've given him.* He grabs a book from the nightstand in his bedroom and shuffles to Hale's room.

"Good evening, Hale. Are you ready to finish your story?" His eyes look up from the floor to the bed, and the book suddenly drops from his hands. The white sheets are on the floor, and the imprinted bed . . . is empty.

Is Hale awake? He dashes from the room and screams, "Hale! Hale!"

Ianna, Rioma, and Greon immediately emerge to Bayo's assistance.

"What has happened?" Ianna asks.

Bayo is frantic. "Where is my brother?" A sneaking suspicion has him enter Kala's bedroom. Why hadn't she come out when he screamed?

To his surprise, Kala is sitting calmly in her lounge chair and gazing out the window. This does not stop the Griffin King from yanking her forearm aggressively.

"Look at me!" Bayo shouts. His face turns red in his panic. "Where is my brother?"

Kala's golem makes no sign of pain, as it is completely unfeeling and cannot speak. Instead, it smiles grimacingly, not a very wise choice for the soulless creature. Bayo releases its arm as he notices Deor climbing the steps. For the first time in his long life, Deor is out of the loop and is trying to understand the dramatic situation upon his entrance.

Instantly, Bayo sweeps Deor off his feet by his collar. "Where are they?" he asks with his mighty power of Endurance coursing through the Elder of the Dark.

Deor winces through his words. "I do not know," he manages.

Bayo's voice escalates. "What do you mean you don't know!"

"I didn't hear any thoughts," Deor explains grimly.

Bayo knows that Kala's magic is strong, but she wouldn't have done this on her own. The pieces of the puzzle are coming together, and he can hardly believe it. *Felix?*

Instantly, Bayo drops Deor and sprints to his study.

In utter hysteria, he shouts, "Felix!"

Behind the second door where Bayo keeps the Three Eyes is a shrinking portal leading into the unknown. Bayo reaches out to it.

"Felix!"

But it is too late. The portal has closed.

Exasperatedly, he orders the orbs to reopen the portal. As if mockingly, they continue with their rotation without following his command. Again, Bayo works his hands over them. No rift appears.

"Open the portal! He took my brother!" Unexpectedly, Bayo pounds his fists against the table.

The Elders are petrified. Bayo hasn't been this enraged since the Griffin rebellion a few years ago or since the last war a millennium prior. Tight-lipped and livid, Bayo endlessly works over his orbs and fruitlessly. He storms from the room and retrieves Kala's golem. His hand is knotted in her hair as he thrusts her face against the glass of the Three Eyes themselves. He has yet to come to terms with the fact this is not really Kala. And he shall never find out the truth.

"Where did they go?" he roars. "What have you done?"

When Bayo beholds the golem's sickening smile, he fills to the brim with regret for bringing this Arketchian witch into his life. *Why has she done this to me? Hadn't I shown her every kindness?* But his confusion toward her betrayal only goes so far. Bayo murderously extends his hands toward Kala and let's his power wash over her. She grips the rim of the table in torment. Her face contorts violently and though her mouth gapes open, she makes no sound. Bayo's wide eyes are maddening. The creature shall soon face death.

Meanwhile Rioma is enjoying the view. Since the Arketchian vixen entered the Griffin Clan and stole away Bayo's attention, Rioma wished she'd die.

Ianna, shaking, dares to speak out of turn. "Bayo, please—"

With one motion of his hand, Bayo, too, strikes Ianna with his power. She yelps and falls back into Greon's arms, who then rushes Ianna out of the room, but not before witnessing what was to come. Kala's grip on the table weakens, and she finally collapses and turns to ash. This has not disturbed the Elders, as it is plausible that the ash resulted from being so old.

Ianna sobs at the sight. "She's dead!"

Greon closes the door to Bayo's study and brings his finger to his lips. "Shhh." He pulls Ianna into a vacant room while she cries.

"We should have stopped it!" she shouts.

For the first time, Greon raises his voice at his true love. "Quiet! If you value yours and Mary's life, you will not speak out of turn."

Bayo has gone to retrieve a strand of Hale's hair from his pillowcase. He dumps piles of his maps of Malphora, Thurana, and Orcura onto his oak table and orders the Three Eyes, "Show me Hale."

Nothing.

Yet Bayo will not stop, not even hours later when he's exhausted himself with every method he knows. Rioma steps forward to place a soothing hand on his shoulder. Maybe this is her chance to bring him back to her.

Bayo shoves her aside. "Leave me!" he barks.

Clearly offended, she flees the room.

In his horror, Bayo sweeps his hands over the surface of the table, and the objects go flying.

With his hands on his hot head, he exclaims, "It's as if they've disappeared from existence! How is that possible? How?" He sinks to the floor, and his panicked sobs surface. "How could he do this to me?"

CHAPTER 24

October 5, 2021

Annabelle awakens with blurry vision in some lavish setting. Her consciousness reunites her with her aching body, and she hazily makes out a figure in front of her. Once her confusion settles, she understands exactly where she is.

Precisely a year had passed since she last came to the Elders' Dome, and she can tell she is in the parlor. It is a room she's seldom visited before, considering Bayo preferred to keep his meetings with Annabelle private. To Annabelle's understanding, it was Rioma, Bayo's wife, who he was avoiding during her visits—though the Griffin King would never admit to it. At the center of this dimly lit space, a firepit hosts a crackling flame. Smoke rises up and out through an opening in the ceiling. Annabelle's vision is focusing. The figure across from the flames is Bayo. His haunting face is illuminated by crimson flames. It's been a year since she's seen him last.

If Annabelle possessed any sort of strength, she'd have immediately risen in Bayo's presence. But she hasn't the will to move, let alone wonder too deeply if he is the same man she once plotted with, for he seems to be a different person altogether. Bayo the dignified, suited with class and refinement, now sits before her with disheveled hair, black clothes, pasty skin, and sunken eyes. Where is his effortless charm and charisma? He looks no better than she does. Perhaps life has not been too kind to the king of the Griffins, just as it has not been too kind with Annabelle . . .

Something must have happened, she thinks. *Will he punish me for failing our plans?*

Annabelle struggles to sit up, though when she does, she sees that on the countered space surrounding the firepit are steaming Bimmorian dishes.

Swallowing her salvation, Annabelle returns her distracted attention to Bayo and says, "Thank you for saving me, High Elder Bayo."

Bayo's voice is low, almost careless when he says, "There's no need for formalities. Eat." Though he stares, it is as though he is looking through her, off in some sort of dark and twisted daydream continually on repeat. The way one looks while they are grieving.

Annabelle hesitates. *Is this meant to be a trick? Is the food poisoned?* Yet her ponderings are short-lived, for the aroma gets the best of her. With a mouthful of food, the once Bimmorian ambassador concludes that she'd rather die full than starving.

Chapter 25

Just beyond the Banshee Forest is the land of Emsequet. Beware, for Emsequet is the home of the once Griffin-consuming Weyling. The Weyling are winged creatures of the night, though they share the higher intelligence and facial features of humans. Shining scales envelop their bodies, the color ranging from ivory to ash. Dragon-like spikes cascade down their abnormally long and curved necks and spines. Vermillion eyes with menacing slits scan the unsteady grounds of Emsequet, adjusting their vision as necessary to detect the smallest movement of potential prey. The bat-like wings of the Weyling outstretch a Griffin's twofold, and with ten times the power, cutting through the air in a fraction of the time with ease.

Since times of old, the Weyling were a dominant nation. They used their brawn and insatiable hunger to conquer the northern and southern hemispheres of the Outlands. Until Bayo's rule over the Griffin nation, Griffins were often a subject of prey to the Weyling. Consumption of a Griffin during a full moon allows the Weyling to permanently adopt the power of that Griffin.

Only the grandest of Weylings knew the secret to obtaining a Griffin's power, and only three princes among the Weyling were ever known to succeed. Two of which are still alive, surpassing the age of us Elders.

Bayo's rule has not only protected the Griffin Clan from the Weyling but also the entire Extraordinary Division. With Bayo's use of the Three Eyes, the Weyling are unable to venture past the borders of Emsequet.

While stuck within their boundaries for centuries, the Weyling have adapted, feeding on the only animals that can survive the desolate scape such as reptiles, insects, and birds.

There is a note on the margins of Felix's writings, a scribble that reads: Avoiding Emsequet will be a safer journey to Bimmorus, but Hale must come to Emsequet. He must meet the Western Prince.

Griffins entering Emsequet must travel quietly during the day and hide at night. This is troublesome, considering the extremely high temperature of the day and low temperatures of the night. There will be no water during the near three weeks it takes to cross Emsequet. Griffins must avoid using their powers and transforming at all costs, for the Weyling can sense magic, even those cloaked with pendants. Likewise, Griffin travelers must keep track of the moon's cycle and be fearful of getting caught by a Weyling, especially the Eastern Prince.

—Excerpt from Felix's journal.

Misty clouds roll in from the west, concealing the crescent moon that hangs high over Emsequet. The muted green terrain is muddy, scattered with sharp boulders and hills. The valley below quakes as the faults crack, separating the land. A river of blood-red magma flows between the fractures, illuminating the desolate surface, bursting upward at random, only to harden into razor-sharp boulders among the thousands.

River, Evan, and Hale travel carefully around the rock structures, far from where the lava flows. Their shoes are caked with mud. Even their socks are crusted and crunch with every regrettable step. While pushing through the discomfort,

River spots the gloomy towers of the Weyling shining in the bleak sunlight and directs his company around several boulders and into hiding.

Beads of sweat cascade down his face. *It should be okay,* River thinks. *The Weyling are nocturnal. I could avoid those towers easily and we should be safe for the night.*

"River—" begins Evan.

"Shh," River whispers. "They might hear."

Evan looks around with a raised brow. There is nothing in sight, and he does not recall Felix's journal warning the trio about the impeccable hearing of the Weyling. Evan opens his mouth in protest, then stops himself. He knows better at this point than to argue with River. After all, River has kept the three of them safe this long.

By midday, the scorching sun has blistered their skin. They travel along a flowing magma river. The heat is unbearable, and so the trio has no choice but to cover their open skin with mud to protect themselves from the sun. And as disgusting as caked mud feels, it soothes and even heals their scorched bodies.

Stomachs begin grumbling in the evening, but nothing is more bothersome than their parched mouths and crusted lips. Evan hands out small portions of dried meat. It's enough to ration for nearly a week.

The sun finally sets behind the peaks of Emsequet, and the trio soon learns the mud masks the freezing cold just as it does the heat. Resting beside a cave-like structure is a small and dimly lit pool of warm lava. This particular pool is quiet, as there are no sudden bursts of magma shooting out from it. It is a perfect place to camp for the night.

Hale lies down, thankful that they had not come across the horrid creatures described in Felix's journal, though he knows he will, for he must meet the Western Prince . . .

A week later, and the trio has slimmed down dreadfully. Evan returns to his stash of meat. There is none left apart from the scraps one could gnaw off the bones. A strange six-legged and two-headed lizard scurries past and Evan pounces. He is unsuccessful, however, as the lizard's six legs are faster than Evan's meager two.

River takes notice. "That thing is poisonous," he explains, gesturing to Felix's journal where he's learned that information.

"You keep saying that. Is everything poisonous?" Evan snaps. Clearly, he hasn't read the entire chapter on Emsequet. Evan was never much of a reader anyway.

"Keep your voice down. They might hear," whispers River.

Evan's eyes narrow. "We're going to starve!"

Without warning, the ground breaks open. River and Evan suddenly are at the edge of the faltering earth. A large pit is made ready for their descent. They manage to keep their balance in this sudden moment when another tremor sends them to their doom!

The rift breaks off into a fiery fork that circles around Hale, and it's widening by the moment! If Hale doesn't jump over the gap now, farther away from his friends, he might die. But River and Evan would perish. He can see them holding on to the bit of rock just above the lava. Hale doesn't have much time, and he doesn't know what to do, as Felix warned them not to transform.

In his panic, he hears Bayo's voice scream as if he were there with him. *Jump, Hale! What are you waiting for! Save yourself.* How can Hale possibly listen to a thing Bayo would tell him to do? The rift has created an island around him, which is slowly sinking. Meanwhile, River and Evan are struggling to hold on. Just then, Felix's steady voice comes from his right. *Act quickly, son! Help your friends!* But how can he listen to Felix? A liar and a thief who wasn't even his true father!

The lava is closing in, and Hale's head is pounding so immensely that everything around him is happening in slow motion. He cannot seem to make a move.

It is now impossible to lean over and pull River and Evan to safety, as the gash in the earth has become too wide.

Hale can feel the soles of his shoes heating up, and he needs to act quickly. It then occurs to him that he cannot not save his friends unless he first saves himself. And save his friends is exactly what he intends to do. He looks around to find the shortest jump from the small island he is on. It is a bit of a reach on his right, but he doesn't have a choice. He dashes, jolts into the air, and crashes on his side of the hard ground. Groaning, he pulls himself to his feet and rushes to the rift where his pack brothers are holding on. The problem is, they're on the other side of the rift and he can't reach them.

What should I do? What should I do? The lava is rising, and Hale can only see one option.

"I'm slipping," Evan shouts.

River holds on to the rock with one hand while the other holds steadfast on to Felix's journal. But his muscles are giving in, and his grip on the rock is wavering. He makes the hard choice of releasing Felix's journal.

In a flash, something swoops from below. Saving the journal with one swift claw a moment before it ignites is Hale in his Griffin form! He grabs River with his other paw, then Evan by the brim of his shirt with his hind claws. They land safely far from the faulty ground, and Hale resumes his human form.

There is a deep fury in River's eyes. "I told you not to transform."

But he is interrupted

"What was that?" Evan dashes at Hale, prepared to grab his collar.

River gets in the way and pushes Evan backward. "Stop it."

"What happened to you, Hale?" Evan asks.

River huffs, "Okay, okay. Leave him alone. He just had a moment there."

Evan is enraged. "A moment? He almost left us to die! The old Hale would never have done that!"

Hale is motionless. Evan's words cut deeper than a knife. *The old Hale. Felix's Hale*, which is now in shambles, as he must battle Bayo's Hale. Perhaps Felix's Hale is preferred. The selfless, heroic, and modest version rather than the selfish, reckless, and confident version of himself. How strange it is that this pivotal moment showed Hale that he is neither of these versions. Should he feel ashamed for turning his back on his father's version in a time of crisis? Though uncertain, he *does* feel ashamed. He never meant to put his friends' lives in jeopardy. But Hale cannot go on like this anymore. His true self is hidden somewhere amid everything he's experienced and who he wishes to be, but he just can't find it, not right now.

River growls at Evan, "I said keep your voice down. This is not the time for this. Hale saved us. You should be thanking him."

A soothing relief washes over Hale's trauma. River coming to his defense is all he needed to remind himself that he isn't a terrible person. River still sees the good in him . . . despite everything.

River commands Hale, "No more transforming," and urges the two along. "Let's go. The Weylings probably know we're here now. We need to lie low."

Hale finds it bizarre to read about the Extraordinary Division in Felix's handwriting. How could Felix ever belong to this world? It is as if all Hale's life, Felix pretended to be another person. Hale remembers his father to be a skilled and smart man, but he was obviously much more than that. He was the Griffin Elder of Prophecy, an inventor, magician—not to mention knowledgeable beyond belief. It's hard to wrap his head around the fact that Felix and Bayo were best friends for a thousand years. The two couldn't be more unalike.

Though Hale cannot doubt his emotions toward the betrayal, one thing is certain: Felix tried to do the right thing. No matter the cost.

Reading every scribble and bit of information Felix jotted is mesmerizing. His fingers brush over the lettering. This old book has somehow brought Felix back to life, and Hale can feel his father's presence through the language he used in the pages. In this way he gets to know Felix all over again and with fresh eyes.

But why did Felix want Hale to meet the Western Prince of the Weyling? Shouldn't Hale be frightened of coming in contact with the Weyling, who consume Griffin flesh?

Hale's eyes strain as the sunlight passes behind the boulder they hide behind. He eventually falls asleep reading his father's journal entry for the billionth time. *Hale is my son. I could feel it in my soul, as if the truth had been sleeping within me for centuries and has now finally awoken.*

Sweet dreams of his childhood grace him. Holding the hands of both parents while teenage Carly sprints playfully in front of them. In that dream, Hale comes to terms with the hard truth. And the truth is . . . the truth does not matter. His father is still his father, his mother is still his mother, and his sister will always be his sister. That love is real and unextinguishable. But sweet dreams are short-lived.

Hissing voices sound nearby, and Hale opens his heavy eyes to spot two silhouettes larger than life, a few yards away from where he, River, and Evan are sleeping.

"Trussst me, Sadafina," hisses a male Weyling. "It would pleassse our massster."

"Let usss take them for oursssselves!" Sadafina whispers. "Their aroma isss—"

"Silencccce."

Footsteps approach Hale, and suddenly two pairs of glowing vermillion eyes illuminate the night. Hale sinks farther into the rock structure and disregards Felix's warning not to use his power. It should not be that much of a risk, considering the Weylings have already sensed the trio by smell.

Hale's vision is replaced by the red color of his Endurance power. Around the bend of the boulder are the beings, and he nearly gasps at the sight of them. They are thrice the size of the average man and are just as Felix described. The Weylings creep over River and Evan with sinister smiles, uncovering a sackcloth filled to the brim with a shiny blue dust that they sprinkle over the boys. Their bodies adopt the bioluminescence of the powdered substance immediately.

The female Weyling, Sadafina, hoists River by his shirt, and River, oddly, does not wake from her touch. *Could the blue powder be keeping them from waking?* Hale wonders.

Sadafina takes a deep inhale. "Mmmm, how delectable! Let usss take thisss one for ourselvesss, Lefang. We ssshall give the other to massster."

"No," Lefang declares. "Princcce Durzaan knowsss there issss more than one."

"How many did he sssay there were? There are only two here."

Hale scrambles to his feet and sinks farther into the rock.

"It wasss not relayed to me," Lefang confesses. "Make hasssste. He wantsss them while the hoursss of dark are upon usss. The other princcce should not know."

Sadafina grabs River, and Lefang goes for Evan. But Hale is not letting them get away easily. He allows his power of Endurance to flood over the Weylings, and yet, there are no screams, no faltering to the ground in dismay. Hale is stunned. *My power doesn't work on them!*

Sadafina turns to the direction Hale hides. "Do you senssse that, Lefang?"

"Make hassste," Lefang repeats, spreading his awful bat-like wings.

Hale's heart is thumping out from his chest. There is no way he can fight the Weylings, especially considering his size, their lust for Griffin meat, and their immunity to his power! Why hasn't his dad mentioned this in his journal? Was their master the Eastern Prince Felix mentioned to avoid? Hale is unsure. *What should I do? What should I do?*

The Weylings take to the skies. River and Evan dangle lifelessly in their arms. Bayo's guiding voice ensues from the depths of Hale's mind once more. It says, *You have the journal. That is the key to your survival. Your pack brothers are as good as dead. You cannot fight the Weylings. Leave them and spare yourself.*

Hale glances over to the journal that lies on the ground, ready for the taking. Then he turns back to the specks in the sky, meant to be River and Evan, who would follow him into the pit of destruction any day of the week. Shaking with nerves, Hale wonders why this decision is so hard to make. It is sickening to know that if he were a year younger, he wouldn't have thought twice about recklessly going after them. But why is he so different now? Could Bayo have changed him that much?

No. Bayo can't change me unless I give him permission. I am who I want to be . . . Who do I want to be? he asks himself.

The Weylings advance to their high towers. Hale grabs his father's journal. The light of his transformation is a brilliant white, and he soars after the Weylings.

I'm going to be me.

CHAPTER 26

At last, a Griffin embraces the skies of Emsequet! Hale scours the dark scape with his mind's eye, using his power of Endurance. Engulfed in red are the Weyling thieves past the accumulation of clouds. *How is it possible for their magic to work on River and Evan when they are both wearing their protective amulets? And why are the Weyling unaffected by my power?*

"I senseee sssomething," Sadafina says to Lefang.

"Of courssse, you ssssap. We're holding Griffinsss," snaps Lefang.

Without warning, both Lefang and Sadafina plummet at immense speed, pulling their monstrous wings back and allowing gravity to take part in their descent. Hale does his best to follow them to the tower's point. The midnight-purple stone of the gloomy tower glistens in the light of the full moon. *The full moon. Great.* Subtle purple light glows from the slit-like glassless windows.

Incredibly, both Sadafina and Lefang descend at the perfect angle in accordance to those slits in the tower. With a tilt of their bodies they miraculously enter the grand palace of their master. Hale pauses as he considers the million consequences of doing the right thing.

No. I'm no coward.

Distractedly, Hale cuts through the air to make his way for that same slit in the tower when several Weylings emerge from the clouds behind him! A piercing shriek escapes Hale's beak. The Weylings expand their striking wings and surround him. Hale swerves above and below, searching for a weak point between their wings, but they are as hard as steel, and Hale is caught in their trap.

"What a speccciman!" hisses the Weyling to his left.

"What an odor!" says a salivating Weyling from below.

They reach out for Hale's limbs and wings with their abnormally long and muscular arms. Pointed claws dig into Hale's skin as he fights his way free. They snarl in hunger and gnash their carnivorous teeth, aching for a bite!

Uselessly, Hale presses his power onto these menacing beings and dodges them when a Weyling sinks its teeth into Hale's shoulder! Immense pain overcomes him, and he shrieks, but the Weyling is not finished with him yet. It sinks its teeth deeper into Hale's penetrated skin, attempting to pull out a chunk of meat.

The excruciating agony of Hale's flesh dislodged from his bones sends him whirling, and in that instant, a spectacular white energy stupefies the Weyling assailants! They are knocked back by this bizarre force, and yet remain hovering in the air, unmoving, as if time itself has frozen. Thus, the otherworldly light pouring out from Hale's eyes is revealed. It pierces the heavens, like beacons, just like it had in the Banshee Forest.

Within their paralyzed and levitating bodies, the Weyling are miraculously dying of the otherworldly pain of Hale's Endurance power, which was ineffective on them prior to this point. They are, however, silent, unable to let out a single moan throughout their suffering. In the midst of this, the blood from Hale's shoulder pours out from his body and floats drop by drop into the atmosphere, against the pull of gravity. The white light then creeps out from Hale's open wounds and wanes while he heals unnaturally.

Peeking their heads through the slit-like windows of their towers are Weylings curiously witnessing the commotion. They are aghast to see the horrifying light show in the western sky, for the flock of fourteen Weylings that have surrounded Hale are gradually adopting his bizarre light before descending to their bloody deaths at the foot of the grand tower.

The surge of this epic power does not startle Hale. It feels warm, comfortable, strong, and familiar. It is like recalling a distant dream. In that bizarre dream he envisions a different version of Bayo. A younger, kinder version, holding Hale in his arms beneath the Welcoming Moon. *Did this really happen? Is this a memory?* Hale is unsure. The only thing he knows for certain is that the light he's emitting is more powerful than anything he's ever known. It could be the most dangerous thing in all the worlds, and yet, Hale is unafraid of it.

Hale returns to his human form midair. The light of his transformation creates a jolt that strikes the ground. The Weylings within their towers duck for cover. Sure as day, Hale soars the skies in this glowing form, entering the Weyling tower through a window, and the beings within cower and flee, all but one who resiliently faces the aerial Griffin.

Prince Durzaan of the West, the mightiest of Weylings, stands erect before Hale, unintimidated and hungry. River and Evan are frozen in blue at the center of the chamber between Hale and the prince. A creaking sounds from above. It is the tower's ceiling gradually splitting apart like a budding flower to let in the full moon.

Durzaan chuckles. His deep-toned voice reverberates the halls. "Dull your light, Griffin princcce," he commands.

Hale's intensity lessens. The Weyling court take their positions beside their master. The moon makes its way to the center of the tower's opening.

Hale takes in the room and spots obsidian amulets on every Weyling, including the prince. They are so much like his own. Now Hale understands why his power was previously rendered useless against the Weyling abductors—the amulets were protecting them from magic. Yet somehow, once Hale was in that ethereal state, he could undo the protective magics of their pendants . . . *But how can they have this amulet? My father is the one who created them.*

"How do you know me?" Hale asks.

The menacing Weyling prince steps forward, towering over Hale. "You are the brother of the Griffin King. The beassst who confined my people to thisss one dominion. You ssshare his likenessss."

His words are sharp, though they might not have meant to hurt as much as they did. Prince Durzaan continues to circle Hale steadily. His enormous wings are folded behind him, dragging with heaviness along the stone floor.

Hale diverts. "How do you have these amulets?"

"Felix, the Elder Prophet, sssought the preciousss obsssidian ssstone that isss only found in Emsssequet. Within the ssstone liesss a grand energy that he believed would make a cloak againsst all magicsss. In exchange for the ssstone and the knowledge he usssed to turn it into a cloaking deviccce, I consssumed his wife'sss Griffin power of Light while keeping her life intact . . . I have heard many storiesss about you from the Elder Prophet. He meant to take you away and keep you from your path of dessstruction. But here you ssstand before me in all your might. I asssume the grand prophet is no more, killed by hisss massster?"

Hale's fists clench.

Durzaan continues, "Why do you come, oh Dessstroyer of Worldsss, into my dominion? You travel eassst, but your home liesss wessst. Do you not ssside with your brother, your king?"

"I fled the Griffin Clan when I learned his true intensions," Hale explains through a tight jaw.

Durzaan widens his golden eyes. "Hmmmm . . . Do you mean to fight me for the livesss of your companionsss?"

Evan and River are lying peacefully at Hale's feet. *I can't fight him . . . Whatever state I was in that allowed my Endurance power to break through their protective pendants is gone now, and I don't know how to bring that back,* Hale thinks.

"Think quickly!" Durzaan booms. "They live until the moon comesss into complete view," he says, motioning to the opening of his tower.

"I will bargain with you. My life for their freedom," Hale says.

Durzaan ceases his stride. "You? The grandessst Griffin in existenccce fleesss the ssside of hisss king and hisss title. Entersss the nation of hisss enemiesss, and laysss down his life for hisss insssignificant companionsss?"

Hale remains silent.

Suddenly Durzaan extends his brawny arm, pressing the palm of his skeletal hand against Hale's chest. Durzaan's slit-like iris dilates, and Hale feels the innermost chambers of his heart are revealed for the prince to see.

Finally, Durzaan says, "You believe the livesss of thossse who raisssed you were lossst in vain. They were not."

How could he know that? Nonetheless, the moon is directly at the center of the tower's opening. Has Hale lost his pack brothers?

Durzaan turns away, climbing his magnificent spiked throne. "I will not take your life, your power, or your companionsss asss I have promisssed your true father. There isss sssomething I musst give you, however. Your new ability to heal your flesssh while in your High Enduranccce ssstate wasss triggered by a rare gemsssstone in my posssesssion. It bringsss out the opposssite of one's nature. The opposssite of anguish brought on by Enduranccce would be the ability to heal . . ." Durzaan reveals a beautiful octagonal clear quartz crystal with an obsidian rim dangling from a shining chain. "Thisss pendant will not only protect you from all magic but give you the power to overcome your given nature."

Hale takes the gift wearily. "Why are you giving me this?"

"To prevent the desssstruction of worldsss . . . to inevitably remove the barrier around Emsssequet," Durzaan answers.

Durzaan redirects his attention to his counsel. "Our Griffin guestsss are not to be touched. Ssspread the word. If Nizakel, the Eastern Princcce, doesss not heed thisss decree, there ssshall be a great war in Emsssequet!"

With that, the Weylings leap from the tower and take to the skies with monstrous howls and shrieks. Hale anxiously watches the full moon pass, wondering if Durzaan will keep good on his word. When the opening of the tower shuts, Hale immediately hurries to shake River and Evan from their enchanted slumber.

Before Durzaan retires into shadow, he leaves most off-putting last words that Hale won't ever forget. He says, "Remember, Griffin princcce—in timesss of your confusssion—which of your loved onesss your natural enemiesss resssspect, ssso that you may recollect what you fight for."

CHAPTER 27

P alla and Garet are striding along the shore on their way back to her bungalow after a long day's work. The scape is colored with a gradient of twilight blue fading into gold against the high tide. Palla notes the strange behavior of the ocean against a cloudless atmosphere. She assumes a storm is coming and urges Garet to hasten his stride, though she should have known better . . .

Dagiel's yellow orb has suddenly appeared near her ear and whispers, "Be mindful, Palla. Do not trust this foreigner. I saw him indulging liquor this morning."

Garet gives the little orb a snide look for outing him.

"Did he hear me? Is he . . . looking at me? Look, Palla, he follows my every move!" exclaims Dagiel while bouncing left and right to test his theory.

"I can see you, spirit," affirms Garet flatly.

Dagiel gasps and becomes invisible. Palla, too, is equally shocked.

"You see them? All of them?" she asks.

Garet nods. "Aye. Beautifoehl dey are."

Palla swallows. "I've never met anyone other than my sister and I who could . . ."

Garet frowns and averts his gaze. "Palla. Dere's moehch I'd like to tell you."

A distinctly familiar and eerie chuckle surfaces. "Oh, do tell her, pet!" There is no mistaking it is Kala, just another orb amongst the many dancing around Palla.

From Kala's conversation with Greon, Palla has gathered that her sister has a long history with the human. "How well did you know my sister?" Palla asks.

Garet flushes. He wants to tell her, but what would she think of him? Though there is no going around it now, with Kala here. *De cahnfooehnded wetch haoehnts me to dis day!*

He sighs. "Naht well. We wahrked tahgether. We've dahne 'ahrreble dings. She needed sooehls, and I wanted to 'inder me sight. Sence a yooehnglin', I cooehld see shadows o' people, segnifyin' dat deir time was nye. A fool I was to troehst 'er." He sucks his teeth.

"*He* is the reason I'm dead," Kala says.

Palla raises a brow. "I doubt that, sister. You brought on your own demise."

Garet cannot seem to hold himself back any longer and claps back at Kala. "You're de mahst repoehlsive wetch I ever ded 'ave de mesfahrtune o' meetin'! I doochght I was red o' you!"

As a bystander, Palla found this reunion very amusing, and she would have laughed, too, if it weren't for what was happening across the horizon. The usually pristine waters of the Arketcha Tribe blacken abnormally. The shoreline is covered with dense seaweed that would block the fishermen's passage the next morning. A foul smell of rotten fish reaches their nostrils. Indeed, Palla makes out several dead catches from where she stands. Without warning, the shoreline recedes, only to tower menacingly above their heads!

Just as the wave comes crashing, Garet pulls Palla away in the nick of time, crying out, "Beautifoehl lady!"

Nonetheless, the pair are struck with water, fighting the pull of the tide, and scramble upcoast and to their feet, hand in hand.

"Are you all right?" Garet asks.

Palla is soaked. And livid. She wrings out the hem of her robe and bellows at the ocean, "Well, you have certainly gotten my attention! Meet me at the temple during your rising hour!" Then she storms away.

The wrinkles in Garet's forehead grow evermore prominent. That was certainly odd, even for him. It is times like these he misses the bottle more, but alas, there's no bottle here, and maybe he should stop drinking, come to think of it. There are many things, it seems, important enough to remain sober for. Like the peculiar woman marching her way through the rocky slopes and into the jungle. A goddess of sorts with silken dark hair and eyes, glistening chestnut skin, modest in all ways, with a heart of finer worth than gold. The very opposite of her witch sister!

While Palla disappears and appears once more through the thick foliage, Garet picks up his speed. Thus, he decides he will follow this woman anywhere, and he'd better do it sober if he is going to be of any help.

"May I go with you?" Garet asks when Palla is about to take the second forked path.

She considers it for a moment. "You will be too frightened."

Garet laughs. "'ave you seen de dings I've seen, darlin'?"

And so, the pair make their way up the winding path through the jungle, a path the Arketchians would take only when burying their dead or visiting them. They come to a plateau where a grand bridge suspends over a gushing pool. On it is a magnificent yet decaying structure. Water pours from its several openings like small waterfalls that merge with the current. The mist of their downpour is a bit too brisk for the evening's cool weather. Palla is stone-faced as she anticipates what is to come.

"Why here, Palla?" Garet asks.

She then explains, "Here, I can channel the spirits of the warriors of the past to protect me."

But there is more Garet must know. "Who is de spirit you were speakin' wit at de pahrt? Why ded dey attack you?"

"It was the ocean," she answers.

"De ahcean itself?" Garet repeats, noting the fear in her eyes.

She nods. "The last time I battled it, Kala and the ancients were my support. Together we were able to conquer both souls of the siren. Now I am alone," Palla explains.

They are at the other end of the bridge. Garet reaches for her hand. She is caught off guard. The way he looks into her eyes makes her feel supported for the first time in a very long time.

He says, "You aren't alahne. And fahr de recahrd, I'd persahnally rather be alahne dan stochck wit Kala's 'elp."

"That ungrateful ingrate!" snaps Kala from somewhere among the millions of orbs above their heads.

"And 'appy to be!" Garet hollers back. "I shan't need to learn dat lessahn twice."

The tension in Palla's shoulders eases with Garet's and Kala's humorous exchange.

The pair enter through the open archway of the temple. Moonlight pours in from the open ceiling and illuminates the stand-colored interior. The circular temple hall is nearly fifty feet high. At the other end is second arched opening leading to the vibrant pastures of the infinite Arketchian gravesites. The pitter-patter of Palla's and Garet's footsteps echo while Palla leads him to the well filled with holy water at the center of the temple.

Palla places her palms into the water and takes it to her lips. She tells him, "Drinking from the well when visiting the temple is a means for cleansing and keeping death from spreading. It is tradition."

He follows her lead and drinks from the well. All the while their eyes remain locked, forcing Palla's heart to skip a beat. How long has it been since any man looked at her like that? She cannot recall. Though rugged in appearance, Garet's eyes are soft like the eyes of a small, furry creature. Palla laughs at herself and averts her gaze.

Monuments of the famous fathers of the Arketcha Tribe stand twenty feet tall against the wall. Garet takes in their appearances. Several of them hold weapons, stationed at their sides. All have stern faces. *Dese moehst be de warriors Palla was speakin' abooeht*, he thinks.

"We still have time," says Palla, observing the black moon from the open ceiling.

"What is de risin' ooehr? A specific time o' night?" Garet asks.

"The moon has control over all bodies of water. Once a month, when its cycle is ended, the ocean has the ability to separate itself from its control, to do as it pleases on its own accord. Near midnight during such a moon phase, the ocean can even embody a humanlike figure and roam the land."

Garet absorbs the information. "Den de ahcean shooehld naht be so frightenin', as 'e is naht in 'is element."

Palla stiffens. "On the contrary, it will be most frightening. I must take this time to call upon the fathers of the tribe now." She turns to the monuments and begins a chant that brings their higher selves forth from the other worlds. Beams of light strike the monuments from above as Palla speaks the name of each warrior. To Garet's astonishment, the monuments begin to shake and move!

"Do not mistake this for idolatry," Palla tells the human. "I have temporarily brought their souls into the stone so they might blockade the ocean from me if the need be."

The newly awakened spirits do not breathe or blink but simply move and look about. A sharp clamoring sounds upon their movement. Absolutely astonishing!

Palla begins, "Friends. It is I, Palla, the Spirit Guide of the Arketcha Tribe, who has brought you in these forms to battle the ocean with me on this night. The siren has been lost to us this past year. Our current chief, Naloo, has banished her to exile out of fear of the lack of control over her vessel. He has done this against my warnings. Now the ocean has come to claim what rightfully belongs to it. Do you choose to help me?"

They nod.

Garet has dozed off against the well. The light rumble of his snoring is interrupted by his drooping head bobbing up and down as he wakes and falls back asleep. Palla smirks. *Even the manner in which he sleeps is bizarre*, she thinks, *and yet, adorable. Palla! You must not think this way*, she tells herself.

The remaining warriors are armed and ready as well as Palla's spirit friends roaming the temple and gravesite freely. The embodied monument of Franto the warrior stares at Garet with disgust, as Franto would regard sleeping in angst of battle utterly careless. Franto even attempts to recall what it is like to sleep, but the memory is too distant . . .

Palla's eyes suddenly shift from her natural chocolate brown to neon green, and she instinctively knows what is approaching. "Fathers of the Arketcha Tribe, the time is nigh," she says, taking her position.

Dagiel's yellow spirit cozies up to Palla's shaking torso. "I am with you."

"The ocean is mighty, Dagiel," whispers Palla. She begins to sense strong vibrations beneath her feet. *He's coming.* "Without the rules of nature set in place, it would bring total destruction. It may even swallow the tribe whole."

Dagiel whispers, "You can do this, Palla. Hold your own. All spirits no matter how mighty have come to fear your name."

"I must," Palla mutters. The vibrations are increasing, sending slight tremors throughout the temple. Oh, how Palla greatly wishes she can somehow return her bravery from whence it came!

Another tremor. Garet topples over and hits his head against the tiled floor. "Ugh, good grief!" he grunts, rubbing his head.

Franto the warrior's stone lips curl into a smile.

The clumsy distraction is just what Palla needs to ease her fright. She laughs. "Have you had a pleasant slumber, Garet?"

Garet's cheeks redden bashfully. *Even 'er laugh 'as me stirred oehp*, he thinks. "Ah, best sleep I've 'ad in ages," he says sarcastically.

"Must be the drink, no doubt," says Dagiel from above.

Garet would have added another snippy remark if it were not for the overbearing gush of water penetrating their ears.

Palla stands firm and ready. "Prepare yourselves," she tells her spirit friends, who enhance the light of their cosmic energy.

Water surrounds the temple on all sides, flooding the bridge and entrance. Palla holds out her hands, and with her power she pulsates white energy to keep the water from flooding the interior.

On the bridge just beyond the entrance, the water gradually grows and morphs into a distinct shape of a giant that makes its way toward the temple grounds! It is beautiful and beyond imagination. The slits of its eyes, nostrils, and mouth as well as its silhouette are aglow in a brilliant aquamarine light.

If one looks closely enough—as Garet makes sure to do—they could make out the lightning-like gash that represents the Great Divide between the two realms of Malphora. On either side of that line where the Extraordinary Division lies, everything that lives inside the ocean is visible in miniature form. Sea monsters, shipwrecks, coral, merfolk, and pockets of seaweed. Tsunamis, hurricanes, and other great storms are scattered along the surface of its body.

In the Human Division are all the above incorporated with countless pockets of black oil lifting and sinking like oil in a lava lamp. Garet wonders what would happen if he should stick his hand inside the ocean's body to pull out all the corrosion. Would the physical ocean be cleansed?

Other great mysteries are hidden within the Human Division as well, such as ancient civilizations and other strange structures. Could they be warcrafts? Spaceships? Garet isn't sure, and the mere thought that many conspiracies were in fact true readjusted his view on life in all but a few minutes. How amazing was it that these beings were able to witness all the mysteries of the ocean just by beholding it in this humanlike form!

The ocean extends its manlike arms. And it is curious as to why, of all the forms in all the worlds, this is the form it chose to take on the night of its freedom.

Its intense booming voice sends shocking vibrations through Garet's and Palla's bones. It is the voice of the ocean. The sound can only be compared to a combination of fierce storms, lapping waves, gushing waterfalls, and harmonious whale song bouncing off the interior of the temple. It says, "Palla, Spirit Guide of the Arketcha Tribe, you have broken our pact."

Palla is trembling, though she does well to fake her composure. "Not intentionally, mighty ocean. Chief Naloo exiled the siren—"

The ocean magnifies over her and roars, "You've allowed a human to decide the fate of the ocean's possession!"

Palla explains, "The siren's soul has become erratic, and I could not prevent Arketchian law with Assella, the angel of judgment, present."

Out from the ocean's outstretched and human-shaped hand grows a long and thunderous body of water. It is as dark as an eye of a storm and arches so steadily that Palla assumes it is a threat and would not cave in. Indeed, it does, and the worn bits and pieces of the temple have already begun to break away.

Palla's stone warriors leap into action by creating a barricade with their bodies to block the blow. But it is not enough. The wave smashes against their bodies and pushes on. Water floods between their gaps and with massive pressure. Palla gasps. The help of the stone warriors will not be enough.

Palla is forced to exude herself once more, protecting herself and Garet with her spirit energy. However, in a moment of weakness, her energetic blockade wanes and the impact knocks Palla off her two feet. She tumbles into Garet's sturdy arms. They share a glance.

"I can't do this," she admits.

The temple is flooding by the moment; nonetheless Garet hoists his goddess back to her feet. Then he does the strangest thing Palla could ever imagine. He smiles. As if poor Palla can take any more madness! Garet's smile is equally as adorable as his batting eyes.

"Dis goehy is no match fahr you, darlin'," he says.

Though no matter how charming Garet is, he is wrong. The ocean's entity is unlike any of the meager demons or spirits Palla has ever battled before. While she appreciates his support, she does not believe she can make it through this. Nonetheless, Palla has no choice but to attempt to try.

A simple incantation in the angels' language turns the color of her eyes to a blazing green. The emerald light reflects off the grey waters. The mystical energy that pulsates from her inner being repels the water in a radial motion, and Garet's jaw drops in awe when he beholds its beauty. No mortal has ever had the ability to behold Palla's magic before this moment.

She's a gahddess! he thinks. Garet inches closer, and the water, too, bids him farewell.

"Wahnderfoehl, Palla. You're doin' it!" Garet's voice is barely audible through the commotion despite his proximity.

Palla turns and her heart skips a beat. She hadn't expected him to be so close. She can feel the heat of his body radiate onto her back, and the gentle rub of his clothes against her thick robe. The Spirit Guide bizarrely finds herself fighting not just the ocean but her longing to sink only a millimeter backward into Garet's chest, to feel his heart beating against her spine and his gentle arms across her midsection.

No, Palla, she tells herself. *You should know better than to indulge in fantasies! Focus!*

She releases a tense breath. Sweat beads down her temples as she dares to expand her power, forcing all her energy to radiate the scope of their bodies, much like what a Griffin of Shielding can do, yet all the more difficult, for this is not how the Spirit Guide is used to depleting her sacred energy. Through the gap of the statuesque figures, Palla spots the ocean spiral upward.

With its arms stretched wide, it strikes the flood below, creating a massive whirlpool that pulls back toward the entrance of the temple, pausing while it gains height. The new threat magnifies over the hundred-foot statues of the Arketchian warriors, reaching the tip of the temple's open ceiling. It holds the intensity of a tsunami with the eye of a hurricane!

Palla gasps. *It can't be possible. It shouldn't be possible.* The ocean's intensions were never to threaten Palla. It was trying to murder her!

The temple surely cannot withstand such a blow—let alone Palla and Garet. The setting darkens as the water conceals the moonlight. There are no foreseeable exits, as the clever ocean created another water barricade over the second archway as well.

Palla's legs go numb. There is no way her powers will save them from this attack. She stumbles into Garet, and he wraps his arms around her torso. Garet is as sturdy as a tree trunk. She'd expected him to be shaken in the moment of approaching death.

Being held for the first time in centuries felt indescribable, as if all Palla's yearning for touch and love were settled in one moment of tripping into the right arms. That support meant everything to her. It had been so long since the living had treated her so. Palla gazes into Garet's honey-glazed irises while he stares at the scape.

"It's okay, Palla," Garet laughs. "Dere are no shadows. You can do dis. You'll stahp it."

He gives her a light shake, grinning from ear to ear, as if he's seen the outcome of this battle long before it's ended. How can he even see shadows when the temple is so dim? Nonetheless, Garet's assurance and sincere smile has somehow magnified Palla's might.

Just then, the stone warriors elongate their bodies and topple over one another, crumbling into a single curved slab of stone to protect Palla and Garet. They have molded and broken to a point beyond restoration. When Palla and Garet huddle in this darkness, Palla intuitively feels the souls of the Arketchian warriors depart from their statues in understanding that they have done all they can. However, their contribution will not suffice.

"Spirits! I require your light!" Palla commands with a wavering voice.

The cave is at once illuminated with the orb-like spirits. Their light reflects off the bits of faces and limbs that once belonged to the stone monuments. Palla takes in a deep breath as she comes into her powers. She feels the ocean's spirit just beyond, and its monstrous creation is about to impact their shelter. There is no time. Palla must act now.

Palla re-creates the barrier. Water is spewing in through the cracks. A moan escapes her clenched jaw as she pushes her powers in a weakened state. She is absolutely certain that her efforts are futile. The stone shield explodes away, revealing the submerged temple. Water continues to leak through Palla's energetic bubble, and the two are up to their knees in it.

The giant face of the ocean spins around the bubble. "Give me the siren!" it bellows.

"I will find her," assures Palla, her hair flying in an inexistent wind. "But she will not return to you. She must stay in the Arketcha Tribe."

Meanwhile, Garet continues to be filled with wonder. In his defense, what now roams the breaking walls of the Arketchian temple is unfathomable! Wrecked ships a quarter their original size come hurling their way. Water dragons and other violent sea monsters with erratic tentacles and gaping mouths filled with rows of jagged teeth have materialized from thin air! The temple is barely containing this one-sided battle. It should cave in at any moment.

Palla and Garet are now torso-deep in water, and she is deeply pale in color.

"Give me yooehr 'ands," says Garet. "Teach me 'ow you're doin' dis."

"You won't be able to," she says.

Garet counters, "I see yooehr magic, de white poehlsations, and I see de spirets. I can do it."

Palla is shocked. *How could he see my magic? Could he be the one I've been waiting for? The one who will replace Kala and help me heal the tribe?*

She grabs his hands and directs him. "Project your energy outwards to blockade the water. Imagine your energy as if it were as real as this water, as strong as wind."

Garet's and Palla's hair flies majestically as they combine their energies. Their bubble grows, and the water that has made its way in is now pushed out. Palla's spirit friends cheer.

Palla can feel Garet's strength, and her eyes widen in disbelief. "Are you straining yourself?" she asks curiously.

"No, I can poehsh it farther," he says, determined.

"Do it."

Garet takes the reins. No matter how hard the ocean roars or smashes against them, it is unable to penetrate their bubble. This is Palla's opportunity to negotiate.

She tells the ocean, "We must come to an arrangement. I seek peace. The siren does not. She is safe with me."

The ocean ponders her offer before responding in its deep voice of storm and whale song, "Return both of the siren's souls to the Arketcha Tribe in three moon's time or your people will pay the consequences."

Finally, the waterworks are at their end, and the ocean returns to its humanlike shape, sucking back in its sunken ships, sea monsters, whirlpools, storms, and flood through its stomach.

The temple walls are cracking. This is to be the last moments the Arketchian temple stands. It is the very last structure in the tribe that dates back to ancient times. Palla was but a young girl when it was built. Her fists clench in fury.

The ocean morphs into a puddle and depletes into the river current below the dismembered bridge.

CHAPTER 28

Lustrous star formations and remote galaxies hover above the eastern portion of Emsequet. Yet not for long as a dark mass of raging clouds are traveling outward. The Griffin trio freely roam the skies in their animal forms. Evan and Hale tail River, their guide, out of the horrid land as quickly as their wings allow.

Pools of bright-red lava illuminate the ground below. Gas faults separate every few minutes, shooting piping hot vapor hundreds of feet upward. But River avoids the geysers easily, for there is a series of cringeworthy scraping sounds signifying the plates pulling apart. The Griffins swoop around the steamy gas when the grimacing black Weyling towers come into view atop the peaks of the sharp mountains.

Hale and Evan share a worried look. The multitude of Weyling towers outdoes the western division of Emsequet by twofold. How could Durzaan offer the Griffins any protection when the eastern Weylings are more in number? Perhaps it wasn't the best idea to pass. Hale squawks to grab River's attention. When River turns, Hale directs his paw to the right, hoping they can go around. But River shakes his head solemnly, pointing to Felix's journal strapped onto the side of his beastly body. And Hale understands that Felix's map has shown this is the only way through. The trio must trust Prince Durzaan's promise and brave the dangerous journey through the abundant Weyling towers . . .

While scaping the skies to ascend the grand mountainside, River lies low, flying just above the rock. The air becomes denser by the moment. The intimidating and growling cloud mass is directly overhead and descends into a thick fog obscuring the scape. Evan and Hale struggle to keep near River, who appears in and out of sight when swerving around Weyling towers abruptly.

There is another sound distinct from the rumbling heavens. Hale cocks his ear and wonders what it could be. It is coming from all sides. Lifting his head, he spots a shadow with long pointed ears and glowing eyes. The span of the black wings is thrice Hale's Griffin form. Hale jumps, nearly knocking into a pillar. The animalistic lilting intensifies. Silhouettes of Weylings spring out from the slit windows of their towers and soar. Their glowing vermillion eyes pierce through the fog.

Hale is suddenly alone. Frantically, he searches for Evan and River, keeping as low as possible. In his panic, he wonders if he can bring on his High Endurance State—as Durzaan called it—if the need be.

Worn wings force Hale to gallop up the mountainside. His claws cling on to the jagged slope. Bits of rock break away with the added pressure and tumble down. A swoop sounds from behind. Hale looks back anxiously. The haze leaves him unable to tell if there is anything behind him. Picking up the pace, Hale channels his inner power of Endurance. The scene is engulfed in an almost infrared light in which he can make out silhouettes. It is just as Hale suspected. The Weylings are onto him. More so now that he has used his power. Hale is confused. None of the Weylings are wearing cloaking pendants. He should be able to use his power on them. And they should not be able to detect him, as he is also wearing Durzaan's pendant.

Using their deep-throated language, they call to one another, and out from the fog comes a swarm of them! Bat-like wings are closing in. Grey, muscular arms with curved talons reach out and graze his skin. Desperate to escape, Hale attempts a jump, but the beasts have boxed him in just as they had in the western division. The close call has Hale shaking. He presses his power onto them, hoping to strike them down with pain, but it is useless.

The best chance he has is to confuse them while he zigzags up the terrain. If there were ever a time he needed to bring on that strange High Endurance State, it would be now. Attempting several more attacks amid running from the beasts proves futile. Hale's power is *weakening*, but it is still allowing the Weylings to find him. He must stop using Endurance entirely. Perhaps it is for the best, for in blindness, he might be truly able to hide from the monsters.

Everything is white and misty. Hale slows his pace and dashes down the slope he just climbed. His useless pendant bounces against his chest while he sprints. The Weylings continue the chase up the mountain, outsmarted for a while. When he gains enough momentum, he returns to the skies when the pendant levitates in Hale's face, and he makes out a cosmic spark from within the stone. At this exact moment, the pendant is matched by the bare and glittering surface of the spiky mountain's wave of white energy cascading toward the snowy summit.

Noticing the obsidian and the mountain do look awfully alike, Hale wonders, *Maybe the matching energy of the mountain is conflicting with my powers?*

The fog is clearing up, and it seems the Weyling towers are long gone, but there is still no sign of River or Evan. Suddenly, a Weyling jumps out and grabs at Hale's wings. He is caught off guard, and the abrupt pull sends him off balance. To have an advantage over the hunger-crazed creature, Hale loops in the air and kicks it in the head, then once again at the base of the neck. The Weyling's balance is unwavering, locking eyes with its prey before it strikes!

Hale's lost his opportunity to dodge the attack as its enormous wings encompass him. Its fanged mouth gapes open while it pins Hale's foreleg to his torso. A powerful kick from Hale's hind legs hardly affects the Weyling, and no matter how hard Hale tries to call forth his power of Endurance, it remains unaffected.

The Weyling wraps its tail around Hale and prepares to take a bite of his flesh when both the Weyling and Hale are mysteriously knocked off balance. The Weyling descends from the heavens and drags Hale down with him. The jagged mountain is gaining on them. Hale must escape its clutches before they make impact. Urgently, Hale slashes its leathery wings until the gashes are too large to enable it to fly. The weight of the Weyling's body is too much to bear, and though Hale strains, the Weyling refuses to let go. It flashes a devilish grin.

Hale prepares to meet his doom when a blond Griffin swoops down, biting at the Weyling's tail just before the crash and catching Hale with a free paw. Evan and Hale lock eyes, and Hale regains his breath before motioning to the levitating pendants around their necks. They must remove them, even if it risks exposing their location to Bayo.

Evan nods. The pair transform midair, landing on the snowy bit of the summit in their human forms. They remove the pendants and place them in Evan's pouch.

"Where's River?" Hale asks.

"I lost him in the fog," Evan explains.

Flapping sounds overhead.

Hale cautiously looks about. "Try to use your power," he tells Evan.

Evan tries calling forth his power of Ardor by motioning his hands. Sparks fly, but they do not burst into flame as they usually would.

"Come on, come on!" Evan mumbles. His face turns red as he strains. Finally, he creates a blazing ring of fire around them.

Snow flurries dust their hair and shoulders white.

"River!" Hale calls. "River!" A cool puff of air escapes from Hale's red lips when an unsettling feeling arises in the pit of his stomach. "Something's wrong. He would have found us by now," he says.

"Maybe he made it through," Evan offers.

"*I* hardly made it through without my powers," Hale counters.

The cries of the Weylings are drawing nearer. Evan positions his body, preparing himself for battle. "We can't afford to think that way."

But Hale can't shake this feeling. "Durzaan must have trapped us. He must have lied." *I should have never trusted him. Bayo was right to trap them here.* Hale resubmerges his sight to his weakened power of Endurance, recoloring the scape in red. Weylings are coming in from the right.

"Hale, can you—" Evan begins.

Hale's jaw is tight as he extends his arms up toward the Weylings. "I'm trying."

The Weylings look uncomfortable. Some pause their flight and plummet to the snowy earth below. Hale is unable to reach his full potential, for the mountain's energy is diminishing his powers despite taking off the necklace.

The Weylings were only stunted yet not removed as a threat. More approach from the other direction when Hale says, "I need to look for River. I can't do both at the same time."

"I got it," Evan responds. Balls of fire pump out from his arms and toward the snarling beasts. While the Weylings swoop low to get at the pair, Evan creates a yellow fire-like whip with his hands. The whip grows and dances in the brisk air, daring for contact with the Weylings.

Hale is unafraid with Evan's protection and allows his mind to venture off, just as Bayo had taught him in the Griffin Clan. As he explores the land with his mind's eye, a deep guilt consumes him. Was it wrong of him to be thinking about Bayo right now and to use what Bayo taught him to his advantage? Was it wrong of him to agree with Bayo about enclosing the Weyling in Emscquet?

Maybe Bayo isn't completely evil; maybe he was doing what he thought was right. But there have been so many other instances that have proved otherwise. *Everything was a lie, Hale. Don't forget he used you* . . . But there were so many little moments Hale can remember showcasing Bayo's goodness.

"Any sign of him?" Evan calls amid battle.

Hale swallows. "No."

"Hale!" Evan is snatched from his place beside Hale, and though his fire cascades up the beast's torso, the beast does not seem to care as it shall soon take a bite of him.

Hale immediately forces his power onto the Weyling, and it howls in torment. Hale is becoming dizzy, but he can't stop now.

"Come on," he mutters.

Weylings were now emerging by the dozens. Evan's fire has run its course over the entirety of his assailant. Evan takes the advantage and kicks his way free, tumbling to his doom. Hale transforms and catches him in the nick of time, then returns to his human form.

"Evan, there's too many," Hale says.

"Can you do what you did in the Banshee Forest?" Evan offers.

Of all the times Hale's unexplained power has come forth, now would be imperative. What exactly triggers his godly might? Is this powerful mountain subduing his gift?

"It's not working." Hale is fearing the worst, and Evan can see it in his glassy eyes.

Rising to their feet, the duo position themselves for combat. They must rely on their next greatest asset: their Griffin forms. The new flock of Weyling are closing in. Evan and Hale are back-to-back, throwing fire balls and aggravating the Weylings with physical pain. The magnitude is no match for their inadequate powers, and the young Griffins must fight physically.

The swarm is upon them.

The two suspect their time is near.

Just then, a massive grey flash cuts through the skies, taking down the nearest Weyling, then the next at an epic pace. In one swift move, the creature pulls at the Weylings' ears, severing their heads. But this avenger is not alone, for an army advances behind him. Hale's vision focuses and recognizes the familiar face.

"It's Prince Durzaan."

Durzaan hovers over the ring of fire, prepared to take on any eastern Weyling that dares attack the young Griffins.

Now that the two diverse houses are side by side, their physical differences are even more prominent. While the western Weylings are larger in build, the eastern's lanky bodies, charcoal-colored flesh, and bright red irises are an intimidating combination. Still, the mere presence of Prince Durzaan has his enemies near retreat.

"Where are you? Facccce me, Nizakel, my brother!" Durzaan bellows. "You dare sssend your doleful minionsss to ssspite my ordersss in placcce of yoursssself?" His resonate voice carries across the mountain.

The western Weylings are motionless for the time being. Their sickening grins and never-blinking eyes study their master's nemesis. Then, out of nowhere, they charge! The Weyling grapple in the skies.

Durzaan has the advantage, taking several at a time, when a searing cry travels up the mountain. Durzaan's elongated ear motions toward it, his eyes wide with fury. He need not tell Hale whose voice the cry belonged to, for Hale has recognized it instantly. Hale furiously begins the chase, pulling up mounds of snow as he dashes forward, his muscles rippling with adrenaline. Evan is not far behind. Durzaan leaves the battle to follow the young Griffins while his army takes over in his stead.

"We musssst enter thoughtfully," Durzaan says. "My brother ssseeks vengeanccce againssst Bayo, for he hasss killed our father. Thisss will be a trap, asss it isss your life he sssseeksss."

Durzaan calls to his army with a Weyling battle cry, and they assemble, finishing the last of the eastern Weylings at the summit. He, Hale, and Evan lift off and enter the distant cave where trouble awaits . . .

It is silent as the company enters the large-spanned cave. The cool chambers are as eerie as the mountain's surface. Stalagmites and stalactites span throughout, and every few moments a clear energy emerges, cascading up and out toward the opening. It is the energy Hale noticed in the skies, though here it is prominent.

Hale takes the lead, using his weakened power of Endurance to hunt River's exact location. He swerves left. Evan, Durzaan, and the army of the west are at his heel. River's harrowing screams pierce Hale's ears and send tremors across the cavern. Straining his wings, Hale flaps as hard as he can.

Hale has never heard River scream like this. Even when beaten by the kids in the Griffin Clan, River never uttered a single cry. He was the epitome of taking his beatings like a man. If this was really River's voice he heard, he is not long for this world. Hale soars recklessly and scrapes himself against the sharpened rock, cutting his skin. Nothing in the entire world matters in this moment. But no matter how hard he flies, Hale doesn't seem to reach the end of the cavern.

The memories he and River shared are playing on repeat. Before Bayo's influence, Hale and River always had each other's backs. They could take on a crowd of ruthless Griffins. River's silly jokes and infectious laughter are consuming Hale's mind. Hale's heart is thumping out from his chest, and he knows he cannot survive another loss.

"Hey, remember me? Your best friend? How's it going?" River said in the arena when Hale was ordered to kill his opponents. How thoughtlessly River jumped

in! River put his life on the line, knowing what Hale was commanded to do, all to bring back his sanity.

Then there's Hale's distant memory of his near-death experience at the hands of a mysterious girl and her song. It was River in his majestic Griffin form saving Hale from death. It was River who cared for Hale while he was comatose after that fateful day. River is the constant in Hale's life when everything crashes down around him. How ashamed Hale is to have turned away from him! He should have never fallen into Bayo's trap. He should have stayed with River, Evan, and Grace.

Hale knows for certain, if he should never see River's bright eyes and joking smile again, he *will* destroy the world. He cannot endure another loss.

The width of the cavern expands to a wider scape encompassed by a luminescent blue rock. *This must be the center of the mountain,* Hale concludes, for this is where the violent energy pulsates out from.

Just then, Durzaan calls out to Hale and Evan. But far too late. Their party is ambushed. The mass that Hale and his company assumed was the ceiling of the cave falls upon them. It is, in fact, an army of eastern Weylings hanging by their feet. Hale and Evan are trampled onto the cool stone, knocked off guard by the sudden attack. Meanwhile, Durzaan swiftly ends the lives of all in his way, hoisting Evan's and Hale's Griffin bodies to their paws.

"Go!" he exclaims.

They gallop through the cave toward River's tormented voice. Durzaan stands before the armies of combating Weylings and bellows, "Nizakel!" His elongated arms extend welcomingly. "Emerge, you coward!"

A mighty Weyling, just about Durzaan's size, steadily levitates to the center of the cavern from the shadows. Nizakel's glassy skin is the color of charcoal. He is menacing, and though he is large in build, he is lanky. He unclasps his cape and tosses it to the side to prepare himself for battle. Beautiful jewels hang from his lengthy ears and are embedded into the spikes along his spine.

Hale and Evan are revealed, held captive within an invisible barrier. It is clear Nizakel possesses the Griffin power of Shielding.

"Nizakel," Durzaan declares. "You have defied my ordersss to leave thessse three unharmed."

Nizakel growls, "You are on the wrong ssside, Durzaan. We mussst repay Bayo for taking our father'sss life and imprisssoning usss in Emsssequet. We wassste away in endlesss hunger." He points his long talon toward Hale. "Hisss life belongsss to me. A debt I will return to hisss brother."

"Reveal the Griffin you hide," Durzaan declares.

With a wave of his hand, Nizakel unveils River, who was invisible until now. *He has the power of the Light, like Durzaan, on top of his power of Shielding,* Hale thinks. The Weyling princes are unmatched with power. Durzaan will surely fail with his lone power of Light.

In his human form, River's puny size pales in comparison to the airborne Weylings seizing his limbs. Fresh bruises are visible across his body. His shirt is wet with blood, and his legs are bent out of shape. He is barely holding his head up and peeks through a swollen eye to spot Hale and Evan banging through an invisible barrier before he blacks out.

At the mere sight of him, Hale's body goes numb.

"How can you help them, brother?" Nizakel says. "After all their kind hasss done?"

"He ssstandsss againsst Bayo, you fool!" Durzaan shouts.

At this point the princes have risen in the air, circling one another while the battle between their people continues behind them.

"I ssshall *not* ssstand down," Nizakel pronounces.

Durzaan widens his animalistic jaw. He bares sharpened teeth and a pointed tongue as he releases a thundering Weyling cry. Nizakel throws a blow across Durzaan's face. Enraged, Durzaan jumps at him, but Nizakel uses his power of Light to make himself invisible. Durzaan follows his lead, and both the princes disappear from sight. A moment later Durzaan reappears, having what seems to be Nizakel's concealed neck tightened between his muscular forearms.

Glitching in and out of sight, Nizakel manages through a clenched jaw, "You've betrayed your own kind for *them!*"

Durzaan squeezes tighter. Just then, Nizakel does a backflip midair, and in a flash his and Durzaan's positions are reversed.

Meanwhile, with Prince Nizakel distracted, the shield around Hale and Evan disperses, and the pair dash forward with balls of fire, striking the power of anguish onto their victims as best they can, for they feel very weak within the mountain. Using their Griffin bodies to their advantage, they swerve through small gaps where the Weylings cannot reach. Their assailants growl and sneer while aiming their arms and tails at them.

"Let usss kill him. Massster will not know. Hisss meat isss ssso tender . . ." whispers the Weyling at River's left.

"Yesss, let'sss," agrees the other at River's right.

Subtly, they make their way to a different chamber. Hale and Evan have followed them to a fork, not knowing which direction they should take. Evan squawks, signaling Hale to go left while he goes right. Hale nods—they have no choice, being so pressed with time to save River's life.

Hale enters the slick chamber. Muffled sounds of River's groaning seem only a short distance away; however, the cave curves, leaving Hale exceedingly frustrated. He forces himself to bring on his power of Endurance to see through the rock walls. River's silhouette is being laid down, and the Weyling are divvying up their share.

"Why doesss it not transsform?" asks one Weyling. "Itsss Griffin form will have more meat!"

"No matter. Make hassste while it ssstill breathesss," the other commands.

They loom over him with unhinged jaws. Vines of salivations drip onto their meal. Hale can't get there fast enough. The Weyling sinks its teeth into River's arm.

"AHHHHHH!"

Even Durzaan pauses just before smashing his brother's face against the cave wall.

"Imbecccile! Do you know what you've done in the name of vengeanccce?" Durzaan declares.

"We feed on Griffinsss. Have you forgotten our nature?" Nizakel counters.

"The Griffin princcce will desssstroy usss!" Durzaan declares.

Nizakel scoffs. "A Griffin could never desssstroy a Weyling."

Durzaan whirls Nizakel over his head and smashes him against the cave ground. "*Thisss* one will." He has his hand at Nizakel's neck. "The time for two divisionsss of Emsssequet mussst come to an end, brother. Choossse, your life and pride or our people'sss well-being."

Nizakel gurgles the words, "What well-being?"

Durzaan squeezes tighter. "We can be free from Emsssequet onccce again."

"Liesss," hisses Nizakel.

"Truth," Durzaan says, staring deeply into Nizakel's eyes. Both his and Nizakel's eyes glow intensely as they share this mental information.

Nizakel throws his brother's hands from his neck and rises, howling. "You wisssh me to hand over my crown."

"Your crown, or your life," Durzaan states. The western Weylings have successfully beaten Nizakel's army and now surround their master awaiting his next command. Nizakel has nowhere to run, and using his power is futile against so many Weylings.

He releases a sorrowed howl and descends, defeated.

Durzaan stands tall before his people. "Let it be known, I, Durzaan, am the king of Weylingsss, king of the wessst and the eassst of Emsssequet! I alone take my father'sss place to rule! I will lead our united people to a new age!"

The Weylings howl in unison.

Hale rushes around the bend of the cave. River's cries send him reeling. He strikes the beasts with his power of Endurance.

"Do you sssenssse that?" one asks the other, neither affected by Hale's power.

"A magical presencccce, yesss. Though no match for the mountain," says the second Weyling.

Evan enters the space like a madman, spitting balls of fire at the beasts. Though it is not up to par with his usual skill, it is more than enough to distract them while Hale sinks his beak into one Weyling's shoulder blade and cuts through the other's wings with his claws. Evan follows on the attack, and before they know it, Durzaan breaks through the cave with a single strike of his tail. The mauve cave wall shatters like glass, and the western minions end the eastern assailants.

Evan's resumes his human form and rushes to River's side. "Oh no," Evan says as he tries to hold in the heavy outpour of blood in various places on River's body.

Blood has pooled beneath the still and pale figure that was once their closest friend.

"This can't be happening," says Evan in disbelief. He places his head on River's chest. "I hardly hear anything, Hale—" Evan breaks down. Evan, who Hale has never before seen shed a single tear, *is crying*. "This can't be happening."

Hale can't bring himself an inch closer. River's lips are blue, and the way his legs and arms are twisted suggests a painful death. The corpse he stares at hardly seems to be River at all, but more like a broken doll. Then Hale sees River's open eyes. His once sparkling green eyes are now bloodshot and unblinking until Evan does him the kindness of closing them. Hale is living his nightmare.

The trio has always made it out of every battle in the Griffin Clan because they always fought side by side. The winning streak made Hale believe his pack brothers were somehow above death. He never thought he'd see them dead, especially not like this. Nobody deserved this, especially not River.

River. Is. Dead.

Suddenly, Hale is gasping for breath. He pales to a pasty white and he stumbles over, dizzying. When he takes in the smell of blood, stomach acid rushes up to his mouth. Hale thought he'd lived through as much pain as a person could experience. He finds himself foolish to have believed nothing could break him after Carly's death.

Prince Durzaan is staring, not at the dead young man, but at Hale. His steady eyes are ever watchful of the Griffin Prince, for in this critical moment, Durzaan believes he shall behold Hale's true nature. Will Hale turn on the Weylings? Is this the beginning to the end of the world?

Durzaan's thoughts are distracted, for Hale is not the only one who caught the scent of blood. The starving Weyling minions wish to quench their everlasting thirst. They approach cautiously, wary of their new master.

Yet Durzaan wastes no time evacuating the area. "Leave the mountain. At onccce!" he bellows.

Evan is dressing River's wounds as if there is hope. Oh, how deeply Evan regrets ever laying a finger on River! River was always forgiving. He was everything Evan ever wanted to be. Regardless of Hale leaving to be with Bayo, River always considered Evan his pack brother, in spite of all Evan had done in the past, and despite what he did in the Banshee Forest. Evan's pathetic feelings of inadequacy have completely washed away, but with poor timing. River is his pack brother. And now he's dead. The very thought of Grace finding out is unbearable.

Evan is stammering for words. "River. Wake up. You can't leave us. You can't leave Grace."

Hale approaches slowly and takes River's cold face in his trembling hands. The touch is enough for Hale to come to terms with the realness of the situation. That is when the grief strikes him.

Hale buries his head in River's deflated chest and cries out. The worst is upon him. A world without River is no world to live in. The person who saved his life, sheltered him, befriended him, and was that true constant throughout every circumstance—*is dead*. Another death. Another death.

The heartache is too much to withstand. Hale's eyes burst with white light. His body goes numb as an ethereal force takes over, lifting him up into their air. The pendant Durzaan gifted him floats up and out of his pocket, and like a magnet, Hale grabs hold of it.

Knowing all too well what Hale is capable of, as he's seen it in the Banshee Forest, Evan rushes backward and shouts, "Hale, stop!"

But Hale is not in control. He is watching, understanding the situation, but the overwhelming flood of emotion and power has him taking the back seat. All he can picture is River's bright smile, laughter, and sparkling green eyes that he shall see no more. *No more.*

Durzaan's crystal throbs in his palm like a beating heart. The vibration courses up Hale's arm and matches with his inner being. Hale understands this as its energy communicating with him. It is balancing his anger, soothing him with its frequency, and speaking to him just as the moon has during the Welcoming Moon celebration. Hale is able to understand it.

The crystal is sharing a gift with him.

A second chance.

Likewise, the mountain counters Hale's strength, but the crystal pendant tells him to push on despite it, to combine their energies, their power. With his inner being, Hale responds, *Okay.* He takes in deep breaths as he allows the waves to enter through him. Finally, the mountain is not prohibiting his abilities but instead strengthening them. All he had to do was give in to its powerful force.

Durzaan's crystal illuminates in white, and so do Hale's eyes, mouth, and nose. A tornado-like gust whirls around him. At this point, Durzaan, the new king of the Weylings, has returned to the scene. With great stamina, he pushes through the storm, with hands in front of his eyes.

"Hale, stop!" Evan shouts in terror.

I'm going to fix this, Hale thinks. *It will be as if this has never happened.*

Durzaan rushes to Evan and blocks him from the current. Then he notices the crystal in Hale's hands.

"Do not fear, Griffin," he tells Evan.

The cosmic wind forces River's body toward Hale. The scarlet liquid of River's blood smears beneath him. Hale places the crystal against River's chest. At once, light engulfs the space, including the mountain's energy. Miraculously, the blood joins together, forming small droplets and reentering River's wounds. The wounds themselves suture together, scar, and heal completely within moments. And yet Hale cannot feel energy return to River's body. Not the beat of a heart or a steady breath. As if agony can be transformed into healing, Hale sends his emotion into the crystal.

Suddenly, River takes in a deep breath and his heart skips a beat.

How cliché River would have thought this moment was, Hale thinks. He would have laughed from the sidelines. He would have said something funny. But this is no fairy tale despite the epic magic present, for River did not wake and have the happy ending of the fairy-tale classics.

Hale's light fades, he drops to the ground, and the storm settles. The strain of his diminished energy comes through with fatigue. Though he is hazy, he grabs River.

"River . . . River?" Hale shakes him. "Wake up. Everything is okay now."

Evan comes forward, astonished. "You . . . you healed him."

River's hands are warming by the moment, though he refuses to wake.

Helplessly, Hale turns to Durzaan and says, "Why isn't it working? He's breathing. His heart is beating. He's healed."

Durzaan's massiveness makes the young Griffins seem puny in comparison. His vermillion eyes seem solemn, and he utters words meant to be of some comfort, though failing entirely. "Young princcce, often, no matter how hard one presssesss on, doesss the circumstanccce improve."

CHAPTER 29

S loshing through the streets of the Arketchian square is none other than Sokos, son of Chief Naloo, with an expensive bottle of liquor in his hand and a girl whose evening he bought clutching his free arm.

Of all the Arketchian tarts, this one was specially picked for her long brown curls and big umber eyes. Eager for her time alone with the high-rolling prince of the tribe, this particular enchantress doused herself up with an innocent glamour before making her way to his favorite smoke and liquor-filled pastime. As long as her pocket is filled with his royal loot, she wouldn't mind a night of simple acting. If she's lucky enough, she might be able to take his mind off his old flame and become his new betrothed. If she's lucky . . .

Those who pass must take a double glance, for this maiden truly resembles the recently expelled siren, Ellionna. However, the passersby go about their way—this isn't new behavior for the chief's son. Sokos can do as he pleases; it's been this way all his life. And it isn't a secret what type of woman Sokos prefers.

Sokos leads her out of the busy square and to a grassy road. The sky is dimming, and the girl questions the prince. "Where do you take me, Sokos?" she asks.

Smiling smugly, he tells her, "Don't you trust me?"

They descend a short slope and gallop through the fauna to a small and private bungalow.

"How lovely. Is it yours?" asks the girl.

Lovely, for a bungalow she can barely make out in the subtle moonlight. Sokos moves her inside and throws her down in the dark. She expects to hit a soft mattress lined with velvet and instead hits her rear bottom on the floor . . . *It is cold . . . no, wet.*

Sokos locks the door behind him and chugs his bottle. She can hear his exaggerated gulping from where she lies. Her backside is indeed wet . . . and sticky, and it smells . . . like rot. The girl scrambles over the floor, looking for candles or a lamp, anything to light the deathly dark space. She reaches farther and finds what feels to be a lamp.

"Are you ready?" Sokos asks.

"J-just a moment," she says, lighting the lamp with an incantation. The room comes to light.

Sokos hovers above her, his voice just above a hushed whisper. "You shouldn't have done that, *Ellionna.*"

The girl's eyes are wide at the sight of her red hands. She is sitting in blood. Shaken, she gazes up at the prince's piercing black eyes. He isn't as handsome as she recalls moments prior. Suddenly she thinks back to a friend who had warned her against rushing away with him.

"He's dangerous," her friend had said.

"How would you know?" she retorted.

"I heard some girls are going missing," her friend explained

"Don't be silly! I shall be his new betrothed," she said with conviction.

Sokos unexpectedly throws the bottle inches away from the girl's head. It smashes into a thousand fragments against the wall. Shards jump back, sprinkling against her tan skin.

Before she can react, Sokos lifts her by her upper arms and pins her to the wall before spinning a single strand of her spiral curls around his finger. He presses himself against her body, leaving her unable to counter the weight.

"Ellionna," he drawls. "Tell me you love me."

The girl shudders. Maybe if she kept up the act, then she could escape. "I-I love you," she says.

She watches as the calmness in Sokos's expression turns to one of rage. Without warning, his right fist smashes against her jaw, and she falls over onto the floor. Sokos walks over to the lantern and extinguishes the flame with a countering incantation that nullifies all incantations to come. The room returns to darkness. The girl begins to plead for her life.

His heavy footsteps approach, and he growls, "You shouldn't lie, Ellionna. You never loved me."

Sokos stumbles out of his hovel not but an hour later. Blood stains his royal clothes, hands, and face, where his victim last touched him. He takes a seat on the stoop and inhales the crisp sea air to sober up. *No girl can compare to her. The rest all scream and cry. But not Ellionna—the real Ellionna*, he thinks.

It has been a year since Sokos had last seen Ellionna. A year since he cannot remove her face from his mind. For every time he laid a hand on her, Ellionna never sang or fought back, no matter how much he pushed her to the brink of breaking. Being with her was exhilarating, death defying! But now—he sighs—*it is not the same.*

A vertical whirlwind emerges from thin air. Sokos looks up to face a clouded window and jumps back. In it is the face of a stern man with pale skin.

"Hello, Prince Sokos," says the man.

"Who are you?" Sokos asks, straightening his posture.

"Bayo. High Elder of the Griffin Clan."

Unaffectedly, Sokos snaps, "What is it you want?"

Bayo cocks his head. "It is not something that I want in particular, but something I have that you clearly desire . . . In my care is your beloved *siren.*" Bayo's image in the floating window is replaced by Ellionna's likeness hanging by iron cuffs. "In exchange for that which you so crave, you will pledge your allegiance to me."

Sokos scoffs. "Why should an Arketchian prince pledge allegiance to a Griffin? For that girl?"

"No," Bayo interrupts. "Pledge your allegiance to me, and you will have all the power you crave. I possess the two halves of the siren's soul, and if you should so accept, you should be the vessel of its *completed* soul. Think of it. The power you always wanted, the woman you crave, to do with both what you will."

"I accept."

Ellionna awakens with blurry vision. Frightening red eyes belonging to a demonic figure are staring directly at her. Her scream is muffled by the rag tied around her mouth. Once her vision sharpens, she understands the demon is only one depiction among the many haunting paintings on the plastered wall she faces. The wall, smothered with black ink, is covered from ceiling to floor with ancient Arketchian hexes only known to the shamans of the tribe. However, no shaman would dare use such hexes, or re-create them in their home. No shaman Ellionna knew of, at least—besides Bezine, the Dark Shaman.

There were infinite rumors that followed the name of the Dark Shaman. Adults of the tribe would warn their children against traveling to the cutoff area of the tribe. No one was to go there, especially children, for Bezine was known to sacrifice them to dark creatures beyond the veil to prolong his life.

Ellionna never believed her grandmother's warnings. She thought it was nothing more than a fictional person the tribesmen created to scare the young ones from leaving the tribe. It was make-believe until her wild eyes beheld the hexes that called demonic creatures from the spiritual realm and into the physical. It is evident that Ellionna is now in Bezine's home. The home in which no one dares enter, unless desperate and interested in dark magic. But more importantly, why did Bayo bring her here?

Someone is chanting somewhere to her left. Rope restrains her to a flat board, and she can only look from the corner of her eyes. Sitting in the center of the room, with his legs crossed, moving his body erratically while chanting, is the Dark Shaman. His half-rotted face is peeling in several areas.

Livia, Ellionna's grandmother, once told her, *"The fewer children he can sacrifice, the sooner he should rot away from this world."*

"But why not just banish him from the tribe?" Ellionna asked as a child.

"He is not in the tribe. Palla, our Spirit Guide placed a spell on the tribe, so he cannot enter. But the tribespeople can still go to him. She cannot take away their free will."

Ellionna's stomach churns. She tries to sing her way to escape, though as soon as she is about to let out the siren's voice, she finds that she cannot make a sound. She gasps. *The siren wants this.* Whatever the siren can gain from this evil man doesn't mean anything good. It is up to Ellionna's cunning to get herself out of this bind. She struggles free from the tight rope when she spots a black figure whirl past. Her heart skips a beat.

It's nothing. It was just the painting on the walls. I'm imagining things. Of course it's not possible. These things don't exist, she thinks. But then Ellionna remembers the angel of judgment, Assella, appearing during her trial . . .

Another black figure flashes by. Ellionna blinks. And just as she tries to talk herself out of the second appearance, it pops up again, right in front of her face with a menacing smile and piercing red eyes. Its likeness is just like the depiction on the wall, however it is alive!

Ellionna screams. Suddenly the torches hanging around the home lose their flames in one mighty gust. Yet she can feel the black figures closing in. She shuts her eyes. Their sickly howls and chuckling fill the room. Bone-chilling hands touch her. Her face is wet with tears, and she is praying as best she can through her rag.

"Those hymns won't save you here," says a raspy voice.

Laughter magnifies among the demons.

At once, Ellionna's tongue clasps to her mouth, and she is unable to continue her prayer. It feels like she is being tormented by them for hours. She is whimpering and too scared to realize the chanting has stopped and that she can now speak.

The soft and sweet touch of a human hand caresses her cheek. She does not know who this can be, and she dares hope it is one of her loved ones. Perhaps it is her grandmother, Livia, her uncle, Atomi, or even her cousin, Robin. Though their touch feels different altogether . . .

"Shh," coos the person. The masculine voice is familiar, though she cannot, at the moment, put a face to it.

Ellionna peeks. *Sokos.* He is older than she remembers. Larger and as frightening as ever. With disgust, she shakes her head to move his hand away. Then she sees it . . . *his clothing.* His robe is blue and red, sacred colors for ancient *marital* robes. These particular robes were worn in the times when the Arketchians worshiped the unholy. Ellionna dares look down, and to her distress, she finds she is wearing them also. Tears well in her eyes as Sokos leans in and removes the rag from her mouth.

Leaning in closer, he whispers, "It will be over soon."

He pulls the board around so that Ellionna faces the room instead of the dreadful wall. Yet the change of direction is just as terrifying. On every surface in the Dark Shaman's home are demonic depictions, dolls, and figurines.

"Sokos," Ellionna says, "please untie me."

He is staring at her longingly yet doesn't fulfill her request.

"I won't run. Please, I've been tied for weeks," Ellionna pleads.

She doesn't expect such kindness of him and honestly assumes he will continue to ignore her. But Sokos *does* untie the ropes, and tenderly, too. He is especially wary of her red wrists and ankles where she's been bound and makes sure not to touch these wounds. When her feet are freed, she stumbles in Sokos's swift arms. His steady hands remain on her waist until she finds the strength to stand. This new behavior of his is most unsettling.

Sokos leans in and steams her earlobe with his hot breath. "Finally, we will be married. We will never be parted again."

Is he delusional? The last time Ellionna saw him was the first time she fought back from his violence. But maybe this is her chance to find some answers . . .

"Sokos," she says gently, "why is the Dark Shaman wedding us? Why are we in his home? Who brought me back to the Arketcha Tribe?"

He stares deeply into her brown eyes. "I will liberate you, Ellionna. You will no longer suffer from the voice. We will be the most powerful beings in all of Malphora."

What does he mean? Ellionna is more baffled than ever—not to mention very disturbed. As far as Ellionna's memory serves her, there was never a romantic moment between them. She parts her lips, intending to ask more questions, but Sokos turns away, indicating he will not disclose more information.

Demons explode from their depictions on the wall and fly around the room. Yet what irks Ellionna more is Sokos's lack of disturbance by them. To distract herself from the frightening sight, Ellionna scans the room for a way to escape. Finally, she spots the door. Lengthening her spine makes Sokos ease his grip. This is her chance. She has no other move.

She bolts for it.

Ellionna is halfway there when a snarling demon appears in front of her. The millisecond pause gives Sokos enough time to cuff her arm and pull her back in front of the Dark Shaman. The Arketchian prince is not amused. He raises his right hand as if he is about to slam it across Ellionna's face, and she winces in preparation for the blow, yet his hand never descends from its hovering position.

To her surprise, Sokos says, "I won't hurt you." He forcefully pulls her close. "Not on our wedding day. Such a magnanimous gift as yours, and you've resented it all the days of your life. And here I stand before you, your saving grace. I saved you from eternal turmoil with the Griffins, taking the burden and responsibility of the voice off your shoulders and onto my own. And *this* is how you thank me."

The chanting stops. "Bring her forward, Prince Sokos."

Sokos pulls Ellionna in front of the Dark Shaman, who then reveals an intricate crystal box with a bouncing water-like soul within.

Annoyed by the bright light and babbling spirits in Palla's bungalow, sleepless Garet enjoys a quiet stroll at the crack of dawn. *It's a wahnder Palla gets any rest*, Garet thinks. Stuffing his hands in his trench coat during the briskness of morning reminds him of home, and more so when it begins to drizzle. He points his face upward, welcoming the refreshing droplets onto his face.

Swallowing down his salvation no longer soothes his dry throat. Oh, how desperately he wishes for a stiff drink! But there will be no more drinking. Garet's gone cold turkey. Afterall, he can't be a total drunk if he's to be at all helpful to Palla, the enchanting Spirit Guide of the Arketcha Tribe. A life of good-doing and helping others is difficult, but it is so refreshing, and he admires Palla for it.

Garet continues on the dirt path and sees a red footprint in front of him as if it were painted on the dirt. But why didn't the pigment wash out in the rain?

Curious. A second set of footprints appear in front of the first. Then another and another.

Garet rubs his eyes. "I moehst be exhaoehsted . . . Dreamin' oehp footprents in me pat."

However, when Garet opens his eyes, the line of blood-red footprints leads up and around the hill where the shadows of death lurks.

"Ahh great!" he exclaims. "I soehppahse I'm sochppahsed to be fahllowin' de damn footprents, den!"

Against his better judgment, Garet *does* follow the footsteps while cursing his sight.

"Why 'aven't I seen soehch dings back 'ahme?" he wonders aloud.

The black shadows lurking behind the trees watch the Irishman ascend the hill. The blood-red footprints lead to an abandoned hut, and just when Garet nears it, the tracks and shadows disappear, which he is very thankful for. Though he by no means wishes to enter.

"Is dis what I get fahr wantin' to be good? Doesn't seem fair, does it?" Garet hovers over the door for a moment. "Ah, to 'ell wit it!"

He pulls the door open and steps inside. Within are five girls no longer among the living. Flies and maggots feast on rotten flesh. Dried blood paints the walls.

Suddenly, the mouths of the corpses open. "Sokos," they moan.

Garet jumps, and the overwhelming stench of rot fills his lungs. He flees the scene at once.

"Palla!"

Bezine has Ellionna and Sokos lie down, hand in hand. No words can describe how much Ellionna detests touching Sokos, even by the hand. Black clouds appear above their heads, and often, terrifying faces jump out at them both. Sokos eerily keeps his eyes open.

Ellionna dares ask the prince, "Do you hear them, too?"

"No," Sokos says calmly. "I imagine I will hear them soon, once the voice is inside me, as they are spirits, and you are part spirit."

"Why do you want this?" she asks.

He squeezes her hands and meets her gaze. Suddenly his human eyes seem much safer compared to the entities above. "For every possible reason, Ellionna . . . I might not be the best, kindest, or even good. But I know I want you, and I want that voice."

This is the first time Sokos had ever spoken to her with a kind tone, but Ellionna will not be fooled. She must use his new act to her advantage.

"How did you save me from Bayo?" she asks.

"He gave you to me," he answers.

Ellionna stiffens. "For what price?"

Bezine dips his finger in a bowl of fresh blood and sprinkles it on their faces. Suddenly, Ellionna can't blink, her tongue is too numb to form any words, and her limbs refuse to lift. She's as paralyzed as the dead. Sokos, too, feels the same. The demon's cackling intensifies.

Bezine hovers over the soon-to-be newlyweds, a knife in hand. The cold blade is pressed against Ellionna's skin. He slashes it against her forearm, and the pain of her separating tissue follows. Bezine collects the warm blood. When he goes to cut Sokos's forearm, he does not repeat the procedure but instead pours Ellionna's blood into Sokos's mouth, nostrils, ears, and navel.

What remains of her blood he offers to the demons. The smoke-like beings float down to consume their fill and after ingesting, they've become less opaque. Their presence is altogether stronger. Bezine drops the bowl. It falls in front of Ellionna's face, licked clean. The satiated demons now circle him, hiding his body within a gloomy tornado.

They part to reveal Bezine's renewed appearance. The Dark Shaman has transformed into a handsome young man, no older then twenty-five years of age. His skin is shiny and smooth. He inhales deeply with restored vigor and yanks off his turban. Long, glistening black hair falls behind him, ending at the base of his spine. However handsome and young Bezine appears, the wickedness in his eyes is perpetual.

"Rise, Prince Sokos," the Dark Shaman commands.

Sokos blinks awake and stands. The enchantment placed on him has broken.

Bezine continues with a monotonous tone, "You are as good as wed. Your vessel should now be sufficient enough to hold the second half of the siren. Let us proceed." With a wave of his hand, the crystal box flies from the air and into Bezine's hands.

He murmurs ancient words to the box, and it vibrates in his palms. By the magic of the dead tongue, the box unlocks for the first time in hundreds of years. The moment they've waited for is upon them. The second half of the siren's soul emerges as a large drop of water defying gravity. It produces a beautiful hum.

Ellionna's throat reverberates and her mouth bursts open with the same song. The sirens are calling to one another, hoping to conjoin in the same vessel. But Bezine takes control of the second half with a great motion of his hands. It flows with his movements like putty. Just then, the siren counters Bezine's force by propelling toward Ellionna rather than Sokos.

Oh no! Finally, Ellionna understands their plan. If the Dark Shaman is successful, Sokos will become the vessel for the second half of the siren. If he is unsuccessful, this second half will merge with hers. Their energy will surely overpower her, and death shall consume the land. Little does she know the Dark Shaman means to add both sirens to Sokos's vessel, but will he succeed? The Dark Shaman is already losing his grip, and the second half of the siren's soul inches closer to Ellionna.

Just then, the front door bursts open, and standing behind it, letting the sunlight into the musty home, is none other than Palla the Spirit Guide, Garet, and Chief Naloo!

Palla's fiery green eyes blaze into the dark space. She shouts in a strange language, which luminates the place with hundreds of her spirit friends. Rather than combat the spirit army, the demons cower and retreat into their wall depictions from whence they came.

Bezine hollers, "Palla, you dare come into my abode!"

"No, Bezine. By order of Chief Naloo I shall not enter yet. You may stand down."

A fuming Chief Naloo charges toward his son. He grabs Sokos by collar of his elaborate marital robe. The chief has always figured his son is eccentric, but until this very moment, it hadn't occurred to him that Sokos is entirely insane.

He feels a great weight of disappointment. Not in his son, but in himself for not being a better example. But he cannot showcase this vulnerability, for Sokos will take advantage.

Blood trickles down Sokos's forearm and stains his nose and mouth, where Bezine has poured it. The awful visualization is coming to the brink of what the chief is capable of tolerating.

"What are you doing, my son?" Naloo asks.

Sokos pushes his father. "Father, do not stand in my way! I am protecting our nation!"

Naloo shakes his son's shoulders. Maybe talking sense will remedy the situation. "We have no idea what the second half of the siren's soul is capable of! Our ancestors have separated the soul in half for a great purpose; a human vessel from a different bloodline cannot host such immense power. You will only harm yourself!"

Sokos pulls back. "Father, let me do it! It will work! He's placed her blood into me."

"You will endanger the tribe with your voice, you will endanger all Malphora! Let us return home."

But Sokos will not give in. "No. I have more self-restraint and discipline than Ellionna."

"You do not! She has lived with it since she was a youngling. Her ancestors were the only ones who could stomach it. While I am chief, you will obey me! We leave now!"

Sokos tenses, yet he agrees. "Yes, Father."

Naloo feels a sense of hope. He turns to leave with his son, but Sokos reveals a dagger hidden within his fabrics and says, "You are correct, Father. It is time for a new age. I'm ready to fulfill my role and will lead this nation to greatness!"

Naloo gasps. "My son! My pride and happiness!" He wrestles the knife away from his midsection. "Don't hurt me. I will not stand in your way."

Yet Sokos presses harder on the dagger, and Naloo cannot combat his strength.

"Ah, Father. I would keep you alive if your life did not stand in the way of me becoming chief," Sokos sneers.

Naloo looks to his eldest son with newfound eyes. There is no other option. Shaking with torment, the chief says, "I give you the title, willingly. If you truly believe all that you say you are capable of, I will move the mountains to give you whatever you need." Naloo then addresses Palla. "Allow them to continue the ritual."

Palla is stone-faced as she braces herself for the consequences of this decision. "Yes, Chief."

Sokos's arm relaxes, and the dagger drops to the floor with a clank. His smile is appalling considering he just attempted to murder his father but a moment ago.

"You will see, Father," says Sokos. "I will make this nation great. We will be most powerful, untouchable!"

Tears well in the chief's eyes. Sokos has reminded Naloo of his older brother who was the chief of the tribe before him and who had murdered an entire family of a werewolf named Atomi and was later killed by the angel of judgment, Assella. He suspects his son will now face similar consequences for his actions. *When did I lose him!* Naloo wonders.

Sokos resumes his place beside Bezine, who continues to whirl the siren's essence above their heads. Finally, the second half of the siren's soul gives in and flies into Sokos's mouth. Sokos's crevices are alight with its turquoise energy, and he inhales in ecstasy.

Garet clutches Palla's arm. "Shadow, Palla," he says.

Palla nods. She's suspected as much.

The prince looks to their dismal faces in dismay. As he is about to question their dissatisfaction, the hum of the siren begins. He grabs at his neck, and his face turns plump red while he chokes. He fumbles into the chief's open arms, and water begins to pool out from his mouth. Demons circle just above Sokos's head in anticipation of an additional meal.

Chief Naloo shouts at the Spirit Guide, "Palla, save him!"

Palla holds out her hands toward Sokos and speaks the angels' tongue. Her eyes flash a cosmic green, and out from her expels a white energy. Immediately Sokos gags until his crevices relight in that turquoise glow. The spirit of the siren emerges from his mouth. Grunting, Palla uses her powers to pull the being back into the opened box.

Through clenched teeth she asks Garet, "Are the shadows gone?"

"Yes," Garet answers.

But the Dark Shaman will not allow Palla to succeed. He holds his arms out, too, and emits his dark energy, compelling the spirit of the siren in the opposite direction, back toward Sokos.

"Stand down, Bezine!" Palla declares.

"No, it must work!" the Dark Shaman says.

"Release it, Bezine!" Palla commands. "Or I shall end you where you stand."

"Lesten to 'er!" Garet pleads.

Palla is losing her grip and is straining.

"I will enjoy this," spits the Dark Shaman.

With his free hand, he makes a fist, and the crystal box that contained the siren for hundreds of years—arguably the strongest container in all of Malphora—smashes into pieces.

Palla's eyes go wide. "No!" She's lost her grip on the siren's soul, but it does not prevent her from striking Bezine with her power, smacking that smug smile off his fresh face and interrupting his mad laughter. He, too, loses his grip on the siren, and it flies right into—

Ellionna.

Ellionna's paralyzed body begins to contort as the two halves of the siren's spirit finally reunite.

"Spirits, attack!" Palla bellows.

"You will regret this, Palla!" says Bezine as he calls forth the demons from the walls.

"Your time has come!" Palla steps foot into the unholy place, quite aware that its energies might affect her powers. But this is no time for backing down.

Meanwhile, Chief Naloo pulls Sokos out of the run-down bungalow, leaving Ellionna on the carpet to suffer while she tries to stay in control of her vessel. The union between father and son is short-lived. In the jungle, Sokos tackles Naloo, rendering him unconscious while he dashes to freedom.

Back inside, the demons dance with glee while the Dark Shaman expels a sickening laugh. Palla is unintimidated and calls on her spirit friends. Whilst the minions fight, Bezine and Palla's energies collide.

Ellionna continues to contort painfully when a pair of arms scoop her up. "Dahn't you wahrry. You'll be ahkay," says Garet while he carries Ellionna out of Bezine's home. He should know. There are no shadows looming over her.

"I've waited a long time for this," the Dark Shaman admits. "Soon the Arketcha Tribe will have their rightful Spirit Guide."

Palla drives her power further into him but is distracted by the voices of her perishing spirit friends.

"No!" Palla shouts.

Dagiel hovers near her ear. "Don't you dare give in, Palla!" he shouts.

"They're dying, Dagiel," she says.

"We chose to fight by your side," Dagiel counters.

Palla's eyes narrow. "No. I will not lose any more lives!" She dares stop her direct attack and spreads her arms to take the blow in the chest. The excruciating crushing pain puts the world in slow motion. But that does not faze Palla. While she flies backward, she makes sure to expel her power directly at Bezine's home. With a hazy vision and aching body, Palla works her way up to her wobbling feet. The Dark Shaman's home is now rubble and ash.

"Sister," says Kala's voice. Palla can hardly hear it through her ringing ears. "Sister, I know how to end Bezine once and for all."

Palla grabs her crown and steadies herself. "Wha—"

"With haste, Palla!" Kala shouts as she materializes as a blue orb.

A furious Bezine surfaces from the rubble. He is surrounded by black smoke, and his eyes are as fiery as a demon's.

"What have you done?" he exclaims. "No matter. Is that little Kala's voice I hear? Is that Kala's blue essence I see? You always did love the color blue."

Kala's orb ignites. "The color of your corpse, I shall imagine," she taunts.

The Dark Shaman smirks. "Goodbye, Kala." He holds both hands out and calls forth his dark powers, striking Kala's soul.

"Ahhh!" Kala screams.

"NO!" Palla exclaims. She is a split moment too late in reacting, but the shock helps Palla regain her clarity. A white bolt of light pulses out from her essence. Their energies clash once more, but Palla holds her focus and chants the angels' tongue with conviction while her remaining spirit friends envelop her with their support.

Kala's soul energy is unwell and dimming, and Palla can sense it. "You must use the Onipa spell to end him. I'm afraid I don't have long."

Palla's face reddens. The veins at her temples are nearly bursting. "With everything I have, you shall have eternity, sister." Palla breaks one hand free from the right and shares her life energy with Kala.

"What have you done, Palla!" Kala cries.

But Palla has no time to worry about the repercussions of what she has just done. Bezine's plague over this tribe must come to an end, and there shall be no more casualties.

"Dagiel," Palla commands, "rally our spirit friends and let them leave this place."

"But Palla—" starts Dagiel.

"Now!"

Dagiel hurries along and the spirits disappear.

The Dark Shaman taunts, "I feel you diminishing, Spirit Guide. You aren't so powerful without them and without your life force, are you."

True, Palla is struggling to keep her legs from buckling. "I could say the same about your demons. Enough chitchat. Ha!" Palla strikes, but the Dark Shaman is quicker. Luckily Palla dodges his attack in time. The trees she stood in front of are now ablaze. Palla scrambles to her feet and hides behind the untouched woodland. Smoke engulfs the jungle, and she wraps her hood around her mouth and nose to barricade them.

The Onipa spell, Palla recalls. *But that is a meager spell used to cleanse homes from old energies and malevolent spirits. It is a mediocre spell that anyone can perform . . .*

"Face me, Palla!" shouts the Dark Shaman as he torches tree after tree and bush after bush.

Palla glances behind her. *What if . . . yes . . . Kala is a master sorceress!* Palla leaps from the shrubs with intense green eyes and catches Bezine by surprise. *"Demoyaye, Demoyaye, tak-ed te manae!"* Which translated means, *Confined, confined, nowhere to hide.*

White bolts explode from the ground and imprison the Dark Shaman. Just as he retorts with laughter, Palla uses the spell of Onipa.

"*Calat tu impuite, def teg ana defe. Nikofeshe nickofesh. Tim-hazaken te hazaken. Bemo kalante te kalante!*"

Wash your impurities, back to whence they come. Sicken sickness. Release darkness to darkness. And bring death to death!

The Dark Shaman knows what Palla is up to.

"No!" he proclaims. He desperately speaks his own spell to counteract hers, but it is too late. Whisps of black energy emerge from him and enter again. He is attacking himself. After centuries, the Dark Shaman finally feels the consequences of his darkness. The energy materializes into tangible black gooey vines that entwine with the trees and branches—while still connected to his innards. He looks to be in the center of a terrifying spider's web.

"And here you shall stay, Bezine, until I come for you!" Palla says.

Bezine releases an excruciating cry, the corners of his mouth exaggeratedly drawn down to his chin. Perhaps he has never experienced physical pain before . . .

"I will end you, Palla. I swear it," he hollers.

Palla has already taken her leave, but that last note has gotten on her nerves. She locks her emerald eyes on the Dark Shaman. Another vine bubbles up from his mouth and attaches itself to the top of the trees. *There. That should do the trick.*

CHAPTER 30

Yellow flames of Ardor lick the top half of Evan's body. Hale does not part from his faint light as he charges through the pitch-black forest. Though Hale carries on as quickly as possible, Evan's light seems to be shrinking by the second. There is a sharp sound of breaking and snapping coming from behind. Hale can barely hear Evan's shouting through his pumping chest.

"Run! Run!" Evan says.

Drips of sweat bead down Hale's forehead. He can't keep up, not with River unconscious on his shoulders. Hale peeks and curses under his breath. Those creatures—whatever they are—are gaining on them.

Why hasn't Evan circled back for him? Maybe he still thinks Hale is behind him. Couldn't he have helped with carrying River a little longer? Apparently not, for Evan could not hold up the journal and illuminate the contents of the map while helping Hale carry River. Nonetheless, Hale is becoming furious.

I should have never listened to him, he thinks. *Why did I let him lead?* It's a rhetorical question, for the answer was that Hale's guilt pushed Evan to take the lead after River's incident. *If River were awake, we would have been much better off*. Even Evan said the same quite a few times.

To keep grounded, Hale reminds himself why they came here. After studying Felix's journal, Evan assumed there would be nymphs in this mysterious wood. He believed the nymphs would have a way to help River's condition, as they were described knowledgeable in Felix's notes. Mindlessly following Evan's lead, Hale would have agreed to running through hell itself to remedy this horrible situation. However, there doesn't seem to be any nymphs here, and coming proved to be the wrong choice.

Hale tries to pick up his pace, but River's body is slipping from his sweaty fingertips. *Come on! Come on!* Evan's light grows faint. There is no way Hale will catch up in time.

If only Hale could use his power and destroy them with a single glance, but he hasn't been able to bring on his power since the mountain incident. Perhaps he's exhausted it for the time being, and it might be for the best. There's been a total of three instances in which he entered the High State of Endurance since returning from death, and Hale often wonders about it. There is no denying it's dangerous, but what is that otherworldly surge coursing through him, and how is he able to become this ethereal being? The way Evan described it to him is exactly how Felix wrote about it in his journal entries, though Felix didn't have any answers. Oddly enough, King Durzaan of the Weyling knew to call it Hale's High Endurance State, though he never elaborated.

Hale's muscles are wearing out, and he has half a mind to transform in the middle of the woods, breaking every bone in his Griffin body to escape through the branches. It would be easier, at least, to go on carrying River's weight. But Hale stops himself. *That could hurt River. Maybe there's another way out.*

He continues onward and blindly through the eerie woods with sweaty hair over his eyes when the advancing snarls divert him in another direction—a direction he was sure Evan took as well. The forest silences. Panting, Hale pauses and looks about.

Evan's light is gone.

"Evan?" Hale calls.

He probably made it out safely by now. But Hale cannot go on. *Those creatures won't find me if I stay quiet,* he thinks.

The atmosphere instantly chills and Hale shudders. A puff of air escapes his lips. He rests River against the trunk of a tree as gently as possible and slumps down to join him. River slides to the left, resting against Hale's shoulder. Hale looks to him worriedly and can feel his light breathing against his skin. River will get cold here. He'll have to get him out of this place soon. Just as soon as he catches his breath.

Hale takes River's ice-cold hand, and shivers rush up his spine. The touch itself has transported him to a distant memory when he had reached out for Carly in a pitch-black forest. A single teardrop falls from his eye. It's been a week since River's incident.

"River," he manages. "It's me, Hale. Would you please wake up . . . we really need you . . . I'm so sorry I didn't get there in time. I'm so sorry for everything."

Just then, a mouthwatering aroma reaches Hale's nostrils. He gets a whiff and it immediately sets off his grumbling stomach. When was the last time they'd eaten? He can't remember. There's a glare shining from the left, and Hale must cover the blinding light with his hand to see past it.

It is a dazzling golden fruit tree.

Another inhale makes him salivate. His mind blanks on every thought and emotion, forcing him to focus on his hunger. The world around this tree no longer exists. Mindlessly, Hale rises and River slumps over onto the cool ground. A second grand light appears. It is a tree just as magnificent as the first. Its smell is equally as potent. Hale swallows. Which tree's fruit should he have first?

Wondrously, more and more trees materialize. This engulfing luminescent light is so picturesque that Hale wishes he can stay here forever. Yearningly stepping forward, Hale's senses are overwhelmed by the unique scent each tree produces. But alas, he cannot wait much longer. *I'll try all of them!* he thinks. Hale trips over a large object and lands harshly on his face. *What was that?* He wakes from his daze long enough to behold the corroded flesh of a strange creature. As the clouded daze of euphoria lessens, Hale spots the hundreds of carcasses dispersed along the ground with half-eaten fruit near their mouths.

Yet one inhale is all it takes to reel Hale back into his enchanted state. The plumpest of all the fruit beckons him. He plucks it and brings it to his wet lips. The sent is so very strong now, like the aroma of a sweets shop. Instantly,

Hale's eyes flash white. His High Endurance State has come forth, but only for a moment, long enough to recall the terrifying beasts lying dead at his feet. There was a passage about this in his father's journal . . . *woodland demons*. The aroma filling the air is no longer pleasing but instead reeks of mold and rot. Disgusted, Hale tosses the fruit and sprints to River.

As soon as he turns, the ground quakes. A series of rips and sickening popping sounds come from behind. Though River is in his grasp, Hale dares to look back at the hundreds of roots pulling themselves erratically from the soil. The trees are contorting and morphing into their true forms!

Their ivory bodies possess the curves of women with hornlike branches emerging from their heads. The alluring fruit dangles from their crowns, which now resemble jewelry rather than food. Wide smiles spew black ooze. Simultaneously, elongated skeletal fingers reach for Hale. The ground splits open upon their advance.

Hale hastily hoists River onto his back and makes a break for it when a woodland demon swings its massive arm around. Hale and River impact the ground harshly. The demons are closing in.

With a raspy voice the closest one says, "There is only one flesh creature in all existence that could resist our scent. I sense the darkness of your soul . . ."

Hale crawls away, his back stings with pain, but alas, mighty roots enclose his leg and drag him back. Branches with minds of their own whip about Hale's torso, hoisting him up into the air until he is upside down and face-to-face with the leading woodland demon.

It inhales his essence. "Almighty Griffin Prince!" This time, when it takes another whiff, it snaps its neck toward River. Hale is released carelessly while it lunges forward. Its skeletal fingers graze River's chest. "But your companion, on the other hand . . . mmm, how scrumptious his pure soul would be!"

"Ah! But his breath fades!" says another, getting in the way.

"Let us have him now! His time on the physical plane is short-lived!" says another.

Hale's heart skips a beat. *What did it mean by that?* He bolts to River's side, yet the growing limbs of the demons are too quick for him. The grip around

Hale's rib cage is tightening by the moment, and he is gasping for air, begging his power to come forward to no avail.

The demons snatch River.

"Don't touch him!" Hale shouts.

The leading woodland demon continues to inhale River's essence. It says, "The mark of your power looms over your companion."

"How do you know me?" Hale asks.

One demon snaps its head at Hale and spits, "We are creatures of old!" The black ooze in its mouth pours out and splatters. "Our roots were inlaid in the soil of Malphora since the brink of time! Through them we hear the whispers of other lands, of past, present . . . and future."

They press their hands on River's chest and it burns a bright red light. River squirms with discomfort as they lean in to suck the soul from his body. But one demon becomes distracted and jerks at Hale. "Tell us, oh Dark One, oh Destroyer of Worlds. When the time will come for the Griffins to consume this world, which side shall you choose? Will you slaughter Malphora if your king so wills? As is foretold . . ."

The other demons taunt him in the same fashion. They say, "Yes. Do tell us! Do you hunger for the souls of the worlds as we do? Will you allow us a portion of your winnings, oh *Demonic One*?"

In this moment Hale recognizes the part of him that is like Bayo. All he can think of now is the cosmic cobblestone bridge where he watched his father say to his mother, "*He looks so much like him.*" Durzaan said the same. Hale knows it wasn't entirely his physical appearance they were referring to, but the darkness within.

An angry thunder rises in Hale's chest. He feels his power emerging, and he welcomes it. A jolt strikes the air. In no time at all the woodland demons are knocked down, severing several of their limbs and roots. And though the demons are battered and broken, bathing in the immense light of his eyes, they continue cackling.

"Aha! Destruction it is!" says one.

"What a pure soul, plagued by dark magic!" says another, referring to River.

Hale is confused. How could his power be dark if combined with Durzaan's crystal, which turns Endurance into healing? But Hale's thoughts are put to a stop, for the woodland demons are advancing, some even crawling with a yearning to taste River's soul.

"Such treasures are so rare . . ."

"Even one cannot be found among thousands . . ."

Hale's eyes flash into their cores and at once, the monsters choke on their own internal ooze. "Help him," Hale demands. "You have magic."

More laughter. "We cannot help him . . . though it is not impossible—"

"You do not understand, Dark One," begins another. "Your plague is not what ends his life. His life is short-lived, as is fated . . ."

Hale is so terrified that he does not maintain control over his power. *No. That can't be true.* Tears stain his cheeks. He dares say, "He already died."

"Short-lived still," it repeats.

"Not meant to stay," another explains.

Hale's arms go numb. "H-how will he die?"

There is no answer.

Hale's voice rises in angst. "Can his death be prevented?"

"You should know more than all . . . the folds of destiny are never certain," answers one demon.

"Yes . . . we might end him tonight," rasps another.

Hale shakes their words from his mind. *It can't be true. River should be all right after he wakes. They must know a way.* "Tell me how to wake him!" Hale demands. The emotional outburst sets him off once more. The demons screech, painfully cowering from the light of Hale's eyes.

One yelps, "The water nymphs! Spirits of the deep! At the brink of the forest. Yes! They might have a way!"

Hale's inner distractions were enough for the sneaky demons to grow their large branches around every dark bend, gripping River tightly a second time. The sight of River's chest aglow with red light, signifying the woodland demons absorbing his soul, sends Hale into a frenzy. Without a second thought, he strikes them with his power. They then turn to stone and crumble to dust as if they never existed.

In one swift motion, Hale swoops River up and over his shoulders with strength he ordinarily doesn't have and resumes his walk through the forest.

CHAPTER 31

Winding paths of trees recede, and in the distance is the shimmer of a bay. Strange whispers travel to Hale's ears. They sound like children's voices in tune with one another. They are leading the way to the water. Hale takes River from his shoulders and into his arms, then removes his shoes. His bare and cold feet step onto the gravel, and he approaches the coastline where Evan is waiting.

Evan rushes to him. "Hale! I thought I lost you guys. I looked for you everywhere." He takes notice of the glow around Hale's body. "Are you okay?"

Hale doesn't answer. There is too much on his mind. *This should be the place,* he thinks.

"What are you doing?" Evan asks as Hale passes.

Small waves lap at Hale's feet. The water is warm. As soon as his skin makes contact with it, he knows he can trust the beings within. Clouds roll in, almost automatically over their heads, hiding the starry sky. A cool drizzle descends, and Hale walks farther into the water. Just as River's lower body dips in, bubbles form and pop continuously around him as if he were made of hot coals.

An aquamarine radiance shines, forming an enchanting path to the center. Though he cannot see the mysterious beings, Hale feels hundreds of separate presences in the water. While they do not form any distinct words, he knows exactly what they are saying.

"*We will help.*"

Hale continues to carry River's body until the water is neck deep and the whispers encompass them.

"*Let him go,*" they say.

There is no good reason to follow their commands, no proof of any kind. Despite this, Hale removes his hands. The thick skies begin to drizzle a piercing, cold rain that forms a cool mist against the bay's surface. The uncomfortable stinging is off-putting, and while River drifts away, Hale is left wondering if he'd made a correct choice. *Where is he? Did he drown? Are they imposters? Was I wrong?* Hale goes after him. But as soon as he propels himself forward, he feels pressure on his chest. It is the spirits of the water, and they utter a single word.

"*Believe.*"

Hale is stunned. It becomes probable that he needn't be afraid at all but simply believe that River would return as promised—alive, awake, and well. Yet believing proves to be the hardest thing he can do even while knowing there are things that exist out of his comprehension—like magic. It is so unnerving that someone possessing the ability to destroy entire worlds can feel so helpless.

Still, Hale cannot give into his thoughts. River cannot die. River isn't just a name to add on a very long list of those Hale loved and lost. He will live. Hale must believe this. Forcefully, he shuts his eyes and commands himself to let go of all fears and worries. All the while Hale repeats, *He will live. He will live.*

Drawing out a large breath, he whispers, "I believe."

Suddenly, a massive water wall shoots into the sky at the exact place River floated to. The petrifying wall meets thick and thundering clouds overhead, and the violent current sends Hale traveling back to the coastline. He hits his backside against the gravel harshly, though this does not faze him. Hale gets a second look at the structure, which doesn't seem like a wall at all but instead a veil between this plane and another. Could this be how the water spirits are returning River's soul to his body? Could River be stuck on the cobblestone bridge in the cosmos, just like Hale was?

Evan rushes over and pulls Hale up. "What happened?"

"The spirits of the water took him. They said they will help," Hale explains. "Didn't you hear them?"

Evan shakes his head. "No."

It seems nobody can hear the spirits the way Hale can. Yet he doesn't find it strange, for he understood the moon, the earth, and all existence during the Welcoming Moon. Then recently, he understood Durzaan's crystal when it spoke to him in the mountain.

Time passes by, and Evan and Hale remain at the edge of the bay, looking on with trepidation.

"What if—" Evan begins.

Hale interrupts, shivering. "They said they will help. We have to believe them." The rain feels like tiny needles piercing his skin. His wet shirt clings to his skin and sends shivers up his spine.

In time with the parting clouds, the veil descends from the heavens and hurls monumental waves to the shore. The fog clears, but there is nothing in sight. The whispers have gone, and the bay is no longer alight with magic. Hale steps forward, searching in the blackness.

River is not there.

Evan tenses up. "Hale."

Hale has no words. The two plunge. The rolling minute feels perpetual. Hale curses himself. How could he be so foolish to put his trust in something he cannot even see? Paddling and kicking recklessly seems to get him nowhere. Evan is the faster swimmer. He cuts Hale off and dives into the deep. Hale follows his lead and comes up first, unsuccessful.

Evan returns to the surface shortly after, exclaiming, "I can't find him!"

Adrenaline has his Endurance surging from within, and he uses it to gain momentum. Hale reenters the water and resumes the search using Endurance to scan the depths that are now entirely vacant. Was Hale losing his mind? At the surface, his sobs break free. They've swam too far out, and the shoreline is a long distance away. They might have even passed the place where River's body floated . . .

"He's gone!" Hale shouts.

Evan attempts to reassure him. "We'll find him. I'll check from the skies." Evan transforms and, with great vigor, leaps from the water, spreading his wet wings wide.

Guilt consumes Hale. He is the reason for the deaths of his family. He is the reason for the death of his best friend. Hale is a natural-born murderer. *I was never any different from Bayo.* As far as Hale is concerned, he is gullible, easily played. Played by Bayo, and now played by mere spirits.

The familiar wave of energy courses through him. It's what Hale's been waiting for. The mysterious High State envelops him, and like a warm blanket, it protects and soothes him. Now Hale has found the answer he was looking for. The way to access this new ability is through his untamed emotions.

Meanwhile, Evan spots Hale's change from above. From this view, it looks like Hale is *absorbing* energy, appearing to the naked eye as pure light. The water repels from him aggressively and the world stops its motion. The waves cease their crashing, and the uncomfortable drizzle hovers midair. Before Evan can call out, he finds his muscles and limbs have stiffened, yet he remains airborne, absolutely horrified at what might come.

Hale, meanwhile, steadily steps forward. His hair and clothes dance about as they would if he were underwater. The water continues pulling apart after his every step.

Then, Hale speaks with a voice so unlike his own. The alien-like voice is amplified a thousandfold, deep in pitch, and ominous. He says, "Reveal him."

Indeed, Hale is conscious, unlike the other incidences of his High State. This is no longer an outburst of his power. Hale is *choosing* this.

Hale motions his hands together, then apart. The water follows his motions and divides. At the center of the bay is a glowing bubble. Just inside is a vague silhouette of River lying flat.

Hale reaches out for it . . . when the whispers return.

"*Wait*," they warn.

Hale abides by their rules. Slender aquamarine arms emerge from the walls of water that Hale has miraculously separated. They push simultaneously, and the bubble housing River floats out toward Hale before falling apart to reveal River in deep slumber, his chest rising and falling steadily.

244 | JK NOBLE

When Hale reaches out a second time, the whispers whirl around his head like looping gnats. "*Wait*," they repeat. "*Allow him to wake.*"

Hale does as they command. River stirs. The lids of his eyes shake ever so gently. Overcome with relief at the sight, Hale releases his power. The whites of his eyes return to their natural hickory brown. Time reverts, Evan is freed, and water refloods the bay, lapping over Hale and River, taking them into its depths.

Yet the water spirits do not allow their Griffin visitors to experience any pain. Hale and River are captured and placed into a large bubble, then are carried to the shore by small cyan hands. Attached to those hands are creatures Hale will never be able to put words to. They are nothing any folklore or myth have explained. They are something entirely different, absent of fins and scales, opaque, and stunning.

Evan is already on the coastline in his human form. He takes in Hale and River from the shore. He is smiling enthusiastically. "You did it, Hale."

Hale beams.

But Evan's expression turns grave. He holds tight to Hale's shoulders. "But you need to stop. Maybe you think you're controlling it now, maybe it feels good, but I've seen you in that state three times and I barely survived them. I don't mean to hurt you in any way—" Evan means to go on, but he is interrupted as River blinks his way awake. Evan pats Hale's arm.

Hale nods. "I understand," he mutters.

"What are you girls chatting about now?" River says groggily.

Unexpectedly, Evan wraps his arms around River, making him groan. "Oh, just about how wonderful our week without you was," he says.

"A week, huh?" River says. His voice is hoarse. "Missed me already, did you? That's shocking."

Evan laughs. "Shocked me, too."

River looks past Evan to see Hale's welling eyes. "What—are you *crying*?"

Hale wipes his face quickly. "No. Crying? Why would I cry?" he says, trying to play it off.

River's half-opened eyes and pasty skin imply fatigue, and yet he spreads his weary arms for a hug. "Come on. Bring it in."

Hale almost plows into River's chest, and all he can say is, "Are you hungry?"

"Starving," River answers.

It is so good to hear River's voice. Having him back feels like a dream. The night continues. Evan and Hale prepare a campfire and roast some leftover meat. River does not yet have the strength to stand, and he is resting against the trunk of a tree with Evan while Hale fetches more firewood.

Hale does not mean to linger near the woods long, for he has unfinished business with the water. He approaches the bay, far from where Evan and River might see, and he sits atop a rock, placing his hand in the water.

"I can't thank you enough," he says in hopes they'll hear him.

A moment passes by before the wind carries their surreal whispers.

"*We did not help him for your sake*," they say.

"What can I give you in return for your help?" Hale asks.

"*We want nothing in return . . . He is important. He is good.*"

Hale feels their presence parting, like when an ocean wave recedes, though he feels the water spirits don't mean to return.

"Wait," Hale says, rising to his feet. "The woodland demons said he is still destined to have a short life. Is that true?"

Hale will wonder forevermore, as he is never answered.

CHAPTER 32

Palla and Garet speed through the jungle. Ellionna is shivering in Garet's arms.

"'ave you seen de chief?" Garet asks.

"No," Palla answers.

"She doesn't look too good," he says.

Palla is scrambling for possible solutions. *Perhaps I can extract a half of the soul as the ancients did before my time. It would seem unlikely, as the souls are united by now, and I'd have nowhere to place it since Bezine destroyed the box . . .*

When they near Palla's bungalow, her messenger spirit rushes to her side. "Palla, you have visitors—"

"Who are they?" Palla asks, preparing for a potential threat.

"We don't know. They are cloaked from our otherworldly sight," explains the spirit.

"Shooehld we leave, Palla?" Garet asks.

"Wait a moment longer; I must defend the siren at all costs," she replies.

The intruders reveal themselves and are but two women. Palla recognizes them. Ianna, an Elder Griffin, and her daughter, Mary, whom she'd met once . . . to give the second soul of the siren to Bayo . . .

Palla gasps. It is now clear that Bayo is the mastermind behind Ellionna's current condition and Sokos was a measly puppet pledging allegiance to the Griffin King's power.

But that is not all. Upon Mary's visit those decades prior, Palla had seen a soul attached to her across the veil of life and death. The soul had sworn to return to reignite their lost love.

Palla's eyes flash green as her spiritual insight takes over. She senses a familiar energy, and it directs her eyes to Garet's arm, where a mark invisible to the naked eye reveals itself. It looks like an arrow piercing through a crescent moon. *The mark of a spirit returned.* Palla's mind whirls backward to that eventful day hundreds of years ago when she sat across from the young Griffin girl and spoke to the attached spirit.

The spirit had given Palla a clue about his new name once reincarnated into this world. *A name representing water,* she told Mary then.

Palla's eyes go wide. *Garet is the Arketchian word for riverbank.*

How could Palla be so foolish as to ever get close to any man? She's even allowed herself to hope for an entirely different life by entertaining the thought of battling grand spirits with Garet by her side. How senseless is she to believe that this human man's spiritual gift is somehow meant to help her, the Arketchian Spirit Guide?

Palla's heart is crumbling inside her chest, and she wishes herself dead. Of all the demons, spirits, and ghouls she's battled in her long life, none of her injuries were as painful as one undetectable by both mortals and spirit. But why does it hurt this badly? Afterall, nothing came of her delusional fantasies.

Garet interrupts her train of thought. The sweetness in his deep tone is all the more sweeter with his strange human accent, and sweeter still since he cannot be hers.

"Do you know dahse wahmen?" he asks.

Palla's vibrant emerald irises return to her natural honey brown. Her lips part, though she is unable to utter any words. In a split second she shall witness two destined souls reuniting after lifetimes of suffering without one another's love.

Perhaps the biggest battle Palla faces is her internal demon. The demon that looks upon lovers and frowns. *No,* Palla declares, *I will not be such a person. They have both undergone so much. Finally, they shall know peace.*

Garet and Mary lock eyes. They hold on to that gaze for a long while, as if they are familiar to one another, though they cannot place where they've met.

Ianna bows respectfully, redirecting Palla's attention, and says, "Spirit Guide, I hope you remember me. It is I, Ianna, Griffin Elder of Shielding, and my daughter. We have escaped High Elder Bayo and seek refuge."

While there is no doubt in Palla's mind that Ianna and Mary shall be safe in her care, she hasn't a moment to respond before Greon bursts from Palla's bungalow at the sound of Ianna's singsong voice—a voice that has replayed in his mind in her long absence, now true as life just beyond the door.

Greon speeds toward the love of his life, and the one whom he loves as his own child. All three are taken aback with shock. Tears pour out from their eyes to blur their blessed vision.

Palla beholds their arms wrapping tightly around each other, their faces nuzzled deep into one another's bodies, their tender kisses and relieved cries. Even though the battle against their villain has yet come to its fated end, Palla decides that she's never witnessed something so beautiful as a family reunited after immense struggle.

Garet gently lays Ellionna on Palla's minuscule bed. "Is dere anythin' else I can do?" he asks.

His body is inches away from Palla's, and he's leaning in. His eyes scan her face, then drops to her lips. She can feel the heat radiate from his body. The proximity brings shivers up her spine. Palla can give in right now and fall into his arms, forever turning away her gift, and keep Garet from his destiny. It takes all her courage to remind herself that Garet belongs to another, and her duty requires her to live without love.

"You've done much. I shall take it from here," she answers coldly.

Garet automatically senses the distance and lingers, biting his lip. Should he just grab her and profess his love? His longing takes him as far as reaching for her delicate hand and bringing it to his lips. The pain of her averting his eyes is unbearable, though he's certain she feels the same way.

Palla pauses in shock, and her senses are almost knocked out of her.

"I'm 'ere if you need me," Garet whispers.

Garet steps out. Palla counts his footsteps and waits until the door swings shut for her tears to fall.

Dagiel nuzzles close to her ear to comfort her. "It will be okay, Palla," he says.

No, it won't.

CHAPTER 33

"I'm okay, Dagiel. I must focus." Palla wipes her tears. "There's no time to waste." She whips out dried herbs, glittering crystals, and amulets from her dresser and works them over Ellionna's shivering and damp body.

Palla can sense the enlarged siren spinning within Ellionna. As suspected, they have merged, and Ellionna's soul is fighting its power. The vessel will surely sicken, and Ellionna's soul might not be able to exist there for much longer— unless Palla successfully separates the siren's soul, as the ancient shamans were able to do in the past. But those shamans are long dead, and Palla is the last of those who remember the former ways in the tribe.

Kala's voice sounds just above Palla's shoulder. "Thank you for saving me, sister. It is more than I've ever done for you," the bouncing blue spirit says.

Palla must focus. "This is no time for such talk. I can hardly take more."

Kala understands. "You do not have the power to accomplish this on your own, Palla. Perhaps the priestesses of the Priestess Sanctuary still remember the old ways."

"Indeed. But we just don't have the time to fetch them, do we," Palla retorts.

The sudden blaze of the Spirit Guide's irises ignites the candle wicks in the bungalow. Crystals encompass Ellionna's squirming body. Palla presses her hands on Ellionna's chest.

"What do you feel?" Kala asks.

Palla answers, "They continue the battle for the vessel. The two have merged; however, the seam is still prominent."

"The dragon's box, where is it?" Kala asks.

"Bezine destroyed it," answers Palla, becoming increasingly stressed.

Kala's spirit rages. "Palla! You cannot do this. This is suicide!"

Palla snaps at the blue spirit. "You must give me more credit than that. The half shall return to the ocean who yearns for it. Dagiel, please show yourself, and bring the others."

The spirits appear as if they were there the whole while, waiting to reveal themselves upon Palla's exact command.

"We are here, Palla," says Dagiel, the yellow spirit, Palla's most trusted, and beloved.

"I must ask you all for help, and we are pressed for time," Palla expresses. "I am in need of your energies. I am so sorry."

"No need to ask permission, Palla. We have pledged our eternal assistance upon our deaths," Dagiel assures, and the rest agree.

"Thank you all."

The spirits huddle around Palla. Their light warms the home, unlike the cold ghouls most would come to know in the Human Division. But their light unfortunately dims as Palla continues her process, and she must watch the essences of her spirit family wain. While mortals would see them as orbs of light, Palla has the ability to look deep into their cores to see their faces. To her, there is no difference between the orbs and the bodies they possessed prior to their death.

Focus, Palla, she tells herself. *You must not allow their sacrifices to be in vain. Succeed, and you shall restore their energies . . . somehow.*

Kala's and Palla's connection grows as Palla continues to draw the spirits' energies for strength. Kala exclaims, "I can see them separating. You must force them. Harder, Palla! Harder!"

Palla moans. Her hands press into Ellionna's chest, so much so that an illumination seeps through her rib cage.

"Harder!" Kala shouts.

Palla's hair flies behind her as she consumes the energies of her friends, for every millimeter she feels them fading to a point of extinction. "I will lose them!"

"You must!" Kala says as she diminishes.

Tears fall from Palla's eyes as she faces the grave choice between saving Ellionna's life or saving her spirit friends from permanent death.

"No!" exclaims Palla. Her eyes return to brown, and a wave of her residual energy wipes out the candlelight. "I cannot do it."

Gravely, her sister responds, "Palla, you are a fool."

Dagiel's opaque spirit floats into Palla's open hands. "You should have continued, Palla. We are dead already. So many people might die because of this. The girl inside that vessel might die."

"You are far from dead, Dagiel." Palla is stern in her decision. "I will find another way."

The light of the sun shines through Palla's small windowpanes and lands directly on Ianna's face. She sighs in her sleep and moves just an inch deeper into Greon's strong chest. His eyes flutter open, and though he is half-asleep, he grins from ear to ear. When was the last time Ianna was in his arms? When was the last time they both slept so peacefully? It felt like eons. He thought he would never see her again. He had defied death so many times this past year, and somehow, by some miracle, she is in his arms, and they are free. It is all he's ever dreamed about and so much more.

He kisses her head tenderly and she wakes with a smile.

"Sleep," he says gently.

She presses her lips onto his and at once their hearts flutter.

"Finally," he says.

She kisses him once more. "Finally."

In the mid of night, Palla tosses and turns on the hard floor of her bungalow. She's been alone for centuries, never sharing her home, and suddenly it's filled with five people—living people, that is. And it's dark, as the spirits have decided to allow the living a sense of normality, making Palla very uncomfortable without their ambient chatter and light.

Subtle breathing sounds in every direction, along with the occasional snoring from the men. Garet, regretfully, has taken a spot somewhere near Palla to sleep, leaving Palla no choice but to shamefully admire his peaceful face. He is pale in color and rugged, unlike most Arketchians. Undeniably strong, however, and on more than one occasion she's witnessed his kindness. Arketchian men have a reputation for mistreating women; however, that is a stereotype, and Palla knows many men, living and dead, who countered that. Like Ellionna's father, Amoz, whom Palla personally crossed over into the next world after the siren took his life . . .

Palla sighs as she glances over to Mary, who is sleeping against the wall as if she hadn't slept in weeks. Against her goodness, Palla wonders, *Why did her soulmate have to be Garet?*

Greon and Ianna sleep in a loving embrace off in the corner. Palla sighs longingly. Witnessing them is proof enough that an all-consuming love can be found in more places than a fable. She removes her heavy robe and throws it angrily in the corner, then rushes out from her own home in nothing but a silken underdress. Palla would normally never expose her body, even in intense heat. Her modesty is her trademark, but she just can't take it anymore. That robe represents her oppression, and it's suddenly much too hot to wear.

Palla can't recall the last time she was ever so angry, so sad, or so disappointed. Tears fall onto her cheeks. The forest comes alive with orbs of multiple colors. Their aura is inviting and pleasurable. She exhales a breath of relief at the sight of her spirit friends.

Dagiel's familiar yellow orb hovers close. "You are never alone, Palla."

Palla wipes her tears. "Dagiel . . . I have failed at every turn. The Dark Shaman and Sokos were working alongside Bayo to place the second soul of the siren in another mortal body. Clearly to use as a weapon for his disposal. Yet Ellionna now houses the entire soul of the siren. She was weak to begin with. I can only imagine what destruction she will cause upon the world . . . It is clear to me now that the rifts are the Dark Shaman's doing. He was tiring my energies to regain power. I lack power and the help that I need. How will the ocean react now that the siren's souls are united? And the chief has disappeared with his son, who has succeeded in taking so many lives without my knowledge, as I was too distracted, I—"

"Palla," Dagiel says, interrupting her passionate rambling. "Release your fears and doubts."

This only enrages her further. He above all should know her failures and the massive weight she bears. "Dagiel, I feel as though I should die right where I stand. I am tormented beyond repair, exceedingly tired. I pray for death."

The flame of Dagiel's orb intensifies with rage. "Speak this way no more! Your road is long and, yes, twisted, more so than others it may seem. But has it not occurred to you that all souls must be tired? We are all eternal. Most souls have faced countless incarnations, repeating lessons and mistakes. But you have lived and learned and needn't begin again. Likewise, each breath you take is a gift that we lack. To enjoy earthly pleasures—in your case, not all—however you enjoy them all the same. You feel the heat of the sun, the soil beneath your feet. We, tethered to this plane, cannot say the same part for recollection and emotion. You have been chosen for heroism; it is no easy task, and that is given. But you forget yourself, Palla. You were never the type to pine for a simple life and turn your back on those in need. And die trying you shall not, for you have not died yet. And more help will come, it is a guarantee. The tides are turning, and old energy revives, but with the trouble it brings will come aid, for no problem exists without its fair share of solutions. Should a problem remain unresolved, that was a solution for prominent issues your blind eyes were too distracted to foresee!"

Palla is taken aback by Dagiel's long speech. But what a wonder it was, for the glooming clouds above her have dispersed. He has freed her from the pains she's given herself in one short moment. She finds herself laughing yet requiring one thing more.

"Dagiel, my closest friend. May I hold you?"

The fire of his orb lessens. "Yes, and ask me nevermore! I shall always relay the same!"

Palla smiles. Her eyes flash their signature neon-green color, and suddenly Dagiel's orb transforms to take the shape of the handsome Arketchian man he once was, long ago. He is opaque, made of yellow light, and hovers above the ground. Although neither could feel one another's touch, they embrace all the same.

He caresses her head. "You are most loved."

Behind Palla, peering through the hundreds of spirits, is Garet. He had followed Palla into the night with great concern. The spirits separate at his approach, and when he witnesses Palla's and Dagiel's embrace, his hands ball into fists.

"I shooehld 'ave known. It wooehld never be me," he mutters, turning back.

The spirits whisper of his presence, and Palla catches his silhouette. Dagiel returns to his orb-like form.

"Call for him," Dagiel says before he and the spirits vanish.

Palla so desperately wishes to heed Dagiel's words. Can she allow herself this slight glint of hope? But then, what would become of everything? Mary would be left without her true love, Palla would lose her abilities, and the tribe would go up in smoke without her. Most of all, she would lose her spirit friends.

For the love of one man, so much would be lost.

Is it worth it?

Palla fights her tears. "You won't remember, Garet, but we've met long ago. You were but a spirit, and we had just one conversation. In that one moment, you filled my heart with laughter. I did not expect to meet you in your new life because you were tethered to another. Yet in this life, you quickly became my sturdy platform. You have a big destiny, Garet. I've seen it, and I shall not hinder it. Likewise, everything I've worked so hard for all these centuries will be lost . . . if I choose to act on my love for you."

Garet hesitates at the foot of the door. His back faces her and his grip is tight on the knob. He wants to tell her that she is wrong. He wants to tell her how she changed his life and gave him purpose. Or how he made peace with his terrifying vision and stopped rushing to the bottle to subdue it. He is now a man who helps others and prevents death. If only he can tell her that his gifts were meant to help her, and that if she should lose her gift over his love, then he would gladly fill her duties for all eternity. Oh, how badly he wishes he can say he is meant for her! *He* is the person she was waiting for all along. All he wants is to take her into his arms and declare his vows.

Alas, he cannot.

His honey-like tone, stricken with grief, settles Palla once and for all when he instead says, "I oehnderstand."

Bayo leans forward in his upholstered seat beside the wooden table with great intrigue. His eyes pierce into the window over the Three Eyes as he watches the series of events unfold. The Dark Shaman is using his magic to put the second half of the siren's soul in Sokos's body. Just when everything is going to plan, three nuisances burst in and destroy it all. Bayo lets out a long, drawling breath and rolls his eyes.

"Pity" is all he says while he assumes he has lost the second soul of the siren for good. While Palla attempts to lead the soul back into the crystal box, Bayo wonders if Mary's journey to the Arketcha Tribe all those years ago was pointless. And it seems he's made a grave mistake in handing over the box so easily.

Just then, Palla loses control over the chaotic spirit, and it crashes into Ellionna. Bayo's eyes light up at the turn of events. But can she stomach the entire soul? Ellionna squirms and contorts, but eventually the siren settles . . .

Bayo cocks a brow. "Hmm." He gets to his feet. With a wave of his hand, the window fizzles, and The Eyes resume their rotation.

Bayo leaves his study, smirking. "Interesting . . ."

CHAPTER 34

May 3, 1920
ONE CENTURY AGO

The Three Eyes have been in Bayo's possession for two centuries. Since then, we have ventured into the Human Division of Malphora countless times. Upon our visits, our magic remains undetected, and we easily blend in and adapt to human cultures and societies. However, the differences between this divide and ours are excessive.

Humans behave the same no matter the era. They mindlessly march to the beat of unseen drummers who have them concentrate on their little lives, jobs, and problems. They believe they are advanced in what they assume is technology, which is created by sucking the earth's energies while ignoring all knowledge of their existential powers. As we know, their natural abilities were recorded in books of old by our ancient peoples before the Great Severance—most commonly known as the universal split between the two realms. Their natural powers are now considered mythical, conspiracy, or taboo according to their many religions.

Still some magic in the Human Divide remains evident—for those whose eyes are opened may tap into very little of it. Some call themselves shamans, witches, healers, and so forth. Yet none of their psychics or mediums can see the future to my extent or come close. Likewise, none of their witches, shamans, or healers perform true magic the way the Arketchians can. Many fake these gifts altogether. To most humans, the very thought of something beyond their egoistic bodies is marked as ludicrous, as if hiding an immense fear that they are certainly insignificant.

Then there's the complete disregard for lands distinct from their own with infinite creative excuses of differences and hate, even though they are all the same species! It is comical to recall the old Griffin empires, whose large scale offered more than one physical appearance to us Griffins depending on geographical origins, difference in sustenance, and exposure to sunlight. Our civil wars had nothing to do with such differences the way the Human Divide believes they operate.

While it has its dangers, there's no denying the beauty of the Human Divide. Beauty in the land, art, and beauty among its peoples. The less ignorant often call upon love, goodness, righteousness, and the Ultimate Being with the many names they've invented for it. At least that knowledge has not died.

We Extraordinary have adapted much differently since the Great Severance. Our numerous wars in the Griffin Clan have crippled us. Our ancient races like the harpies, centaurs, and fauns became nomadic species to avoid genocide at the hands of the animalistic vyrtrusks, banshees, woodland demons, the Weyling nation, and so forth. Several weaker species of the Extraordinary Division have unfortunately died out.

Keeping most of the native monsters in our divide proved beneficial for the humans, who've only had to deal with a fraction of the monsters that remained. Monsters that favor isolation and continue to hide in remote places, oceans, at the poles, and what the humans call space. It is not that the humans are negligent of their existences, but more so that their rulers collectively hide and deny proof, perhaps for good reason. There's also the matter of beings that are present in all realms and worlds, which are universally known in the

Human Division as angels, demons, and the spirits of the deceased. All of which continue to be an ongoing debate among the humans.

No, the humans are not as advanced as they believe.

Bayo and I often discuss these topics amongst ourselves. We also determine our strategies for a better future in the Griffin Clan, the Extraordinary Division, and later the entire world of Malphora. He tells me he'd gift our people with knowledge and not treat them as cattle, he'd awaken their powers, and we'd live in peace. I believed that Bayo could accomplish such daring feats, especially so when he confined one of our greatest predators, the Weyling, to the desolate lands of Emsequet. But as of late, I see a deep change in my oldest friend.

I have reason to believe the power of Endurance is overwhelming Bayo's entity. I've seen it during the annual Welcoming Moon celebration for the past fifty or so years as a visual interpretation gifted to me by my power of prophecy. I find it difficult to put what I've seen into words. From what I can describe, while we are gaining another year of life, a piece of the soul of the Endurance moon enters through Bayo's body.

I have proof for my theory. Even though Bayo does not show me his changes firsthand, I've witnessed a shift in his subconscious behaviors. He now desires ruling over nations, not for the good of all, but because anguish and submission give him pleasure. Perhaps he's fighting his feelings and fears his corruption. This must be the mysterious reason he stalls his epic plans.

He refuses to discuss his new theologies with me, as it is important to him that I continue to think highly of him. Still, his Endurance outbursts are growing more prominent, and while all around him have been touched by his anguish, I have not. No matter what happens, I know he would never hurt me.

—*Excerpt from Felix's journal.*

Hale, River, and Evan huddle around a weak fire one chilly night. With his shivering arms around his torso, Hale leans in and blows at the fire's base, then gently feeds it twigs. The fire picks up, but it is no match for the wind. Hale wastes no time. He gathers large branches to build a canopy over their heads.

"Let me help," Evan says, catching onto Hale's plan. When they complete their shelter, heat immediately radiates from the fire. Hale, River, and Evan crawl in.

"Wow, that's so much better," Evan says.

"How did you know to do that?" River asks.

"My dad taught me. We used to go camping a lot . . . back in the Human Division."

"Even with all its faults, I really miss the Human Division," Evan says.

"Yeah, but none of us had it easy there," River adds. "I was homeless; you and Grace were orphans."

Evan holds out his hands toward the fire's heat. "I still miss it. It was a million times better than this crazy world. There were stores, cars, televisions, phones. Every year there was a new gadget. There were no monsters . . . well, that's not true," he chuckles.

River says, "I miss playing my guitar and singing in the city streets. Making people smile was the best feeling. Right before I got warped here, an agent gave me his card. I kept it." River digs in his jeans pocket and reveals the crumbled paper whose writing is faded. "This would have changed everything for me. I would have given back to Lana, the woman who took me off the streets and raised me as her kid."

"Maybe we'll get back someday," Hale offers.

There's a moment of silence. It's clear Hale's pack brothers don't believe that to be an option.

Eventually, Evan goes on. "Oh boy, do I miss the movies! Grace and I would sneak into the theaters all the time."

River smiles. "So did I, all the time, with Lana's kids."

"What was your favorite movie?" Hale asks them.

"*Fast and the Furious* . . . all of them," Evan says.

"*Seven Pounds* was my favorite," River says. "What about you, Hale?"

"Ha ha . . . I think *The Avengers* . . . each one was great." Hale scratches the back of his head.

"My gosh! *The Avengers!*" Evan exclaims.

They reminisce.

Hale smiles. "There's probably hundreds of *Avengers* movies by now."

"Yup, back when we thought it would be so cool to have superpowers," River says, lying down.

Hale laughs. "I used to hate the idea of having superpowers. My sister and I talked about it all the time . . . Then once I got them, I felt so empowered . . . Remember what Spider-Man's uncle said—"

Evan and River repeat the famous line simultaneously: "With great power comes great responsibility."

Hale looks down shamefully. "Yeah . . . I should have remembered that."

An awkward silence is overcome when Evan slaps Hale on the back.

River gasps, "Oh no. Don't tell me we are your Mary Jane and Harry Osborn!"

They laugh.

Hale shakes his head. "No, you guys are waaaay better."

CHAPTER 35

The elites of Bimmorus would concur that the most prestigious post for any Bimmorian guard is near the bridge connecting the kingdom to the outer lands—as so they were trained to relay. Conversely, no such elite has ever visited the southern post in the middle of nowhere—since it is the middle of nowhere.

Truth be told, every guard hopes to be positioned *within* the palace, where the juicy secrets of the royals may be overheard through the glistening walls. And anyone knows which of the two positions gets paid more. No, the position on this very bridge is one no sane person wants, unless they're desperate.

The two fellows positioned here on this foggy and brisk morning are indeed desperate. Desperate for a job in which there is nothing to do, that pays enough for the bare minimum, a job perfect for those on the bend, those who could not finish their education, or those who *hated* supervision. To this pair, this job is a dream!

The two are enjoying a hot cup of lanka spiked with homemade liquor made from fermented sranu fat. They hop gleefully on the muted grass, playing and singing to their heart's content.

"Ten zaire says I win," says one guard, shoving the other. He aims a large rock high, prepared to throw it into the water. This is one of their pastimes. Who throws farthest?

Their metal uniform is carelessly cast aside. And why should they wear their uniform at all? There are never threats in this part of Bimmorus, and no one to walk by and see. Likewise, the azure-skinned guards have no care for their appearance beneath the armor, nor for hygiene, as a matter of fact. Yellowed teeth and matted hair conceal the fact that both are so young. Most would not judge, though—these are hard times in Bimmorus.

"That's more than half my pay!" shouts the other guard, who is far too lean for his height.

"Oh fine, then! How about an evening with your fair sister," chuckles the stout one.

The lean man throws an unexpected right punch, smashing against his partner's left jaw, which is beneficial—even though his last good tooth loosened—because he spots something across the horizon.

"What on Malphora are those beasts?" he queries.

"Where?" asks the lean one.

The stout one points just ahead of him. "There."

The lean one then notes, "They are rather large, aren't they. Do you think they are—"

"No, no," interrupts the stout one. "It is impossible, unfathomable." He squints his eyes. "Or . . . ?"

"It is! It is!" exclaims the lean one. "Oh, what do we do? There's never been an intruder before!"

The stout guard slaps him upside the head. "Get it together, man!" he shouts, though he, too, is at a loss for what to do. Stammering for words, he offers, "M-maybe we should call for help?"

Before the count of ten, the guards scurry off and ring big ol' rusty bells that are worked into the bridge's entrance, then scurry back. These bells signify an attack or approaching threat, and they've never been rung—as far as they know.

"Our uniforms, our uniforms!" they shout, dressing themselves clumsily.

Several of their items hang backward and sideways. In no time at all, regal Bimmorian guards flood the bridge with shining weapons and armor, making this pair feel utterly inadequate.

TWENTY MINUTES AGO

During a very informative lecture at the Royal Academy of Bimmorus, Marcus's irises have rolled back. His elite classmates would have laughed at the drool dripping onto the desk if they hadn't known better. Marcus is experiencing another vision. It is one of lesser impact, as he has not fallen over convulsing, thanks to his instructor, Lady Meir. Thankfully, the numerous visions have gained Marcus popularity in the academy, despite his pale color and Griffin origins.

He speeds out from his classroom. Lady Meir does not bother to stop him. What would be the point in preventing the general's right-hand man from his important missions? In the middle of the stairwell, Marcus pulls out a pocket watch from his breast pocket.

He unlocks the silver contraption and presses on the crescent moon engravement. An enchanting projection of the sun and moon revolving around the earth displays itself before his eyes. Tiny notches along the rim indicate specific minutes rolling by. If Marcus were to turn the dial, the image would zoom out to include the entire galaxy, stars, nebulas, and planets in the Extraordinary Division. This is how Bimmorians track time and all such astrological changes.

"I'll make it!" Marcus proclaims a bit too optimistically.

He clicks the knob thrice to transmit a message: "Camden, this is urgent!"

There is no return transmission—and that can mean only one thing. Camden is in the throne room, standing before the elites and the king himself. This leaves Marcus no choice. He must break into the throne room . . . yet again! At this point, Marcus might as well consider this reckless action a hobby. For with the number of times he's attempted a break-in, he's gotten rather good at it.

Marcus spots the sparkling palace across a narrow white bridge, with piercing eyes signifying his determination. He cannot fail this time. He must make it into the throne room undetected before the idiotic guards from his premonition ring the bells. Raging water laps over the jagged rocks below. The rough back-and-forth movement of the ocean's surface and white skies signify an approaching storm. *Befitting*, Marcus thinks. Lanterns on either side of the bridge ignite a yellow flame as he races past.

Entering the palace unnoticed is no easy feat. Guards are positioned on most entrances. Using blind spots to his advantage, Marcus ingeniously ducks for cover, then proceeds on the tips of his toes. His catlike agility has taken quite some time to practice, as have the secret shortcuts he's memorized through the mazelike structure. More often than not, Marcus's position was compromised, and he'd not like to repeat his time in the cold dungeon alongside criminals awaiting their execution. The guards have likewise stopped informing Camden about Marcus's imprisonment to prolong his punishment; they go so far as to search and strip him of his transmission device!

But not today, as Marcus has just skidded past the leader of the palace guards, Officer Luciel, who belly-laughed at Marcus for missing an entire two days from the academy in the dungeon and called him a *flying rat.*

"Aye! It's that flying rat again!" bellows Luciel.

Oh no. They're onto him. Marcus makes haste. He'll have to make a right even though it is a longer route. A pack of guards with silver armor is charging from the right. *Okay, maybe not.*

"After him!" they shout.

Marcus is wide-eyed. The guards are exceedingly angry this morning, and if he should not succeed in finding Camden, the dungeon will be the least of his worries. Hale might not be allowed to enter Bimmorus! With a heaving chest, Marcus bolts through the stairwell that leads downstairs rather than upstairs to the throne room.

"Where's he headed?" they question.

He needs to confuse the guards, which might not be too hard a task, considering he finds them incredibly dense. They chase him down the dark corridors, and back up he goes through a stairwell decorated finely with cobwebs and loose stone. His lungs are on fire and his hair is drenched with sweat, but oh, he can't deny this is fun!

It seems the guards have continued along the wrong path on the floor below, giving Marcus a moment to check the time.

"Nine minutes," he mumbles exasperatedly.

He hasn't a chance to catch his breath, though he now doubts any success at this point. Marcus sprints up three flights of stairs and appears on the topmost floor, peeking his head out of the dusty entrance. The guards are on their way up the main stairwell. He'll have to race them to the throne room.

Marcus bolts whist the guards shout at one another, "He's fooled us again!"

"There he is!"

"After him!"

"Don't let him into that throne room!"

Marcus is inches away from the door. Pointed staffs brush against his back. Desperately, he sinks his body into his knees and plunges forward, bursting through the double doors and skidding across the freshly waxed tile on his belly.

"Whoaaahh!" he exclaims, catching the attention of all the elites in the midst of very important government business.

Officer Luciel bows before the king, "Your Majesty, we humbly apologize for the intrusion—"

King William erupts from his golden velvet-lined seat. "You've been outwitted by a mere adolescent for the last time, Luciel! Release your staff."

Luciel hesitates. The highest form of embarrassment a Bimmorian guard could possibly live through is to be forced to release their staff in public, as it will not be returned to them. Turning deeply lavender while he ponders his family homelessness upon losing this source of income, Luciel works at the straps on his uniform and prepares to unhinge his staff.

Marcus, meanwhile, springs up to simply bow before the king, his ash-blond hair sticking up in odd places from his fall. "Your Majesty! It is entirely my fault. I'll go to the dungeon straightaway—"

"You will not, prophet. You will do what you came here to do. Camden!" shouts the king.

Camden steps forward from the sea of blue. His sky-blue skin glistens with silver freckles. He looks rather confused, though Marcus cannot tell why.

"I will see to it, Your Majesty," Camden tells the king. His silken indigo cape floats behind him as he departs with Marcus on his arm.

Camden is not a fool. He knows his uncle was lenient with Marcus, for it played to his advantage that Camden be absent from the conversation proceeding. Thankfully, he's left a small recording contraption beneath the historical throne itself. An undetectable bug he found in Lady Thelmure's Gadgetry. King William's sneaky affairs between his shady council will not go far, no matter how he shall try.

But this matters not, for Marcus is hastily relaying information and urging Camden to the courtyard outside and into a flying chariot. The golden two-seater is lined with red velvet, and the magnificent piece is carved to look like the national bird of Bimmorus, the femu. Once Camden pushes a perfectly carved stone into the center of the dash, the carvings of the contraption illuminate, and a pair of golden wings emerge from the belly of the machine.

No matter how many times Camden has taken Marcus for a ride, ascending the skies by machine is not as wonderous as stretching his own wings. Alas, they cannot rebel against King William's decree nonsensically.

"How much time do we have?" Camden asks.

Bells ring in the distance.

Marcus cusses under his breath. "*Jufanax,*" which is Bimmorian slang for sranu droppings. Why specifically a sranu dropping? Well, anyone who's seen one would understand. "They're here."

Camden's eyes widen at Marcus's use of speech. As if the young Griffin were his own kin, he exclaims, "Marcus!"

Marcus gives Camden a sideways glance for his double standard. He learned such slang from the general himself.

The emerging guards look like busy ants from above, and Camden swoops down to command them to follow his lead toward the southern border. They zoom through the skies and spot the three Griffins yonder, dodging Bimmorian arrows.

But Marcus leaves Camden with a warning. "You need to be careful of Hale. He has dark energy around him."

"Why, then, is he meant to be here?" Camden asks.

Marcus explains, "He is supposed to meet you."

"Me? Why?" Camden is baffled.

"I don't know everything, you know," Marcus remarks.

"It will piece together in due time, I suppose," Camden adds.

The black Griffin among them creates an impenetrable bubble around the trio to protect them. *It is the power of Shielding*, Marcus notes, the same power his pa, Eliath, has.

"Cease fire!" Camden bellows.

He brings the flying chariot in the way. Arrows strike its metallic belly as it slowly comes to a stop.

"Fall back!" Camden commands.

The guards lay down their weapons, allowing the trio to land majestically. In a blinding flash, they turn into three teenage boys protected by a bubble of Shielding and enflamed arms of Ardor.

Marcus is in awe. *Wow, a Griffin of Ardor, just like my ma!*

Then there is the third young man, the one that Marcus has been eagerly waiting for. Someone who he's come to know well, though the two have never truly met. A seemingly timid brunet with loose brown curls, tall, and lanky from extensive travel.

Hale.

With the assistance of the Elder Prophet's journal, the Griffin trio has withstood their long and perilous path across the Extraordinary Division. They've escaped banshees, vyrtrusks, Weylings, woodland demons, death, and fate, all to find salvation in the Kingdom of Bimmorus. The feeling of sturdy soil beneath their weary feet is enough to bring tears to their eyes. Perhaps it is too good to be true; perhaps they shall find another enemy beyond the gates. But for the time being, all that is true are the tales of their pilgrimage, their strength, and their bond.

They spot the person commanding the Bimmorian army. A distinguished man with light-blue skin and platinum-blond hair, dressed in silken indigo, who proceeds to climb out from his chariot to make his way down the bridge. There is no doubt that the three have now come to an advanced civilization, yet Hale, River, and Evan instinctually brace themselves for yet another fight for survival.

One glance of their frail and dirtied flesh and clothes tells Camden all about the horrors they've faced, and he finds himself releasing his worry for not putting the wall up around the kingdom sooner. He locks eyes with the one in the center, the one Marcus foretold had a great destiny. Eyes he finds innocent and frightened. Odd, coming from a boy of such power . . . Still, they settle General Camden all the same, and he knows in his heart he has done the right thing.

Camden ceases his stride. "Greetings, Hale, prince of the Griffins. We've been expecting you."

EPILOGUE

In the Griffin Clan, countless Griffin soldiers fall into their ranks. A monstrous shadowlike figure observes them from the skies, coming in and out of visibility in tune with the moonlight peeping through the clouds. Griffins reach such a grand stature with age and power, explaining the Elders' enlarged second forms. Though unlike most, this particular Griffin lacks the vital gleaming fur thus bestowed by the Welcoming Moon. The muted color and ratty texture suits this being all the same. Its long claws rake the atmosphere as if the air were tangible. The jagged movements of its body are most unnatural, for its sharpened joints are nearly poking through skin, in harmony with its blackened irises.

The Griffin transforms near the ground, at the head of the fleet. Its transformation is as shadowy as the Banshee Forest, mysterious considering all Griffins—even the grimmest of Griffin villains throughout history—have had no such transformation. Once the black mass of energy disperses, Elder Deor's human form is revealed, inhaling the air as if for the first time.

The ivory skin of his human vessel is ever duller in the moonlight. His shoulder-length light-brown hair sways as he paces before his army, giving them mental commands. The unblinking young Griffins complete artistic sequences in exact unison. Griffins of Shielding blockade the army fronts, Griffins of

Light make the entire company invisible and visible again, and Griffins of Ardor practice their flame. Each warrior wields their glowing huanim spears like masters of their craft.

Lost among them is a redheaded girl who once answered to the name Grace. Could she recall her name? Could she relay the life she has once lived? The people she loved? She would not, if asked. All anyone in the waking world will witness is a mindless being whose mechanical breathing and unblinking eyelids are most bizarre. They'd probably wonder how long her mind's been lost, or if her soul is fighting for escape from within.

Indeed, it was.

Banging at the walls in a narrow tunnel is Grace's essence that feels and recalls. She watches what has become of her body through the window she has fashioned with what she perceives as fists, like an outsider.

Lost, though not entirely at a loss. Grace has been busy at work in this prisonlike space. It is a solitary place in the constructs of her mind that she's certain Deor has no access to—or possibly does not know of. Here, she is free to think and free to exist while he keeps her vessel to play. *He won't play for long,* Grace thinks.

The channels that he has worked to link her mind to his are somehow opened, and Grace has occupied herself on reversing the signal in secret. A single slipup will compromise her position. It will be the end of it all.

Grace releases her spirit up through the tunnels. It feels like a massive exhale that allows her to soar. Up above, she witnesses the physical world, the young Griffin soldiers, their timely sequences, and Deor pacing before them. But Grace is not spirit free to roam; she exists within the channel. Channels of infinite energies webbing together and combining at the source that is Elder Deor. The colorful system is completed to perfection, and Grace wonders where its magic meets science, how this is possible, and most importantly, how to cut it at the root.

Another exhale allows Grace in the center of it all, where Deor's commands burst out from him like waves into the individual tunnels of the young Griffins. She tolerates his energy; however each command he gives seems to bring her closer to his essence. It is eerie, grimy, and off. She lets her heart linger on the one thing that matters: her motivation, the reason she continues to fight. *River.*

Another forced release has her riding Deor's wave, allowing her focus to shift. Immediately, Grace connects with the Griffin soldiers. Most are silent, as if beyond any reach. She wonders if they are trapped within tunnels as well, or if their souls remain at all. Too grim a thought, though she does not doubt it. Then there are the fighters, screaming out from within. Yes, she can hear them well. For every shout, they are punished with darkness, pushed further into the constructs of their minds, into mazes within mazes, until they are too weak, too broken to attempt escape.

This is the farthest Grace has ever roamed, and now she knows just the trick to inch closer without the Elder's detection. The waves of energy expelling from his mind have quickened. Grace struggles to keep afloat and allows them to push her back to whence she came, for if she remains, he will find out soon enough. Back in the black hole, she curses Deor's perfect system, which is even inlaid whist he slumbers . . .

Grace gasps. *That's it! His subconscious is at its weakest point when he sleeps!*

The field is suddenly engulfed by the ultimately blinding transformation of the entire Clan. Immense snarling beasts gallop through the grass, spread their wings, and ascend the heavens. Around and upside down they go like an airborne tsunami gaining on Deor himself.

The Elder of the Dark sits cross-legged before his creation, quite pleased. The Griffins leave him unscathed, though their shrieks and caws drum in his ears, and the weight of their flight sways the grass.

He thinks, *This accomplishment alone will set a new age among Griffin kind!*

Miraculously, Grace hears the reverberating of his thoughts in her mind. This has never happened before.

She smiles. *No. The new age will be mine.*

A deep-pitched chuckle bounces off the walls of Grace's prison, paralyzing her with fear. *You fools underestimate my power time and time again. There is no escape. You are but a meager pawn . . .*

The walls are closing in around her. The window she has fashioned into the waking world bubbles to black. Its slimy ooze clings to her, suffocating her essence. Deeper and deeper into it she falls, until it consumes her whole. What remains is an empty vessel made of sinew, bone, and nerve, decorated with auburn hair and doe eyes, somehow more mechanical than the rest of the conquered. Thoughtless. Soulless. Empty. Neither the flap of her wings, her path, nor her speed are of her own making, whoever she is . . .

ABOUT THE AUTHOR

J.K. Noble grew up and resides in the Big Apple, where fantastical inspiration lives among the bright lights and colorful personalities. She envisions unique mythological creatures majestically roaming bustling streets and skimming the skies between skyscrapers.

Absorbing fantasy stories, in awe of the great magic each possesses, Noble soon learned that she too holds the same power as the mystic writers of old. Her debut novel *Hale: The Rise of the Griffins,* was an introduction to a world of magic, adventure, and romance. Noble makes her return to the world of the Extraordinary in the fantasy sequel, *Hale: The Prophet's Journal.*

A free ebook edition is available with the purchase of this book.

To claim your free ebook edition:

1. Visit MorganJamesBOGO.com
2. Sign your name CLEARLY in the space
3. Complete the form and submit a photo of the entire copyright page
4. You or your friend can download the ebook to your preferred device

Morgan James BOGO™

A **FREE** ebook edition is available for you or a friend with the purchase of this print book.

CLEARLY SIGN YOUR NAME ABOVE

Instructions to claim your free ebook edition:
1. Visit MorganJamesBOGO.com
2. Sign your name CLEARLY in the space above
3. Complete the form and submit a photo of this entire page
4. You or your friend can download the ebook to your preferred device

Print & Digital Together Forever.

Snap a photo

Free ebook

Read anywhere

Printed in the USA
CPSIA information can be obtained
at www.ICGtesting.com
JSHW021757251023
50871JS00002B/6